WARRIORS OF CAMLANN

BRITANNIA
OF THE N
Glevum
Corinium
Mons Badonicus
SABRINA AEST
Caer Baddon
(Aquae Sulis)
DUMNONIA
Fort
Cado
Gevisse
Moridunum
Vectis
OCEANUS BRITANNI
Armorica
(Brittany)

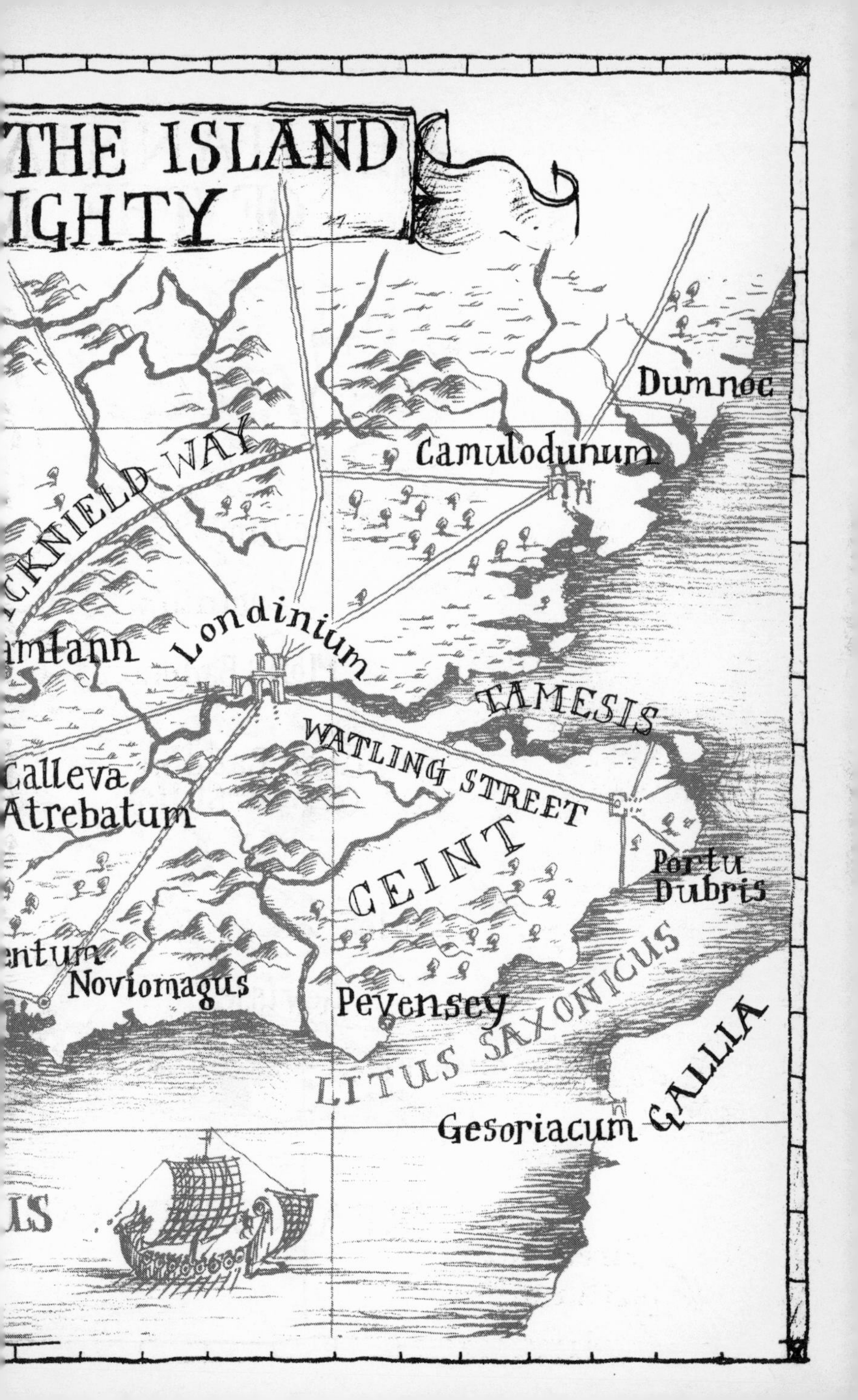
THE ISLAND
IGHTY
Dumnoc
Camulodunum
ICKNIELD WAY
Londinium
amlann
TAMESIS
WATLING STREET
Calleva
Atrebatum
CEINT
Portu
Dubris
entum
Noviomagus
Pevensey
LITUS SAXONICUS
GALLIA
Gesoriacum
IS

Acknowledgements

I would like to thank: my test readers, William Browne and Jessica Liebmann for their helpful comments, Dan Shadrake of Britannia, the Arthurian Society, for his insight into the military and other details of the period, and my agent Mic Cheetham for her ever sound advice. Thanks are also due to my husband Paul for his boundless support and enthusiasm and, of course, my editors at Bloomsbury. All mistakes are, as ever, entirely my own.

Published by Bloomsbury, New York and London
Distributed to the trade by Holtzbrinck Publishers

Library of Congress Cataloging-in-Publication Data:
Browne, N. M.
Warriors of Camlann / N. M. Browne. p. cm.
Summary: Armed with their respective powers as warrior and magician, Dan and Ursula attempt to return to their own time through the Veil but instead find themselves in the turbulent era of the early Middle Ages in the service of Arturus Ursus, War Duke of Britain.
ISBN 1-58234-817-0 (alk. paper)
[1. Space and time--Fiction. 2. Arthur, King--Fiction. 3. Magic--Fiction. 4. War--Fiction. 5. Great Britain--History--To 1066--Fiction.] I. Title
PZ7.B82215 Wat 2003
[Fic]--dc21
2002028222

First U.S. Edition 2003
1 3 5 7 9 10 8 6 4 2

Bloomsbury USA Children's Books
175 Fifth Avenue
New York, New York 10010

N. M. Browne

To my sister, Laura,
without whom I would never
have become a writer

~ Chapter One ~

Dan gripped Ursula's hand as if his life depended on it. It was possible that it did. The oily ice of the yellow mist clung to him. It made his flesh recoil. He fought the urge to run through it in panic. He did not want Ursula to know the extent of his fear. He could not see her. Only the warmth of her calloused hand reassured him. He felt her grip tighten as she moved ahead, pulling him, then he too was through it. His body shuddered with shocked relief. He was through the mist. There was an all but inaudible pop and they were through it together, but in a place of total darkness.

To his surprise Ursula did not release her grip. He was relieved to feel the slight tremor of her hand. Good. She was scared too. It was Ursula who spoke first.

'We managed to stay together at least.' Her voice was little more than a whisper. She sounded unusually vulnerable. Maybe because she thought they were back home, in their own world where she would have no sorcery and no strength. She would no longer be Boar Skull the great Combrogi warrior or Ursula Alavna ab Helen, the sorceress; she would just be Ursula Dorrington of 10G, unpopular and powerless. Ursula would feel the loss almost like a bereavement. He knew just how she felt. His own throat seemed dry, unused. He croaked a question.

'Are we home?'

'How, by Lugh, should I know?'

Dan grinned. She had answered him in the language of the Combrogi. At least they would still have that. Back in their own world they would be the only two who spoke what he supposed must be a form of ancient Celtic. Now, that would raise a few eyebrows.

In the darkness he felt for his sword 'Bright Killer'. It made him feel safer. It was still there. He had been worried about arriving in a twenty-first century car park, a Celtic longsword at his hip. He had been worried about a lot of things, perhaps the wrong things: a twenty-first century car park would have been an embarrassing place to arrive, dressed as ancient Celts from another world, but at least they would have known where they were. This not knowing was far worse. The darkness seemed to press against his eyes. He felt the familiar pulse of adrenalin – fight or flight. There was no one to fight and nowhere to run. His warrior's readiness threatened to degenerate into panic.

'What do we do now?' At least his voice was still steady – croaky, but steady.

'Did you bring a tinder box?'

'I didn't think we'd need one.' Dan did not add that he'd hoped to arrive home in the twenty-first century.

'Dan, I'm scared. What if this isn't home?'

He heard the slight break in Ursula's voice, the rise of panic. Ursula did not panic.

She carried on: 'And then, what if it is?'

He knew what she meant. They had left their ordinary lives months, maybe even years, ago. The mist had claimed them then too. They had wandered into it and found themselves transported into something very like first-century Britain; found themselves fighting with Celtic warriors under the leadership of the young Celtic king, Macsen, against the might of Rome. They had become accustomed to strangeness, to magic, and to fear, but such familiarity didn't help Dan much now. He was still afraid, and so was Ursula. In that place which he thought of as Macsen's land, she had discovered a gift for sorcery. She had learned to call up the mist and bend it to her will, or so they had thought. They believed she could control the mist, use it to bring them home – to Dan's sister and Ursula's mother, to school and normal life. It looked like they'd been wrong. They had wanted so much to go home but even the thought of it brought its own worries. Could they live a normal life? Dan had been a warrior, more than that he'd been a berserker. The Bear Sark, they had called him – a title synonymous with murderous madness. He had killed not once, but many times, in a frenzy of savagery. He could not undo what he'd done and what he'd done would always set him apart. What if it happened again when he was back home? What if he killed again? He'd be locked up. In first-century Britain he'd been a hero. He had seen terrible things, done terrible things; he knew his own wild capacity for violence and it frightened him.

Dan squeezed Ursula's strong hand. He did not know how to answer her. He knew exactly what she meant.

It was a cold and strangely quiet night. Dan strained his ears for the sound of traffic but could hear nothing. By twenty-first century standards he had become a good tracker. He'd learned to listen and to feel, to take in all the information his senses could offer, to analyse and to react. The soundless darkness offered no information. By the standards of any time he had become a formidable warrior. He had learned to use his mind and body as a weapon, a honed instrument for his will. Here in the stillness of this nowhere landscape he felt as vulnerable as the schoolboy he'd been before. A large part of him wished he were still that boy. He licked dry lips and shivered. They could be *anywhere* or any *when*. If by some miracle Ursula had brought them home, then how long had they been away? Would his sister be worried about him? Would she have given him up for dead? If Ursula had got them back to the right time, had she got them back to the right country? Long-suppressed doubts assailed him. He did not want to share them with Ursula. She might think he didn't trust her. He held her hand more tightly. Her powerful fingers squeezed his.

'Can you see anything?'

As his eyes adjusted to the near total absence of light, he found that he could, a little. The ground all round them seemed grey and featureless. His instinct told him they were on a grassy hill but he could not account for that feeling. That did not matter. Instincts could keep you alive when rational thought left you for dead.

'I can see enough.'

'Let's go then.'

'Where?'

'Wherever there is to go.'

Dan almost suggested Ursula speak English again – to get back into practice. He didn't quite have the heart. The rhythm of the Combrogi tongue gave him an obscure sense of comfort. It helped to dispel some of his disquiet, his discomforting sense of foreboding.

They walked for a while. The terrain was not difficult. They had become more used to horseback than hiking over the previous months, but even so Dan set a good, ground-eating pace. He had been long enough away from a wristwatch to have given up thinking of time primarily in minutes and hours. He estimated they had walked for the best part of a duty watch. The darkness dissipated in the characteristically gradual way of a clouded dawn. In all that time they had seen no lights, no house, and no road. They walked on uncultivated land, endless fields of coarse grass broken only by thickets of gorse and scrub. These were not good signs.

'I've messed up, haven't I?' Ursula sounded sullen. She'd let go of Dan's hand some time back. He knew that she was grinding her teeth. In the wan light her face looked grim and distant like she'd looked before – when she'd been just the big lumpy girl no one had liked at school. He hated that look. It was a reminder that the bond between them must weaken. Ursula's wild courage had saved him more than once. He had trusted her completely. Once they were home things would not be the same – could not be the same. He didn't like that thought.

He looked at her, really looked at her, as he had not done for a long time. That surly look of hers was almost the only thing about Ursula that had not changed over their time together. Her pale, blonde hair had grown and now hung almost to her shoulders framing a fine boned, but strong-looking face. Ursula was over six-foot tall. Where once her height and bulk had marked her out as almost freakish, now her taut-muscled frame marked her out as beautiful. She was unlikely to be unpopular or powerless again. Would they still be friends?

Her face creased with a frown and he realised she was still waiting for him to answer.

'We don't know that you've messed up – not yet,' he said encouragingly.

'Dan, we *can't* be home. Don't try to humour me! We'd have found some sign of civilisation before now. Wherever we are – I hate it. I feel so lost. I can't feel anything anymore.'

The new, beautiful, Ursula sounded as distressed as he'd ever heard her. If he'd not known her better he would have thought she was about to cry.

'What do you mean?'

'I can't feel the magic here. It's not home, Dan, but it's not *there* either; it's not Macsen's world. It's horrible. I feel all empty. I'd forgotten how it was before. Dan, how am I going to manage without it?' She looked at him in desperate appeal with eyes that were no longer the emerald green of a sorceress but the cool blue of the schoolgirl Ursula.

He opened his mouth to comfort her, then stopped, silenced by his awareness of an abrupt movement in the bushes. A figure appeared suddenly from the dark thicket, moving swiftly towards them. Dan's hand was on Bright Killer faster than thought. Something struck him, a hard blow. He never saw what.

Ursula watched open-mouthed as four men rushed towards her. She saw everything in one frozen moment: the bearded men in tunics and leggings; their bare heads, their long hair the colour of her own; their swords and small knives thrust towards her; their mouths open, screaming something – a war cry, a shout of triumph? The sound ripped the air, there was a thud and all else was silence. One of them had thrown a stone with deadly accuracy from a slingshot. It lay where it had landed, stained with blood. In the grey light the crimson blood welling around Dan's head showed up bright as neon against the pale yellow green of the grass. Ursula could not react. She stared at the spreading redness. She could see nothing else.

It was as if she had never been Boar Skull, never spent months in training, never defended herself in hand-to-hand combat. Numb with shock and loss she let them take her. She had left her sword in Macsen's land but she could have tried to defend herself. She made no attempt to fight as they snatched Bright Killer from Dan's lifeless grip. She made no attempt to run when they roughly bound her hands. She did nothing when they ripped the eagle brooch that Macsen had given her from her tunic. They spoke to her in a language she didn't know – they were not of the tribes – that much she knew – she spoke all their many dialects. The strangers smelled powerfully of peat fires and stale sweat and the pungent stench of fish. They stood close enough for her to smell the alcohol on their breath. Dirty, calloused hands caressed her roughly. It was as if it was happening to someone else. They refrained from doing her harm. She was not sure why. The tallest, who was still a few inches shorter than Ursula, cooed endearments and then signalled for her to be lifted bodily away. She did not resist. She had never been more lost. Once, when she was a sorceress, when she had wielded magic, when she had been able to shape-shift, she had almost become trapped in the form of an eagle. Even then she had not felt more lost than this. The world had shrunk until there was just one thing in it: the blood welling around Dan's pale face and his utter stillness.

She had let Dan down. She had not known their attackers were there. Always before, she had sensed danger. This time, she had sensed nothing. It was her fault. Dan relied on her for such things. She tried to reach for the magic. She needed the magic, had never needed it, never wanted it more. But she expected what she found – nothing. There was no magic in her. She was alone and helpless in an unknown place. Dan was dead.

~ Chapter Two ~

The sun was high in the sky before Ursula had recovered her wits sufficiently to take in her surroundings. She was not back home. Her attackers, whoever they were, tied sound knots. Straining on them only tightened them further. They had carried her bodily to a cart and had transported her, bound and gagged, to some other place, a dark place that smelled, like them, of fish and filth. The road they had travelled had been uneven and pitted with holes, and the wooden cart in which they'd thrown her was no more than a wooden box on wheels. Ursula had been thrown against it so constantly that she was sore and badly bruised. She did not think she had broken any bones.

All the long, cold, painful journey, Ursula had wept for Dan. She had wept silently until her vision blurred and her head throbbed to the rhythm of her grief. Dan was the only friend she had ever had – the only person who had risked death for her – and the only certainty in all the strangeness they had experienced since they first went through the Veil. She could not believe he was gone. It had happened too quickly. There had been many times, after she and Dan had joined the Combrogi, when she had readied herself to die or to see Dan die. Today, death had found them both so unprepared. How could Dan, the Bear Sark, the mightiest fighter the Celts had ever claimed for their own, be killed by a stone from a well aimed slingshot? Her memory was full of Dan: Dan smiling, Dan listening, Dan fighting in his berserker madness. Most of all she thought of Dan falling, Dan falling as the stone hit home, and blood surrounding him like a dark halo.

Why had she not fought their attackers, grabbed Bright Killer herself to avenge Dan? There was no doubt in Ursula's mind. Dan could not have survived the force of that blow. There was no doubt in her mind that she should have saved him. There was no doubt in her mind that it would be a struggle to survive this new strangeness without him, but her own life was in danger and she had to try. She had to concentrate on staying alive.

Ursula had become practised at a certain kind of mental discipline – the kind she'd needed to release her sorcery. She called on that practice now and almost broke down again at the emptiness she felt. There was no sensation of power. There was no awareness of electric energies thrilling through nerves and neurons.

She listened to her own trembling breath and only then, in this new and fragile state of calm did she become aware of some other presence in the cold, dark place where the men had trapped her. Someone or something else was breathing quietly, raggedly.

She could not get up. Both her hands and feet were bound, though fortunately not together. She had seen prisoners tied that way – hands to feet, their backs arched like a bow. There had been charred corpses in that position in Alavna. She was not tied like that – and she was grateful. With some uncomfortable manoeuvring, jarring fresh cuts and bruises from her time on the wooden cart, she managed to get herself into a semi-seated shuffling position. With painful slowness she explored her prison. She was inside some large rectangular stone structure. There were three bodies lying against the wall furthest from her. Two were unquestionably dead, though not yet cold. The hard impacted earth of the floor was wet and sticky there. Ursula was glad of the darkness. She did not want to see what had been done to them. Fear tightened in the pit of her stomach. She remembered Alavna, and the slaughter she had seen there. No sight could be worse than that. She forced herself to continue her exploration. She had been a warrior. She could bear whatever she had to face here.

The darkness disorientated her. Her thighs cramped

with the effort of movement. She gritted her teeth against the pain. After an agony of shuffling, she reached the third body. It still breathed. Reasoning that anyone imprisoned with her was at least an enemy of her captors and might thus be her friend, she started to speak. She did not attempt to speak in English. English was not for her the language of blood and pain and fear. She spoke instead in the languages of the Combrogi, in the tongue of the Silures, the Carvetii, and the Ordovices, in the ancient warrior tongues. 'Are you hurt? Are you sick?'

A dry voice whispered from a parched throat, 'Water. Give me water!'

The sandpaper voice shocked Ursula. She found herself trembling with more than the awkward muscle-straining exertion. He spoke in Latin, the language of her old enemy, the Ravens.

She recovered herself quickly and answered in the same language. Even without the power of her living, pulsing magic she could still remember words she had learned with its aid.

'I have no water. I'm a prisoner too. Do you know where we are? Do you know a way out?'

The man was wracked with a spasm of something that, in other circumstances, might have been a laugh. Ursula failed to see the funny side of their predicament.

Eventually, he calmed himself sufficiently to rasp,

'You can't *not* know who has captured you. Where have you been living? The people who captured us are slavers – Aenglisc slavers.' The man struggled for breath. 'We'll be dead or shipped a long way from here before the day's out.'

Dan would have known who the Aenglisc were, but she could no longer ask him. The realisation of that was like a stab wound – she almost buckled under it. She shied away from the pain of it.

Were the Aenglisc the same as the English? Why were they fighting Romans?

Ursula had fought Romans before. In Macsen's land, the land she had just left, they had been known as Ravens and there they had been her enemy. She would not jump to any conclusions about this new situation. This Roman might yet turn out to be her enemy, but he may also be able to help her.

'We'd stand a better chance of escape if we could free my hands and feet. They've tied me up.'

It was inconceivable to Ursula that she would try to escape without trying to release her fellow captive – even if he were a Roman.

'Do you have a buckle or anything sharp I could use to cut the rope?'

Ursula had seen rope bonds cut with miraculous ease in many a film. It had to be possible. Could a hundred Hollywood action movies be wrong?

'You are wasting your time. These men are professionals. Once you're caught that's it.'

Never overly blessed with patience, Ursula's tone was shot with steel.

'Do you have anything sharp or not?'

'No. But ...' There was a pause. 'Lady, are you of gentle birth?'

Ursula was taken aback.

'What do you mean? What has my birth to do with anything?'

'Marcellus – the corpse beside me – he carried a knife strapped under his tunic. They may not have found it.'

Ursula swallowed hard. Did she want to grapple with a corpse or did she want to be an Aenglisc slave? She rested a moment, gathering her strength and her courage.

'Tell me, Roman, what is your name?'

While the man, Ambrosius Larcius, spoke. She listened hard and thought of Kai, the warrior who had been almost like a father to her in the world she'd just left. He might have *boasted* that he could rob a corpse with both hands tied behind his back. She smiled a grim, private smile. The Combrogi did things like that. He would have found her squeamishness amusing. She could hear his amused laughter in her mind. Kai had respected a man's spirit as much as anyone, but he regarded an enemy's corpse as no more than a carcass.

Thinking of Kai brought tears to her eyes – eyes she thought had been drained of them, but it helped her to do what she had to do. Fumbling a little because everything was slippery with gore, she managed to get her cold fingers around the knife. She dropped it several times and cursed – Combrogi warriors' curses she rather hoped the man Ambrosius Larcius would not understand. If he did, he would certainly never again ask her if she was of 'gentle birth'.

At last, she had the knife, a serviceable Roman knife, kept sharp as a good soldier's blade.

'I have it!' Ursula told Larcius rather curtly. She liked the thought of giving a Roman a weapon about as much as she had liked the thought of recovering it from a dead man. Nerves made her voice sound more brutal than she had intended. 'You must cut my bonds with it. Nick so much as a hair on my arm and you will join Marcellus. Believe me, I'm not of gentle birth and I would kill you.'

She did not think that was true. For all her experience as a warrior among the Combrogi, she had not become so brutalised that she could kill a wounded man in cold blood. Larcius believed her though, which was what mattered. She heard his sharp intake of breath. He was injured in the upper arm, a sword wound deep enough to disable but not to kill. He had not been bound, but was too shocked to pose much of a threat to the

Aenglisc. He was almost too shocked to be any use at all to Ursula. She kept the steel in her voice as she told him what to do. The rope was sturdy and Larcius was shaking, though whether from fever, fear, the shock, or the blood loss, Ursula did not know. She did not much care. It took a long time to cut through the rope and Ursula had to curb both her tongue and her temper but in the end she was free. The return of blood flow to her hands and feet was painful. She stamped her foot to relieve her cramp, and then heard something. Someone was coming. She grabbed the knife from Larcius and threw herself to the ground. Her movement was so sudden and the floor so hard she had to muffle a cry of pain. Outside, someone was talking loudly. A door opened and light flooded the room. Ursula was almost blinded as the tallest of her captors threw another bloodied body into the prison. She only saw the body's face for a moment but she would have known it anywhere, instantly. It was Bryn, Dan's Combrogi squire. The last time she had seen Bryn it had been to say goodbye as she left him in Macsen's land, before stepping into the Veil. How could he be here? What was going on?

~ *Chapter Three* ~

Bedewyr gingerly approached the prone figure on the ground. The huge dog guarding the body was the size of a donkey and its slavering jaws were large enough to engulf a man's head.

'Is he dead?' Petronax's voice was harsh.

'I don't know. That hell hound won't let me get close enough to find out.' Bedewyr sounded embarrassed. He did not like to admit to fear but then the beast threw back its head and howled like its wolfish antecedents. Bedewyr could feel each hair on his scalp lift in atavistic terror.

'Have you no meat left? Throw the dog some food!' Petronax did not attempt to keep exasperation from his tone. Keeping his eyes on the beast, he groped in his saddlebag for the remains of their lunch. The meat was dried and far from tempting but Petronax was good with animals. He knew it would serve.

'Here boy! Look! We mean no harm to your master.

We can help.' He kept his voice low, his tone, comforting, and his movements steady. The wolf dog ceased his howling and took the gift of meat but its eyes never left Petronax's own.

The body, sprawled on the ground, was that of a tall, dark-haired youth. There was a wound at the back of his head, the side of his neck and jerkin were caked in the rusty brown of dried blood. Petronax extended his hand cautiously towards the body to feel for a pulse. The man lived.

'It's all right, boy, we'll take him with us. Here, Bedewyr, lend me your strength.' The hound growled, but permitted him to lift the unconscious man, with Bedewyr's help, towards the spare mount. What Bedewyr lacked in initiative was more than balanced by his powerful physique and youthful strength.

The unconscious man was hardly smaller than Bedewyr himself, with the hard muscles of someone used to heavy labour or the butchery of war. He was clean-shaven and youthful – probably no more than sixteen or seventeen summers. His long dark hair was tied back in a braid – a soldier? Petronax looked at the youth's hands – they were as calloused as any swordsman's. He was a soldier; there could be no doubt. The proof lay in the scabbard of unusual intricacy and beauty that hung from his hip. It was of ancient design, gilded, in perfect condition and empty – a rich soldier then, maybe a mercenary without his sword. Petronax helped Bedewyr secure the stranger as comfortably as possible to the horse and surreptitiously inspected him for further clues as to his origin. There were none. His clothes were nondescript – good quality tunic, cloak and trews – though somewhat unusual in style. He had no visible tattoos, no crucifix and no amulet. Petronax's characteristic curiosity would have to remain unsatisfied.

The warrior's war hound loped forward to stand guard over his master. It was time to go. There was a chance that whoever attacked the youth might still be in the vicinity.

'These Aenglisc get bolder with every passing moon.' Petronax spat his disgust. 'Let's get out of here.'

'You think this was Aenglisc work?'

Petronax suppressed his impatience with his companion whose youth did not quite excuse his stupidity. 'Read the tracks Bedewyr! Read the tracks! Look here.' He knelt and picked up a couple of glass beads that lay all but hidden by the churned earth. He picked them up and held them between his thick workmanlike fingers so that they caught the light. 'Are these trinkets Combrogi? Besides, who else would ambush two men here, in this godforsaken place?'

'Two men?'

'There are tracks that suggest two men and a boy

were attacked here. Look! See for yourself.'

'Then two have been taken?'

'From here, yes.'

Bedewyr looked sceptically at the flattened grass and mud. 'It is far from the road. Why should anyone set an ambush here?'

It did indeed seem an unlikely place for an ambush. It was miles from any hamlet and the nearest Combrogi settlement of any size; the city of Camulodunum was a six-hour ride away. It had been grazing land but even the sheep seemed to have moved on. The ground was littered with droppings but they were all old – the land had been abandoned no doubt when the Aenglisc moved inland.

'Why are we here, Bedewyr?'

'Because the Druid sent us?'

'Good – and why do you think he did that?'

Bedewyr was about to answer that the ways of wizards made no sense to him, when a glimmer of unexpected insight illuminated his handsome features.

'We were here to meet these people who were ambushed?'

'Bedewyr, you delight an old man when you discover your wits. While such a miracle of understanding can issue from your lips there is hope for the world.'

Petronax's tone was light, mocking, but there was no mistaking the urgency with which he continued.

'It looks as if the Druid was not the only one expecting these particular visitors.' He sighed and muttered to himself, 'We should have travelled faster, but it is too late now.' He fixed Bedewyr with a stern look. 'Bedewyr, you will take this poor unfortunate to the Druid at Camulodunum. The Druid insisted that we bring the men we found here back to Camulodunum before the Council meets to choose the new High King. He will be well cared for there. I will track the whereabouts of his companions. Guard this young man well. He is important to the Druid – and what is important to the Druid may be dangerous for the likes of us.'

'You think he is a wizard?'

Petronax grinned and shrugged.

'By his build he is a soldier, but I do not know that he is not also a wizard. What signs would I see on his body if he were? If he is, you may be sure that Duke Arturus will not tolerate his presence in Camulodunum for long. You know what he's like about unchristian superstition. I don't know why he keeps the Druid so close by. Necessity probably – it keeps you pagan Combrogi happy.' Petronax was suddenly serious. 'Bedewyr – baptised Christian that I am – I would not lightly see the Druid upset. Ride swiftly and keep alert for trouble. I smell magic and I don't like the stink of it.'

Bedewyr nodded, trying to disguise his anxiety. Petronax made him nervous and the thought of magic, in which he fervently believed, terrified him. He fingered the lucky amulet that hung round his neck; it had been three times blessed and was a gift from his mother. It ought to serve. He forced himself to sound matter of fact: 'Do you have a message for the War Duke, Arturus?'

Petronax shook his head. 'No. But tell the Druid I'll find the others – the ones taken from here, and bring them back to Camulodunum. He has my word.'

Bedewyr nodded and spurred his horse onward. If he could deliver the unconscious stranger safely to Camulodunum, he might finally win some respect from Petronax.

It took longer than he would have liked to get back on the main road and when he had reached it, the echoing sound of the horse's hooves on the packed gravel surface only served to emphasise his loneliness and vulnerability. The road ran arrow straight for as far as the eye could see. Although it was overgrown in places and he had to be alert for the occasional pothole, it was still the fastest route to the fortress. It was also the most exposed. His neck prickled with the sensation of being watched.

He rode with one hand on the hilt of his sword, ready for trouble. When the injured man stirred and his hellhound barked, Bedewyr jumped so violently that he almost removed his horse's ears with an uncontrolled slash of his sword. Trembling from the shock of the sudden sound, he guided the two horses towards a small thicket of trees, where he dismounted and tried to tend to the man. The dog no longer growled but bared his teeth menacingly as Bedewyr attempted to untie and lift the man from the saddle. It was a task he managed without grace and he feared that his clumsy mishandling of the man may have hurt him further.

'My thanks.'

The man's voice was soft and he spoke Cornovian, Bedewyr's own tribal language, with an odd accent. Bedewyr was so startled it took him a moment to frame a stuttered reply.

'Y-you are welcome.' Bedewyr laid him gently on the dew-damp grass, then regretted it and tried to lift him onto his cloak. The man winced with pain at each movement so Bedewyr settled instead for giving him a drink from his canteen.

The right side of the man's head was dark with dried blood and a deep gash was visible, where the white skull had been partly exposed. Bedewyr tried not to stare. The dog immediately started to lick the wound. The man patted the huge beast somewhat absently, but seemed unperturbed by the great beast's ministrations.

'You were attacked?' Bedewyr asked.

'I don't remember.' Again the soft voice spoke clearly but he stressed the wrong syllable of each word.

'Who are you?' Bedewyr would not normally have

asked for a man's name so bluntly but he was intrigued – he could place neither his accent nor his nationality.

'I don't know. You don't know me?'

Bedewyr shook his head regretfully.

The man's dark eyes darkened further. 'I have a head wound?'

Bedewyr nodded and the man's expression cleared.

'Then I'm sure I'll remember soon.' He fingered the empty scabbard, tracing the inlay with his finger.

'It's no good. I almost remembered something then, but now it's gone.' He shook himself in irritation, then continued. 'I see I am without a weapon. I would be indebted to you and your tribe if you could lend me the use of a spare blade.' The man's elaborate politeness was both courtly and archaic. It confused Bedewyr further but, though he knew Petronax would have thought him a fool, he unpacked the spare sword he always carried in his pack and gave it to the man. According to the War Duke the new swords, recently forged, were vastly inferior to the ones their ancestors had made. A wise man, who could afford it, carried more than one, as they were apt to break. Bedewyr did not entirely trust the Druid and knew that he could be arming an enemy, that his spare sword could end up sheathed in his own chest, but his sympathy was roused by the man's confusion and gentle courtesy. When the man clasped the blade in his hand all doubt and uncertainty disappeared from his eyes. The darkness lessened. Bedewyr, too, was reassured. Surely no wizard would hold a sword with such easy familiarity, as if it was no more than an extension of his arm. The large dog suddenly paused from tending his master's wound and stood, tense and ready. The stranger tightened his grip on the sword and staggered to his feet. The two of them, dog and man, stared intently at a distant clump of thorn bushes. The man's face was hard and focused. A small band of Aenglisc raiders were charging towards them.

Bedewyr reached for his own sword. There seemed no question but that they would have to fight. Fear made his hand shake. It also made him blurt out, 'If you have no name, I'll call you Gawain after my brother who died. A man should not die nameless.'

The young stranger spoke with all the authority of a battle-hardened soldier. 'We are not going to die, at least not now. Stay away from my sword arm and leave the rest to us!' He indicated his hound with a slight inclination of his head and flashed Bedewyr a smile of surprising warmth. 'And thank you, it will be an honour to carry your brother's name into battle.'

The dog stood beside 'Gawain', something of his master's certainty evident in his stance. The low growl that issued from its throat had an almost jubilant quality. Gawain reached out and patted his head.

'I have misplaced your name, old friend, but I have

not forgotten you. You have fought by my side before.'

The look the war hound gave him was one of pure adoration.

The Aenglisc were shouting now, the ragged vain-glorious shouts of a mob urging each other on. Gawain found himself seeking something in his own mind, an inner habit of calm. He found it. His mind and body unified in a state of total concentration. The world narrowed. There was his sword, his dog, and his enemy. He may not remember his own name, but he remembered who he was. He was a warrior and this undisciplined mob was doomed.

~ Chapter Four ~

Gawain took in several pieces of information at once. The five men charging towards him were not enemies he had fought before – he knew that. They were simply dressed in long rustic tunics and trews. They wore no armour and ran bareheaded so that long dark-blonde hair streamed behind them. Even from several paces away they stank of cask courage. They waved long knives rather than swords in the hope of intimidating him, but he could sense their underlying fear. One of them, a big man built like a blacksmith wielded an axe, but it was a wood-cutting tool and single-headed, not a war axe. They carried no shields and they did not seem to his discerning eye to be experienced warriors.

Gawain felt no fear – a part of his mind ran through the best tactic to employ to despatch so many men without injuring himself. The dog beside him waited for the signal. The men were scarcely more than a metre away.

He could see small rivulets of sweat trickling down the face of the nearest man; see the glazed look of unfocused aggression. Now! The dog leapt forward and at the same instant Gawain attacked. The first man raised his long knife but Gawain slashed his sword in a sideways motion to slice through the muscle under the man's arm and open a deep wound across his chest. As the shocked man lost his balance and cried out in pain, the hound leapt for his throat.

Gawain felt a searing agony of pain across his own torso although the man's weapon had not so much as nicked his skin. At the same moment a picture of a smiling, blonde-haired child flashed across his inner vision – the child meant nothing to Gawain. He shook the image away just as he dismissed the pain from his mind. He had no time for weakness. He had no time for anything but the moment, the movement of the fight. He had not been touched and so, he knew, there could be no pain. Gawain's attention was focused on the axe man. He was taller than his unfortunate companion and heavily built. The man's face was set in a rictus of rage. He was screaming something in a language Gawain did not know. Spittle flecked his beard. The sound of the hound's growls and the weakening cries of the dog's victim sounded too loudly in Gawain's ears. He imagined he could feel the war hound's teeth ripping through his own flesh. He felt dizzy but he forced himself to concentrate. He could not remember previous fights in detail, but he knew that something was different about this one, something was wrong. Something that had once insulated him from the awareness of the pain he inflicted was gone. This new awareness made it much harder to keep to his task: to stay alive; kill his enemies. The axe man, who was now within hacking distance of Gawain's exposed body, hesitated as if steeling himself for the blow – it was all the time Gawain needed. He sliced down with all his sword's weight on the man's shoulder and all but severed his left arm. The nerves of his own left arm screamed out in agony but Gawain refused to listen to their lies; he was unhurt! The axe man tried to land a blow with his intact right arm but the shock of his injury had enfeebled him. Gawain ducked the blow, kneed him swiftly in the groin and kicked him so that he fell forward. At the same time, with a swift, horizontal, slicing blow he severed the jugular of the third man, who followed his fallen companion and stepped into the breach. The last two attackers slowed their charge. Three strong men were down and dying in a space of two or three paces. The hound had finished them off by tearing out their throats. Their screams of pain had ended as abruptly as they had begun. There was a strange kind of silence. Gawain could feel the terror of the two who remained, their conviction that they were about to die. Shock had sobered them up sharply, but they did not run. Somehow, Gawain knew that it would shame them to leave their leader on a battlefield; though they were not warriors they chose to die like warriors. They exchanged a look and charged together. Gawain mentally saluted their bravery while readying himself for the kill. Without signal or warning the war hound leapt for the smaller of the two men and with his considerable weight knocked him over. The second man tried to slice at Gawain's sword arm, but Gawain abruptly swapped his sword to his left hand and in one incongruously graceful motion sliced across his opponent's belly. He hunched forward whimpering, clutching his spilling guts. Gawain brought his raised sword down with all the force he could muster and severed the man's spine at the neck. He touched his own stomach and was surprised to find it whole and unmarked. His whole body burned with pain, though he was unharmed. Every limb shook and he felt sick at the carnage and the stink of blood and faeces that assaulted him. The man the dog was savaging still lived – just. Gawain whistled. The dog obediently moved away from the fallen enemy, though his low-pitched growl indicated his dissatisfaction. His victim was scarcely alive. Gawain ended the man's suffering with a clean blow across his bloodied neck.

Gawain staggered backwards, fascinated and appalled by the scene. He allowed the sword to fall from his hand. He patted the war hound who nuzzled him contentedly with his gory muzzle; the hound's breath smelled of fresh blood, his strong teeth were still stained with it. This all felt so wrong. Gawain knew he had killed before. He knew what to do and thought he knew what to expect and yet he had never felt like this before he was sure of it. He had never suffered with his victims before, never imagined what it was to feel the full force of his own blade. For a vertiginous moment he had even glimpsed his own face, contorted with a terrible, grim joy as he hacked with all his strength at another man's flesh. He sat down shakily on the damp grass. The bump on the head had affected more than his memory.

Bedewyr was looking at him, his own sword drawn but unbloodied. Bedewyr's face was pale and he spoke in little more than a shocked whisper.

'I have never seen anything like that – you are so fast …' The whole fight had been over in a matter of heartbeats. 'Where did you learn to fight like that?'

Gawain found his voice. 'I don't remember, but I fear that I have had much practice.' He wanted to vomit but knew that he would not, he wanted to cry but could not. He knew that his body had done all this before and was responding with the blunted reactions borne of experience. His mind rebelled. He had done a terrible thing. He had killed five men. He had felt them die. This had not happened before. He wiped his hands on the grass and cleaned Bedewyr's sword – automatic gestures. He handed the sword back to Bedewyr.

'I'm sorry – the blade is slightly nicked and a little blunted. It cut through bone without shattering – it is a good blade. Please take it – I don't think it is safe for me to have such a weapon.'

Bedewyr flinched at the word 'bone' and did not disagree. He was more afraid of Gawain than he had been before. His eyes had a wariness about them that had not been there scant minutes earlier. To Gawain's eyes Bedewyr looked too young to have seen butchery like this before.

'I would have helped, you know,' Bedewyr began. 'But it was over too fast – and the dog ...' Bedewyr shuddered.

'Do you not fight with wardogs?'

Bedewyr nodded, 'Yes, but I have never seen any hound half this size or half this savage, I—'

'There is no need to fear him. I can't remember his name but he will not harm you if you do not harm me.' Gawain tried to make his voice as gentle and unthreatening as possible.' Do you have some more of that water?'

He rinsed his mouth and spat on the ground.

'What do you do with the dead here?'

'We do not bury our enemies.'

Gawain nodded. 'Do you wish to claim their skulls?'

he asked matter of factly and was surprised by the horrified reaction on Bedewyr's face.

Gawain shrugged. 'Some people find it potent to keep the heads of their enemies. If you are not one of them, that is fine by me. Now, where were you taking me? I think we should go quickly before there are more of these – what do you call these people?'

'They are Aenglisc. They are trying to take over our land. I was asked to take you to the War Duke Arturus and the Druid.' Bedewyr watched Gawain closely for his reaction to either of the two most important names he knew, but he was disappointed. Gawain merely swung himself easily into the Roman style saddle and nodded.

'Lead the way, Bedewyr, and don't worry – I am not a mad man and I do not think you a coward!'

Bedewyr blushed at the accuracy with which Gawain had guessed his thoughts, and spurred his horse on. He knew that Gawain fought less like a man than a demon. Bedewyr grew cold. Could he be a wizard after all?

~ Chapter Five ~

'Bryn?'

As soon as the door of her prison slammed shut, Ursula ran to the crumpled figure of the boy.

'Bryn? Answer me, Bryn. Are you all right?'

The black shadow, that was all she could see of Bryn in the sudden darkness, struggled to a sitting position.

'I've lost a tooth,' he said thickly. 'But I think it was one I was meant to lose.' Ursula restrained herself from hugging Dan's squire. Although he was little more than eight years old, among his own people he counted as a man and Ursula had learned to respect male Combrogi pride. She contented herself with a manly clasp of the boy's thin shoulder.

'How do you come to be here? I thought you were going to stay with Kai and King Macsen.'

'I was going to, but Braveheart bolted after Dan. I tried to catch him but by the time I'd grabbed his collar we'd got caught up in the Veil. I could see Dan's back and then, when we stepped through ...'

Ursula found she was holding her breath. Bryn had seen his own father die and much of his tribe slaughtered, she did not want him to have seen what had happened to Dan, his Lord, his protector, his hero.

'I saw Dan and the blood and everything. I was going to go to him but I heard voices. I couldn't hear what they said and I was afraid they were Ravens or whoever had hurt the Bear Sark.' Ursula heard the slight hesitation in his voice, the trembling that told her that he wept bitter tears of shame that he had not immediately run to his Lord's side.

'I hid – I was a coward – and they put Dan on a horse and took him away. Braveheart stayed with him. He was braver than I was. There were two of them but they separated. I was going to track the one who took Dan's body. I started to, but then this big foreigner – not a Raven, something else – caught me and knocked me over, and when I came round I was outside this hut,' he used a derisory word for 'hut' that meant something closer to 'hovel'. 'And then they threw me in here.'

Ursula sought his shoulder again, felt the stiffness in it, the effort he was making not to sob out loud.

'Bryn, I think Dan was past your help. You did the right thing. No one would hurt Braveheart – he's a valuable animal—'

'He won't fight for foreigners he's Combrogi!' Bryn

flashed back, outraged that she could even suggest such disloyalty from his father's former war dog. Once more Ursula had said the wrong thing. It was a gift she'd got. She let her hand fall heavily from his shoulder.

She sensed rather than saw the slight relaxation in his posture.

'You think Dan is dead don't you?' Bryn's voice was low now, low and tightly controlled, bound with pain and the memory of pain. Ursula nodded and, realising she could not be seen in the darkness, answered him in the same tight, quiet voice.

'Yes, there was a lot of blood and—'

'He's not dead. I'd know it – I'm his squire I pledged my life to him – I'd know it!'

Ursula didn't argue. What would be the point? Instead, she took the knife, and feeling her way, silently undid his bonds.

'We've got to get out of here,' she said in her most matter of fact voice. 'There's another prisoner here, a Raven – the other lot who brought you here are Aenglisc or something. We have to take the Raven with us.'

Bryn appeared to be wiping his face. There was a pause, then he said, 'I think they're preparing some sort of ceremony – they are taking things to the grove of trees near this place. I don't know, but by the way they looked at me – I don't think I'll see the spring.'

Bryn had something of Kai's black humour. Ursula

earnestly wished that Bryn had stayed with Kai, in Macsen's land. She trusted Kai – he would have cared for him and ensured that he stood as good a chance as any of reaching adulthood. Now, the odds on him living that long were severely lengthened. It was up to her to keep both of them alive.

'Hey, Larcius! My friend here thinks we might be used as part of a ceremony. What do you think – do these Aenglisc go in for that kind of thing?' She spoke in good soldier's Latin; it was the only kind she knew. Larcius's version was different but still comprehensible. Anyway his groan told her as much as his words.

'Sometimes they sacrifice victims for auguries – most of them are pagans.' He spat his contempt. That surprised Ursula. All the Ravens she had met before were pagans too. She wondered what he meant, but had more pressing things on her mind.

'We'll have to be ready to make a run for it when they take us outside. Larcius, you're going to have stand up – I'll support you all I can but we'll only have one chance!'

The man grunted what might have been an affirmative. She switched languages – Bryn's Latin was rudimentary. 'Bryn, you'll know something of battle wounds – see if you can do anything with Larcius. Be gentle, we don't *know* that he's a bad Raven – call him a Roman if it helps, you know, like Rufinus who helped King Macsen.'

Ursula returned to the corpses by the wall. She had not checked them for weapons. She steeled herself against the gruesomeness of her task. Their captors had been careless – she took that as a good omen – they'd left two other belt knives – short but sharp and serviceable.

She would have liked to have a plan but, ignorant of where they were held, the lie of the land and the number of their enemies, they would have to improvise. But before that they would have to wait. She had always hated waiting. Her muscles knotted and it was by force of will alone that she stayed calm and outwardly controlled. Larcius and Bryn didn't have a hope in hell without her.

Bryn had bound Larcius' wound so tightly that the man had cursed, which was unfortunate as Bryn was at least familiar with all the Latin expletives. Only Ursula's swift intervention prevented Bryn from punching his patient. When she had calmed them both down she questioned Larcius closely. With what she could glean, she managed to piece together a picture of their situation.

They were in a coastal settlement that had recently been established by the Saxons or the Aenglisc as they called themselves. The Combrogi were fighting to keep the Aenglisc from gaining more territory. Oddly, Larcius seemed to regard himself as Combrogi, though he couldn't understand Bryn at all. Ursula concluded that the word must mean something different to Larcius, as to Ursula the word 'Combrogi' described the Celtic tribes she had fought with in Macsen's world, her own adopted people. It was clear that some considerable time had elapsed since Macsen's reign. Exactly how long it was impossible for her to ascertain, but it was time enough for the distinction between the Combrogi and their old enemies to have blurred. Anyway, it wasn't relevant to their escape – she would worry about the wider world when she was no longer imprisoned and when Bryn was safe.

It was hard to gauge time in the dark but it was a long time before the Aenglisc finally came for them. Ursula had wrapped rope around her hands to simulate the bonds she had cut through. She had done the same for Bryn. Each of them was armed with a belt knife, a weapon she would not have chosen to pit against a sword but which was considerably better than nothing.

They allowed themselves to be manhandled into the bright sunlight of late afternoon. Ursula's eyes streamed in the sudden brightness. Bryn looked terrible. His face was pale and strained beneath its liberal coating of blood and grime. Larcius was the biggest shock of all. He was dressed well, in fine wool, badly stained with blood from his wound. He was not tall, several inches short of her own height, but it was his face which so startled her – she had never seen a man so handsome.

His eyes were the most piercing blue she had ever seen, his hair dark and crisply curled, worn short in Roman fashion. He favoured her with a smile of knowing complicity. Something strange happened to her stomach.

'Lady, you are beautiful as well as courageous—'

Any further compliments were silenced by a hard, back-handed swipe across his mouth from the burliest of their captors. That focused both their minds. They were surrounded by Aenglisc and were being marched in the direction of a small wooded glade, as Bryn had guessed. The men around them were armed with spears, but to Ursula's experienced eyes they seemed old weapons, badly maintained, and the men who wielded them did so without conviction. They had a chance here; she could feel it. She did not take it yet. She did not know where they could run to and they needed horses if they were to get Larcius to safety. He could not straighten up and he stumbled ahead of her on unsteady legs. The men stopped a few metres away from the centre of the glade by a large tree. It might have been an oak – Ursula was not too good at such identifications. Dan's sword, 'Bright Killer' barred the way, thrust almost up to the hilt in the soft earth. It glinted with a cold, silver light. Ursula blinked back tears. This was not the moment to grieve for Dan.

'That's Dan's sword stuck in that rock!' hissed Bryn.

What was Bryn talking about? There was no rock,

though Ursula could see that magic distorted the air around it like a summer heat haze. Then an elaborately dressed woman walked into view, her long dark hair a silky curtain almost covering the heavily scarred portion of her face. Rhonwen! Ursula struggled to retain her composure; their chances of survival had plummeted again.

Rhonwen was Macsen's sister, a princess, and a powerful sorceress who had run away through the Veil when Ursula had proved the more powerful. Ursula's head had always ached when Rhonwen was near, as if the magic warned her of Rhonwen's presence. This time she had received no such warning and she could think of no reason why Rhonwen should be here. It was Macsen's sister who had called Ursula from her own time, had helped her, been helped by her and still, Ursula knew, hated her. She was no friend of Ursula's, and Rhonwen, unlike Ursula, clearly retained her magic in this world. Though Ursula could no longer wield it she could feel it crackle like static against her skin. With an almost physical ache of longing she wanted to be able to command it as she once had. But she could not. She would not let that loss hurt her. She could not afford to blunt her wits with a useless emotion like regret. She flexed her fingers surreptitiously. If she did not have magic she would have to rely on brute force, cold steel and the implacable firmness of her will.

~ Chapter Six ~

Rhonwen smiled. It was not a pleasant smile. Her emerald eyes met Ursula's briefly. Rhonwen's look was cold and did not acknowledge the history between them. The one-time princess raised her face to the heavens and began to chant. Ursula had heard her incantations before, but the sound still raised the hairs on her neck and arms. Rhonwen looked more unearthly than ever. Her face was unchanged; though Ursula was surprised that Rhonwen had not attempted to mask the pink rawness of her burnt face as she once had. To Ursula's clear perceptions one side of her face was beautiful, flawless, the other a puckered contusion of scars. But the air was so thick with magic it was hard for her to know what others saw. Rhonwen had always dressed to impress in Celtic splendour but what impressed these Aenglisc was strange indeed. Rhonwen was wearing a slightly stained silk robe of deep green under a fur mantle. The fur mantle was little more than the skin of a wolf hung with the bleached white of animal skulls. Around her neck she wore a series of bone amulets and two or three small leather pouches decorated with feathers. They contrasted oddly with the sophistication of the gown. Five or six sizeable objects also hung from the leather belt at her waist, most did not bear close scrutiny but Ursula recognised a beautifully mounted crystal ball in an elaborate gold setting and a polished boar's tooth also on a gold chain. She looked wilder, more savage than she had before.

Ursula licked dry lips. She did not know what function was served by Rhonwen's apparel. Maybe the Aenglisc believed the objects had ritual power but there was power here, for sure. Rhonwen's chanting had released it. Ursula felt like she was imprisoned in glass, she felt as if some vital nerve connection in her body had been severed, like she had lost the use of a limb. Smelling it, tasting it, needing it so badly maddened her. It made it hard for her to concentrate.

'This is our Heahrune, that is what you would call "Priestess". You must walk alone to stand by her. It is sacred ground fit only for the Heahrune and for the sacrifice.' The man who spoke, stumbled a little over his Latin but conveyed his meaning well enough. He and the others stood aside to let the three prisoners – Ursula, Bryn and Larcius – walk towards Rhonwen. Bryn looked scared, and Larcius resigned. Rhonwen saw

Larcius and ceased chanting.

'Ah, Ambrosius's boy.' Her still beguiling voice was lazily insulting. 'It is a pity we couldn't make a common cause. We could have achieved much together.'

Larcius managed a smooth smile. 'I came to you in good faith, Priestess. I do not think much of your hospitality. It is indeed a pity that I could not have found something to do with such a beautiful woman as yourself, that would not have shamed my noble father's house. I have never much liked the idea of death rather than dishonour but ...' he shrugged, somehow emulating Rhonwen's air of careless indolence. It was quite impressive for a man about to be murdered and only slightly marred by the beads of sweat that glistened on his forehead.

Ursula tore her eyes away from Larcius to focus on her surroundings. The village was no further than a field away, a field in which sturdy ponies grazed. She caught Bryn's eye. He'd spotted them too. Bryn was good with horses, had been raised with them. He appraised them through narrowed eyes and gave the briefest of nods.

Rhonwen's musical voice was continuing, in Latin: 'These people trust me to prophesy their future and their fortunes in the war that is coming. Soon the warriors of this tribe will return and these men would know their chances. Will it be feasting and ale over the hearth fires or libations over the grave goods of the buried dead? We shall see.' She smiled serenely.

'I'm sure Bryn knows how the druids once read the future in the death throes of their chosen sacrifice. Agony can be so very instructive.' She repeated her remarks in Bryn's own tongue. He paled still further and looked sick. 'I have learned much since I have been among these people. Their faith in the goddess Nerthus is strong – she has ever been a demanding woman, the goddess, and here she likes her feast of suffering.'

Ursula found herself wondering what had happened to Rhonwen, since last they had met, to make her so openly sadistic. She had not been like that before.

Rhonwen continued. 'I will make my foretelling from the direction you fall when the men send their spears to impale you, the position of your limbs as your fingers implore me for mercy, and after.' She smiled again, a careless smile. 'I will study your entrails as you writhe and see our victory in your agonies.'

Ursula believed her. Rhonwen would do that. Rhonwen too was a stranger here – her clear, uninflected Latin gave her away. She had to perform this ritual to keep her position with the Aenglisc; it was what they expected of their Heahrune. Rhonwen would not meet her eyes and Ursula felt the first intimations of uncontrollable, visceral fear. There would be no mercy here. Until that moment Ursula had thought that love of Macsen might temper Rhonwen's fury with one of his oath-bound warriors. She knew now that it would not, could not. But Ursula was not ready to suffer the fate Rhonwen had planned for her, and only her own wits would save her. She thought rapidly, desperately. She turned her attention to Rhonwen's hands. When she raised them in invocation Ursula was ready. She had her knife out in an instant and screamed, 'Go! Go!' in both Bryn's language and in Latin as she sprang forward to grab Rhonwen. Ursula stood behind the priestess pulling her head back by her shining hair. Ursula laid her hard knife against Rhonwen's soft throat. Instantly, with reflexes that were a credit to his tough Combrogi training, Bryn rushed to Larcius's side and helped him towards the ponies on the other side of the copse. The armed men raised their spears but dared not tread on sacred ground. One man let his spear fly, but it fell short and landed close to Rhonwen's feet. Ursula grasped Rhonwen tighter and shot the men a warning look. No one else made the attempt. Whatever Rhonwen had told them about treading on hallowed ground had clearly frightened them more than the fear of her displeasure, as no one made any move to perform the obvious manoeuvre of sneaking round the back of the trees and attacking Ursula from behind. Ursula's knees were shaking, but she kept her hand steady. She was taking a huge gamble. She did not know what she was up against. She was acutely aware of how she towered over the tiny priestess and how useless her physical advantage would be if Rhonwen had improved her mastery of magic.

'Speak and I'll kill you!' Ursula kept her voice low and vengeful.

It took Rhonwen an instant to recover from her shock then bright flames leapt round them as Rhonwen summoned fire from the air. Tongues of fire roared and licked at Ursula's feet; she could feel the heat of it singeing the leather of her Combrogi made shoes. She could smell the burning leather and yet, though she no longer commanded the magic she could instinctively recognise it and know its nature – and this time all Rhonwen had done was to create a complex illusion. Ursula understood exactly how she had done it. Rhonwen's skill at weaving an illusion had improved but it remained an illusion nonetheless.

'You'll have to do better than that Rhonwen,' Ursula snarled, pulling Rhonwen's head back, and nicking the skin of her neck with the knife so that a small ruby of blood appeared on Rhonwen's white throat. Envy of Rhonwen's magic made Ursula more brutal than she had intended.

'It will take more than illusion to frighten me!'

It was a challenge and Ursula knew it, but every moment she could distract the Aenglisc from the escape of Bryn and Larcius increased their chances of survival. Rhonwen raised her hand. There was a sulphurous smell and black smoke swirled around Rhonwen's ankles, dark shapes blossomed from the fire; horned demons with the torsos of men and the hind legs of goats; goblins with huge misshapen faces, hairy as apes. Each of the apparitions was armed with a shining spear. They closed on Ursula menacingly hissing, grunting and brandishing their spears. Their eyes burned with malevolence, the goblins drooled and slavered and stank like the dead. The stench almost made Ursula gag. The Aenglisc stumbled back further from the glade in horror and fear. To Ursula the figures lacked solidity. She knew how they were made. Could Rhonwen only manage illusion or was there more? Rhonwen had made real fire once, in Macsen's land, and bore the scars on her face to prove it – could she still? It was that power she feared, the magic that changed things, not this ghoulish, insubstantial, spectacle.

'Do you think I'm afraid of your puppets of air, Rhonwen – have you still not mastered real magic?'

Ursula had mastered real magic, in Macsen's land, and now it was lost to her. The bitter taste of loss was nastier by far than the acrid smoke and putrid odours of Rhonwen's conjuring.

Ursula had known she could not kill Rhonwen in cold blood. She lacked Rhonwen's ruthlessness. She was surer of it as she felt her warm flesh under her knife;

saw Rhonwen's blood well from the tiny puncture mark she'd made with her stolen knife. Rhonwen was brave. She was Combrogi and she did not flinch. How was Ursula to break this stand-off? She was hampered by her ignorance of the Aenglisc language. She dragged Rhonwen closer to the assembled men, closer to Dan's sword, stuck so strangely in the ground. The apparitions followed them of course and the men shrank back from the black smoke and the grotesque gathering of fiends. Ursula wasn't even sure that the men could still see her. For all she knew they might believe that she was being slaughtered by Rhonwen's demonic allies.

'Hey, you!' she called towards the man who had spoken in rude Latin. She made her voice as strident as possible and hoped that Rhonwen's magic would not distort it.

'Tell the men I will kill the Heahrune if anyone approaches my friends or me! I am a Heahrune too and her magic can't hurt me. Now, pass me the sword and get me a horse and I will leave you in peace.'

The man looked fearful, the more so as Ursula was clearly unafraid of the unnatural creatures that threatened her. He said something to his companions – she could only hope it was a fair translation. She squinted past the ugliest of the goblins to see one man, who did not appear to be armed, back away. She trusted that he had gone to get her a horse.

'Lady, Heahrune,' the Latin speaker began respectfully, 'I cannot take the sword as it is trapped in that boulder.'

Dan's sword was not a metre in front of her, trapped in nothing more than the soft loam of the earth, though it seemed that only Ursula and Rhonwen herself could see that truth.

'Try!' Ursula said shortly. The man looked at Rhonwen who appeared to blink her agreement. Ursula tightened her grip on her captive and tensed. The man pulled at the sword with all his strength but was unable to move it. Ursula could see his muscles straining as he pulled, but the sword would not shift. He signalled to his younger friend, who had the sturdy frame of a man well used to hard physical labour. He too strained convincingly without moving the sword hilt so much as a millimetre. Perhaps Rhonwen's magic was more potent than it appeared. It looked like Ursula would have to get the sword herself. She was trying to work out how she might manage that manoeuvre without relinquishing her grip on Rhonwen when she heard the approaching rumble of horse's hooves.

'Ursula!' It was Bryn's voice. He sounded petrified.

'I'm fine, Bryn. I have Rhonwen, but I need to get Dan's sword.'

She paused. She could not ask Bryn to walk through the circle of monsters that would seem both real and substantial to his eyes. Anyway, although he was not small for an eight-year-old he was too small to restrain Rhonwen. She made a decision – she would have to rely on Larcius. The illusion of menacing demons still grunting and waving their silver spears was just dense enough to block her view in Bryn's direction.

'Is Larcius with you, Bryn?'

'Yes.'

'Larcius! I need you to hold on to Rhonwen while I get the sword. Walk through the circle of demons – they won't hurt you!'

'How can you be so sure?' Larcius sounded scared.

'I was a sorceress once – trust me.'

'Lady, I fear you are a sorceress still – you have enchanted me!' She could tell from his voice that he was dismounting and moments later, passing through demons, wielding his knife like a sword. The demons ignored him and having no independent reality, they continued with their incomprehensible series of grunts and ineffectual spear waving.

'See – it's not real!' Ursula added, encouragingly.

Sweat poured down Larcius' perfect face, leaving rivulets of clean skin through the grime, like a tear-stained child. He bowed to the two women and, keeping his knife extended, walked cautiously to Ursula.

'Keep the blade at her throat – if she tries anything, kill her.' Ursula said harshly, indicating Rhonwen with a dismissive jerk of her head. Larcius looked at Ursula, warily.

She was fleetingly aware of how frightening she herself must look, then dismissed the thought. If she kept them alive, did it matter?

Ursula deliberately walked through the demons and goblins in front of them. Realising the illusion was destroyed, Rhonwen allowed the apparition to dissolve. Ursula marched forward to the place where Dan's sword protruded from the ground. She turned to face the Aenglisc and indicated that the Latin speaker should translate her words.

'This is a Combrogi sword. It was borne by the bravest man I have ever known. It shall never rest in enemy hands. Men of your people killed that man and this sword will have its vengeance!' Afterwards, she would have found it impossible to explain why she made such a speech, but it felt fitting. Her eyes blurred with tears as she lifted the sword easily from its sheath of earth and held it aloft in triumph. There was a gasp from the Aenglisc. Through the blurring effect of her tears, Ursula could make out the illusion that Rhonwen had created round the sword – a huge boulder surrounded by a cairn of smaller stones, a more fitting memorial to Dan than to his sword.

One of the Aenglisc had returned with a horse complete with leather bridle and Roman saddle. Ursula saw the fear in his eyes as he handed her the reins. She kept her own face impassive as a rock. It was hard not to break down and weep. She had forgotten Dan's sword had moulded itself to the very shape of his hand. She was almost overwhelmed by grief. She managed to mount the horse without assistance – there were no stirrups but she was used to that. She rode over to Rhonwen and Larcius. Rhonwen's face was closed and grim. Larcius looked astonished.

'Tie her up!' she said to Larcius. 'And gag her! I want no invocations following us.'

She kept Bright Killer pointed at Rhonwen's throat.

'I will not kill you, Rhonwen, though I could. I give you your life for Macsen's sake but in all this' – she slashed at Rhonwen's belt with its assortment of fetishes – 'I fear you bring him shame. Is this the way a Combrogi priestess and princess debases herself!'

Like the previous speech the words came to her mouth unbidden. She did not know why she was saying them but Rhonwen flinched. Ursula knew enough about Rhonwen's past to be able to hurt her. She picked up the crystal ball and boar's tooth with her sword, an idea forming in her overheated brain. Maybe she could buy them more time. Taking the ball and tooth in her left hand she held them up for the Aenglisc to see.

'I am a great and powerful Heahrune. If you untie this woman before sunset all her power will fly to me. If you pursue us she will die! With these things of hers I can kill her however far apart we are. Without her you are powerless against me. Do you understand?'

Ursula's translator looked grave and it seemed as if her guess about the importance of these objects was a good one. He trembled as he translated her words to the other Aenglisc. She hoped they could reach some kind of safety before sunset.

Rhonwen lay on the ground beside the magical cairn of stones, trussed up like a chicken and gagged with a strip of fabric from her own robe. Ursula had a bad feeling that she would pay for this one day.

'Come, Larcius, let's get out of here.'

'Bryn, well done! Let's ride!'

Trusting to the power of her words she turned her back on the armed Aenglisc spearmen and rode away. She hated to turn her back on an enemy but some instinct told her that it would give credence to her claims of power. It must have worked: no spear buried itself between her shoulder blades and they rode on unhindered. It took a long time for her breathing to return to normal and the palsied shaking of her hands to cease.

~ *Chapter Seven* ~

Bedewyr and Gawain rode on in silence. Bedewyr was too afraid to speak – he did not know what kind of man or monster rode with him – while Gawain struggled to obliterate the memories of the recent fight from his mind. His body ached as if he had received the blows he'd dealt. He did not want to think too much. He trusted that his memory would return, as he trusted that the youth Bedewyr would take him somewhere safe. It was by far the easiest recourse. He trusted as the giant dog trotting at his side trusted, and relaxed into the saddle.

He did not recognise the land they travelled through. They saw no fellow travellers on the overgrown Roman road and the land on either side of them was untilled and abandoned; it was like riding at the end of the world. They stopped a couple of times to drink water from a nearby stream and Bedewyr shared with him some coarse unleavened bread and poorly dried meat.

Gawain ate both with quiet gratitude.

'Do you remember anything now?' asked Bedewyr tentatively.

Gawain shook his head. 'If I may borrow your brother's name a little longer, I would be grateful.'

'Your courage and skill in battle lends it honour,' replied Bedewyr without conviction, though it was mostly true. His own brother would have been proud beyond description to have possessed even a quarter of this man's skill with the sword – for himself he had never seen such savagery and Bedewyr feared it as much as he admired it.

It was growing dark when Gawain became aware of a change in the appearance of the countryside. Even in the failing light it was obvious that they now rode through land that was farmed and cared for. He became uneasily aware of hidden eyes observing him. The road ahead was blocked by three mounted men riding abreast towards them. Gawain wished earnestly that he had not returned Bedewyr's sword. The men were dressed as Ravens. All three wore helmets that covered their cheeks and shaded their faces; the helmets gleamed, bright with silver. They each carried flaming torches and their mail shirts glinted fire in their reflected light. Bedewyr relaxed perceptibly and Gawain was confused. Bedewyr was Combrogi; were these Ravens allies?

Bedewyr rode ahead of him and eagerly greeted the

mounted men in Latin so heavily accented it took Gawain a moment to recognise the language he knew as well as the Combrogi tongues. 'Petronax went to track this man's companions. Tell the Druid I have brought one of the men he sought.'

Two of the mounted men turned the horses round and spurred them back the way they'd come, the third man listened as Bedewyr spoke in a low voice, with rapid frightened glances in Gawain's direction. The war dog's teeth were bared.

Gawain spurred his horse forward, determined not to be excluded from a conversation that might bring him trouble. 'I fear that I have not my true name to offer you but for now I am Gawain. You are?'

Gawain spoke good Latin to Bedewyr's evident surprise. His companion's face remained closed, unreadable. He was a big man, broad shouldered and heavily muscled. His face was wide and his nose, broken more than once, gave him the pugnacious air of a boxer. A thin scar that ran down one side of his face from temple to chin – a knife wound by the look of it – gave his mouth a slightly twisted look.

'I am Medraut, rightful King of Ceint and Count of the Saxon Shore. I believe you are a friend of the Druid.' The man's eyes were grey and cold, but he made no move to draw a weapon.

Gawain felt his heart pump faster. There was danger

here and he was unarmed. This man had the eyes of a killer.

'I was attacked and sadly my memory of the Druid, as of all else, eludes me. But I am grateful to Bedewyr, for he helped me when I was wounded. I am in his debt.'

Medraut gave him a bold, appraising stare. 'I see you are unarmed.'

'But for my dog.'

The dog's teeth were still bared and he gave a low growl.

'A fine specimen,' said Medraut.

Gawain made his gaze as uncompromising as Medraut's own. It was a kind of challenge, as blatant in its way as the dog's warning growl.

Medraut seemed to accept it as such, but continued: 'Welcome to Camulodunum, the seat of Arturus Urbicus, War Duke of Britain.'

Gawain inclined his head slightly in acknowledgement of the reluctant welcome and signalled for the war dog to cease his growling. Keeping a close eye on Medraut he rode on beside him.

It was dark by the time they reached Camulodunum proper. The great Roman walls of stone were mixed with layers of red tiles; clear even in the flickering light of the braziers that lit the walls. The stone structure was topped by a well-manned wooden palisade. To Gawain it seemed that the whole area thrummed with nervous tension, with the anxieties of many men at battle readiness. It made his own stomach churn with nerves. The gate to Camulodunum was massive and heavily guarded. It swung open to admit them and Gawain found himself facing a small cluster of strangers, all armed, he noted warily, and all were staring at him expectantly. A soldier took his horse and Medraut indicated that he should dismount. Gawain laid a warning hand on the war hound and stood to a kind of attention, though in truth he felt dizzy from the head wound, the long ride and the after-effects of the bloody battle.

One man stepped forward from the waiting throng. He was wearing a dark hooded cloak that covered most of his face and body, but there was something familiar about his movements, something that hovered on the very edge of Gawain's memory. The man clasped him in a warm embrace.

'*Daniel*, by Lugh, it is you and you are safe.'

'Do I know you?' Gawain's voice was hesitant.

The man by way of answer threw back his hood and fixed him with a searching look. It was the bard, Taliesin. He looked older and his beard was greyer than the last time Dan had seen him, standing at Macsen's shoulder, saluting him in farewell, but it was unmistakably Taliesin. He did not think to wonder at the change in him for in that one instant Gawain felt his personal universe tilt and realign. He moved from being Gawain, the unknown soldier, to Dan, schoolboy and former Combrogi warrior. It was a strange and dizzying realignment.

'Taliesin? But what—?'

'Later, Daniel,' Taliesin whispered under his breath. 'There is too much to say. But where is Ursula?'

'I don't know. We were together, and then there was an attack and there was no time. My God, Ursula!' Dan paled. How could he have forgotten Ursula even with concussion? He felt flooded with appalling guilt. 'I banged my head, and forgot who I was.'

'And who is this boy, Druid, that you have brought to this citadel?' It was Medraut, unmoved by the reunion.

'Why, Medraut, I thought that a fighter such as yourself would recognise another in the same heroic mould. This is the Bear Sark of legend, come as I have ever promised to help us in our hour of darkest need.' Taliesin paused for dramatic effect. 'I have told you before of the prophecy given to me in the sacred grove by the wisest of sages. "As the bear on the high hillside protects the cubs, so *The Bear* of Ynys Prydein, the Island of the Mighty, protects its own. Remember *The Bear* and cherish it, for when *The Bear* is gone the hillside falls." This man may yet fulfil the prophecy.' Taliesin beamed triumphantly and Dan had the uncomfortable sensation that he had walked in on someone else's dream. The world darkened and he felt a thundering in his ears like the sound of a thousand horsemen at full gallop. For the first time in his life he passed out.

Dan woke to find himself in a chamber of some magnificence. He was lying on a sheepskin stretcher in a warm room. He heard voices arguing. He shut his eyes again the better to listen.

'Look, whatever Taliesin has said to us in the past – he's exaggerated. This *Dan* is a youth – no more. I don't doubt that he knows how to fight in a skirmish but he's no heroic fighter. He's no older than Bedewyr.'

Dan recognised the first voice as belonging to Medraut, the second was new to him.

'And Bedewyr claims that this youth killed five Aenglisc single-handed – well, with the help of that dog of his.'

Dan opened his eyes to see 'that dog of his', Braveheart, his faithful hound, mounting guard over his stretcher. Dan lay still, trying to orient himself. He was in a room of apparently Raven design and luxury. The complex mosaic of the floor was warm to the touch and the air was scented and clean. He was in Camulodunum, which even in Macsen's day had been a major city – though admittedly less major, once Boudicca had burned it to the ground. Taliesin was there, surrounded by Ravens. What could be going on? He had left

Taliesin with Macsen and the other Combrogi when he and Ursula, having defeated the Ravens, had entered the Veil. How could Taliesin be here, now, ahead of them, aged, and working with the Ravens? It made no sense. Did it matter? Whatever was going on, his first duty was to get out of the city, find Ursula and try to get them home. His thoughts were interrupted by the warm wetness of Braveheart's tongue greeting his renewed consciousness with noisy enthusiasm.

'I see you have awoken.' It was a man's voice, the same voice that had been speaking to Medraut.

Dan struggled gracelessly to his feet with a little assistance from Braveheart.

'Sir,' he began, in Latin. 'I apologise for the display of weakness – I sustained a head wound earlier, I—'

'Please, no apology, come and make yourself comfortable. You would have wine? We still have wine to offer honoured guests.'

The speaker was a slim young man, clean-shaven with short blond hair worn in a clipped military style. Dressed in a knee-length undyed tunic decorated with red roundels at the shoulders, he lay in Roman fashion on a shabby gilded couch. He waved Dan in the direction of a second couch, covered in a sheepskin to disguise its much-mended upholstery.

I am Arturus Urbicus, War Duke of Britannia, and I believe that you are the Bear Sark of legend.'

Dan did not know how to respond to that, but sat awkwardly on the couch as if it were a sofa. He took the wine offered to him by a young servant boy in a home-spun tunic, and sipped it. It was strong. He dare not drink more. He needed what remained of his wits.

'I'm not sure what you mean.'

Medraut laughed abruptly. 'You are not alone in that. According to the Druid, our merlin-man, you fight like a demon from the very bowels of hell and are exactly what we need to help our cause.' His tone was mocking.

Dan said nothing, being uncomfortably aware, for the first time, of the silent audience of men observing him from the furthest walls of the chamber. It was a very large hall and the domestic nature of the arranged couches had misled him from its public function. It was a kind of audience chamber and any impression of intimacy was illusory; all that was done here was done for display. That thought did not make him any more comfortable.

'Are you the Bear Sark that the Druid has told us so much about?'

Arturus looked at him with piercing blue eyes that seemed older and more harrowed than his youthful demeanour suggested. Dan felt compelled to honesty.

'I was the Bear Sark, yes, but …' He paused aware of how strange his words would seem. 'But, I do not think I am that person now.'

There was another loud guffaw from Medraut who spoke rapidly to Arturus in the language of the Carvetii. 'See, I told you. He is a fraud and a weakling – the Druid plays a game of his own. I don't know why you trust him.'

Dan wondered if the assembled men could understand Medraut's rapid Carvettian, or had he changed languages only to keep his thought from Dan? In the same tongue, Dan replied, 'I may be a weakling, but I am no fraud. I was called the Bear Sark before, when I fought for King Macsen …' he paused not knowing how to explain the gulf between that place and this. He understood now what Ursula had known at once at an almost cellular level: this was not Macsen's world and they were not what they had once been. 'I don't know what you have been told about me but I'm not sure I am what you need. Anyway, I can't stay here. I have to help my friend who is in trouble.'

'The Boar Skull?'

If Arturus had been surprised by Dan's grasp of the tribal language he did not show it, his tone was measured, calm.

'Yes, the Boar Skull.'

Medraut murmured to Arturus. 'I don't like it. We should not trust this man.'

'But what if he is the Bear Sark? To have such a figure with us would surely inspire the men. We would be fools to throw away such a prize! And then there is the prophecy …' Arturus speaking in little more than a whisper glanced appraisingly at the waiting men, who were fidgeting slightly as they watched the scene played out. 'And morale is not all it might be, since the High King Ambrosius died,' he added in a harder undertone.

Medraut smiled his twisted smile again.

'There is only one thing to do! He has to fight. If he is the Bear Sark he will prove himself in battle; if he is not, then we will quickly be rid of him.'

Medraut's voice was cold and firm. Dan felt the sinking sensation in his gut that was a precursor to real fear. He never wanted to fight again. In the moment that his recognition of Taliesin had opened the floodgates of all his memories he had realised one thing. He was no longer a berserker. He was sane and whole and could not lose himself in the wild killing frenzy that had earned him his name. Now he was himself again, Dan, he did not think he could fight without it.

~ Chapter Eight ~

Six soldiers in variations on Roman military dress escorted Dan to the barracks training ground. He was not under arrest, for Arturus smoothly assured him that he was their honoured guest, but he was unarmed and the soldiers weren't, so Dan drew his own conclusions. They had let him sleep in a guarded room with Braveheart but Taliesin had not come to visit as Dan had hoped. Maybe Medraut had prevented him. Dan was aware that for some reason the bulky soldier had taken a determined dislike to him. He did not know why.

Dan had slept well, exhaustion overriding all other considerations. He had tried to think about the mystery of Taliesin's presence, tried to think about what might have happened to Ursula, but his body had its own ideas and oblivion had overcome him. He had breakfasted on oatcakes drizzled with honey and ale of the kind that Macsen's men had drunk, though not so finely brewed. It was weak enough not to worry him. His body, so many months among the Combrogi, was used to it.

It was not long after dawn, and a cool morning. As Dan was marched through the straight streets of the Roman city, Braveheart by his side, his curiosity almost overrode his nerves. What he saw was not quite what he had expected of Camulodunum. They passed a vast temple decorated with brightly painted statues, but the paint had peeled to reveal the white marble beneath. Someone had placed a large rustic cross at the entrance and grass grew between the stone slabs that formed the steps. There were weeds too in the roads and many of the stone houses and shops were tumbled down or ruined. Some had been roughly mended with timber or straw with scant regard given to their appearance. There were some soldiers dressed in the Roman style but many more wore simple homespun tunics and cloaks, sporting just a helmet, a belt or a sword that bore the marks of Roman origin. The whole population had turned out to watch the fight and few of the townspeople wore Roman dress; the checks and plaids of the Combrogi were more in evidence, though their colours were muddier and less vibrant than those that Macsen's men had worn. There was little evident display of wealth and Dan was disappointed. He had always wondered what a Roman city looked like. This one was clearly past its best.

Dan was led into the amphitheatre, a vast arena, surrounded by tiers of ruined benches. Arturus's men had formed a circle around the perimeter to make a smaller arena, and to make sure he could not escape, they stood with swords drawn. Crowds of people had followed them and were arranging themselves on the broken benches. Dan began to sweat in spite of the coolness of the morning. He wished he had his sword, Bright Killer. He wished he were still the Bear Sark. He wished he still possessed his capacity for madness. He looked out for Taliesin's familiar form but saw no one he recognised except for Bedewyr, who rushed towards him.

'Gawain—I mean, Dan!'

'You can call me Gawain if you want to, Bedewyr. I'm not sure I know who I am anymore.'

The oddness of that reply seemed to confuse Bedewyr further. 'Well, I heard you are to fight Arturus's champion, and I thought you might need me, as you didn't know anyone else – I mean, besides the merlin-man.'

'Who?'

Bedewyr made some rapid sign against the evil eye. 'I mean, beside the Druid you call Taliesin.'

'Thank you. I—'

'You will need a second to hold your cloak and to be sure that the fight is fair.'

'Thank you, Bedewyr, I didn't know that. Would you also take care of Braveheart for me and see that he is looked after if—'

'Medraut won't beat you.'

'Medraut?'

'He's got a reputation, but he must be thirty years old! You would make a lot of people very happy if you finished him off.'

'Finished him off? Is this a fight to the death?'

'Oh yes. Arturus says it's like the old games and a bit of old-fashioned gladiatorial killing is good for the men – gets their blood up. It's the only thing he really disagrees with his priests and monks about. He'd bring back the gladiators if we had any fighting men to spare, which of course we don't.'

It was worse than he'd feared. Dan patted Braveheart's head absently. He wished Ursula were there. She might have come up with something that meant he wouldn't have to enter that arena of armed men and try to kill the formidable Medraut. He had only ever fought as a beserker or, in his brief period as Gawain, as an amnesiac working on instinct. He still couldn't understand how, when he'd fought as Gawain, he could have experienced in his own body the blows he'd dealt his enemies. It seemed unbelievable and yet he was sure it was so. He needed Ursula's calm common sense. Even if she had been unable to find a reason for him not to fight, just her presence would have helped. He felt very alone. He managed somehow to fake a smile for Bedewyr.

'Thank you, Bedewyr, I would be very grateful if you would be my second. You couldn't lend me a sword as well could you?'

'The Duke Arturus will give you each a sword, to make sure there's no foul play – poison and the like.'

Bedewyr said it so breezily Dan was quite taken aback. What kind of a world was this?

The guards guided him towards the lean figure of Arturus, muffled against the morning in a long, richly dyed cloak of emerald green. It was lined with fur and very beautiful but somewhat ineptly patched in places where the fine wool fabric had torn and pulled. His eyes were flint hard and unreadable.

Medraut already stood before the Duke in his chain mail and elaborately decorated, gem encrusted, crested helmet. Dan had no armour or weapon of any kind.

'For this to be a fair fight I will arm you both,' Arturus began, but Bedewyr interrupted.

'Excuse me, Duke, but Gawain—I mean, Dan has no armour. Surely the Count may not fight in his if his opponent has none?'

'Do you challenge my justice, Bedewyr?' Arturus did not raise his voice but managed to make it sound subtly threatening.

Bedewyr flushed. 'No sir, but—'

'Your point has been noted but, in Dan, Medraut must fight a hero, while Dan fights a mere man, battle-hardened veteran though he may be. Be ready.'

No one it seemed argued with the Duke for long. Dan signalled for Braveheart to stay at Bedewyr's side, and accepted the sword from Arturus. It was not of the quality of Bright Killer, though fortunately it still had a killing edge as well as a stabbing point. It would have to do. He smiled more genuinely at Bedewyr as he gave him his cloak.

'He favours his right hand and side but he's very tricky,' Bedewyr whispered, and Dan felt the dampness of his own sweat, suddenly cold on his skin. Now that he had regained his memory he knew he had always found his quiet place of inward focus before any major event in his life. When he had been a berserker that place had been red with blood and wildness. Now, it was, as it had always been when he raced or played football in his almost forgotten schooldays, the place where nervousness ended and where concentration began. He could still fight. He had fought as Gawain. The memory of that bloody battle sickened him. He did not want to kill again, but neither did he want to die. He closed his eyes briefly to prepare himself for combat and had an alarming vision of a young man in a soft woollen tunic, lean and well muscled, dark hair bound back in a braid. He opened his eyes in horrified confusion and for an instant he saw the young man's eyes open; dark eyes, harder than his years suggested. He recognised the vision. It was himself.

Dan started to sweat, his palms were damp and unless he was careful the hilt of the sword would become slick – he could not afford to lose his grip on his sword, or on reality. Something weird was happening to him, stranger and more frightening than even his beserker rages – he had been largely unaware of them. Now, he was suddenly aware of too much.

Dan closed his eyes again to test a growing suspicion. His mind was assaulted by unfamiliar sensations. His left leg ached with an old wound. He stretched muscles that were ox-strong but aching with the stiffness that afflicted them each winter. The hand that held the sword was huge and gnarled by the harshness of an outdoor life. He tested the weight of the blade, a little light but it would serve. The mail shirt and the two layers of clothing he wore underneath it was heavy but comforting. The familiar weight of his helmet made him feel invincible. He felt confident and yet there was fear too. He was glad of it. Living with fear made him what he was. There was no way that a pup, scarcely on the road to manhood, could beat him – Medraut, Count of the Saxon Shore – in a fair fight, and it would be a fair fight, he had promised Arturus.

Dan opened his eyes, and almost lost his balance with the sudden abrupt change of perspective. His own heart pumped faster, he felt the steely strength of his own youthful limbs, his own lightness and his own explosive energy, barely contained. He was afraid now. He may no longer be a berserker but he had a whole new strain of madness to contend with: he could feel his enemy's thoughts.

'Gawain? Dan? Are you all right?' Bedewyr's face was wrinkled with concern.

'I am well, Bedewyr. Wish me luck!'

'May Cunedos and Mithras grant you victory this day!'

Dan strode to the centre of the circle of men to face Medraut. He had to get a grip of his hectic fear. He could not fight in this unfocused state. He sought his place of stillness and to his profound relief found it – still and calm and unpolluted by his opponent's thoughts.

Medraut was a big man, no taller than Dan himself, but broad and very intimidating. Medraut's helmet protected his face and skull and even offered some protection to the back of his neck. The mail shirt protected his torso and the leather of his under-tunic protected his upper arm and groin. At first glance Dan stood very little chance at all. He knew from experience that Raven helmets fitted snugly; there was no chance of removing this one without also removing the head that wore it. He did not want to take that option. He also doubted that the poorly fabricated sword was up to such a task –

it took a sharp and heavy blade to behead a man. Medraut was circling him warily, his body lowered into a fighting stance.

Dan prayed that he would not see himself again through this enemy's eyes – he could not deal with such a dizzying dual perspective. He dropped his right shoulder and adopted the familiar fighting stance, which offered the enemy the least access to his vital organs and the greatest access to his sword. Medraut stabbed forward with his sword and Dan parried it, lightly stepping backwards. He wanted to tire the older man till his joints ached. He was reluctant to attack. He was afraid of feeling the man's pain. He let Medraut make all the moves, defending himself easily. Dan's reflexes were lightning quick and in any case he could not quite blot out all awareness of his enemy's thoughts. He was always aware of Medraut's next move a heartbeat before it happened.

The audience were bored. The soldiers started to bang their spears against the ground and shout. Dan longed for the madness, which had always let his unconscious take over. He was not used to thinking in a fight. He had never fought defensively in his life before. He had to make a move. Medraut's face was red with anger and effort. Dan needed to finish it. He could not be the Bear Sark but he could still be Gawain. He had to forget himself and let his battle-honed instincts take over. He urged himself to let go, to stop thinking. Suddenly, he found the knack of it. It happened in an instant as if someone had flicked a switch and the whole pace of the battle changed. Dan suddenly started to attack. His speed was devastating, the sudden change in pace confused Medraut whose anger was beginning to cloud his judgement as surely as the sweat now dripping into his eyes clouded his vision. Medraut found himself stepping back from the relentless thrusting of Dan's sword. Twice, Dan almost got through Medraut's defences. Twice, he was stopped by the older man's blade at the last moment. The third time Dan sliced through the protective leather tunic and drew first blood. A sharp, stinging sensation reminded him of what he already knew to be true. He would feel every blow in this contest – those he dealt and those he received. He backed off and wiped the sweat from his eyes. Medraut was bleeding freely from his upper thigh but it was a scratch, nothing more, though it initiated a new round of more enthusiastic spear thumping from the crowd. Dan wiped his right hand on his tunic, switching the blade to his left hand. Medraut rushed forward, eager to take him at a disadvantage, except that it was no disadvantage. Medraut thrust forward at his undefended right side as Dan sliced through the exposed under-arm of his opponent with a left-handed thrust and slash. Blood welled and Dan bit his lip against the pain. Medraut swayed but did not fall. Dan knocked the sword from the man's strong right hand, twisted, and had his own blade to Medraut's throat. Their eyes were level. Dan experienced another strange moment of double vision: he saw Medraut keeping the fear from his eyes, defiantly refusing to yield to the pain and the recognition of defeat; and he also saw his own eyes, dark and ferocious, staring back. Dan shook his head to dislodge the unwelcome awareness.

'Be sure I can rip out your throat before you can knock the blade from my hand.' Dan made his voice loud and threatening, but he knew Medraut believed him because it was true. Medraut's strength was no match for Dan's swiftness.

'Duke Arturus, I do not want this man's death on my hands. Do you now believe my claim?'

The Duke crossed the arena to stand alongside him, and in a very public gesture accepted Dan's sword and proclaimed, 'You are very welcome, Daniel Bear-Sark. You are all that Taliesin promised.'

Dan longed to deny that, longed to explain that his old berserker self would never have had to fight so hard for victory. How could he explain that even now as blood dripped down Medraut's side, Dan felt the man's wound in his own flesh? He needed to talk to Taliesin. There was too much he did not understand.

~ Chapter Nine ~

Dan had been guided to the bathhouse; they were not unlike Macsen's Roman-style baths at Craigwen. Taliesin joined him there. The blue, spiralling, druidic tattoos on his aging, too-thin frame made him resemble some strange exotic lizard. His hair grew long now and like his beard was streaked with grey; only his eyes were unchanged. These differences like so much else in his new situation troubled Dan. Still, it was good to feel the cleansing heat and to wash the bloodstains from his body, which ached with the effort of the fight and hurt where he had hurt Medraut. It was difficult to accept the evidence of his own eyes that his own flesh was whole and uninjured. He felt battered, confused, and more than a little afraid. Only some of the tension left his body in the warmth and quietness of the baths. Taliesin had sent the servants away and had been granted privacy, as a boon of Dan's victory. Or so it seemed.

Dan knew he needed to find Ursula but had been assured that a man with the unlikely name of Petronax had been sent to look for her. Dan had not the strength to argue. Bedewyr seemed to believe that Petronax could be trusted. Dan, bone-weary and bewildered, accepted his judgement. Dan would have no chance of finding anyone in the state he was in, of that one small thing he was certain. He had reached the limits of his strength. But it was good to stop for a moment, to rest. He relaxed a little more. Taliesin said nothing but watched Dan with that strange, still intensity of his, and Dan knew he would have to ask, knew that the older man had always been miserly with his secrets. Dan was afraid of what Taliesin might tell him and yet he hated to be ignorant. He tried to keep his tone light as if nothing mattered.

'So, how did you do it then?'

Taliesin looked at Dan, his expression inscrutable. Dan thought he was afraid, felt it strongly, but could not understand why. What had Taliesin to fear from a question – less, surely, than Dan had to fear from the answer?

'What do you mean, Daniel?'

'How did you leave Macsen's time after me and end up here before me – wherever *here* is? It doesn't make sense.'

There was a long pause, several heartbeats, and

Taliesin sighed. Dan knew he was gathering his internal resources, fighting his fear. He still did not know why.

Taliesin's voice was quiet, undramatic, as if he deliberately eschewed his bardic skill to tell the bald truth. 'After you left Craigwen, things went well with us. Macsen managed to consolidate his position and there was peace. The loss of Rhonwen played on his mind – whatever else she was and is, she remains his sister and he loves her. He begged me to find a way to get her back and to learn more about the Veil – it had after all proved useful to him, to us. Years passed for me while you and Ursula were outside time, inside the Veil where there is no time. I travelled in search of the remaining druids, to find the secret of raising the Veil. I learned what I could of the fading magic of the druids and their link with the Veil, their knack of calling it and guiding it. I used it to travel to many places in times very different from Macsen's and my own.'

Taliesin's eyes seemed very dark and old to Dan as he listened, excited in spite of himself.

'I saw things – I couldn't tell you.' Taliesin gave him a quick glance from under bushier eyebrows than Dan remembered.

'At last, I found a man who could help me – Igris, a philosopher, wiser than any druid, from a people who had explored the potential of the Veil over the ages. He found Rhonwen for me. She was at what he called a "turning point" – a moment in time when big changes depend on small events. He said that the descendants of my people, the Combrogi, were fighting for survival and that Rhonwen was hastening our end.'

Taliesin looked at Dan again with appeal in his eyes. 'The prophecy you heard me speak of – that was real. Igris talked in terms I rarely understood, but one night we sat in something like a sacred grove and he explained quite clearly that if no leader emerged to guide us, all that the Combrogi had been, all that we had loved and fought for would not just die, but vanish as if it had never been. That our land, Island of the Mighty, that I love, would be possessed by others. *The Bear* is the key to our survival but he could not or would not say who *The Bear* was.'

'What was the prophecy? I heard you say it but I didn't understand.'

'Igris told me, "As the bear on the high hillside protects the cubs, so *The Bear* of Ynys Prydein, the Island of the Mighty, protects its own. Remember *The Bear* and cherish it, for when *The Bear* is gone the hillside falls."'

'Well, that could mean anything!'

Taliesin's smile was brief and humourless. 'I don't think members of his order were supposed to interfere in the ways of the worlds revealed to them through the Veil, though they were allowed to comment – as long as they did it poetically and—'

'Uselessly?' Dan finished for him.

Taliesin's smile was still wan and troubled. 'My first responsibility was to find Rhonwen and send her back to Macsen. I knew from what Igris had said that she was advancing our destruction by allying herself with our people's enemies. I found her, begged her to return with me to Macsen. She laughed in my face.'

His expression was momentarily unreadable but Dan could sense Taliesin's deep shame. 'I did not intend to remain here but discovered that I could not leave. I do not understand why but each world we visit through the Veil changes us. There were worlds I visited where my limited and hard-won journeyman magic was very strong, where I could shape-shift as easily as think; while here, I have little gift and that which I have is a strange, fey, capricious thing – different from anything I have ever known.' Taliesin spread his hands expressively.

Dan found himself nodding – it was his own experience. He was no longer a berserker here, and Ursula no longer a sorceress. Thinking of Ursula, the anxious knot in his stomach tightened.

'But how—I mean, where were we during all this time?'

'You were caught like a fly in amber, in the Veil. Time only starts again when you are free of it – and I got free while you were still trapped in the timeless Veil. Eventually …' Taliesin hesitated and Dan could feel his trepidation. 'I called you here.'

It took a long moment for Dan to understand, then he felt his face flush hot with fury as the implications of this quiet statement sunk in.

'Wait! Hear me! Let me explain!' Taliesin reached out to touch his shoulder but Dan jerked his arm away.

'I cannot call the Veil anymore – that power is lost to me, but Igris spoke sometimes about ways in which those who had stepped outside time could always find each other again. I thought I could husband my magic to influence your destination – influence Ursula. I have touched her mind – when we helped her return from her shape-shifting. I knew her and I knew I could find her again, though it took me years to do it.'

Dan turned away from the bard, not wanting to hear more. He had trusted Taliesin and yet it was he who had prevented them from going home, he who had deliberately brought them to this place. Because of Taliesin he might never see his sister Lizzie or his father again. He was too angry to speak.

'It was not just that I thought Ursula would get me home – after Rhonwen refused to help me. When I thought about what Igris had said I thought I knew what the Combrogi needed. I wanted – still want – to help them.' Taliesin was pleading with Dan to listen, to understand, to forgive.

'Rhonwen has great influence here with the Aenglisc, and I believe her influence could destroy this island. She plays old games – making alliances with her people's enemies, as if she had learnt nothing from Macsen. The Combrogi are fragile here, a shadow of what they once were. They were ruled for generations by those we might call Ravens or Romans. When the Roman armies left and many of their senior people were kicked out, the people who remained were Romanised Combrogi, neither one thing nor the other, somehow lacking the strength of either. There were those who rejected Roman ways and wanted to be true to their ancient roots but they lost their influence a generation ago. Their heritage is weakened but these Combrogi are still my people. I feel it and I know Igris was right – there is a turning point here. All they need is a leader to believe in – to revive their spirit.' Taliesin paused, his eyes alight with sudden passion. 'I thought Ambrosius might have served to unite them but the hill people, those who clung to older ways, would not follow him and Arturus – well, you have seen him. He is a good general but not a hero. So I tried to rekindle their pride and I did what I had once lived by doing – I told them heroic tales.'

Dan thought he knew what was coming next. 'Of Boar Skull and the Bear Sark?' He couldn't keep the sneer from his voice.

'Yes, and of Igris's prophecy because I thought that one of you might be *The Bear.* Ursula's name means little bear – while you, Bear Sark, what could be more obvious?' Taliesin glanced quickly at Dan. 'And, yes, I admit it, I wanted you to be the answer, for then Ursula might be able to get me home. I know my own weakness and am wise enough to know I'm a fool. I was able to find her in the timeless, frozen moment when you entered the Veil and I called her to me. I sent men to wait for the coming of the Veil. I did not want to work magic too close to Arturus and his bishop, as there are many here who do not think he needs the company of even an apprentice druid like myself. It was a mistake because my men got to you too late. I fear that Rhonwen, sensing the closeness of the Veil, sent men of her own to investigate. Her magic here is all trickery but her affinity with the Veil remains.'

Dan's face contorted with horror. 'Rhonwen! You think Rhonwen has captured Ursula?'

'I don't know, Dan. I hope not. I'm so sorry. It has all gone wrong, and how could it have gone right when I went against all that I have ever believed in to bring you here. I've brought trouble on you, lad, and I never meant for that to happen. I wanted to help these people; I wanted to get home. I was desperate and I was wrong. Can you forgive me? I knew I was wrong as soon as I saw you.'

Dan was struggling to digest this new piece of information. Rhonwen hated Ursula and Ursula without her magic was vulnerable. Dan remembered how anguished Ursula had been in the moments before they'd been attacked. He should have had his wits about him, should have paid more attention. He spoke in a terse, hard voice.

'Your plan didn't work, Taliesin. Ursula has no magic. She can't raise the Veil, and I'm no longer the Bear Sark. We're trapped here, all three of us. We none of us can get home.' Dan was angry beyond reason and in danger of thumping Taliesin who was now an old man. Worse than that he was very afraid he might shame himself by crying tears of fury and frustration. What the hell did Taliesin think he was doing, interfering in all their lives?

Taliesin let out a low groan of anguish and prostrated himself on the floor. 'By all that is sacred and holy, by the One, and by my own vows as a bard, I beg your forgiveness, Daniel.'

Dan looked at him without really seeing him; he had no time for histrionics. 'Oh get up, Taliesin. As if that is going to make any difference.'

Taliesin raised his head from the hot floor, and scrambled to his feet. The hypocaust was directly beneath the mosaics of the floor and even for penance it was too hot a place to lie for long. Dan could feel Taliesin's anguish, feel his guilt as if it were his own. Dan's empathy was a curse, for he did understand exactly why Taliesin had done what he'd done, just as he knew exactly how earnestly Taliesin now regretted it. There was little point in recriminations. It was done now.

'This is giving me a headache, Taliesin. I can't forgive you now. Maybe, if Ursula is safe, I will try but, Taliesin please, leave me out of any of your future schemes for saving whatever world you find yourself in.'

Taliesin clapped his hand on Dan's shoulder and forced him into unwilling eye contact. Taliesin's eyes blazed with fierce conviction.

'I swear to you, Daniel, that I am your true friend and ally here. I will do all I can to get you home. I swear the triple oath of the druids of my blood, by fire, by water and by the earth and by and the holiness and wholeness of the One.'

The tiles around the bath had cracked in places and with a sudden movement Taliesin dragged his wrist across the sharp edge of a broken tile so that his blood welled. He crossed the wound against his heart and bowed his head. Dan felt the sudden smarting pain in his own wrist.

'OK, Taliesin. You win!' he said in English, under his breath, before stepping forward to enfold the old bard in a warrior's embrace. 'It *is* good to see you again. I would have missed you, had you given me the chance.' Dan sensed Taliesin's deep gratitude and warmth threatening to engulf his own precarious self-control. Celts!

*

There were soldiers ready to escort Dan from the baths. He was given fresh clothes, a tunic in the Roman style, a soldier's garment. He asked instead for a homespun tunic of the kind Taliesin wore, and asked Taliesin if he might borrow a long cloak like his, if he had a spare. Taliesin's eyes narrowed as Dan dressed himself but he said nothing, not even when Dan fastened his empty sword belt under his cloak. Dan knew that Taliesin longed to ask him what he was doing.

'I am no longer the Bear Sark. I'm not Dan either really, am I? Taliesin, I don't want to fight any more – it hurts too much. I'll be … I don't know, whatever I can be that doesn't involve killing.'

Taliesin's eyes were sharp.

'Something is going on with you, Dan. What is it? Can you feel the magic?'

Dan shook his head. 'No, it would be useful if I could, wouldn't it? But I can sort of feel other people's feelings. It's awful.' He faltered. 'When I injured Medraut, it felt like I had injured myself. It's hard to describe, but I can't hurt people any more.'

Taliesin's compassion was an invisible embrace.

'You should be a bard, lad, you take that empathy and mix it with other things and you can make men laugh or cry as the need dictates. I had the beginnings of such a gift once, long ago. I understand the burden.' He patted him on the shoulder and Dan struggled against the overwhelming urge to cry again. What was wrong with him? He was tougher than that.

'I should have known.' Taliesin shook his head. 'Nothing stays the same through the Veil – not me, not you, not Ursula.'

The use of her name made Dan aware again of the anxiety that underlay all his other emotions: 'Ursula!'

'Hush! Don't worry, lad, I know Petronax. He is a good tracker. If anyone can find her he will.'

Dan tried to believe it and to control his wayward, excessive emotions as he followed the soldier anxious to guide him back into the presence of Arturus. Dan took a deep breath. It was not going to be easy to explain that he was not the Bear Sark of legend but some other thing. Perhaps in this world of Arturus, the War Duke of Britannia, he should be Gawain, a good and gentle man, a man of empathy, not of death. He missed the familiar feel of his sword as he followed the soldier towards the villa which Arturus used as his headquarters. The empty scabbard was a potent but uncomfortable symbol of what he wished to become.

~ Chapter Ten ~

Arturus looked up from a rough wooden table strewn with documents as Dan came into the room. He scowled at Dan's appearance. It was still early in the day and in the harsh morning light Dan could see that Arturus's face was crossed with lines etched by worry and the open air. He was harder than Dan had first appreciated.

'Bear Sark, these are not the garments of a hero.'

'I am no longer the hero you want, Duke Arturus. I trust the Count is recovering from his wounds.'

Arturus waved his hand, dismissively. 'Medraut is a tough man, it will take more than that to kill him I'm sure.'

Dan did not like his attitude – a good commander cared more than that for his men.

'May I see him?'

'I think that unnecessary. You beat him fairly. There is no need to rub it in.'

'Still, I would like to see him and make my peace with him.' Dan was not entirely sure why he was so insistent, but felt it was something he should do.

'If you insist.' Arturus looked displeased and the fine vertical lines between his fair brows furrowed. He spoke to one of his guard. 'Ramio, escort the Bear Sark to the barracks, where the Count is resting.'

'Duke—'

'Yes.'

'I would prefer it if you would call me Dan or, failing that, Gawain. Truly, I am not the Bear Sark any more.'

Arturus's face darkened. 'As you will it, but the name Gawain is unlikely to inspire my men.' He stepped closer and Dan could smell his sweetened breath.

'I have heard how you assisted King Macsen against a conquering enemy. My need is greater, for the Romans were a cultured people compared with those who oppose us now. We are at the mercy of pagan barbarians who slaughter women and children for pleasure. In the south and east we are attacked by Aenglisc, in the north by Picts and to the west by the Scots. Our High King and my dear friend and mentor Ambrosius Aurelianus is dead and those left to rule this land are gathering here to choose a successor. The future hangs by a slender thread. There are appeasers among us who would placate the enemy. If they gain power the Combrogi will not survive. Over the last ten years I have fought too many battles, against too many enemies and lost too many men and yet I have hardly begun. There are those who think the battles are over. They have no idea!' Arturus banged his fist down so hard on the table that his goblet of ale juddered and almost spilt.

'I beg of you. If there is any way you could lend your strength to my cause, do not turn away from us in our hour of need! Taliesin promised to call you at our darkest hour, and surely he has chosen his moment well. We have never needed a hero more than we need one now.'

Dan sensed the passion that underpinned Arturus's whispered words. 'Duke, have you ever killed a man face to face, so close that your breath mingles, that you can see the fear in your enemy's eyes, the scar he got in childhood, the curling eyelashes adored by his mother?'

Arturus hesitated. 'I am the War Duke of Britannia. I have been fighting since I was sixteen years old. Do you think I let my men do all my fighting for me?'

'Do you?' Dan looked straight at Arturus, challenge in his eyes.

'I am a leader, my men protect me as best they can, but I have killed and done my penance for it. Leaders cannot afford too sensitive a conscience. I do God's will.'

Dan's voice was very quiet, 'You do not know what you are asking of me.' And he turned away.

'I think I do. Are you a priest then, a follower of the

Christos? We fight under his banner. Will you not fight for that?' Arturus's voice rang after Dan as he followed Ramio to the barracks.

Ramio was distinctly wary of Dan, even though he was unarmed, and seemed glad to leave him to the care of a man in dark robes, not unlike Dan's own, who tended Medraut.

'I am Gawain.' Dan noticed the large wooden cross the other man wore on his breast and added 'Father' as an afterthought.

'Not "Father", brother Gawain, but "brother" only. They call me Brother Frontalis. I am Arturus's chosen confessor. I have spoken already to our Merlin. He was expecting you here. Be welcome!'

'Merlin?'

'Taliesin. He and I speak often. He is much travelled and has many things to teach anyone who is prepared to listen.'

Dan's confusion deepened. From what he knew of the druids, and Taliesin had aspired to be a druid, they had little enough in common with a Christian monk, and why had this man called Taliesin, Merlin, the name of a famous magician?

Dan allowed himself to be guided to Medraut's bed. The wound had been salved with some foul smelling stuff and bandaged, but Medraut was white-faced and clammy. He tried to rise when he saw Dan.

'Come to finish me off? You would not have beaten me if I were ten years younger.'

'I would not have fought you now if I'd had a choice,' Dan retorted more sharply than he had intended. He could feel the sickening, dragging pain of Medraut's wound.

'I came to see if I could help heal you,' Dan whispered, uncertain of whether Brother Frontalis would approve of what he was about to do. 'It might not work but – it's an idea I had …' Dan ran out of words at the sceptical, not to say antagonistic, expression on Medraut's face.

'You have the power of miracles?'

'No. I don't think so, not miracles, but I think I might be able to make it hurt less.'

'Healing always hurts,' put in Frontalis. 'It is the good God's way of teaching you not to play with swords!'

Dan smiled grimly. He did not disagree with that. He did not know why he thought he might be able to help – it was just a feeling he had. He was thrown into a world where feelings were all round him and maybe, as Taliesin had said, he too, like a bard, could change some of them.

Dan shut his eyes and cleared his mind. Once more he saw the world from Medraut's perspective. The pain dominated his thoughts. That, and mild irritation with the young man who had defeated him, coming to crow over his defeat. Medraut had no confidence in Dan's healing powers. You got cut. It hurt. His life was predicated on that fact.

Dan struggled to distance himself from the seductive power of Medraut's thoughts, to feel his own healthy arm, strong and whole, and to bring that idea of painlessness into Medraut's consciousness. It was hard, holding two ideas, two sets of sensations in his mind at once but he was rewarded by an awareness of Medraut's sudden stillness. Medraut relaxed as if the ache had ceased.

Dan slowly withdrew to his own single perspective. His own arm hurt like hell, but the look of gratitude and astonishment on Medraut's face was extraordinary.

'What—?' he began.

'I haven't made it better,' said Dan hurriedly. 'I can't work miracles, but I've taken the pain away for a while. I don't know for how long.'

Brother Frontalis crossed himself, a look of wonder on his face. 'I wouldn't mention this to anyone else, Brother Gawain. I know from my many talks with Taliesin that all good comes from the one God, but others are not so certain.'

Dan nodded, having no idea what the monk was talking about, and staggered out of the room. He felt dizzy and sick and he wanted to check that it was sweat not blood that poured from his own arm. He was distantly aware of Medraut thanking him and then he collapsed in the yard outside the barracks.

'Gawain, Dan, Bear Sark, your friend is come!'

Dan opened his eyes to see Bedewyr stooping over him, and Braveheart licking his face.

'Ursula!'

'Taliesin says the Boar Skull has been spotted with three others. He thinks you should go and meet her. She has Petronax as a prisoner!'

Dan could not help a grin of pure happiness. Ursula was safe and in charge. He tried to seek her out with his mind. Would his new gift allow him to reach her, feel her presence? There had been a strong link between them in Macsen's world. The inside of his skull ached as if someone had hit him over the head with a heavy blunt object and his vision blurred. He moved his right shoulder surreptitiously. It worked and it no longer pained him. Maybe Medraut felt the pain again now? Dan could not take on the burden of that pain again; he had done his good deed for the day. His exhaustion no longer mattered. He used Braveheart's strong back to help him scramble to his feet.

'Can you lend me a horse?'

'The Duke said you were to borrow the Count's. He wants you to take five men including Taliesin.'

He wondered what Ursula would do when she found out that it was Taliesin who had brought them to this world. Perhaps it would be better if Dan primed her first. Ursula could be unpredictable and, even without magic, was no mean fighter.

'I think it would be better if she met with Taliesin later. I would be glad if you would accompany me, Bedewyr, and four other steady men who will follow orders. You don't want to upset Ursula.'

Bedewyr flushed with pleasure to be chosen. It made Dan uncomfortable; they were more or less the same age. He had been happier when Bedewyr had been repulsed by his killing prowess. Dan did not want to be Bedewyr's hero.

Ursula was growing tired. They had ridden for too long. She had been worried that the Aenglisc might track them and had insisted that they ride hard away from the settlement. They had had to stop far more frequently than she had wanted to in order to staunch Larcius's wounds. She was jumpy and bad tempered. Bryn had been certain they were being followed and she trusted the young Combrogi's sharp ears now that she no longer had her magic to sense danger. She and Bryn had ambushed the old man, Petronax. He had been wise and surrendered on hearing them speak to each other in the common Combrogi tongue. He was of the tribes, or claimed kinship with them. He had no tattoos and his grasp of the language was sketchy, but it was enough to convince Ursula to take him prisoner. She did not in any case want to kill him, though she was pumped full of adrenalin and her reflexes were hair-trigger sharp. Even Bryn thought she was over vigilant and persuaded her not to tie the old man quite so tightly lest he lose his hands along with his circulation. She was working hard to compensate for the loss of magic and the loss of Dan. It made her mean. She had thrown away Rhonwen's possessions. They smelled of magic and she could not stand to have them near her. Bryn tended to Larcius, reassured Petronax that 'the warrior woman' was not going to kill him, and kept very quiet around Ursula who rode her horse as hard as if she was fleeing from demons.

It was around late afternoon when Bryn rode alongside and told her that he could see riders.

'What do you want me to do?'

Ursula drew the sword Bright Killer. She had fastened it from a loop of rope at her hip. She held it ready in her right hand. 'If we are attacked, Bryn, ride for whatever safety you can find. Take Larcius if you can, but don't put yourself in danger. I owe it to Dan to keep you alive. Promise me you will flee at my word.'

Bryn shifted uncomfortably in the saddle, it was not what he wanted to do but Ursula scared him. She had been a sorceress, and who knew what she could do to him if he disobeyed? He nodded reluctantly.

'What will you do to Petronax?'

'Let me worry about that, Bryn, eh? Be ready to ride like the wild hunt.'

There was little cover around, just tilled fields and the distant sign of buildings, a few sparse looking trees and something that looked like a watch-tower. There was no high ground from which to make a stand, but she was in no mood to die cheaply. She was no berserker but she was going to fight like one and pay back the monsters who had felled Dan. She squinted at the distant sight of figures riding towards her – four, no, five riders. She did not think she could take them all. She could see silver helmets flashing in the sun. Romans, or Aenglisc wearing captured helms? She was not going to risk them being Aenglisc.

'Ride, Bryn!'

'What if they're allies?'

'Then I'll still be alive and I'll call for you. If I'm dead, stay away! *Go*!'

Ursula yelled the last with such authority that Bryn gave up the argument, grabbed the reins of Larcius's horse and rode off the road towards a small clump of wind-stunted trees in the distance.

Ursula rode towards Petronax, her sword at the ready. His eyes widened in fear.

'I'm not going to kill you, you fool! You have a right to defend yourself if these are Aenglisc, but I warn you,

you attack me and you'll die painfully and very slowly.'

With unexpected skill she rode alongside him, cut his bonds and handed him his sword, which she had kept tied to her own saddle.

'Die well, Petronax!'

She shot him a grin of such ferocity that his blood ran cold. Recklessly, she spurred her horse forward to meet the advancing horsemen.

As she drew nearer she saw they were in Roman dress – more or less, though she had never seen Romans in the short leather trousers that these men wore. One of them, who seemed to be leading, was wearing a long, dark grey hooded cloak but he rode like a Combrogi. She tried to get a grip of the fear and desperate energy, which fired her blood. She had not Dan's skill, so she could not afford his total foolhardiness. She had always been a calmer, more deliberate fighter. She needed to keep her wits; wildness was not her style. The grey man broke away from his escort, urging his horse to a gallop. He did not seem to be wielding a spear, or angon, but she kept herself ready to wheel her mount just the same. He seemed to be shouting something. She strained to hear.

'Ursula!'

She faltered. She thought he'd shouted her name. No one here knew her name did they?

'Ursula!' The man in grey threw back his hood.

'Ursula! Sheath that sword! It's me, Dan!'

It took several moments for that information to percolate through her adrenalin-charged system; longer still for her to recognise Dan's familiar face and form in the unfamiliar clothes. Tears streamed down her face and she could not see at all as she rode blindly towards him.

It was not magic; it was no trick. He was real. Dan was alive!

~ Chapter Eleven ~

They rode back to camp on one horse, the fine stallion belonging to Medraut, Count of the Saxon Shore. Ursula had disregarded her usual caution to leap, with Bright Killer shining, from her own horse over on to Dan's. She needed to touch him to be sure that he did still live.

Dan was relieved beyond measure to see her. She clung to his back as they rode. Her unfamiliar touch and her profound joy at finding him shook him a little. He hadn't realised that Ursula's feelings ran so deep – so little showed on the outside. He wanted to tell her about Taliesin, and about his own new power, his determination not to kill any more, but riding like the wildest of wild Combrogi for Camulodunum was probably not the time. Instead, he savoured her happiness and his own – pure and unsullied for the duration of the ride.

Bedewyr welcomed Petronax home and did his best not to show his amusement that the proud veteran had been captured by a woman. Dan sent the other men Bedewyr had chosen to find Larcius and Bryn.

The summons from Duke Arturus came almost at once, before Dan had done little more than outline what had happened to him and sketch in Taliesin's role. Ursula seemed less concerned than he had expected.

'Well, you know, Dan, it's not certain that I'd have got us home anyway. There are places I could have taken us to that are a lot worse than this. You don't want to know some of the nightmares I've had about the Veil – back in Macsen's world! I'm just grateful we've both survived.' She was – he could feel it clearly. For the moment, all she could think about was that he lived, and so did she – against the odds. Ursula pushed her hair back from her grimy face unselfconsciously and continued, 'Anyway, what's this Duke Arturus like?'

'Not like Macsen. He's cold somehow – not such a leader.'

'Is he one of the good guys?'

'He's against Rhonwen and he says the Aenglisc are savages. Are they?'

'I don't think I saw their caring-sharing side. They were going to kill me and let Rhonwen tell the future from my death throes. What does Taliesin think?'

'I think he sees these people as Combrogi, even though they seem more Roman to me and some of them don't even speak the tribal languages.'

'You don't seem convinced, Dan.'

'I've had enough fighting. All I want to do is go home.'

With that, they were escorted back into Arturus's council chamber where Dan greeted Bryn with a warrior's embrace. Bryn almost glowed with joy that his Lord still lived. Dan fought a lump in his throat. He'd never realised how much he meant to the Combrogi orphan. He made a private vow to be more worthy of the boy's absolute and unqualified adoration.

There was a tension in the air that must have been obvious to anyone. Taliesin stood silently to the left of Arturus while Medraut stood to his right, looking remarkably cheerful in spite of his wound. He did not seem to be in any pain but was being persuaded to sit down by an insistent Brother Frontalis. The walls of the chamber were lined with men. The man Ursula knew as Larcius was lounging on the sheepskin-covered couch. Dan sensed Ursula's sudden confusion when she saw Larcius in clean garments. He realised bleakly that she was very attracted to him. She even blushed. It made him feel acutely uncomfortable.

Ursula had been too busy talking with Dan to change her clothes. She was caked in dried blood and dirt and stank of horses and stale sweat. Her pale blonde hair was filthy and hung like rat's tails around her face. Dan thought she looked beautiful, if in an unconventional way.

The Duke eyed her coldly.

'Do you claim to be the Boar Skull of legend?'

'I have been called that, sir, yes,' she said calmly, undeterred by the tension in the air.

'But you are a woman.'

'Yes, that's true. Didn't Taliesin tell you that bit?'

She was joking but Dan knew the moment she said it that Taliesin had omitted that part of the tale. Dan glanced at the bard; his lips were drawn into a thin line but his face remained otherwise impassive. Perhaps he'd thought her transformation into the mighty Boar Skull too unbelievable. Ursula was smiling; her joy at finding Dan had put her into an uncharacteristically buoyant mood. It worried Dan because to him she seemed enormously vulnerable. She was taller than almost all the men there, strong and athletically lean, but compared to the burly men all round she seemed young and slight and horribly, innocently, unaware of the disapproval she was generating. Dan felt the waves of it combined with anger that the hero Taliesin had promised was this tall, filthy, straggle-haired girl. He wanted to warn her. She had learned to fight well as Ursula but without her magically-enhanced alter ego, she was no more the Boar Skull than he was the Bear Sark. He sensed trouble.

'Taliesin neglected to mention that you were a girl, yes, and it makes me wonder how true the rest of his tales were.'

Taliesin said nothing, but Dan felt Ursula's anger begin to blaze. He wished he still had his sword. If they hurt her he was not sure he could keep from killing them all or dying in the attempt. His sword, still moulded to his own hand, was in Ursula's strong grip. They had not thought to disarm her, which summed up their expectations of her.

'I don't know why Taliesin did not mention my gender; perhaps he did not think it important. I have fought as a Combrogi warrior and I have proved my worth to those whose opinion I respect.' Dan noted how she tightened her grip on the sword and subtly altered her stance. She was not unaware then. He could feel her rising anger but also her battle readiness.

There was a murmuring from the assembled men, a wave of challenge: let her fight.

Ursula glanced around quickly at the assembled men and spoke to them directly. She was afraid now, Dan knew it, but she was ready to do some damage. He prayed silently that there would be a way out. Ursula was good, but without magic, she could be beaten. Ursula herself brought his earnest prayer to an unexpected halt. 'Come on then! Try me!' She shouted in the commonest Combrogi tongue, accompanying the challenge with a white-toothed smile that had much in common with Braveheart's warning teeth-baring. She dropped into a fighting stance. She turned off her grimace of a smile – her face became sullen and expressionless, as it always did when she was under threat. Her blankness was strangely intimidating.

The assembled men ceased their muttering as Larcius rose to his feet, somewhat awkwardly due to his wound. 'For those of you who do not know me, I am Ambrosius Larcius, son of Ambrosius Aurelianus, High King of Britannia, and grandson of Ambrosius Aurelius who wore the purple.'

There was a sharp intake of breath from the assembled men and Dan finally grasped the reason for the underlying tension in the air. Ursula was only part of it. If this Larcius was the son of the High King was he not the new High King? Did he now outrank Arturus?

Larcius waited until silence was restored. 'I am here now, alive before you due to the courage and strength of this young woman. She has proved herself to me and I stand as witness to her many stalwart qualities.'

There was silence, then someone from the back shouted, 'You fight her then!'

Dan sensed Ursula's shock; her mixed pleasure and annoyance at Larcius's somewhat patronising accolade. She did not want to fight him. Dan knew that.

'He is injured!' Ursula objected, angrily.

'And you are a woman,' Arturus said softly. 'Give him a sword!'

Someone took Larcius's cloak and gave him a sword,

not a gladius but a longer Roman spatha. Ursula looked at it in distaste. She spat on her hands and wiped them on her grimy tunic. Dan was worried. If this handsome Larcius were a prince he would have had the best available tuition in the arts of war. Ursula had learned with a hard taskmaster, Hane, himself Roman trained, but even so. Maybe Dan could help her as she had once helped him. Maybe he could enter her mind.

'Ursula?'

He knew she'd heard him, felt the connection between them, the marrying of minds. It had happened before, in Macsen's world, this strange intimacy at once shocking and familiar. Her answer came back firm and uncompromising, and shocking in its crystal clarity.

'Get the hell out of my head, Dan. Can't you see I'm busy?'

Larcius circled her with a professional eye. Ursula contrived to look bored. He made a move and Ursula turned his blade away nonchalantly. Her extra height and reach and her longer sword gave her an advantage that Dan had, in his panic, failed to acknowledge.

She parried several more of Larcius's more probing attacks. He was a confident swordsman but Ursula came from the hacking and thrusting school of survival; she looked unimpressed. Dan watched her with growing respect. She was not as quick as Dan himself, but she was always where she should be. She moved without particular grace but with great economy and she was strong. She turned aside Larcius's blade again and again. The crowd was silent now, watching. If any of the assembled men were true Combrogi they would be betting on the outcome even as Ursula fought. Dan began to get the feeling that Ursula was spinning this out, trying to make Larcius look better than he was. He saw several opportunities she didn't take, and he knew she'd seen them too.

'Ursula, get on with it. Finish it!'

She did not answer him but thrust forward suddenly with a well-aimed attack and knocked the sword effortlessly from Larcius's hand. It skittered across the mosaic floor amidst silence. Taliesin clapped and Arturus scowled.

'I hope I didn't reopen your wound.' Ursula sounded genuinely anxious.

Larcius smiled shakily.

'You have already pierced my heart with your loveliness – the rest is nothing.'

Ursula blushed again! Dan could not believe it.

There was some clamour at the back and yells of 'Fix!' and 'He let her win!'

Dan knew Larcius had not let her win, though his overly courtly response might have been designed to suggest that he had. That man had been afraid.

Ursula's irritation got the better of her caution and, with a sinking feeling, Dan heard her shout, 'Oh, for

Lugh's sake! I'll fight anyone you like but can we do it outside. This room is stifling!'

They walked en masse to the amphitheatre where Dan had fought Medraut the previous day. Dan pushed his way to Ursula's side, though she was effectively under guard. They spoke in English.

'You heard me didn't you?'

'Yes, Dan, though I don't think much of your timing. I don't know why you're so surprised, you forget I was once a sorcerer!' Her triumph over Larcius had put her in playful mood.

'Seriously, how did you hear me and speak back to me?'

Ursula looked suddenly earnest. 'Things have changed, Dan, but not the connection between us. Have you forgotten how I passed power to you? How you learned the language from me? We are linked somehow, as we have been since Rhonwen first called us.'

Dan was confused by that earnestness, the uncomplicated affection she had for him. 'No, I've not forgotten. I just didn't think it would still work here. Oh, I don't know. It's all too weird.' He found it increasingly difficult to get his mind round what was happening to him, the strange feeling that his own mind was not a closed entity but receptive to the mind's of others. He changed the subject. 'Listen, are you OK with this fight even though you're not Boar Skull now?'

In Macsen's world, Ursula's magic had first manifested itself in her ability to take on the form of a huge and extremely effective male warrior.

Ursula's grin was mischievous. 'The funny thing is, I think I am. I don't look like him … er, me – whatever. I don't seem to have his physique and all the rest of it but I feel like I've got the strength and the reactions he, I mean *I* had when I was Boar Skull. It's great! I loved having that power. I tell you, whoever fights me next is in for a surprise.'

She laughed, a laugh not too far from hysteria. Even reading her mind Dan did not understand Ursula, but he no longer worried about the coming fight. He'd bet on Boar Skull against all comers.

Three men offered to fight her in turn within the arena formed of Duke Arturus's soldiers. The first man was a heavily muscled tribesman who, unusually it seemed, still sported tribal tattoos. He was of the Deceangli, a tough people. Ursula disarmed him quickly enough and when he continued to charge at her, hoping to use his strength against her, she rugby-tackled him and finished the contest straddling his chest with Bright Killer held against his throat. He conceded ruefully to loud barracking from his friends. Ursula spoke to him in his own language and told him not to underestimate women. He was almost as startled by that as by his defeat.

The second challenger was a smaller man, named

Viridias. He had the compact build and economical moves of a born fighter. That contest lasted longer, but again Ursula disarmed him and this time he conceded at once. He had quite a reputation in Arturus's force and when he bowed to her in courtesy at his defeat, the men grew silent. Dan saw him shaking his head at his fellow soldiers; he knew he'd met his match.

The third man, Quiriac, was a giant, at least as tall as Ursula herself and built like Kai, their friend from Macsen's world on whom Ursula had modelled herself as Boar Skull. He had a Combrogi weapon and wielded it as Ursula held Bright Killer in the three-fingered grip of the tribesmen. Betting started in earnest. Quiriac was supposedly the best fighter in Arturus's army. Ursula was tiring. She took a goblet of water from one of Arturus's men, drank some, and poured the rest over her head.

Quiriac was a worthy opponent. He did not waste time circling her. The makeshift arena rang to the clash of Celtic sword against Celtic sword. Ursula's height was no advantage here and her opponent's sword was as long as Bright Killer. Ursula's concentration was total. She could not disarm him; he was too good for that. She raised the sword as if to slice down with all her strength and as Quiriac lifted his sword to parry the blow, she suddenly twisted the blade and slashed sideways so that the cutting edge sliced against his torso. She stopped the blade before it bit too deep, but it could have been a fatal attack. Quiriac conceded defeat and Ursula's reputation was assured.

Breathing hard she approached Duke Arturus.

Dan was startled to hear her voice in his mind. *'Do you want to wield Bright Killer again, Dan, or can I pledge it to this Arturus.'*

Reluctantly, he replied. *'I do not want to kill with it again, Ursula, it's yours – pledge it.'*

It seemed to Dan the right thing to do. Arturus's men banged their spears on the ground so that the earth seemed to shake to their rhythm. They stopped as Ursula started to speak:

'Duke Arturus, I trust I have proved to you that Taliesin does not lie. I am Boar Skull and I am a Combrogi Warrior and I offer you my sword at your service if that is what you will.'

The spear banging started again with even more enthusiasm. Dan was surprised to see a scowl on Taliesin's face.

'Forgive my mistrust, Lady Boar Skull. You have indeed proved yourself a warrior of surpassing skill. Larcius tells me that you tore this sword from a great pyre of stones from which no man could release it. It is a magical sword indeed.'

Ursula quickly grasped what Arturus intended.

'Duke Arturus, it is a great Combrogi blade worthy of

a man willing to bear it to unite Britannia, the Island of the Mighty against her enemies. Take it as a gift and a pledge of my service.'

The spear thumping became maniacal as Arturus raised the sword to the sky.

'I name this sword, torn from the very rock of this land, the sword from the stone, given in our country's hour of direst need: *Caliburn*.'

Dan felt a shiver run down his spine as he heard the name; there was something familiar about the name 'Caliburn'. More than that, the powerful image of a sword being lifted from the stone suggested a conclusion so obvious it was ridiculous.

'*Ursula, I've just remembered 'Caliburn' was another name for the sword in the Arthur legend – you know, Excalibur. You don't think …?*' he tailed off and Ursula's incredulous mental voice finished the idea.

'*You don't think Duke Arturus could be Arthur do you? He couldn't be!*'

~ Chapter Twelve ~

Dan tried to speak to Taliesin but Duke Arturus, having proclaimed the day a feast day, swept him off somewhere. Dan could sense that Taliesin was in some way disappointed with what had occurred in the amphitheatre. As it was inconceivable that he would have wished Ursula to lose, Dan gathered that the bard's dissatisfaction had something to do with the sword.

Bryn, Dan and Ursula were shown to their lodgings in an inn by one of the War Duke's retinue. It was a ramshackle looking place, close to Arturus's villa in the main town. Duke Arturus sent his deepest apologies, apparently, but all the rooms in his villa were already filled with high-ranking visitors from throughout the Combrogi territories, preparing to choose a replacement for Ambrosius as High King. It would not be politic, Arturus's messenger, announced gravely, to request that such guests be moved to less prestigious accommodation. But as a sign of the esteem and honour in which Arturus held them he had sent them precious gifts and the messenger himself would assist them in dressing should they have need of him.

The inn keeper was a short broad woman, more concerned with sorting out barrels of ale for the feast than with them. She treated Bryn like one of her many children, forcefully persuading him to wash and change before allowing him to check on Braveheart in the stables. She left Dan and Ursula alone.

They sat hunched by the fire on low wooden stools. Arturus seemed to have no urgent need for them before the feast and Taliesin had not appeared, as Dan had half expected, to speak to Ursula or comment on what she had done. Ursula was chewing thoughtfully on some bread the innkeeper had given them. It was tough and adulterated with hard lumps of something she'd rather not think about, but the fights had made her hungry. She spoke unselfconsciously, with her mouth full.

'I don't understand how Duke Arturus could be our Arthur of legend. I don't think I even like him much and he looks wrong. Shouldn't there be a fine castle, Camelot, and a wizard called Merlin and—?' Ursula stopped, irritated. She did not want her idea of a mythical Arthur to be no more than a rather cold, cross young man in a patched robe.

'But think about it!' Dan launched his theory with conviction. 'This place – Camulodunum Bedewyr called it but I heard some of the soldiers refer to it as the Fort of Camulos. Well, that could be Camelot, couldn't it? You've got to admit it sounds like it and then, well, I have heard Taliesin called Merlin – I'd almost forgotten with everything else that's gone on. Medraut called him merlin-man and Frontalis called him Merlin, and I'm sure Caliburn is another version of the name Excalibur, and you've got to admit Arthur is just a modern version of Arturus.'

'But he's a king in the stories, not a miserable duke.' Ursula was scowling. She did not want to believe it. 'And there wasn't a Boar Skull in the stories or a Dan or an Ursula,' she added triumphantly.

'No, but I think there was a Gawain.'

Ursula looked at him curiously.

'It's the name Bedewyr gave me when I couldn't remember my real name – anyway, I think Arturus could be appointed High King. Didn't you realise? That's why so many people are here.'

'I don't know, Dan, it makes my head ache thinking about it. Ursula sighed her dissatisfaction. 'It doesn't matter anyway, does it? If what you said about Taliesin is true and he can't raise the Veil, and neither can I, unless we can persuade Rhonwen to do us a favour and raise it for us we're stuck here with him whoever he is. And I've pledged myself to his service.' She looked suddenly exhausted. 'I'm cold and fed up of not having proper clothes to wear and this bread's awful and I don't want to be a bloody hero and I ache all over.'

The inn's Roman heating system no longer worked and the fire, which replaced it, smoked badly and was not up to the task of heating the large main room. Dan put his arm round her in comradely fashion and felt her tense. He spoke before he thought.

'Come here, I'll warm you up!' He said it lightly and meant it innocently, but Ursula looked startled. He felt her discomfort and flushed.

'I meant, you could share my cloak.'

Ursula had jumped awkwardly to her feet, her embarrassment showing through her attempt to sound casual and unconcerned. He knew she did not want to offend him.

'Thanks, but I think I'll try and use the bathhouse and get warm there. I should change – I think Arturus's gifts are probably clean clothes and stuff.'

She was gabbling as Ursula rarely did.

Dan tried to adopt the same friendly tone of voice. 'I'm sure Arturus will send a woman to help you.'

She would need assistance to strap on Arturus's gift of armour and though he'd helped her when they had trained together in Macsen's land he knew he couldn't do that anymore.

'I'll see you at the feast, then!'

As she left he swore inventively under his breath and

squirmed internally. He didn't know quite when it happened but he found himself – well – he found that he fancied Ursula. It didn't seem right; she was the best friend he'd ever had, Boar Skull, his comrade in arms. He was closer to her than he'd been to anyone and now, of all times, he had to start noticing how beautiful she was. He didn't want her to know; he was sure she didn't feel the same way – yet how could he hide his feelings from someone who could sometimes read his mind? He struggled to his feet, stumbling over his long priestly robe and tried to excise the embarrassing moment from his thoughts.

Dan tried to decide whether or not to wear the gifts that Arturus had sent. They were soldier's clothes and he had the strong feeling that Arturus had granted him great honour by offering these garments. They were largely of Roman manufacture and of a quality absent from the cruder garments that many of the men wore. They felt old and valuable. There was a felt shirt, a soft woollen tunic and a shirt of silvered scale armour. It was much polished and showed not the slightest sign of tarnish. There was an elaborately decorated belt, not as finely made as his scabbard, but of good, well cured, dark leather and an elaborate silver buckle. There were long, soft, woollen trousers dyed a deep red colour, dark leather pointed boots with a strong sole, and a thick, blue cloak with a large and heavy gold brooch in the shape of a crossbow. There was also a spectacular heavy, crested, silver helmet, decorated with huge coloured-glass stones. Dan was tempted by the splendour of it all. He was vain enough to know that he could not fail to look suitably heroic in such a costume, that it might impress Ursula, but it would only be a costume; he was not the Bear Sark any more. He dressed himself in the tunic, belt and leggings; the pointed boots were too small for his size ten-and-a-half feet. Then, with a slight pang of regret he put on Taliesin's grey cloak and his empty Celtic scabbard and walked alone to Arturus's villa.

The first person he saw was Ursula. It took him a moment to recognise her because she was dressed as a Roman, complete with gilded helmet and fine-linked chain mail. She looked magnificent. Arturus had obviously decided that if she fought like a man she should dress like one. She gave Dan an embarrassed grin.

'You didn't put your stuff on?' she said accusingly.

'Nah, it didn't seem right.'

'This helmet is really heavy and so is the mail shirt. I feel a right nerd. I don't think I can keep it on for long.'

'I think you should, you look like Taliesin's hero.'

'But why won't you wear yours?'

'I'm not a berserker any more, Ursula, and I can't fight when I know how it feels to be my own victim. You do understand don't you?'

'Not really, I mean, you can fight without being a berserker. I heard that you beat a horde of Aenglisc. Bedewyr told everyone in Camulodunum about that.'

'It just doesn't feel right.'

Ursula saw Dan's pained expression. His face was more strained than she'd ever seen it. His eyes had a haunted look. She had once been terrified of his berserker madness, but now she missed that capacity in him. Even without her magical perceptions she knew it was gone and that what he was going through now was every bit as frightening for him as his madness had once been. He had told her about his new gift of empathy; she was not sure it was a gift at all. She wondered if he could feel her own conflicting emotions. She wanted him by her side, Bright Killer in his hand, making everything safe for her. There had been a kind of security in the knowledge of his killing power. In a world where she had already faced death more than once such knowledge was comforting. In Macsen's world he had been her anchor in an alien land. Here, he was so unlike himself, so uncertain in his plain druidic robes. She was worried about him. She put her hand to his shoulder as if she were still Boar Skull.

'Dan, I don't have to understand. If you say you don't want to fight anymore that's enough for me. I know you're no coward. We're in this together, right?'

He grasped her arm, Combrogi fashion, relieved

beyond belief that she had chosen this moment to reassure him. He felt nervous without his sword, diminished, less a man, in a place where battle skills seemed as important as ever they had been to Macsen's Combrogi. He smiled.

'I don't know what you've committed us to with all that pledging, Ursula. We'd better go and find out.'

Dan removed his arm from hers, quickly, so there could be no misunderstanding and the two of them walked together, comrades once more, towards the soldiers guarding the villa.

~ *Chapter Thirteen* ~

The feast was a curious mixture of Combrogi and Roman. Low tables had been set in a square so that all present faced one another. Duke Arturus sat with Medraut and Larcius at his right hand and a woman in long flowing robes on his left. He rose when he saw Dan and Ursula enter the room. The assembled guests started to bang their horn goblets on the table in what Ursula hoped was approval. Taliesin sat next to Medraut. He looked grave when he saw Dan's grey clothing.

Arturus gave a tight smile 'Welcome to the heroes of the Celtic wars! We are honoured to have you with us.'

Dan nodded in acknowledgement of the welcome, conscious of too many emotions eddying round the room. Taliesin and Arturus were displeased that he had failed to arrive in the resplendent armour of a warrior. The woman sitting next to Arturus gave Ursula a pointedly envious look, though whether it was because of the splendour of her apparel, her athletic figure, or the warmth of her reception from the assembled guests, Dan could not tell. Ursula herself was exultant, basking in the approbation of the men. He realised with a small shock that she was a girl for whom acceptance and affection were relatively new experiences; she had always been an outsider at school. Here she looked happy and relaxed, as though all that had happened to her in Macsen's land and in this one had been for the better, and all the horrible sights, the mutilation of battle, the pain and the hardship they had seen had only made her stronger. It was amazing. He could not blame her for it. He was glad she was happy. All *he* felt was guilt.

Arturus introduced him to many of the assembled dignitaries. Most were soldiers although some had brought their wives, whose bright robes and flashing jewellery vied with the splendour of the military armour. There were also a few elaborately dressed civilian men who held positions of importance. Dan guessed that it was a gathering of almost all the powerful members of the Combrogi alliance. He touched the arm of each guest, even the women, and murmured words in whichever language was their mother tongue. He had learned the commonest idioms when he had served Macsen. They seemed surprised and pleased. He felt horribly disoriented as in the brief moment of contact he was engulfed by the emotions of each individual. He felt like a cork bobbing in a vast ocean of sensation and was in danger of being overwhelmed. As had happened so many times before, Ursula, saved him.

'Dan, come and sit down. No one can eat until we do. You're not the bloody Queen – you don't have to greet everyone by name. Come on, please, I'm starving.'

The clear voice in his head reminded him he was Dan and he went to take his place by Ursula as Arturus introduced the envious woman next to him.

'This is my Lady Gwynefa, daughter of the Count of Britannia, King Meirchion Gul of Rheged. We are to be married when Taliesin says the time is auspicious, when Brother Frontalis can organise the service, and when her father arrives with his five hundred heavy cavalry, which is her dowry.'

He tempered this blunt remark with a smile of unexpected warmth for his Lady and an oddly boyish grin. Perhaps he had the makings of a leader after all.

The Lady Gwynefa smiled too. She was plumply pretty with dark curls swept up in some complicated arrangement of combs and decorative clips, pale green eyes and olive brown skin. She was no older than Ursula and may have been younger, but she was remarkably self-assured and confident of her own beauty and seemed determined to engage Dan in flirtatious conversation. He was glad of the distraction. Keeping his mind on her prevented it straying to the many undercurrents of tension within the room and almost prevented him from noticing Ursula giggling with Larcius. There was something incongruous about a fully armoured Roman soldier giggling but no one but Dan seemed to notice. Try as he might he could think of no other occasion on which Ursula had giggled.

The interminable meal was not over when he became aware that something very bad was happening. Unconsciously, his hand reached for the sword he no longer wore. He could feel a terrible menace, like storm clouds gathering to block out the sun. Dan glanced in Taliesin's direction and saw the older man pale and put down the morsel of meat he'd been about to eat. Their eyes met. Dan felt sick. Horror was moving in their direction. He saw the laughing, drinking, feasting faces of those around him in a kind of horrible slow motion. They did not know it but the bad thing was almost here.

The shrill bugling call of a trumpet sounded an alarm.

Arturus was at his feet at once. 'Arm yourselves men!'

He rushed from the table as men threw down their drinking vessels and raced for their weapons which, in accordance with old Combrogi ways they had left outside the hall.

'What is it? You felt it too, didn't you?' Dan whispered to Taliesin.

'Death and destruction and human misery, Dan. I would guess the Aenglisc have attacked a settlement nearby and will now be cutting down all those who've tried to escape. It's happened before.'

'You can't be serious?'

'I don't joke about massacres, Dan.'

Ursula ran to his side, strapping on a borrowed sword, a second sheathed weapon tucked underarm.

'I took this from Bedewyr,' she said, thrusting Bedewyr's spare sword into his hand.

'Please take it. Don't use it if you don't want to, but have it near.'

He could not resist the mute appeal of her eyes. He sheathed it in the fine Combrogi scabbard under his robe, and joined the others who ran for the city walls to see what was coming their way.

Perhaps fifty people were hurrying in their direction. Some were in family groups some supported injured men and women staggering along the Roman road. Many were bloody and all were distressed beyond measure. Dan could feel their anguish and grief. Unwanted pictures flashed through his mind: whole families being hacked to pieces, houses set on fire with the inhabitants still in them. He heard the screaming and the shrieks of pain of those now dead, forever remembered in the minds of the survivors. As if that were not bad enough he felt the terrible fear of the people now fleeing to Camulodunum. They were being pursued.

'Ursula, the Aenglisc are harrying them. Get a horse.

Arturus. Get archers – the Aenglisc are coming!'

Dan ran for the stables. Ursula was only a pace behind.

'What's going on, Dan?'

'They're refugees. There's been a massacre – like Alavna. I think some of the Aenglisc are chasing the refugees, hunting them on horseback. They're terrified, Ursula, and a lot of them are carrying children.'

He turned to see that Bedewyr and Quiriac were within earshot. Bedewyr said something to the grooms, who quickly had all four of them mounted. Braveheart, hearing his master's voice leaped up at Dan. Bryn was moments behind.

'Bryn, stay here!' Ursula snapped in a tone that brooked no argument. Her face was grim.

'Let's go!'

Townspeople hurried out of their way as they set off at a canter for the city gate. The great door was already open to let in the first few refugees. A woman bleeding profusely from a deep head wound, her eyes blank with shock, muttered, 'The Aenglisc have come – they killed hundreds!' Then she sunk to the ground.

Ursula noted the deep gashes on her arms where she must have held up her hands to protect herself. They did not pause but rode forward. Dan glanced up and saw the top of Arturus's head as he gave rapid orders to the archers on the ramparts. They galloped past the few groups of refugees close enough to the city gate to be safe. Braveheart ran at Dan's side, elated to be free of the confines of the city. Dan could sense the dog's excitement; it was the only positive emotion he could perceive. He had to fight to block out the horror and the fear that was pouring from these people as freely as their blood and tears. There were Aenglisc ahead, he could smell them.

'There they are!' Quiriac shouted.

In the distance, Dan could make out three men on horseback, whooping and shouting with wild pleasure at the chase. The bulk of the Aenglisc had obviously stayed at the village while these few pursued their sport. One of them rode past an unarmed girl and cut her down with his sword so she fell on the tilled earth.

Dan could feel his fury build. He spurred his horse on and unsheathed his borrowed sword.

He was close enough now to feel the mad joy of the mounted Aengliscman as the young girl died, screaming for mercy. He was close enough to feel her terrible fear and pain. The man's eyes widened as he saw Dan, his grey robes flying, ride screaming towards him. Fury blinded Dan to any thought of his own safety – he was as reckless as he had been in his deepest berserker frenzy. Dan rode hard till he was parallel with his enemy. The man spoke to him and though he could not understand the words he knew they were said in mockery because the Aengliscman believed Dan to be a priest. The man was a warrior unlike the other Aenglisc he had fought. He wore a boar-crested helmet of gilded iron, a loose mail shirt, and carried a sword. He raised it in his own defence but Dan was too quick. Carefully timing the blow, Dan hefted Bedewyr's sword two-handed at the enemy's neck. The momentum of Dan's still moving horse carried the powerful stroke forward and the Aengliscman's head was hacked from his shoulders. Dan had little experience of fighting on horseback and was grateful that the combat had been brief. He did not know how effective he could have been if his opponent had taken the offensive. A short fight was bad enough. He had felt the man's surprise as the sword severed his spine. The man's last thoughts were the horrified realisation of the inevitability of his own death. They were imprinted indelibly on Dan's mind. He would never be rid of them.

He looked down at the sprawled form of the girl. Her head was tilted a little to one side and he could see the soft curve of her youthful cheek. He did not need to dismount to know that she was dead and it was her life's blood that had ebbed away to soak the earth.

He had not meant to kill again. He regretted the act at once. What good had it done? The girl was still dead and now her corpse was joined by another to pollute the fertile fields outside Camulodunum.

'Dan!' Ursula's scream of warning inside his head shook him from his regrets. Two mounted men were bearing down on him with spears raised. The first threw a viciously barbed wooden spear in his direction. He ducked neatly and it whistled over his head to land harmlessly in the rain-softened ground. The Aenglisc's sword was out and he was charging towards Dan, screaming something unintelligible. Dan prised the spear from the ground. His only reasonable response was to turn his horse to gallop towards his attacker. A good enough horseman not to worry about losing his seat, Dan clutched his sword in his left hand and the smooth shaft of the spear in his right. It was a well-made weapon. He had never thrown a spear at an enemy, but had excelled at javelin throwing at school. He found the point at which it balanced and tried to estimate how far ahead of his enemy he should aim in order for the spear point to hit its mark. He had no experience to build on, only his normally reliable fighting instincts. Twisting slightly in the saddle to avoid damaging his horse, he let the weapon fly. He sensed rather than heard it punch through the boiled leather breastplate of his adversary, and the man toppled from his horse. Dan was doubled over by a sudden pain in his own chest; he could hardly breathe. The Aengliscman was dying in agony and Dan found himself fighting for his every breath. He swayed in the saddle and would

have fallen but he knew he was still in danger and with huge effort pulled his thoughts from the dying man's pain. The second mounted man had taken some time to arrest his horse's charge and steer it in Dan's direction. He readied himself for another attack, but then Ursula's voice came clearly into his mind.

'Dan, there are many injured here. Help them! Leave this pig to me.'

Ursula was an awe-inspiring sight. Her blonde hair streamed behind the gold and silver helmet and her tense, white face was locked in concentration. She looked like an avenging goddess. She galloped towards Dan's opponent with her sword drawn. Dan felt the sudden fear of the man she was charging. He unaccountably dropped his spear, screamed '*Waelcyrige!*', wheeled his horse and rode away, with Ursula in pursuit.

Ursula's own feelings were kept under very tight control. Dan felt her focus on her businesslike attack, distancing herself from her task. Dan tried not to know what she was seeing and feeling; tried not to know how the sole-surviving Aenglisc was feeling. His own thoughts and emotions were quite enough for him to deal with on their own. He turned away as a cry of fear and pain informed him that Ursula had dealt with the last Aenglisc. Her sword, when she returned a few moments later, was red with gore and her face was pale as paper.

'Should someone take their horses?'

Dan shrugged. 'Arturus can sort that out. Are you all right?'

She nodded. 'I don't like doing it, you know.' She sounded bleak, her voice shaky, almost tearful.

'I know,' he said, because he did. Her feelings mingled with his and it was difficult for him to separate them.

'Thanks, Ursula, you saved me again. I lost it after I killed that guy. I didn't want to do it.'

'I know.' She smiled a sad, weary smile and the two of them rode back towards Bedewyr and Quiriac.

~ Chapter Fourteen ~

Between them they managed to help many of the very badly injured. They loaded the horses with as many as they could bear and escorted the sad survivors into the City of Camulodunum. The archers who had watched the whole encounter from behind the palisade cheered them as they came within earshot. Ursula and Dan had done what heroes did. Brother Frontalis and Taliesin met them at the gates to take the injured to the army hospital in the barracks. Arturus met them there.

'The Aenglisc grow very bold, to chase these people to the gates of Camulodunum. It would have been good to bring one of them back for questioning.'

'Yes, it might have been a good idea but I was too busy trying to stay alive to think of it,' Ursula answered tartly.

Bedewyr, nodded in silent agreement.

Arturus smiled. 'I am of course grateful for your heroism, Lady Boar Skull and, of course, that of the

Bear Sark.' He met Dan's eye and amended his thanks. 'I mean, my thanks to Gawain.'

Ursula was equally unhappy to be known as Lady Boar Skull. 'Please, call me Ursula.'

'I will, if it pleases you, call you Ursa, meaning 'she-bear' for it suits your courage and ferocious skill much better.'

Arturus was doing his best, but he was not a natural charmer. Ursula struggled to answer him with a suitably gracious response. She was suddenly so tired she could scarcely speak. She smiled and nodded and begged his permission to seek her lodgings. She had ridden for eight or ten straight hours, fought three men, killed a fourth, and reaction had just set in. She swayed and would have fallen but for the timely intervention of Larcius.

'Lady Ursa, I do not know how you can still be standing. You truly have the strength of ten men and the courage of twenty. What you did out there was nobly done. You have given the men an example of heroism that will inspire them through all the dark days to come. Allow me to escort you to your lodgings.'

Ursula found she was not quite as exhausted as she had thought. Her heart started to beat rapidly and she was acutely conscious of his hand at her hip, where her mail shirt ended. She was several centimetres taller than Larcius but leaned gratefully on his shoulder, until she remembered his injury. 'I'm sorry – I forgot, your wound.'

'It is much restored through the prayers of Brother Frontalis and the herbal knowledge of Taliesin.' It was quite possible that much of Larcius's incapacity was the result of shock. Certainly, he looked fine – more than fine in fact.

Larcius gently removed her helmet, then the sheepskin hat she was wearing under it for a closer fit. She was aware that her hair was plastered to her head with sweat, that she had been perspiring heavily in the padded leather jerkin she wore under her mail shirt, and that she was too tired to care. He returned her helmet when they reached the door of the inn.

'If you need help with removing your boots and mail shirt, don't hesitate to call for me.'

She must have raised a knowing twenty-first century eyebrow because he added smoothly, 'I will send one of my retinue to assist you. Duke Arturus has been good enough to furnish me with servants. When we first met, I had nothing, but thanks to the War Duke's largesse I have acquired some of the accoutrements of a prince. My lands were sequestered when I moved to Armorica, over the sea. I came back only because I heard Ambrosius, my father, was sick and now I can reclaim what was once mine, Ursula. You will not find me powerless again.'

She knew there was information contained in that

sentence that she ought to understand, but she couldn't for the moment make sense of anything. Even with Boar Skull's strength magically contained within her own frailer body, she had come to the end of her endurance.

'Thank you, Larcius,' she murmured, conscious of her slurring speech.

'My Lady – Ursa – you saved my life today and I will never forget it. I returned to Britannia too carelessly, anxious to seek my father's pardon before he died. I came back too late, but without you I would not have come back at all. You have restored me to my rightful place when otherwise I would lie dead and unburied in a Aenglisc sacred grove. Arturus is to hold a Mass for my safe return to the bosom of the Combrogi peoples. All I can say is that I am for ever in your debt and will give you anything you ask of me.'

He looked at her meaningfully, his handsome face alight with earnestness.

Ursula had no idea what he was talking about.

'It was a pleasure,' she mumbled, more or less incoherently, and staggered off to her chamber and the merciful oblivion of sleep.

Dan tried to help Taliesin but the dizzying multiplicity of images and feelings from the traumatised survivors of the Aenglisc raid was too much for him. Many of the injured kept reliving the events they had witnessed in brutal flashes of memory, like cinematic flashbacks. They were not just visual memories either, but multi-sensory. Dan relived with them the sounds of terror, the screaming, the meaty thud and thump of boot and sword meeting flesh, and the odours: the metallic smell of blood and human excrement and the choking smoke from burning homes. He felt with them the still-present pain of scratches, bruises, lacerations, abrasions, and large gaping wounds. It was all too much. Taliesin, staunching a wide leg wound with professional calm, spotted Dan's white face.

'You can't help, Dan. Preserve your sanity for all our sakes. Get out of here!'

'I could hear them when they were outside the city wall – I don't think I can get away from it.'

Taliesin looked at him with an unreadable expression in his eyes.

'Brother Frontalis,' he said with a slightly odd inflection, 'I need your good right arm.'

Dan never saw it coming. The broad-shouldered monk swung round from the child he had been tending and took in the situation with one swift appraising glance. Without a warning flicker of an eye or twitch of a muscle he withdrew one powerful arm and threw a punch that sent Dan reeling into unconsciousness and blessed peace.

*

Dan woke in the darkness of the inn. Someone had put him to bed. His head throbbed. The chamber smelled sweetly of lavender and of some other pleasant but unrecognisable fragrance. Someone had left pots of oil and a wooden crucifix at each of the corners of his straw-stuffed pallet. He did not understand why. He inhaled the clean, sweetness of the aroma and was grateful that his mind was his own again. He was in a small private room, which seemed strange after the communal living of his time in Macsen's world. By the quality of the light that filtered through the shuttered window it was long past dawn – long past the time when he should be up.

He dressed quickly and joined Ursula for breakfast before they headed off for the barracks together, in search of Taliesin.

As they approached the guard on the barracks they were surprised to receive a smart Roman style salute. They both nodded at the guard in some confusion: 'Where will we find Taliesin?'

'Who? Oh, the Druid. He is with the Duke in the Commander's quarters.' The guard pointed at a squat single-storey building at the other end of the parade ground.

'Arturus doesn't seem to know what to do with us, does he?' Ursula said reflectively to Dan as they walked towards the building.

'I think we've arrived at a bad time.' Dan said distractedly. He was again beginning to feel oppressed by the fear and pain emanating from the barracks. 'Talk to me, Ursula. Are you sure you have no magic left? You've still got Boar Skull's strength – that must be magical.'

Ursula glanced at his tense face. 'No, I would know if I still had the magic, Dan – it races through your veins like electricity – it's like raw energy surging through your body. It's as if you've been plugged into the earth itself. I can't tell you how much I miss it, Dan. I don't feel I'm enough on my own.'

It was true. Dan could feel the terrible awareness of its absence in her. Her pleasure at finding him alive and then her determination to prove herself a warrior had masked her underlying sadness at the loss of her power.

Dan grabbed her hand and she squeezed his back, clumsily.

'Ouch! You don't know your own strength, you don't.'

They both grinned and then fell silent. As they approached the Commander's quarters, Dan was taken aback by the passionate fury emanating from the room. He let go of Ursula's hand.

Two soldiers stood guarding the door, and Medraut's voice could be heard bellowing, 'I will not leave my fort unguarded. If we move men out of here we are wide open! You saw what happened yesterday. They are getting bolder every day and they're greedy for good land. They're just waiting for a chance! We have lost Ceint. I will not lose the rest of my land to the barbarians!'

Arturus's response was quieter but clearly as angry. 'And I will not let one of my oldest friends down. More than that I will not let the Aenglisc get behind us like that. Look at the map, man. If they take Caer-Baddon we're lost – they'll have free rein over all the west – Caer-Baddon is undefended and we might all just as well pack up like our good friend Ambrosius Larcius and flee for Armorica. We have good intelligence that they're gathering forces. They have not had such effective leadership since Hengest was in his prime. Now they have Aelle as their Bretwalda – he took Pevensey, he's no fool – and a very ambitious leader in Hengest's son Aesc, not to mention the pernicious influence of the enchantress, Rhonwen. We have to beat them now and beat them decisively. We can use some of the troops from Fort Cado and bring the heavy cavalry across the Icknield Way. We could make a stand here, at the old fort at Mons Badonicus, you know, Baddon Hill.'

Dan was surprised by the passion in Arturus's voice. It seemed that he did have the spirit of a leader in spite of first appearances. The guard at the door saluted them, notably awestruck by Ursula's appearance now that she was clean and obviously female, no longer the grim and filthy warrior of the previous day. She gave him one of her rare smiles, causing the young soldier to blush and almost fall over his spear in his effort to open the door for them.

The door opened on five men in various stages of exhaustion scowling over an ageing map, which was laid out on a large wooden table. The room smelled of stale sweat and sour wine and men too long together in close quarters. Arturus looked up to greet them.

'Boar Skull and the Bear Sark – I mean, Ursa and Gawain, welcome! You catch us debating our strategy for ridding ourselves of the Aenglisc menace for good. You are most welcome to join us. I have just ordered some breakfast. It has been a long night. You know Gorlois Cerdic of Dumnonia and Helvius of Caer-Baddon?'

Arturus rubbed one be-ringed and elegant hand over the light stubble on his chin. His robes were crumpled and he looked altogether more like a War Duke than he had the day before. He was flanked by Medraut, Taliesin, and two other men dressed in Combrogi plaids, who inclined their heads in acknowledgement of the new arrivals.

'Thank you,' Dan said courteously, 'though we might be of more use if we had a little more background on this … conflict.'

Taliesin spoke in reply. 'My Lord, Duke Arturus, it may be as well that I speak to our heroes in private and brief them on our recent history. I know you are anxious to continue this debate. Perhaps we may rejoin you later?'

Nodding and bowing, Taliesin ushered Dan and Ursula out of the room and into the clean cold air of the parade ground.

'Taliesin,' Dan wasted no time in interrogating him. 'What on earth did you do to me last night?'

'Oh, that!' Taliesin looked sheepish. 'Brother Frontalis is the great grandson of one of the last legitimate gladiatorial champions of Rome. Before he took up the cross of the Christos he used to dabble in some unofficial, not to say illegal, gladiatorial bouts in Gaul. He knocked you out! You looked terrible – we thought it might help.'

'And what of the scents and the crosses around my bed?' Dan did not look pleased.

'I know some herbs that seem to calm the fevered brain and Brother Frontalis blessed the crosses and prayed for your soul to be at peace. By the look of you, something worked.'

Dan's scowl cleared. 'I slept well – but do you know what I could do to control this …' he searched for an appropriate word, 'empathy, while I'm awake? It is just too much.'

He felt a wave of sympathy from the older man.

'I know, Daniel, but you must find your own way

through it. Brother Frontalis will pray that you find the strength to control it – there is little else anyone can do, my friend.'

Dan felt choked by emotion, his own this time. He could feel Taliesin's sympathy shading into pity, Ursula's worry and fear that he was no longer the Dan she thought she knew. He could feel the anguish of the Combrogi refugees, their silent, potent keen of grief, and the controlled fury still radiating from the Commander's quarters. He just wanted it all to stop.

He put his hands over his ears in a pointless attempt to cut out the noise that was not noise, and somehow found the strength to mumble, 'Then please, can we get further away from here – if distance will make any difference. Is there somewhere quiet we can go to talk about what's going on?'

Ursula looked momentarily puzzled as she surveyed the deserted training ground. She shared a quick glance of complicity with Taliesin and, following Brother Frontalis's example, punched Dan squarely on the jaw. For the second time he was knocked, unprepared, into the peace of unconsciousness.

~ *Chapter Fifteen* ~

When Dan revived it was to the cool, dark interior of a small, rectangular, stone building, dominated by a large wooden cross.

'Dan, I'm so sorry, but you looked so terrible, so lost, I didn't know what else to do?'

'Well, I'm glad you pulled your punch and didn't break my jaw.'

He sat up, feeling woozy but the background noise of other people's pain had at least faded to a distant hum. He could deal with that. 'I'm sorry, I'm not being much help.' He swallowed down his distress. 'I just don't know how to control it.'

Taliesin smiled. 'Is it better in here?'

'Yes – it's not so overwhelming.'

'Perhaps the suffering Christos bears the burden here,' Taliesin said enigmatically.

'Anyway, I need to apologise to you, Ursula, and explain why you're here.'

'It's done now, Taliesin, Dan told me what you did. We're stuck here. What more is there to say?' Ursula sounded resigned. Dan tried to dampen down his awareness of her own distinctive brand of sadness.

'I want you to know why I called you. It wasn't only that I thought you could get me home. These people need you as much as Macsen needed you, they are Macsen's heirs in every sense that counts.'

'But they're Ravens! How can they be his heirs?' Ursula interjected, anger evident in her voice.

'In this world the Ravens are Romans, and they and the Combrogi have a common cause. Arturus is an able man, a sensible, intelligent leader, but he is not a hero. You know, men don't fight for able men, they fight for heroes. The men need to know that you two are with Arturus – you will inspire them.'

Something in Taliesin's voice made Dan look at him sharply; he seemed disappointed as he had when Ursula pledged Dan's sword to Arturus. Taliesin acknowledged Dan's look.

'I will not lie to you – I had hoped that Arturus himself might look to you for leadership, not the other way around. I thought you, either separately or together, might be *The Bear* of the prophecy.'

'What?'

'Dan will explain. When I was searching for Rhonwen I met a philosopher, Igris, he said there was a prophecy associated with the Combrogi here.'

'Go on.'

'The prophecy said, "As the bear on the high hillside protects the cubs, so *The Bear* of Ynys Prydein, the Island of the Mighty, protects its own. Remember *The Bear* and cherish it, for when *The Bear* is gone the hillside falls." '

'So?'

'Your name, Ursula, means *bear* and Daniel was always the Bear Sark. I had prepared the Combrogi to see you as the culmination of the prophecy but by pledging yourselves to Arturus you threw all that away.'

'Well, I'm sorry, Taliesin that I didn't do what I didn't know you wanted.' Ursula's tone was tart. 'Anyway, couldn't Arturus be *The Bear*? I thought he was the great leader.'

Taliesin looked puzzled. 'Does he strike you so?'

Ursula shook her head. 'No, but I've only just met him.' She wrinkled her nose 'I'm sure he *will* be a great hero – that's what all the stories say.'

'What stories?' Taliesin's eyes were sharp and suddenly calculating.

Dan was getting irritated. 'Never mind all that. What does it matter? What is the background to this fight – what were they talking about in that room?'

'It matters, Dan, believe me,' Taliesin said firmly. 'And Ursula has just given me an idea – why shouldn't

Arturus Urbicus become Arturus Ursus, *the bear on the hillside*, the saviour of the Island of the Mighty?'

Taliesin smiled. 'Arturus must become High King, and then, if you are prepared to help him, it could still all work out to the Combrogi's advantage.'

Dan sighed.

Taliesin continued, 'All right, Dan, I will give you the background. The Romans occupied much of the 'Island of the Mighty' but most of the standing army left three generations ago to fight for Rome nearer to the heart of the Empire. The Aenglisc, came to help fight the barbarians in the north, but this is good land and they have not been content to stay where the Combrogi would have them. There was confusion and civil war between Valerius Vortigern, the High King, and Larcius's father Ambrosius. Ambrosius was more in favour of the Roman ways than Valerius and, in the end, he won. Ambrosius managed to raise an army levy from round here, where the land is most at risk. We've won more than we've lost but when we have lost, we've lost badly. Larcius tried to take on Aesc, the son of Hengest, who was a formidable leader among the Aenglisc. More foolishly, he tried to beat them in their own territory. Hundreds died, most of them young men. Larcius lost so badly he ran away rather than face his father. He fled to Armorica, across the sea, only returning when he heard of his father's imminent demise. No one knew he was back until you found him, Ursula, and we still don't know if it was to make his peace with his father or … well, suffice to say it would probably have been better for Arturus's security if he'd remained in Aenglisc hands. Arturus loves him like a brother, but …'

'But what?' Ursula demanded.

'But I don't entirely trust Larcius, he has always been ambitious. There are even rumours that he intended to ally with Rhonwen, though perhaps that cannot be true if she tried to kill him.'

'She did,' said Ursula fiercely.

'Anyway,' Taliesin continued, 'Larcius has always had a personal following and many hoped he would take over as High King when his father died. He's been away for five years but even so he could sway the vote. Arturus is good strategist and a great war duke but he's no charmer of men. Indeed, he has made enemies – compromise does not come easy to him. Men follow Arturus because he wins, not because they love him. Whereas, both men and women,' he gave Ursula a quick glance, 'tend to like Larcius.'

Under Ursula's antagonistic gaze, Taliesin changed tack.

'The Aenglisc are not all the same – they call themselves different things and come from different places. Anyway, there is always the risk that some of the Combrogi will desert Arturus to join the Aenglisc – if there's profit in it. Rhonwen has allied herself with the Aenglisc and is highly regarded by both Aesc and Aelle, their Bretwalda, leader. Rumour has it they don't blow their noses without consulting her and they are unifying the various Aenglisc factions so that now they are trying to push us back to the far west and we need to make a stand. We have intelligence that they are planning to take Caer-Baddon, you may know it as Aquae Sulis, a major Combrogi city. It's not as stupid as it sounds, as they are renowned sailors and can get their war bands to the southwest by sea as well as across the land. Medraut is Count of the Saxon Shore and is afraid if we take our troops from here we will have no one to reinforce the remaining forts. Camulodunum is the last outpost of civilisation. North of here is almost wholly Aenglisc. I'm not sure we can ever get that land back. We stand at a turning point – without strong leadership some of the Combrogi will as ever ally with whoever has the most to offer them. That could be Aelle or Aesc as easily as Arturus. Before we can win we have to make everyone believe we *can* win so that our allies do not desert us and make failure inevitable. That is the importance of the prophecy – I have made sure that men will fight for the Bear Sark and, indeed, for the Boar Skull. It has been my chief work here. I may now have to change my approach and try to support the idea of Arturus as *The Bear*. Given time, it could be done.'

Ursula was thoughtful. 'I can't imagine what you are talking about, Taliesin, until I see these places on the map. What do you think, Dan?'

Dan scowled with concentration. 'I think Aquae Sulis is the Roman name for Bath, which is in the southwest, isn't it?'

Taliesin nodded. 'We are in the old Trinovantes land, in the southeast of the island. Some people now call it the Kingdom of Caer-Colun, the more common name for Camulodunum. Since Ceint was lost to the Aenglisc, Caer-Colun is all that is left of Medraut's land. There are good Roman roads between the two cities. We could get to Caer-Baddon to reinforce the Combrogi if Arturus can persuade the rest of them that it is a good idea.'

'Is Arturus not the leader then?'

'He is War Duke – but not yet High King. The War Duke persuades, he cannot command, and tomorrow the Council of Britannia decides who will become High King.'

'The two other men in the council – I did not catch their names who were they?'

'Gorlois Cerdic, the Dumnonian King and Helvius of the Kingdom of Caer-Baddon, formerly the Belgae lands. They are important leaders with the most to lose if Aquae Sulis, Caer-Baddon is overrun.'

Dan was concentrating hard, determined to understand. 'You said you had intelligence – where did it come from?'

Taliesin looked uncomfortable. 'I had husbanded all my power to call you when you were caught in the Veil, but Arturus begged me to do one thing for him before I lost all my limited powers of sorcery. I cannot shape-shift as Ursula did but I managed to make part of my mind into a bird, a merlin, and spied on Rhonwen and her allies.'

'Did she not sense the magic?' Ursula sounded incredulous.

'Rhonwen is not what you were, Ursula, she doesn't have your gift or your grasp of what magic can do. I don't think she did know I was there, no. We have heard corroborating reports anyway.'

'Arturus wants to defend Caer-Baddon and you want us to fight for Arturus in this big battle.' Dan sounded aghast.

'I think Arturus will try and reinforce the old fort at Mons Badonicus, just outside Caer-Baddon, it is in a key strategic position, but yes, I think it will help a great deal if you fought. You are legendary throughout this land. You will give the men heart and hope and victory. For now, you two and you two alone can help keep the tribes united.'

Dan stared directly at Taliesin. 'I cannot fight again, Taliesin. I will help in any other way I can, but I do not want to kill again.'

'But they are our enemies, Dan,' said Ursula, desperate.

'They are not my enemies! You don't know what it is like! You can talk about enemies, but all I feel is the pain these so-called enemies feel when I hurt them, their fear and their horror of death. These enemies are men and nothing is worth doing that to a man, *nothing*.'

Ursula's face had taken on its most obstinate sullen aspect. 'Well, from what I can see, what these Aenglisc did to those people yesterday was as barbaric as anything the Ravens did in Alavna. I fought then, and I'll fight now. You know better than any of us what the refugees have gone through. How can you not want to avenge them?'

'I just can't, Ursula. You said you understood, but you don't do you? I will not get involved in this war of Arturus's. Who is to say which is the right side? What is this prophecy that Taliesin holds so much store by? He thought *we* fulfilled it and now he thinks he can change Arturus's name so that he fulfils it. What is that all about? Anyway, haven't you guessed yet? These Aenglisc you're so anxious to kill are probably your own ancestors!' Dan glared at both Taliesin and Ursula and stormed from the building.

'Let him go!' said Taliesin gently, resting a restraining hand on Ursula's arm.

'We each follow our own path. I don't envy him his – he has chosen the hardest road.'

Ursula was torn between fury and despair. Dan was

alive but he had changed. She so needed him to be her ally and support, in this world as in the last.

'Let's get out of here!' she said to Taliesin. Is there some place I can do some training now? I really need to hit something – very hard.'

It was not magic that surged through her but Boar Skull's brute energy and her own frustrated fury. If she did not get rid of it soon she could not answer for her actions.

~ *Chapter Sixteen* ~

Dan ran from the stone church, ran from the strength of Ursula's disappointment. He could not bear it that she did not understand. He could still feel the waves of other people's feelings threatening to engulf him. He had never felt so intimately connected with every person he met, nor so alone.

He hitched up his long robe and lengthened his stride. He had to get away from here. He did not notice the commanding presence of Brother Frontalis and all but ran into him.

'Gawain! What ails you, man?'

Dan looked up into the frank and kindly gaze of the gladiator-monk. He did not know what to say. He drowned in waves of the monk's compassion.

'I can't stay here. Do you know of anywhere I could go?'

Brother Frontalis looked thoughtful. 'It seems to me, Gawain, that a man of your gifts, if gifts they are and not demons in need of exorcism, needs to spend time in quiet prayer and solitude. I could try exorcism, by the grace of our Lord, the Christos, but I fear that if you have a gift of the spirit it would go ill with any who tried to tamper with it.'

Dan looked blank, he was not at all sure he knew what Brother Frontalis was talking about.

'I don't think I'm possessed with demons, Brother Frontalis. Maybe if I could just get some peace, even for a few hours ...' Dan eyed the other man's right arm suspiciously, 'without losing consciousness, then, maybe I could cope.'

Brother Frontalis guided Dan towards the shelter of the barracks hospital. Dan winced at the horrifying memories of those who lay there.

'Gawain, there is a place where most of my brothers remain to prepare for the coming of the Kingdom of God on Earth. You will be needed here tomorrow for the Council of Britannia but I could guide you to the retreat after that.'

'What do you mean, "I'm needed tomorrow"?'

'The High King is chosen by lengthy debate and each man or woman present at the Council votes. You are a Combrogi hero; it is inconceivable that your opinion will not be sought. You cannot go anywhere before then.'

Dan looked into Brother Frontalis's broad face and found it implacable. Dan knew there would be no escape from Camulodunum before then.

'Thank you, Brother Frontalis.'

Dan turned away from the stables and would have left but there was a sudden flurry of movement as men and women ran from their homes towards the city gate.

Bedewyr saw Dan and smiled delightedly. 'It's King Meirchion Gul of Rheged with his Sarmatian Cataphracts.'

'His what?'

'Cataphracts – his heavy cavalry. Come and see.'

Now that Dan stopped to listen he could feel the ground tremble from the deep, reverberating rumble of many mounted men. It was a noise at once threatening and exhilarating, more rhythmic than distant thunder. He felt the vibrations through his spine and shivered.

Ursula stood on the parapet and watched the dust rise like a mist to mask the approach of some five hundred mounted men plus their baggage carts, servants, wives, and camp followers. It was a breathtaking sight, even through the haze of dust. Each man was dressed in a conical helmet and an elbow-length coat of scaled armour. Some shimmered blue-green and seemed to be of horn, others were of red lacquer or the rich brown of rawhide, and some few wore metal armour. Most of the horses were similarly apparelled with bronze or red-lacquered head guards and mail skirts that protected their chests and sides. The men also wore tunics and trews of Celtic brilliance: greens, reds and yellows only dimmed by dust and mud. They carried sheathed swords and light bows across their back as well as the long slender lance, the kontos, favoured by horsemen. As far as Ursula could see many were unusually dark-skinned and dark-eyed, though she spotted some with the light eyes and dark skin that so distinguished Gwynefa. King Meirchion Gul of Rheged, Gwynefa's father, rode at the head of his troop, a tall lean looking man, notable for his elaborate golden helmet and metal armour. Next to him rode standard bearers carrying great red-and-gold dragons – these Sarmatian dracos were an infinitely more impressive version of a wind sock. The wind blew through the open maw of each dragon so that its long, hollow body was inflated and it undulated like a live creature in the breeze. It was an awe-inspiring sight – the proud stance of the riders carrying their decorated lances, the horses riding three abreast in a column that extended as far back as the eye could see. The sound they made was deafening, not just the pounding of the horses' hooves against the stone road but the animal snorting, breathing and occasional whickering of five hundred weary horses, the clatter of mail and weapons and the jingle of harnesses. It continued long after the first arrivals were safely stabled in the barracks' mews or housed in the temporary shelters that had been erected on the parade ground. According to Taliesin these Cataphracts were descendants of the

Sarmatians who arrived in Britannia from the far reaches of the Roman Empire. They had intermarried with the local women and a substantial number of them chose to remain when the rest of the troops left Britannia. The armour and the technique of training and breeding the horses had been passed on down the generations and were part of a unique heritage. The Cataphracts of old shared their barracks with their horses and their great grandsons prided themselves on keeping to the same tradition. Ursula, breathing in the overpowering stench of hot, damp horses, was inclined to believe him. She took Taliesin's advice and returned to the inn to dress herself in heroic splendour before joining Taliesin at Arturus's villa to greet the leaders of the Cataphracts. She agreed with him that it would be best to make a good impression. She wished she knew where Dan was. She was worried about him and had struggled to see the old Dan in the strained, hooded figure of their last encounter. Her urge to fight something had dissipated suddenly. She felt empty and lonely and too far from home. She was trying to phrase an apology, which was not really an apology – but might persuade Dan to speak to her – when she noticed the extravagantly dressed figure of Larcius hurrying to greet her. Her stomach did that thing again where it seemed to twist and knot her insides to leave her breathless. Larcius was wearing leather scale armour and a fine purple cloak with some kind of fur collar. His dark hair was clean and he smelled fragrantly of spices.

'My dear Lady Ursa, might I escort you to the War Duke's presence?'

At a loss for words, Ursula smiled her assent. Her palms felt suddenly hot and the sheepskin fez she was wearing under her helmet caused small beads of perspiration to form on her forehead. Larcius chatted lightly about the Cataphracts and their great skill as horsemen, not unlike Ursula's own ability. Her leap from her own horse to Gawain's was now famous.

'You will like King Meirchion Gul – his is very much a Celtic kingdom. He prizes strong women, and Gwynefa is the light of his life.'

'You know him?'

'I know everybody. He and my father were allies. After my mother died I often stayed with them in Rheged. I've known Gwynefa almost since she was born.'

'She is very beautiful,' Ursula offered, half expecting one of Larcius's elaborate compliments for her own beauty to follow.

'Yes. She is.' He said shortly and changed the subject. 'You will, of course be voting at the Council of Britannia tomorrow?'

'Will I?'

'As a Celtic hero you will surely help choose the new

High King at the Council of Britannia tomorrow. Arturus is still here and not mounting campaigns from his Castle at Cado as he would prefer it because he is a candidate.'

'I don't understand – who is the choice between?'

'Well, the main contenders are Meirchion, Medraut, Cerdic and Arturus. But if Arturus marries Gwynefa, King Meirchion will waive his right and back Arturus. Medraut, well, he's not very popular, and the fact that half his kingdom is in enemy hands doesn't help his cause. Then Cerdic of Dumnonia, he's the elder half-brother to Arturus so ...' he shrugged, 'who knows? Of the others, many are young or too old and don't have the standing yet, though Agricola of Dyfed shows promise, and then there's *me*, the great Ambrosius's son, Larcius said with a sardonic smile.'

A heavily laden horse and cart wobbled in their direction and he placed a protective arm round Ursula's waist. It made her feel uncomfortable.

'Well, my lady, be sure that even if I were High King you would always be Queen of my grateful heart.'

Ursula was distracted from his words by a glimpse of a man in dark robes, running from the villa.

'Larcius, thank you for your company, but I need to go. Please give my apologies to the Duke. I will be back soon.'

She extricated herself from his arm and ran in the direction of the dark-robed figure. It had to be Dan and she had to speak to him.

~ Chapter Seventeen ~

Ursula failed to find Dan in spite of her best efforts. He did not return to the inn that night, but when the call came to attend the Council of Britannia he arrived, pale and haunted looking, to take his place in Arturus's hall. It was an odd meeting. All the furniture had been removed – the Roman-style couches and small tables bearing wine. Everyone sat in a circle on the mosaic floor, like small children at school assembly. Various elaborately dressed people spoke, apparently randomly, about the purpose of kingship and the pride of the people. No one spoke in Latin, which was awkward, as for many it was clearly their native tongue, and Ursula squirmed with embarrassment at the mangling some of those present gave the familiar language of the Combrogi. It was dull beyond description to listen to the endless round of self-congratulatory speeches, and her mind drifted. She watched Larcius and admired his handsome profile. Arturus looked sour and said little,

Taliesin looked bored, and Dan looked tortured. She wanted to reach out to him and find his mind, but what could she say? She fidgeted with her sword belt and traced the pattern of the round medallions of Roman designs that were woven into her tunic. It was somewhat worse than double physics on a Friday afternoon.

Then Arturus clapped his hands and servants brought out the best ale and Taliesin brought out his harp. Ursula felt her scalp prickle as Taliesin used all his skill to change the atmosphere of the room. There was little enough real magic in it, just enough to taunt Ursula, to remind her of what she had lost, but Taliesin's musical talent had if anything increased. The tune he played was familiar, redolent of Macsen's great hall, but the words were new. She recognised them with a shock. The bard was singing of the Battle of Craigwen, the battle in which she and Dan had helped to save King Macsen and the Combrogi from the Ravens. Ursula met Dan's eyes and he pulled a face. He was clearly as embarrassed as she was to hear their role in the battle sung of in such heroic terms, but his face looked less anguished as if Taliesin's last remnants of magic had eased his discomfort, salved the rawness of his sensitivity.

Afterwards, Taliesin introduced Dan and Ursula to the assembled crowds, though there was no one present who had not already heard the story of their exploits. Taliesin invited them to sit at either side of Arturus, as his honoured guests. Perhaps it was Taliesin's revenge for Larcius's arrogance in arriving in purple, the imperial colour, and upstaging the Duke. As the ale was consumed with customary Celtic rapidity, the real argument began and things began to get interesting. Cerdic was becoming increasingly heated about the significance of his territory and its pre-eminence because of its mines and link with Roman Gaul. As Arturus's elder it became clear he felt the decision should be made on some ground that favoured his claim. The assembled men were watching and listening carefully. Ursula began to feel edgy and to regret that like all the others, she had been obliged to leave her sword and knife at the door. Her heart began to beat faster. Cerdic had drunk too much and was losing his self-control. Dan had also tensed and his face resumed its worried expression.

Suddenly, Cerdic leapt up, his dagger in his hands, and threw himself at Arturus. Dan and Ursula responded as one, instinct overriding all else. Ursula flung herself at Arturus, knocking him backwards, while Dan tackled Cerdic for the knife. Checking that Arturus was safe, Ursula waited for her opportunity. Dan and Cerdic were rolling around on the ground. No one else was going to intervene – it was sport of a kind and the spectators watched for the outcome with barely concealed glee. Ursula was not risking Dan's life for entertainment. Cerdic had gained the advantage and lay on top of Dan, gripping his neck firmly with his powerful left hand while straining to gain complete control of the knife with his right. Ursula, relying on her Boar Skull strength, grabbed Cerdic by the neck of his tunic, heaved him backwards and away from the prone and sweating figure of her friend. She kneed Cerdic casually in the groin and twisted the knife from his hand. His strength was no match for hers. She twisted his right arm behind his back and held it there.

'What would you have me do?' she asked Arturus. She was only vaguely aware of the astonished response from the assembled men. Out of the corner of her eye she saw Medraut's swift intake of breath and something like a smile flit across Taliesin's craggy features. If he had planned this she would kill him.

Dan got to his feet. His neck was red and already bruising from Cerdic's ruthless grip. He clasped Ursula's shoulder in gratitude and moved to check that Arturus was all right. Ursula had never been taught to tackle and Dan was afraid she may have winded Arturus in her enthusiasm.

Arturus got to his feet rather clumsily and addressed the rulers of Britannia.

'King Gorlois Cerdic has brought a blade into this sacred gathering, the Council of Britannia. What is to be his punishment?'

Cerdic struggled under Ursula's grip. She tightened it

and he grimaced with pain.

Dan, too, looked distressed. '*Thanks Ursula, but please, you're holding him too hard – it's hurting me!*'

Ursula loosened her grip marginally and was warmed by Dan's swift smile. Then quite unexpectedly amongst all the muttered chants of 'Kill him!', Dan spoke.

'Honoured kings and rulers of Britannia, I would beg for this man's life. I am neither priest nor druid, nor even the Bear Sark any more, but I know that this man's heart is full of remorse – he is shamed and will be loyal to whoever is chosen High King this day. I ask you for mercy.'

There was much mumbling at this. One man, Dan did not know his name, asked, 'What says the Lady Ursa?'

Once, in Macsen's land Dan had granted Ursula status by making her the keeper of his sword; here it seemed the tables were turned and she had the opportunity to repay that debt.

Ursula cleared her throat. 'I will do whatsoever my lord Gawain desires.' She turned to look at Dan with what she thought was an appropriate expression of humility.

'Perhaps we should leave the final judgement for the High King when he is elected. Is there anyone else who wishes to speak?' Arturus said.

'It seems from their actions that our heroes support Duke Arturus – is this so?' One of the assembled dignitaries asked.

Dan glanced at Ursula who was once more looking at Larcius, her usual expression altered by some other emotion. He could not bear for her to choose Larcius; he had disliked the man on sight. Dan had not intended to do Taliesin's work for him but the words suddenly came to him.

'Yes, I support the claim of Duke Arturus to be the High King of Britannia. He bears my sword, Bright Killer, now known as Caliburn as a sign that he is the one with the strength to defeat the enemies of this land.

All eyes turned to look at Ursula who was still holding Cerdic in a bone-breaking grip. Her arms were beginning to tire. Larcius was looking at her with a curiously direct gaze. Had he not said that he had some claim to be High King? She remembered that he was the son of the last High King, Ambrosius. Dan looked resolute. She could not contradict him and, more than that, if Arturus were the Arthur of legend he had to be King. Under Larcius's scrutiny she felt her mouth go dry. She licked her lips and hoped that her voice would not squeak.

'It is as Gawain says. I gave the sword, once Bright Killer, now Caliburn, to Duke Arturus for the defence of this realm. How can he not be High King if he can rid us of the scourge of our enemies?'

There was silence.

Brother Frontalis broke it. 'In the absence of our

bishop, who is still sick, it is left to me to remind you that we stand at a crossroads in the life of Britannia. Let us kneel and pray that we may be guided in our choice by he who reigns in heaven and by the Holy Spirit.'

Some of the assembled, the pagan elements, started to mutter at Frontalis's words, but most, including Arturus struggled devoutly to their knees.

Taliesin walked over to stand beside Brother Frontalis, and all muttering ceased: 'Let us pray for our land and all that is sacred in it. Let us pray by all that is sacred that a leader will be chosen, joined, wedded, made one with Britannia, our Island of the Mighty, and we its people.'

After a long pause Taliesin spoke again.

'I propose that Arturus Ursus, son of King Uther of Pengwern and Ygraine of Dumnonia, Dux Bellorum of Britannia should be High King of Britannia. Who agrees?'

Was it Ursula's imagination or did Arturus look a little startled to be named as 'Arturus Ursus'? No one commented as one by one the rulers spoke.

'I, Meirchion of Rheged, Count of Britannia, agree and pledge my sword and my men to his service in the defence of Britannia.'

'I, Medraut of Ceint, Count of the Saxon Shore, agree and pledge my sword and men to his service in the defence of Britannia.'

It took a long time. At some point Larcius made his pledge. Ursula did not meet his eyes. She did not know if he had thought she would act otherwise for, indeed, it seemed to her that he would have made a better High King than Arturus, but who was she to stand against history?

Ursula dared not relax her grip on Cerdic and she was relieved when Arturus stood to acknowledge their words – it was a sign that maybe the meeting might soon end.

Arturus walked to the centre of the circle of men, and then prostrated himself towards each quarter of the circle in turn.

'As our Lord washed the feet of his followers, so I promise to be your servant, to act only for the good of Britannia and for her people. I thank you for trusting me, and I promise you I will not betray that trust.'

Arturus stood up. Ursula was a little taken aback by his self-abasement, and by the startled expression she saw on some of the other faces, she was not the only one. She earnestly hoped that they had not made a terrible mistake in choosing Arturus over Larcius.

'It saddens me that my first act as High King must be to stand in judgement over my mother's eldest son, Gorlois Cerdic. I would not take up this sacred office with blood on my hands, so my judgement is this: King Gorlois Cerdic of Dumnonia is to sacrifice his lands and crown to the High King, and pledge to use his skills as a soldier and horseman to lead and train the Cavalry of Camulodunum and be their Commandant.'

Many of those present looked displeased. It was not tactful of Arturus to have immediately added to his personal wealth and status by taking land from his brother.

Arturus continued. 'As a sign of the love and respect in which I held his father, I grant the title of King of Dumnonia to Larcius Ambrosius, for as long as he shall live, after which it shall revert to my brother's heirs. As Larcius is the son of my lord, Ambrosius Aurelianus, whom I so deeply mourn, it is my dearest wish that we two might work together for the good of Britannia.'

That was better. Ursula released her hold on Cerdic. In spite of her greater height there was something incongruous about seeing a comparatively slender woman restraining the heavily built warrior.

Cerdic knelt before King Arturus. 'I thank you for your clemency. I, Gorlois Cerdic, son of Tanicus Cerdic of Dumnonia and Ygraine, once of Calchfynedd, lay my sword and life at your service.'

Ursula loosened the muscles of her arm and shoulder and took her place beside the new king. She was at the court of King Arthur, and it was not at all what she had expected.

~ *Chapter Eighteen* ~

The decision to choose Arturus as High King changed everything – fast. Bishop Petrus recovered sufficiently to officiate at a small formal oath-taking ceremony at which the High King's status was confirmed, and Arturus and Gwynefa were married. There was surprisingly little fuss. Arturus was a practical man and too concerned with the coming campaign against the Aenglisc to permit himself to be distracted. The various kings and civic leaders left Camulodunum at dawn the day after the ceremony. They were escorted by their private retinues, their wagons and their men at arms, fully armoured and prepared for trouble. Camulodunum was close to the occupied territories and the risk of an ambush was high. Perhaps the other rulers of safer territories needed to be reminded of the imminent danger. Either way, none left before promising grain, cattle, horses, weapons and men to swell the ranks of the Combrogi. Arturus hoped to raise a force of more than a thousand men to occupy the fort at Mons Badonicus in readiness for the Aenglisc onslaught. It was not a large force by the standards of their ancestors but it was enough to pose considerable logistic problems. Such issues kept Arturus cloistered in the Commander's room at the barracks, poring over maps and supply lists and the precious handwritten, vellum copy of the Roman military manual by Vegetius that had belonged to Ambrosius's own father. Medraut spent long hours debating strategy, until it was agreed that he would stay with a minimal force, so that should the Aenglisc mount a opportunistic attack on Camulodunum or his own fort of Dumnoc neither would be left undefended.

Taliesin was concerned. In his view, Arturus was not playing the role of Celtic High King sufficiently. He was failing to dispense gifts and hospitality – failing to spend time with the men, failing to win their loyalty.

To compensate for Arturus's absence Taliesin insisted that Ursula trained with the cavalry troops during the day and mixed with the military commanders at mealtimes and during the evening entertainments. He insisted that she learn the names of the men, their interests, and their strengths. It was not an arduous task. She enjoyed the training, riding with the long lance, learning how to fire an arrow at a target from horseback. She loved the feeling of fitness and strength that was Boar

Skull's inheritance. It was so different from the way she had felt at home. Larcius was often around, though she found his presence unsettling. Ursula had spent time enough with warriors to handle herself like one of the men. It was easier for them to look at her as some kind of precociously gifted boy rather than as a woman and she did nothing to make that more difficult. Larcius had the good sense not to treat her as he treated Gwynefa, with endless complicated compliments that made her laugh, but it was hard for Ursula to deny that she was a woman when he was near. She was not entirely sure that she wanted to. She missed Dan, though, all the time.

Dan stayed out of everyone's way, sequestered in the chapel with Brother Frontalis or talking with Taliesin. He had become a semi-nocturnal figure, sleeping in the small room at the back of the chapel for much of the day and only emerging after dark to talk to the night sentries. He also exercised in Combrogi fashion, silently, alone in the training ground when all but the watch, slept.

Ursula was hurt by his avoidance of her. She tried to meet his mind but it was closed to her, so instead she waited for him outside the chapel – a small ambush of her own. She waited a long time. When Dan finally emerged, she noticed that he moved heavily like a much older man, like a man in pain.

'Dan,' she said softly, 'Why are you avoiding me? Why are you hiding like some kind of freak in the shadows?'

'You know why.'

Ursula looked puzzled.

'It's not you, Ursula, but I can't stand people anymore, not when I have to feel their fears, their bitterness – it's all more than I can bear. And for a couple of nights now I've been sharing their dreams.' He shuddered and lifted haunted eyes towards her.

'I don't think I can deal with much more of it, Ursula. I need to find Rhonwen and beg her to raise the Veil. She has no particular enmity towards me. I've got to get home – get back to normal.'

'You'd try and get home without me?' Ursula was shocked.

'You seem happy and you're important. All the soldiers in the camp hang on your every word. The Lady Ursa is everybody's idol. There are men in the barracks who dream about you every night – you'd be shocked.'

'And this makes you think that I wouldn't want to go home?' Ursula's voice was dangerous.

'Well, at least you're having a better time than me.'

Ursula could feel her temper flare. 'You sound like a spoilt—'

'What, Ursula? What do I sound like? Like you

would know! You have no idea.'

Her punch arrived at the speed of thought, but Dan dodged it anyway, and before he knew what he was doing he had bunched his own fist. His father had drummed it into him as a small child that he should never ever hit a girl, but he found that Ursula did not count. She had the power of a Celtic warrior in her fists. His own fury temporarily blocked out his awareness of her feelings, so he was taken by surprise when a second punch made contact. That was it. He attacked Ursula like a wild animal, kicking and punching – she was nowhere near as agile as he was and she took it for a while, until a blow from her right fist sent him reeling backwards into the wall of the chapel and Brother Frontalis.

'My children! What in the name of our Blessed Lord is going on?'

Ursula stood up, bruised and bleeding. She felt like a schoolgirl again – ashamed and awkward.

'Not exactly a fight for heroes,' Brother Frontalis said dryly.

Dan stood up and shook his head.

'I'm sorry, Ursula.' He knew every place where he had hurt her, he could feel the sting of the abrasions and, worse still, he knew she felt betrayed. He looked up to see her eyes were no longer angry but moist and injured looking. He allowed himself to hear her voice in his mind.

'You are my friend – you were oath-bound to help me. You would have left me – here alone – how could you?'

'Ursula, I'm so sorry.'

Dan did not know if the lump in his throat was because he'd hurt her and he was sorry or because he'd hurt her and he knew exactly how it felt for her, but when he went to hug her and she hugged him back, the tears flowed. It was a relief to hold on to Ursula and let all his fear and horror of the past few days wash away. She felt the same way and there was no shame among the Combrogi in showing emotion. Ursula clung to him as if he was the only stable thing in an unstable universe.

'Dan don't leave me – promise you won't. I've hated not talking to you these last few days. I don't want to be the Lady Ursa – I just want to be Ursula. I want to see my mum again. Please don't even think of leaving me again!'

'I won't. I won't. I'm sorry. It's all wrong, all this feeling other people's feelings makes me selfish – you wouldn't expect that would you. I promise I won't leave you.'

Dan stepped away from her, though he kept hold of her hand as he wiped his streaming nose on the back of his other hand.

Ursula pulled a face.

'I'll make a new oath if you want,' Dan said.

Ursula shook her head vigorously and wiped her face.

Her eyes were pink and puffy looking, and her nose seemed to have swelled to about twice its normal size.

'I don't need your oath – I believe you. I'm your friend Dan – you shouldn't need to keep away from me.'

'What about Larcius?'

'What about Larcius?'

It seemed impossible to Dan that she could not acknowledge the strength of the attraction she felt for the man. He could feel it charging the air, whenever she was with him. But it wasn't the time to argue. They had only just made up.

'It doesn't matter. I wondered if he was your friend too.'

'Not like you,' she answered firmly. 'For a start, he's sane.' Ursula grinned and let go of his hand.

Dan found it impossible not to smile back. His spirits felt lighter than they had for days. His problems no longer seemed quite so insurmountable.

When they separated, Brother Frontalis gave them a very odd look. 'I think you had both better come to the barracks and get cleaned up. I've just had word from the High King, Taliesin is sick and Arturus says we must move tomorrow.'

~ Chapter Nineteen ~

Taliesin lay insensible on a pallet in the barracks hospital. Dan approached cautiously, afraid of what he might feel from the sick man.

Ursula held Dan's hand. 'Do you think—?'

Dan squeezed her hand. 'I don't know.'

Ursula had a terrible sense of dread. Dan squatted down beside the old man. Taliesin was thin and the flesh of his face seemed inadequate to cover the skeletal structure, he was bone pale and scarcely breathed.

Brother Frontalis hovered around his friend, his fleshy bulk accentuating the frailty of the bard.

'Do you know what is wrong with him?' Dan asked hesitantly. 'Do you know if he has done anything unusual in the last few hours?'

'If you mean, do I know if he's been practising sorcery, the answer is yes.'

'What did he try to do?'

The Christian holy man dropped his eyes.

'May the Lord forgive me if I have done wrong, but he asked me to stay with him while he meditated. He went into a trance, as he has done before, and I thought I saw a bird, a brown bird, a merlin falcon, fly round the room, though the shutters were closed, and then it disappeared. Taliesin had told me once that he imagined his soul to be a small swift hawk, earthbound in his ageing form. He liked to imagine that it could leave his body and soar. I wondered if he was right, if his druid soul really was a merlin falcon and if I had seen it go to its home.' Brother Frontalis looked worried. 'But he lives yet and I do not know if I should have prevented him.'

'Did the bird return?'

Frontalis shook his head. 'I don't know. Taliesin has told me before to note what he says when he …' Words seemed to fail Frontalis for a moment. 'When he does this thing – for what Taliesin the merlin knows, Taliesin the man knows also. A little while ago he mumbled something about Aelle mobilising and ships off the coast – twenty or thirty Aenglisc ships. I ran to tell the Duke, I mean the High King. He takes Taliesin's visions seriously. That's why Arturus took the decision to march at dawn. If his troops don't get to Mons Badonicus in time the Aenglisc will attack Caer-Baddon and the west will be taken. When I returned to Taliesin, not long after, he looked like this. I should not have left him. I hoped that you might know what to do with him – it is beyond my power to save him except through prayer alone. I was on my way to fetch you – well, when I found you, er … disagreeing.'

Dan had himself gone pale.

Ursula glanced from Dan to Frontalis and saw the same grave expression on each of their faces. 'Well, what is it?'

Dan sighed. 'I don't know how to explain it, but Taliesin isn't here. I mean he's not asleep – I can't feel anything from him at all.'

'You're not telling me his soul – whatever – really was that bird?' Ursula sounded sceptical.

'I don't know, Ursula. I'm not trying to tell you anything, but that is what Brother Frontalis thinks.'

'Indeed,' agreed Frontalis. 'If the body and the soul cannot be separated how can the life of the one survive the death of the other?'

'Do you think that could happen the other way around?' Ursula looked horrified.

'I have never believed it, for the soul is immortal, but …' Brother Frontalis paced the room. 'I have always thought Taliesin, in his own way, served the One, but what if his soul is held now by the devil?'

'Dan, what do you think?'

'I think he's got lost, like you got lost when you shape-shifted into the form of an eagle in Macsen's land.

It is not quite the same but he is every bit as lost as you were.'

'Taliesin saved me then – he and you. What can we do, Dan?'

'I don't know. Maybe just hope he finds his own way back. Can anyone else here play his harp?'

Brother Frontalis shrugged. 'He was always trying to recruit people but the boys here grow up to be farmers or fighters, or follow the church. There was not as much interest as he'd hoped for. But I think your boy Bryn has been spending time with him while you've not been around.'

Dan felt sudden guilt. He'd not had much time for Bryn of late, he'd been so wholly self-absorbed. He'd assumed Bryn had spent his time in the stables or with Braveheart, who he'd also neglected.

'You can't learn the harp in a few days,' said Dan.

'No, but Bryn had begun to train as a bard, before his father died.'

'He never told me that.'

Brother Frontalis said nothing – he did not have to. Dan was already very aware that he knew very little about the boy who had pledged to serve him until he died and who would, Dan knew, lay down his life for him. It was a humbling realisation.

'I'll go and find him.' Ursula was on the move as soon as the words were out of her mouth.

'No! I'll go. I need to apologise to Bryn – I've been very selfish – I haven't even thought about how he might feel and I've stayed away from him and everyone else so I wouldn't have to find out.' Dan straightened his bowed shoulders.

'Don't worry, Ursula, I'll find a way to get Taliesin back. Why don't you go and find out what Arturus wants of you? I'm sure you're an important part of his plans.' Dan spoke without rancour, as if his tears had washed away all the resentment that had been building up against her, all the jealousy at her freedom from the burden of other people's feelings with which he was afflicted.

'But I can't leave Taliesin ...'

Dan turned to look at her – he met her eyes and held them.

'Ursula I cannot fight any more, please let me do what I can do and trust me to do it. I know you will do all that Arturus needs you to do, please trust me.'

She could not refuse, and he knew it.

'OK,' she said in English, 'but send me word.'

He nodded tersely.

'I'll walk with you to the stables. I expect Bryn will be there. Will you also take Braveheart? He will not want to be left behind.'

'But Dan—'

'Ursula, I don't think I have behaved very well just lately. There's lots of different kinds of courage and I've been cowardly over facing up to what has happened to me. I was jealous of the way you've found a place here, and I felt bad that I wasn't able to beat Cerdic.'

'But he's a massive man – no one would have expected you to beat him – not without the berserker madness!'

'But *you* did!'

'Dan, you know that I'm still Boar Skull, that I've got his magical strength. If I was just me I wouldn't have stood a chance.'

'I know it with my head, Ursula, but I still felt pretty stupid being rescued by a ...'

'You can say it, Dan.' Ursula sounded angry.

'OK then, by a girl!' Dan flung the word at her like an accusation.

'I never thought you were sexist.'

'Neither did I! But I didn't like it.'

'So next time, I'll let someone kill you, shall I?' Ursula was still furious.

'No, I think I'd rather be jealous.'

Ursula glared at Dan, who glared back, and then began to laugh.

'Cerdic did look ridiculous.'

'What do you mean?'

'Well, if you think I felt bad about it, imagine how he felt.'

Ursula started to grin in spite of herself. 'You won't do anything too risky to save Taliesin, will you?'

'Only if you don't do anything risky to help Arturus.'

She shrugged. 'Well, OK. Good point. But try and talk to me – you know, with your mind, if you can.'

Dan smiled shyly and nodded.

'Good luck, Ursula.' He kissed her lightly on her cheek. She lowered her eyes in embarrassment, but something else too – relief, pleasure?

'Good luck, Dan. Will you follow us to the fortress?'

'If I can.'

She watched him walk to the stables. The whole training area of the barracks was now given over to horses, their riders, and their kit – it smelled like a zoo and the task of feeding men and beasts was a full time job. Bryn had found himself a home there. He had not wanted to stay on at the inn without Dan. Ursula ought to have checked on him. Dan was right. They had both let Bryn down.

She walked back to the inn to collect her own things and get some rest before their departure. She did not want to begin the march half blind with exhaustion. She was nervous of leaving Camulodunum behind, worried about what was to come. She did not want to leave Dan and Taliesin and Bryn, and yet she knew she could inspire the men. She knew that to them she wasmore than a fighting hero; thanks to Taliesin's influence they saw her as a gift from God to ensure their victory. She was all too aware of the heavy weight of their expectations.

It was close to midnight, scant hours before they would start to march. She left the stench of the barracks behind and saw King Meirchion's second, Cynfach, the commander of the Sarmatians walking alone. She knew him quite well and liked him.

'Cynfach! What have I missed?'

Cynfach started, then recognised Ursula's tall figure.

'Oh, Ursula, you were missed at supper. Are you well?'

She nodded, and then realising it was too dark for him to see her properly she said, 'Of course, I had to see Gawain, that was all. What was said?'

'The High King has had word that Aelle is mobilising. Ships have been seen off the coast. If we don't leave soon we may be cut off. The reconnaissance group leave at dawn, so they can lay out the camp and get everything organised, then the light horse under Cerdic, then Arturus and the command group and the infantry, then us and you, I believe, and finally the baggage train. The good news is that by the time we get to camp all the work will be done, the trenches dug, the fortifications built, and all the rest of it. The food might even be ready.'

'It sounds very complicated.'

'The High King does things in the old way, the Roman way. It is the way the Caesars of old did things in hostile territory and what was good enough for them ...'

Cynfach clearly approved, but then he would. The Sarmatians, like Arturus did things in the old way as passed on from one generation to the next.

'How are the men?'

'Oh, glad to be moving.They're rested now, from the ride here. They've had enough training. They're ready for action.' Then he added in a quieter voice. 'Nervous too.' He flashed a grin, a sudden whiteness in the darkness – he had good teeth. 'Like me! For some it will be their first real battle, as it will be my first real command.'

'They and you will be fine.'

'Do you think so?' Cynfach sounded unexpectedly eager for her reassurance.

'I know so.'

'And you will ride with us?' He sounded almost painfully anxious.

'I hope so, Cynfach, I'm looking forward to it.' She yawned. 'I'm going to grab a couple of hours sleep. See you at dawn.'

'Good-night, my lady Ursa.'

It was a strange feeling for a twenty-first-century schoolgirl to know that five hundred heavy cavalry and their leader depended on her. She did not need Dan's gift to know they did – it was simple fact and she could not, would not let them down.

She wondered if Dan had found Bryn and if they

could help Taliesin. She pushed that worry from her mind. She had to trust Dan. She crept into the inn with its now familiar smell of grease, wood smoke, and hops. She thought that with so much to think about it would be hard to sleep. It was not.

~ Chapter Twenty ~

Dan could sense the anxiety, fear and excitement of the men sleeping fitfully in their barracks, or lying alongside their horses in the makeshift stables that all but filled the parade ground. He managed to distract himself from the fragments of other people's nightmares and odd dreams that trickled into his mind. He could learn to ignore them, he was sure he could, given time and resolve and some of Brother Frontalis's faith.

He found Bryn curled up in a grubby blanket near the lantern of the watch. Dan wondered if maybe he was afraid of the dark. Bryn's arms were wrapped around Braveheart's neck and his small body was snuggled into his flank. Braveheart had been Bryn's father's war dog. It was possible he'd slept like that in his own home. Bryn looked small and vulnerable in sleep, his fierce eyes closed, just like any small boy in need of a good wash. A louse crawled across Bryn's forehead and Dan fought the urge to pick it up and crush it. He was surprised at the wave of tenderness he felt towards the boy, and was reminded painfully of his own little sister, Lizzie. He ought to be ashamed of his neglecting Bryn. He was ashamed. Nodding at the officer of the watch, who recognised him and sketched a salute, Dan gently touched Bryn's shoulder. Braveheart opened his eyes at the sound of Dan's approach, but refrained from leaping up in a greeting. Even the great war dog was respectful of Bryn's vulnerability and stayed quite still, only thumping his tail and raising his huge head to gaze adoringly at his master. Dan stroked the rough wolfish coat of the huge hound and tickled him behind the ears. There was no rebuke in the dog's dark eyes but there should have been. Dan had not even checked that he'd been properly fed.

'Bryn!' Dan whispered.

Bryn was instantly awake, his hand at once on his belt knife.

'Bryn, it's Dan.'

Bryn's eyes creased into a smile of pleasure. 'My Lord! Do you need me?'

With something of a lump in his throat, Dan nodded. 'I believe you've been hiding your talent from me.'

Bryn frowned, puzzled. He rubbed his eyes with a dirty hand and scratched his hair.

'I don't know what you mean.'

'You can play the harp.'

'Oh, I never thought to tell you, sir. I was only at the beginning of my training.'

Dan could feel Bryn's growing anxiety that he might have displeased Dan. 'It's fine, Bryn but I need you to do it now.'

'Of course.' Bryn disentangled his cloak from under Braveheart's side and was on his feet without further questions.

'Braveheart, stay here until Ursula comes. You understand?'

The dog whimpered and looked questioningly at Dan.

'You must fight alongside Ursula. Good dog.' Dan made a picture in his mind of Braveheart running alongside Ursula's horse. He did not know for sure what Braveheart understood, but with a small whine of protest he lay back in the straw of the stable floor, only following Dan with his eyes.

'You're not going to fight?' Bryn looked bemused. He was trying to hide his disappointment and his shame on Dan's behalf.

'It's hard to explain, Bryn, but I'm sure there is another way to help the High King Arturus achieve his victory.'

Bryn nodded without conviction but said nothing. They waited until they had left the stable behind for the cool darkness of the training ground. Still speaking in a low voice, Dan asked, 'Do you know how to play Taliesin's harp?'

'It is a very great instrument. He let me touch it once.' Bryn sounded awestruck.

'Yes, but in an emergency could you play it?'

Bryn must have wondered what kind of bardic emergency was likely to arise in a world where the songs of Bryn's world had almost been forgotten.

'I can play a simple accompaniment to a couple of the great song cycles – but I don't know all the words. At home, I would have been an apprentice for five years before I would be allowed to sing them in public. I have only studied and practised for maybe half a year at home before Da died and then for some days here. I am not really worthy.'

Bryn's doubt was contagious. Maybe Dan's plan would not work.

'Bryn, I think you are my only hope.'

Even in the darkness, Dan could see Bryn square his shoulders.

'I will try, Dan – whatever you want.'

'Taliesin is in a trance – I thought his music might bring him back like it once did for Ursula.'

'But Taliesin, is a great bard, Dan, the most skilled our world had known for generations. He was famous – more famous even than Prince Macsen, before the Prince fought the Ravens. I don't know any of the secret knowledge, I was too young. I was good, mind, for my age,' said Bryn quickly, so that Dan might not think too ill of him. Dan could not find the words needed to reassure Bryn. He patted him awkwardly on the shoulder and said the first thing that came to his mind.

'I trust you, Bryn, I know you will do all you can.'

Brother Frontalis knew where Taliesin kept his harp, a smaller instrument than its descendent in Dan's world. Bryn carried it as though it were a holy relic to the room where the former bard lay, still and pale as a dead man. Bryn was nervous and afraid. Brother Frontalis knelt at the foot of the bed praying. He looked up only to acknowledge them with his eyes and carried on. He was so focused on his task that Dan could feel no emotion coming from him at all, his whole self had become like a light beam from a torch, intent on prayer.

Dan nodded at Bryn who washed his hands in the bowl of holy water Frontalis kept for his ministrations. Brother Frontalis either did not notice or did not think it inappropriate, because he said nothing.

Dan could not help but admire the self-control with which the young boy set about his task. He was trembling when he first took the harp from its case, but by the time he had carefully tuned the strings he had regained his composure.

'What do you want me to do?'

Now that he was faced with the reality of the small

boy, the harp and the unmoving figure of Taliesin, Dan was not at all sure. 'Is there something special that Taliesin taught you?'

'Everything Taliesin taught me was special – he is Taliesin.'

Fortunately, Bryn seemed to understand what Dan meant. Concentrating very hard, he began to play. The first two notes were tentative, the phrasing clumsy, but despite that the incredibly sweet tone of Taliesin's harp triumphed. Bryn continued and as he grew in confidence Dan could feel himself enraptured by the sound of the harp as if it were itself magical. When Bryn started to sing, all the hairs on Dan's neck rose at the unearthly purity of his soprano voice. His voice took a more complex melody than the simple accompaniment of the harp. It was a song Dan had not heard before, about hearth and home and longing and the boy put all his experience of loss and loneliness into the melody which soared with such loveliness that Dan suddenly ached for home. He held the song in his mind, imagined he was broadcasting it through the night, calling out to the lost bard.

'Come Taliesin, come back! We need you!'

Dan kept repeating the thought like a homing beacon to bring Taliesin home. For a moment, Dan saw the barracks from another vantage point high above the city, flying by moonlight in an unfamiliar night. He could see the warm light of lanterns, bright in the blackness and abruptly he was back in the room, listening to Bryn end his song. There was a fluttering of wings and for a fraction of an instant he thought he saw the image of a small bird hovering over the prone body of Taliesin.

Dan did not know what to say.

Luckily Brother Frontalis did. 'God has blessed you, Bryn, with the voice an angel would sell his soul for. I have not heard you sing before. You have a gift that you should offer to God.'

'It was a beacon of light in the darkness, and he didn't do so badly on my harp.' The voice that croaked so dryly was Taliesin's own.

'My thanks to all of you, for you have brought me home.'

Dan rushed to Taliesin's side. 'Are you all right?'

'I will be. It was no more than an old man's arrogance overestimating my strength. Did Arturus get the message?'

'We are mobilising at dawn.'

'Good. I will sleep now. Mind how you put the harp away, Bryn – you did it justice tonight.'

Bryn was stunned into silence by the compliment.

Dan patted him on the shoulder. 'I wish I'd known you had such talent. Bryn, you should not be a warrior but a bard!'

'I chose the way of the warrior when my father was

killed, when you saved me and I laid my sword at your service. I don't think I chose badly.' Bryn spoke pointedly, reminding Dan of his own obligations to his sworn man.

'Don't you?' Dan asked, sadly.

'A song cannot destroy the Aengliscs and give us peace.'

'No, but a voice like yours can be a torch of beauty and hope and the promise of joy in men's darkest hours. It is part of what we fight for and hope to attain – a glimpse of heaven on Earth.' Brother Frontalis stood and looked at Bryn with his frank gaze. 'If I could sing like that I would never speak again!'

Bryn looked embarrassed.

'It's late, Bryn. Do you want to sleep in the stables or would you rather I arranged for you to have a bed at the inn again?'

'Why – because I can sing?'

'No, because I should have asked you that before. You are my squire and I have not treated you with enough respect.'

Bryn smiled. 'Thank you. I would have liked that before, but now I think I'd rather stay with Braveheart. I help to keep him warm and make sure nobody bothers him in the night. He'd miss me.'

Dan's smile of response was strained. 'Come on, I'll walk you back there. You have done good work tonight.'

~ Chapter Twenty-one ~

Ursula waited with the Sarmatians at the city gate. It was shortly after dawn and in the thin grey light five hundred horses and as many armoured men waited to ride out to battle. The cobbled city street echoed to the sounds of the low murmurs of men steadying horses too tightly packed together, and of well trained mounts showing their discomfort in the tossing of manes and pawing of cobbles. She leant forward to pat Dan's hound. Though as a war dog he was well used to horses, he did not like to be so close to so many and showed his uncertainty in the flattening of his ears against his huge, wolfish head. He growled a low rumble of warning for anyone foolish enough to stray too close. Although there was a lot of noise it was curiously muted. Everyone was waiting. Everyone was anxious to be gone.

Ursula had seen Arturus before he left at the head of the command column. His manner had been unexpectedly warm. He had looked more like a king than she had ever seen him, his eyes bright and blazing with a kind of certainty. She found, rather to her surprise that she trusted him. He had briefed her swiftly but clearly. She was to stay with the heavy cavalry and if trouble should arise be ready to ride back to warn and defend the baggage train. The journey would take three days for Arturus's army. It did not help at all for Ursula to reflect that the journey could have been covered within hours in an ordinary family car.

The air was still damp and cool. The feeble light did little to warm up the morning. In the unforgiving dawn light the assembled men looked haggard and strained, creased by sleep and the stress of action promised but not yet begun. Ursula shivered with cold and with a kind of fear. She was grateful for the many layers of clothing she wore to protect her from the chafing of her mail shirt. Her upper body was warm but, even though she had quite well fitting leather boots, and what passed for socks, her feet were far from warm. It didn't seem to bother anybody else – it was one of the disadvantages of her soft twenty-first century upbringing. The horse's breath steamed in the air making a kind of mist around the Cataphracts. Someone blew a horn loud and shrill, sending a shiver through the waiting company. As they passed through the city gates she briefly saw the distant banners of the light cavalry far away down the straight

Roman road. They were off. Men reined in their mounts to let her and the giant war dog, Braveheart, pass to join the head of the column. The scent of damp horse flesh, dung and leather and the complex stench of stale sweat and oiled weapons, ale flavoured breath, and men's hair made for a heady mixture, pungent and unfamiliar. It reminded Ursula, should such a reminder be necessary that she was far from home. The rhythmic sound of so many horses on the stone cobbles, the jangle of harnesses, the creak of leather armour and saddles, and a hundred other noises which she could not identify made the experience of riding with these men indescribably alien to Ursula – yet some atavistic instinct made her blood sing to its strange music. A light wind lifted her hair and brought with it the powerful cocktail of smells that was an army on the move. She felt invulnerable. So many competent horsemen, well armed and trained; so many powerful horses, strong and fast, and she was part of it. She rode to the living rhythm and yet common sense told her there was risk in the tight formation, the rolling tide of horsepower. There was little room to manoeuvre should there be trouble. The road was narrow and they rode three abreast, a metre maybe more between ranks. She turned in her saddle to see the breathtaking sight of fully armoured, Sarmatian horsemen riding to war in a column that stretched half a kilometre back from where she rode with Cynfach at the head. Directly behind her in scarlet-lacquered leather and gleaming silver helmets rode the standard bearer with the crimson and golden draco, fully inflated as he rode. Next to him came the two horn blowers, one with the long bronze lituus and the other a tuba. They, like many of the cavalry, carried full face masks over their shoulder, which they would use only when they charged in battle. The masks bounced at their shoulders like a second silver face. The effect was disconcerting.

Cynfach smiled at Ursula's obvious awe. He could not know how primitive, how barbaric and yet how frighteningly powerful it all seemed to her and she did not explain. Cynfach was enormously proud of the unbroken tradition of which he was a part and she encouraged him to talk about it. She had always preferred to listen rather than talk. When Ursula had first begun training with them, Cynfach had explained about the various musical signals used for commanding troops in the field and delivery instructions at camp. Now, he was anxious to tell her how that complexity had been distilled or debased down to a very limited number of blasts, to which his troops were trained to respond. Ursula knew the ones that related to charge, retreat, and turn, but was interested in the others which in the camp would mark the hours of the watch. Even that was a less scientific task than in the glory days of Rome, as no one had contrived to preserve a working water clock to mark the night hours.

She was interested in what he had to say at first, but found her mind drifting as he warmed to his lecture. It was a relief when Larcius, having galloped along the fields beside the roads unexpectedly caught up with them.

'Is there a problem?' Cynfach's tone was only just polite – he disapproved of Larcius.

Ambrosius Larcius looked magnificent in a short red cloak and polished metal scale armour. His handsome face glowed with health and vigour under the shining bronze and gold of his helmet. He smiled, flashing unusually good teeth, unbroken and white.

'Not at all. Everything is going according to plan. It's just that I was delayed persuading Gwynefa that she ought not ride with us against the High King's orders – that took a while. She was determined to ride with her father's Sarmatians.'

'I did not know that she had an interest in war,' said Cynfach coldly.

'It is wholly due to the inspiration of Lady Ursa,' Larcius continued, apparently impervious to the chilliness of Cynfach's response. 'I think the Queen aspires to be a great war leader, since her father's troops are surely the best in Britannia.'

Cynfach remained stony despite the compliment.

'You are to ride with us, Larcius?' Ursula asked.

'The High King asked me to escort you, Lady Ursa, to ensure no harm comes to you.'

'Are you sure it was not the other way around?' Cynfach asked pointedly, but before Larcius could reply he added, 'I will check my men. Excuse me.'

Larcius and Ursula rode in uncomfortable silence until Ursula asked, 'Why did you not let Gwynefa ride with the men – surely it would have done no harm?'

'She is a young girl – the Sarmatians may not always mind their language in her company. Moreover, this is not a festival ride – we could be attacked.'

'I would have thought she would be as safe in the middle of five hundred heavy cavalry as in the keep of any fortress and I don't think she's going to die if she hears a rude word is she?'

Ursula found herself quite irritated by Larcius's attitude. From the little she'd seen of Gwynefa she seemed entirely able to handle herself in any company. Half of her own Latin vocabulary would probably never be taught in school

'Gwynefa is not like you, Lady Ursa. She has been raised more or less as a Roman lady. She is used to the comforts due to a princess of Rheged and now those due to a queen.'

Ursula bit back a retort that she herself was used to central heating, electric light, the internal combustion engine, and warm feet.

'Lady Ursa you seem annoyed – have I offended you with talk of the Queen? I fear she is too much on my mind.'

Ursula was about to launch into a diatribe about his patronising attitude to women when she became aware that Larcius was trying to tell her something quite different. Larcius so contorted the Latin language to emulate what he considered to be good archaic Latin that she often had trouble making sense of his mangled syntax. This time she really did think he was trying to be direct. She responded more cautiously.

'And why is that, Larcius, why is Gwynefa on your mind?'

'I told you we knew each other when we young. Well, it was a bit more than that. We were at one time informally betrothed – while my father lived and before I went to live in Armorica. King Meirchion wanted an alliance with my father. It was always assumed that I would be his successor.'

'Oh!' Ursula flushed, uncertain why Larcius was confiding in her and equally unsure as to how to respond.

'Did Gwynefa not object to marrying someone else?'

Larcius looked at her oddly. 'Gwynefa was a princess of Rheged – she was always going to marry to cement a political alliance.'

Ursula said nothing but remembered that Rhonwen

was a princess, too, and she had kicked up quite a fuss when told who she might marry.

'And you?'

'I wish I had not gone to Armorica. Things would have been different. There would not have been a rift with my father and—'

'You would have been High King?'

'Perhaps.'

Larcius smiled at her and she felt a sudden weakness in her legs. He was so much more attractive when he stopped trying to turn everything into a compliment. He had the most beautifully expressive eyes, which turned her sinews to water. She was not used to feeling that way.

'You could help me if you chose, Lady Ursa. You are so beautiful and different – I know that if you would accept my courtship, I would more easily forget my past.' He sounded earnest and Ursula was ambushed by conflicting emotions – a larger part of her than she had expected was thrilled that he thought her beautiful and wanted to 'court' her. He was the most handsome and desirable man she had ever met, but the Ursula who had spent her life being mocked and excluded because of her appearance felt a resurgence of all her old stubborn pride. It was that Ursula who responded.

'Where I come from, Larcius, being second best is not a compliment.'

There was nowhere to go on the narrow road. She wanted to spur her horse forward and gallop away from him and the hot flush of embarrassment she could feel on her face.

'I meant no insult, Lady Ursa, I have the greatest respect for you – for your beauty and your skill.'

The unspoken 'but' angered her more. 'As we have already established, Larcius, I am not of gentle birth, the bad language of the Sarmatians is perfectly suitable for my ears and I could kill you in combat without breaking sweat. Your respect for me is very different from your respect for Gwynefa – I won't be second choice, a kind of consolation prize.'

'My what?'

Inadvertently, Ursula had resorted to an English expression for which she could find no equivalent. She had run out of words to express her own confusion. She did not want to be treated like Gwynefa, she could not stand the fawning compliments, the constraints under which she was forced to live. On the other hand, she did not want to be seen as some kind of exotic animal, a wilder, freer woman whom Larcius might want for reasons she didn't want to explore. She was aware of the contradiction but could not possibly explain it.

'I am sorry if I have caused you offence, Lady Ursa.' Larcius spoke with more sincerity than she had expected. 'Ursa, you saved my life, I don't want your ill will. You are not like the other women I know, I thought I could be blunter with you. I see now that I have erred.'

She was moved in spite of herself by his apparent honesty. 'I'm sorry Larcius. I find you very attractive but I don't want to be used as a distraction from the love of your life. I want to be the love of your life – or nothing.'

She choked on the last word. Ursula could hardly believe she was saying this stuff. She never used the word 'love'. She squirmed in her seat and shrank away from the words as if to disown them almost as soon as she uttered them. She dropped her eyes and began to be fascinated by the fineness of her horse's mane, the texture of his glossy coat.

'We are not so different then,' said Larcius softly. 'Two romantics in an unromantic world.'

A denial was almost on Ursula's lips, but it was true. She had never realised it before. She was a romantic. She wished she'd kept her mouth shut. She did not want that to get around the Sarmatians, it was not the image she fought so hard to project.

Fortunately, further conversation was avoided by the return of Cynfach.

'All is in good order.' He gave a terse smile of relief.

Ursula remembered that for all his knowledge and apparent confidence he was an untried commander of

Arturus's best troops. She smiled too, 'How long to camp?'

'We will eat in the saddle and make full camp tonight.' His anxious excitement was scarcely suppressed. 'We're on our way now. The Aenglisc won't know what's hit them!'

Taliesin sipped soup cautiously, struggling to control his shaking limbs.

'I think you might be able to help me, Dan. What you've got, this empathy thing is one part of a wider gift. I think you could lend my merlin form more strength and power so that I could scout longer and further without this happening. It would be of huge use to Arturus.'

Dan, picking at his own meal of bread and soup, looked uncertain. 'I don't know. You're not exactly an advert for it.'

'What?'

'I mean the state you're in does not encourage me to follow your example, but I suppose we have to try it.'

'Tomorrow,' said Brother Frontalis firmly. 'The High King has asked for the three of us to follow on to the fortress. We're to travel in one of the wagons. Arturus wasn't sure Taliesin would be in any state to ride. I think, Gawain, that you should wear your armour under your cloak – just in case.'

'Just in case of what?'

'Oh, ambush, insurrection, armed confrontation, that kind of thing.'

'I have told you, I will not fight.'

'But our enemies don't know that. They have heard the stories about the Bear Sark. Having you looking like a warrior will make the men feel safer, and morale is important.'

'I already thought of that,' said Dan with a grin, opening his cloak to show the splendid scale armour that Arturus had given him.

'And it's a pity the Lady Ursa is not here to see you in all your splendour,' said Brother Frontalis with a knowing smirk. 'I think she prefers her men with a bit of military style.'

Taliesin snorted into his soup.

'Brother Frontalis if you had seen Dan in his Bear Sark days you would put a tighter rein on that tongue. Help me up! I'll not ride in a wagon like a pregnant woman, nor will I wait for tomorrow. I'm Combrogi, not a bloody Roman!'

~ *Chapter Twenty-two* ~

Ursula ached in every bone and muscle of her body by the time they rode into the fortified camp. It was an impressive site. Deep trenches had been dug to enclose the camp and each ditch was surmounted by a high turf embankment from which protruded an object of sharpened stakes, shaped like a Christmas star and designed to impale anyone who tried to leap the ditch for the comparative safety of the turf embankment. The embankment itself was patrolled by armed infantrymen. They were given hot food and directed to the site, which had been marked out for their tents. Ursula being of high status had a tent of her own near that of the main command. She was relieved not to have to sleep near the disturbing presence of Larcius or, indeed, any of the other men. Although she had lived in Macsen's world for many months she found the lack of privacy that everyone took for granted very difficult to accept. The men even sat next to one another and chatted on the loo. It was a relief to be alone. She removed her boots which were damp and cold. They ought to have been rubbed with fat to preserve and soften the leather but she was too tired. Instead, she warmed her feet on a hearthstone she had begged from the containing wall round the fire. Her feet were so cold and numb that the warmth was almost painful. When at last her feet were warm she slept, almost at once – the deep sleep of the physically exhausted, without fears or dreams. She was not sure her body could survive two more days of such heavy riding; the novelty had worn off and she wanted to go home.

Dan arrived at the camp several cold, wet, hours later. He too, had been forcibly reminded of the discomforts and privations of this world. He also wanted to go home. Taliesin had managed to ride for about half the journey until his weakness forced him to hitch a ride on one of the wagons containing supplies. Brother Frontalis, who was built like an ox, had difficulty finding a horse that could manage his weight and so he joined Taliesin in the wagon from time to time under the pretext of resting his mount. Bryn rode stoically at Dan's side; his endurance and good humour only increased the respect Dan had for him. Dan had always thought that he'd had a difficult time. His mother had died when he was fourteen and his father spent too much of his time and their money at the pub, but Dan's difficulties were minor compared to Bryn's. Dan had known that he was the sole survivor of his tribe. Dan himself had seen the corpses of Bryn's sister and father. What Dan had not known was that Bryn's four elder brothers had all died in conflicts with the Ravens and that his mother had died in childbirth, bearing him. Dan's own shame at abandoning him in the Roman fortress increased. It must have been hard for Bryn to understand the difference between the Ravens who had wiped out his tribe and the Romans with whom Dan was allied. Dan was not sure he understood it himself.

The next two days passed in much the same way as the first. Dan talked a lot to both Taliesin and Brother Frontalis about the various techniques of mental and spiritual discipline they knew of or had heard about. Dan was determined to find a way to deal with what he now regarded as an affliction. Sometimes the troops sang marching songs and war songs and even fragments of the great songs to pass the time. Dan stayed with the rearguard and did not try to contact Ursula: the news that Taliesin was restored was common knowledge and he did not want any further disagreements about his decision not to fight. He was not yet strong enough to deal with her disappointment.

Ursula talked to Cynfach and Larcius by turns. She found Larcius much the easier company; he joked and told her humorous tales of his travels, whereas Cynfach kept trying to teach her about Roman military tactics. For the first time she began to relax in Larcius's company and even to enjoy the disturbing effect he had on her body. Perhaps if they began again as friends then gradually he might find that she was not second best at all? Larcius even dropped his ridiculously complicated way of talking and even Cynfach laughed a couple of times at the account of his exploits overseas.

They arrived at the fortress at dusk on the third day. It was some way from the Roman town of Aquae Sulis more commonly known as Caer-Baddon and some distance from the road, so that they had to ride across fields worn to mud by the feet and hooves of the vanguard. The fortress was not what Ursula had been expecting, lacking the grandeur of Macsen's cliff-top fortress at Craigwen. It was merely a flat-topped hill surrounded by three perilous escarpments, and a gentler slope surrounded by a series of ditches. It was surmounted by timber ramparts, which enclosed the whole of the top of the hill. Nonetheless it was an awkward climb to the top even using the easiest route. The only entrance to the fort, a stout and narrow gate, was situated at the top of the most difficult slope. They had to walk the horses in single file to this gate and it was very fortunate that no horse was injured in the process. The land was boggy and treacherous and the conditions at the summit were not much better. There was a large, timber, feasting hall, though it had not been occupied for many years. The blazing fire and cooking smells that greeted the Sarmatians could barely disguise the damp, mouldy, smell of disuse that permeated the building. It was a defensible site, but quite why anyone would want to defend it was rather beyond Ursula. There was dry straw for the horses and makeshift stables had been hastily erected from the remains of several smaller buildings. Ursula hoped that there were no high winds expected – it looked less than substantial. Tents had also been arranged in the same formation as at the camp to provide shelter for the light cavalry, the infantry and the servants who helped feed the men and horses. Conditions were crowded and seeing the state of the place, Ursula's mood plummeted along with her hopes of getting a bath. She would be lucky to find somewhere dry to sleep; the ground was a quagmire. She gave the care of her horse over to one of Arturus's civilian grooms, fully aware that the Sarmatians never allowed any one other than themselves to tend to their horses. She did not think they would think badly of her: they did not appear to believe her bound by the same rules as everyone else. Braveheart followed her into the hall where long tables had been set up and where the light cavalry and infantry were already eating. She called and waved to the many familiar faces of the men she had come to know in Camulodunum but was more concerned with working out how to get her share of the stew. Eventually, a servant brought her a generous portion. The baggage train arrived just as she was finishing eating. She ate standing up as close to the fire as she could decently get. She was too sore from the long ride to even consider sitting down. Arturus was nowhere to be seen. A horn blew and men disappeared to help unload the wagons of the supplies, which had to be carried up to the summit. The supplies included not just food but a variety of weapons, a large supply of boulders, numerous heavy barrels and a great wooden machine that had to be pulled up the slope on rollers using thirty of Arturus's strongest men. She was told, with pride, that it was the last Roman ballista in working order in Britannia. She did not know what that meant. Ursula was also surprised to discover that the wagons were not to be fully unloaded but that some supplies of weapons and grain were to be taken on to Caer-Baddon itself, which was to be occupied by Arturus's forces from Fort Cado. Ursula found this confusing. She was not at all sure that she had understood Arturus's plan.

'Ursula!'

'Dan, I didn't know you were here. How is Taliesin?'

Braveheart leapt on his master and enthusiastically washed his face with his tongue, nuzzling him so energetically that he struggled to stay on his feet. When

Braveheart had calmed down, Ursula gave Dan the remains of her stew, as the efficient feeding system that had prevailed at camp seemed to have broken down.

'Thanks, I'm starving. Taliesin is fine. He's with Brother Frontalis and Bryn. I came to look for you. How long have you been here?'

'Not long. Why are we here? It's a bit of a dump isn't it?'

'It's not what I expected.'

'How are you, you know, coping?'

Ursula forced him into eye contact.

'Really how are you?' Ursula's voice was insistent in his mind.

'I'm coping better. I can sort of distance myself a little. Taliesin talked to me about it and so did Frontalis. I can still feel more than I want to but it isn't swallowing me up like it once did. How are you?'

'Confused. I've said I'll fight for Arturus, but I don't know why we're here in this place. It feels like it was abandoned for years. Do you know what Arturus is planning? What are we doing here?'

'I haven't seen Arturus but Taliesin seems to understand him. According to Taliesin the Aengliscs want to gain a foothold in the west and are going to try to take Caer-Baddon. Arturus is hoping to lure Aesc and Aelle, the Aenglisc leaders, into trying to wipe out Arturus's entire army here, before moving on to Caer-Baddon.

Arturus believes that with the Sarmatians and the advantage of the fort we can wipe out the combined Aenglisc war bands.'

'But won't they realise that if Arturus wants them to attack him here it must be because he thinks he can win? Why should they fight where he wants to?'

'Arturus thinks they will take the opportunity to take his forces out completely. Both of them will be prepared to bet everything on their own superiority. It's a real showdown.'

'And what if Arturus is wrong and they attack Caer-Baddon first?'

'Apparently some of Arturus's light cavalry from Fort Cado have moved there, but Taliesin was a bit vague about how many – around fifty I think.'

'Fifty horsemen won't save them!'

'Arturus has been fighting the Aenglisc for ten years – he is sure Aelle will come here first – but he could move us to Caer-Baddon easily if he's wrong.'

'Where are the Aenglisc now?' Ursula still sounded and felt unconvinced by Arturus's grand plan. It struck her as far too risky and she wasn't sure she would put all her eggs in one rotten basket like this fort.

'That's what Taliesin and I hope to find out as soon as he is rested.'

'You're going to try and help him be a merlin again aren't you?'

Dan nodded.

'It's really dangerous.'

'So is war, Ursula. I've not lost my bottle you know, just my taste for killing.'

'I never said that.'

'You thought it.'

'Kindly stay out of my head, Dan. As it happens I didn't think you were a coward – you're not. I was worried about you. I was afraid you'd lost it – not your courage, more your sanity. You were very odd back in Camulodunum.'

Their discussion was interrupted by the arrival of Cynfach.

'I've a message for you, Ursa, the High King wishes to see you in his tent and you too, Gawain. You can leave the dog with me – he got used to me on the ride.'

Dan glanced at Ursula. She had gone quite pale.

'What is it?'

'Can't you feel it?'

'What? No!'

'It's Rhonwen – she's using magic, a lot of magic. She's very close. Dan, I think I'm going to be sick.'

Dan helped her to the door where she fulfilled her promise and was violently ill.

'I'm so sorry, Dan.'

'Don't worry – I'm not going to clean it up – I doubt if anyone else will in this place. The latrines stink already. Are you all right?'

He knew she wasn't. He could sense her inner keening for the power she once had, and something else – fear.'

'What are you afraid of, Ursula? I don't understand.'

'She's trying to call to me, to pull me to her somehow. I can feel her dragging at me. I don't know what she wants but it can't be good. I bested her last time we met, Dan, and she didn't like it. She knows I'm here – you can bet she knows Arturus is too.'

'That's all right. It was no secret.'

'She wants me dead, Dan. I've no magic left but I know she is trying something that will kill me.'

Dan grabbed her hand, which was trembling as Ursula's hand did not normally tremble.

'I won't let her hurt you, Ursula. I promise. Come on, let's go and find Taliesin.'

Ursula grasped his hand as if it was a weapon against fear and silently followed him to Taliesin's tent.

~ Chapter Twenty-three ~

It was rapidly getting dark. Soon the only light would come from the flames of the braziers, which marked each row of tents and from the torches fixed at intervals along the fortress wall. Ursula thought the whole camp a fire hazard. She would have liked to wash her face and wash the acrid taste of vomit from her mouth but water was in short supply. They did not now how long they would have to remain in the fortress where the only source of water was one deep well and a number of barrels brought from Camulodunum along with the ale and other foodstuffs. The flickering flames made dark, bulky shadows of armoured men. Order was gradually emerging from the chaos of their arrival. Everyone was again in their right places and the watch was set. Guards patrolled the walkways above the wooden battlements, protected by its wooden palisade. There was little noise, only the whisperings and rustlings of nearly one thousand exhausted men and horses settling to their rest, the regular footfalls of the watch, and the crackling flames of the braziers. It was difficult to talk except in murmurs.

To Ursula's surprise, Arturus was talking with Taliesin when they arrived. He had removed his armour and was dressed in the ordinary homespun tunic favoured by most of the civilians Ursula had seen. He got to his feet when she and Dan ducked into the low tent.

'Please join us,' said Arturus courteously.

Taliesin gave Ursula a hard, appraising look. 'What's the matter?'

'Rhonwen!' As she said the name, Ursula felt her gorge rise and she was very afraid she was going to be sick again.

Taliesin looked questioningly at Dan.

'I don't know. I can't sense anything, but Ursula always *was* affected by Rhonwen.'

Dan spoke calmly, working hard to ignore the emotions he could feel battering against his awareness, demanding to be acknowledged and shared. Arturus was awash with nervous excitement, Taliesin with weariness and trepidation, but it was Ursula's feelings that were the most disturbing. She was afraid, with a visceral fear that twisted at Dan's own guts and made his stomach churn.

'Well, try harder to sense *something*, you're the one with all the empathy,' Taliesin said testily.

Arturus intervened smoothly.

'I'm sorry to ask you to do something that might be painful to you, Gawain, but I believe you could help us. We know that Rhonwen is Aelle's Begrunen, his wise woman. He does what she advises. We need to know what she is up to. I know she is a witch and uses the Devil's power to deceive. Our men need to be prepared if she has anything planned, particularly if it is aimed at Lady Ursa, who the men revere.'

Dan looked at Ursula, doubtfully. She was looking at him pleadingly.

'I don't know what Taliesin wants me to do. I think he wants me to fish about in your thoughts to try to feel what you feel – at least we might be able to find Rhonwen that way. Do you mind?'

There was a pause before Ursula answered, but Dan knew that she shrank away from such an intimate invasion of herself as much as she did from Rhonwen's unspecific malevolence.

'Can you do that?'

'I don't know. Taliesin seems to think I can.'

'I don't know, Dan. This mind talk is all right because you hear only what I want you to – don't you?'

Dan nodded, which mystified Taliesin and Arturus who were watching the two silent Combrogi heroes expectantly.

'I don't think I want you to hear more than that. I suppose

I have to let you, but I'm scared.'

'Me too.'

Dan reached out to hold Ursula's large hand. Her palm was sticky with sweat, in spite of the coolness of the evening. She did not withdraw.

'Here goes then.'

Dan closed his eyes and Ursula gripped his hand with almost painful force. As he tried to feel what Ursula was feeling the pressure on his hand eased. That was a relief, she'd been crushing his bones. Then he realised why the pressure had eased – he was feeling his own hand holding Ursula's! It felt cooler. He perceived that it made him/Ursula feel calmer. At the same instant he perceived something else, something fearful, something bad that made his thoughts skitter in panicked confusion. Something was hunting him/Ursula, a malevolent presence. Dan could feel it waiting for him/her, like the memory of a nightmare. He was swallowed up by this feeling and was also peripherally aware that there was a kind of confusion of consciousness – that things were not usually this way. Dan no longer existed. Dan did not feel uniquely Dan feelings nor Ursula feelings. There was a losing of himself in Ursula-ness, a drowning in the mental flow of Ursula, her stream of consciousness. Somehow, at some instinctive level, without a question ever being raised, a decision was made to pursue the nightmare to its source. The Dan/Ursula awareness was very afraid, but there was no other choice. They were blind and deaf hurtling towards the source of the nightmare, feeling the mental chill of another hostile mind, yet having no senses with which to perceive.

'Bird! Be a bird!' *A part of them shrieked silently into the emotional maelstrom.*

Ursula/Dan, tried to be a dove and a pigeon at the same time. They became something and it flew. With that becoming came sight and hearing and the dizzying perspective of flight. There were Aenglisc everywhere, an army of foot soldiers, in mail shirts and ridgehelmets, or spangenhelm. *Rhonwen stood in front of a huge crowd, her face ravaged by fire, her dark hair wild and matted. Her garments were hung with skulls and bleached bones so numerous that her own form was lost beneath them; so many that they clinked and scraped together as she moved in some variant of the* danse macabre. *She now seemed a half-mad figure, frothing at the mouth, her eyes glazed and her pupils eerily dilated as though she were drugged. She was chanting. Her beautiful voice was as ravaged by hard use as her beauty. The words were hoarse and harsh and were screamed rather than sung. The meaningless syllables sent shudders down the bird form that was the eyes and ears of Dan and Ursula. The air thrummed with magic and fury. Rhonwen was pouring her venomous hate into a roughly made, clay figure that may have been intended to represent Ursula. There was no time for thought, or rather thought and action were one with this bird that was made of thoughts. It flew down towards the upturned face of Rhonwen and dived for her face, pecking and beating its wings, which became entangled in the mass of her heavy, dark hair. To the Ursula/Dan bird it felt as if talons clawed the scarred flesh of Rhonwen's burnt cheek. Whatever happened, the chanting stopped abruptly and with it the malevolent power died away, and the fear dissipated and the strange fusion of being ceased.*

Dan felt Ursula's hand crushing his and opened his eyes at the same instant that he gasped for air. He saw, with his own eyes, Arturus cross himself and Ursula let go of his hand. He was himself again. He breathed deeply and shook his head like Braveheart did when wet, as if to rid himself of the strangeness that still clung to him.

'Are you all right, Ursula?'

There was a pause. Dan could see intelligence return to Ursula's frightened eyes. She swallowed hard and wiped the sweat from her hand on her tunic, almost as if she were checking that she still was what she had been before. Ursula took a deep breath and answered, woodenly, reflexively as if in shock.

'Yes, thank you. That was the weirdest thing that has ever happened to me.'

Given the number of weird things that had happened to Ursula in recent months, that was no inconsiderable claim, but Dan agreed with her. Taliesin was still looking at him expectantly.

'We found Rhonwen. She was acting like a mad woman, shrieking and wearing all these bones. She'd made a model of Ursula – I think she was trying to harm her through the figure.'

Arturus did not pause to question how Dan had gained the information. He accepted that Dan had found the means to spy on the army and was only interested in what he had discovered.

'How many men were with her? Please think, Gawain.'

'I would say near a thousand – wouldn't you agree Ursula?'

Ursula nodded thoughtfully. 'I think they were all infantry. I sensed no large numbers of horses. There were a group of maybe fifty archers and I saw a good number with throwing axes, but most had only swords and shields. I don't think there were more than a thousand, no, not more than a thousand.'

'And where were they?'

Ursula and Dan looked at each other. It was hard to accept that their recent experience had taken place in any real time or place. They had arrived wherever Rhonwen was, instantly.

'I don't think it was far from here,' Dan volunteered hesitantly.

'It was near the sea – I could taste the sea.'

'Yes, yes, you're right.'

'If they camp there tonight the vanguard could be here by midday tomorrow.' Arturus looked thoughtfully from Dan to Ursula, and back. 'It is clear that Gawain and the Lady Ursa can speak without words, yes?'

Dan and Ursula nodded.

'We could use such a talent. I will think about it. Do you know what the witch plans to do?'

Dan and Ursula both shook their head, and with a half smile of regret, the High King left. Ursula thought there must be some residual link between herself and

Dan because for one instant she felt Dan recoil from the thought of having to repeat their recent experience. It had not been as bad as she had feared but it must have been worse for Dan. She could almost taste the flavour of his thoughts in her mind. It had been a terrible, intense, self-destroying closeness but a small fraction of Ursula was newly aware of loneliness without him. She felt a little hurt that he did not feel the same way.

~ Chapter Twenty-four ~

Arturus was right. By noon of the next day the vanguard of the Aenglisc army began to pour onto the land beneath the fortress. Only their leaders rode. The majority of the men walked together in no particular order, each carrying his own personal kit. There was little in the manner of their dress to distinguish them from the less Romanised of their enemies. They all carried shields, mainly large, oval, wooden shields with heavy, metal, central bosses that were themselves pointed enough to be used as weapons. Some carried slightly smaller round shields, but all walked with pride and a certain ease with their weaponry which Ursula recognised as the mark of a warrior. They were more threatening than the Aenglisc she had already fought. They were warriors not soldiers, closer in their demeanour to Macsen's Combrogi warriors than to Arturus's trained Romanised forces. It hit her then, the realisation that these men were dressed like those she had seen in a re-enactment of the Battle of Hastings before she first entered the Veil. Like her classmates she had been shouting encouragement to the men in the Aenglisc shield wall as they were charged by the Norman knights. Dan was right. These men might very well be her own ancestors. Few were as tall as herself, but that was probably the result of their diet. Many were blonde as she was, blonde with faces that would not have been out of place in any street in modern England. She had agreed to fight these men and some of them she would kill. She was after all still Boar Skull where it mattered – in the strength of her right arm. She would kill some of these men, unless her own luck ran out quite spectacularly. She moved away from the walkway on the battlements with a growing sense of unease. Could she back out now? Bedewyr, Larcius and Cynfach had also been watching the arrivals. As Ursula turned to walk away she noticed that all of them were watching her closely. There was no way she could back out without harming Arturus's cause. She was committed. It had seemed so much clearer when she had rescued the Combrogi villagers from the brutal invaders. Here and now the Aenglisc were just another band of men, wanting what was not theirs. Did they deserve to die?

Arturus's servant saw her walk away, and hailed her.

'Lady Ursa, the High King and Taliesin would like to see you in Taliesin's quarters.'

She smiled and the young man flushed, embarrassed to be acknowledged by a hero. It made Ursula uncomfortable, but it was a common reaction. Damn Taliesin and his clever ideas. It was all his fault – he'd turned her into a legend.

Dan was waiting in Taliesin's tent, his dark cloak giving him a distant, monkish air.

The High King was speaking in furtive whispers to Taliesin but stopped when Ursula entered.

'Lady Ursa, thank you for coming so swiftly. You have seen them – the war bands?'

Ursula nodded.

I have been talking over our tactics for the battle with Taliesin. We agree that it would inspire the men if you were to lead the charge of the Sarmatians.'

Even in the dimness of the tent Ursula must have looked stunned because Arturus added quickly, 'It is important that the men have heart. Were not so many of the men Christians, I fear that they would regard you as a goddess.'

Ursula hesitated, and then said cautiously, 'But, Arturus, you are their leader, their High King, their War Duke – would it not be best for them to follow you?'

Arturus's teeth flashed brightly in the gloom, a swift, rare smile.

'Lady Ursa, I am not a fool, and though I wish my

men gave me half the adoration they reserve for you, they do not. I win battles. I won battles for my dear friend, the High King Ambrosius; I will do it now for myself. The men and the kings of this island respect my competence, but I have never had their love …'

'But—'

'Leave it Ursula – he's right. You don't know how these people feel about you. I do. They would follow you to the gates of hell and back, which is just as well because there are enough Aengliscs to send you there. Taliesin agrees. It's why he called to us through the Veil.'

Dan's mental voice was firm and strong. She trusted it. She let her 'but' trail away. All she could do was accept the inevitable with the best grace she could manage. She sighed, the smallest, least dramatic sigh she could produce – no more than an exhalation of breath.

'You'd better tell me what you want me to do.'

By late evening, the land around the ancient hill fort was bright with campfires. The songs of their enemies, raucous and warlike rang loudly and discordantly through the still night. They stoked the flames of their courage and hate with their fires, their war songs, their sea songs and their sagas.

Dan stood with Braveheart on the battlements. He was protected by the high, wooden parapet and the darkness of his hooded cloak. His body quivered, with an involuntary nervous spasm as the waves of aggression and hate from the Aenglisc threatened to overwhelm him. There were more than a thousand men. Either his earlier estimate had been wrong or more troops had joined the battle force.

The Aenglisc were convinced to a man that they had caught Arturus this time. They could not fail. They saw war as the duty of a man and they gloried in it. They were afraid, of course, but they believed they could win, that they would win and the victory would inspire a hundred tales to fuel the fireside sagas for a thousand years. Somewhere out there in the darkness Dan could feel Rhonwen, readying herself for her own battle. Was she the source of their confidence? Dan was not skilled enough to pick up her particular brand of hate among so many, but he knew it was there. He swung round as he sensed Taliesin approach.

'I have brought you comfort, Dan.'

Dan tried to smile. He managed a grimace, a twitch of the lips, no more.

Brother Frontalis and Bryn came into view. Bryn carried Taliesin's harp in a leather case, lined with fur. He removed it reverently. Taliesin settled himself in Combrogi style on the muddy wooden boards of the walkway. He took something from the cord he wore round his neck and began to tune his harp. It was a dark night but for the slight, transient, glimmering moonlight, but Taliesin needed nothing but his harp and his talent, hard won through endless years of practice in Macsen's world it had not been lost in the movement between worlds. Taliesin's quick fingers spun a magical web of musical threads, wove sound to insulate them from the menace in the night. A hush fell over the soldiers in the hill fort. They paused in their clattering and cleaning of kit, stilled and silenced by the haunting harmonies, as Brother Frontalis added his rich baritone to Taliesin's harp. The night should have swallowed one man's harp and another man's voice, but it did not. When Bryn raised his own pure treble, it was as if the stars themselves sang, piercing the darkness with silver clarity. Where Bryn's voice and Taliesin's harp sounded there was only beauty and belonging. While they played Dan was free of any feelings but his own.

It was a kind of spell and even when the last lingering chord died Dan sensed a change around him. Arturus's men were calmer and he was no longer overwhelmed.

'Thank you.' Dan's response was heartfelt. 'I did not think anything could help but that did.'

'Can you sense Rhonwen out there?' Taliesin nodded in the direction of the Aenglisc camp, which now surrounded the hill fort like a sea.

'She's there. I know that much – but I don't know what she plans to do.'

'We'll find out tomorrow. I've no doubt they will try

to provoke a battle, they're not well placed for a siege. The harvest is in and most of it is in Caer-Baddon or here. Arturus will try to delay the fight until they're hungry and sick – a few dead sheep in the river will sort them out nicely. The men from Cado have their orders.'

Dan absorbed this information for a moment. 'But what about our water?'

'Our barrels of water are guarded night and day.'

'Rhonwen couldn't poison us through magic could she?'

'I don't think so. If she had the power to strike us all down with a real sickness she would have done it by now.'

'What are you expecting then?'

'Only trouble, Dan, no more than that. Let's get some sleep.'

'What if they attack tonight?'

'Then we'll fight them tonight. But they won't. They're too drunk.'

It was true. There was a different quality to the emotions still raging over the fortress wall. Without a further glance at the sprawling enemy camp, Dan followed Taliesin to the neat rows of tents, the familiar stink of the latrines and the powerful odour of horses. When his mum had been alive she had grown roses and had bought manure from the stables. He was not sure she would have been impressed by the association he made between her and the reek from the stables, but nonetheless it gave him comfort and he went to sleep dreaming of home, of his mother and Lizzie, and a carefree, sober father he had not known for years. He longed for those lost days when he had always felt safe. He longed for them so badly that his chest ached and he woke to the sound of the lituus, the morning battle horn, with his face wet with tears.

~ Chapter Twenty-five ~

Taliesin was right. The Aenglisc did not attack in the night. Soon after dawn, the smells from the Aenglisc cook fires drifted across the hill fort. Ursula had slept badly. She had been cold and the thought of leading a charge of Sarmatian horsemen down the steep scarp slope of Baddon Hill filled her with panic.

She was terrified of failing them. She kept on imagining herself falling off as she led the proud horsemen in the charge; or worse, failing to jump the broad ditch at the foot of the hill and breaking her horse's legs. Moreover she had relatively little experience with the long spear, or kontos, which the Sarmatians used to such good effect in training. She was out of her depth and drowning in the hostile waters of 'what if?'.

More prosaically, Ursula hated not being able to shower or bathe. Like everyone else she had slept in her clothes and she felt dirty and unkempt. Larcius had lent her a comb and she had braided her hair, though it was too fine to stay in place for long and she would have to tuck it into her helmet when it came to the battle. She felt sick at the thought of battle. She was not ready.

Dan was eating his breakfast standing up, chatting to Frontalis. She felt a pang of envy and annoyance. He had abdicated his role as a hero, why had she not had the wit to do the same? Suddenly, the air around her crackled with static, lifting the fine golden hairs on her arms. Magic! Rhonwen!

Ursula ran for the battlements, followed a moment later by Dan.

'What is it?'

Before she could think her reply it became all too obvious. The sky darkened and the air became black with demonic forms. Rhonwen had modified and improved the trick she'd tried against Ursula earlier. Above their heads, hideous dog-faced men feasted on Roman soldiers, while great vultures with monstrous beaks and human eyes flapped their black wings and seemed to drop severed heads onto the terrified Romans. It was like a scene from some vision of hell painted by Hieronymous Bosch.

'Sorcery!' screamed Brother Frontalis and he began to sing in his strong baritone, 'Yeah, though I walk in the valley of the shadow of death, yet will I fear no evil ...'

'It's an illusion!' cried Ursula, wishing she had a more powerful voice.

Men were kneeling on the ground and crossing themselves, while the pagans spat curses at the demonic host.

Arturus took control. He raised his own shield, which was painted with a golden cross, outlined in crimson against a ground as white as chalk and egg white mixed could make it. The cross was vivid in the eerie light. Arturus shouted, 'What you see is *not* real. It is sorcery and illusion. We are not men to flinch from the semblance of evil. We must be strong and be ready to repel the real enemies – the Aenglisc. They are counting on our disarray to conquer us. To the battlements!'

Arturus's ringing cry was echoed by the clarion call of the lituus signalling action. Overhead, the demonic throng darkened and deepened like a thundercloud and the air was filled with a cacophony of screams, shrieks of pain, and bestial cries that made Ursula shrink with fear. She knew it was an illusion but it was a powerful one that blotted out the sun and made everything, even Arturus's shield, grey and colourless. It made even her allies look ghastly and cadaverous. The men followed orders but many covered their heads with their shield. They rallied a little at Arturus's courage, but the horses reared wildly in their stables and not even the skilled Sarmatians could keep them calm. Braveheart raised his massive head and bayed an unearthly cry. A chill settled round Ursula's heart. Dan was battered by the overwhelming tide of fear. He grabbed Ursula's hand and dragged her towards Taliesin, who was inspecting the illusion with a critical eye.

'Rhonwen's improved, I'll give you that. Not bad.'

'Taliesin!' Dan forced the one time bard to face him. Taliesin seemed to react to a crisis with unhelpful levity. 'Taliesin! What did you do to make the sound of Bryn's singing so loud yesterday?'

Taliesin looked shamefaced 'I wondered if you'd realise. Because you helped me when I was stuck in merlin form, I was able to use a little of your mental power to amplify the sound, so it rang in the minds of those around me.'

'You did what?' Dan sounded both angry and bemused.

'Dan, it doesn't matter,' Ursula broke in urgently. 'If you have an idea, tell us! This is horrible even for me and *I* can feel the magic Rhonwen's using and I *know* that what is up there is not real.'

Dan spoke rapidly and urgently. 'I need Bryn to sing something strong and powerful, loud enough to deafen the enemy and show Rhonwen we're not afraid. It would hearten the men and it might make her stop this monstrosity.' He waved at the hellish apparition that was still raining severed heads down into the fortress, though no solid object thudded to the ground.

'Bryn, can you sing something really powerful? Taliesin can you help me?'

Taliesin smiled. 'You can do it yourself – what you must do is imagine you are shouting something as loudly as you can, something good, something that makes you feel safe and cared for. Don't actually shout, of course, but mix that good feeling in with Bryn's song. It isn't as difficult as it sounds.'

Brother Frontalis stepped forward and held Dan's hand. He met Dan's worried look with his frank and confident gaze. 'I told you all that is good comes from God. I know it, and Taliesin knows it too. All will be well, Gawain, take my faith and send it out to all the men, for no evil, real or feigned, can fail to fall at the Lord's name.' Frontalis was unafraid and totally sincere.

'I don't know if I can make this work,' Dan faltered.

'Dan just do it! I know you can!' Ursula clapped her hand on his shoulder rather hard, which gave him the jolt he needed.

Dan looked at Bryn, who was terrified of the horrible drama taking place overhead. Bryn's eyes were huge and frightened looking, but he did not say anything nor did he cower away as many of the grown men were doing.

'Sing the *Alleluia* I taught you, Bryn,' said Brother Frontalis. 'Let the sound soar, like I showed you.' Brother Frontalis's confidence seemed to relax Bryn slightly.

'Do we need to stand at the battlements so Rhonwen and the Aenglisc can see us?'

'That's a good idea. But take Bryn away, Ursula, if it looks like he's in danger.'

Bryn was about to protest but Dan added sternly. 'You are our secret weapon, Bryn, and a good soldier does not expose such a thing unnecessarily.'

They followed the men still forming a defensive wall along the battlements and found their place next to Arturus, who waved his shield defiantly at the enemy.

Rhonwen's magic was even more disconcerting from the height of the battlements. It seemed as though they stared into a sea of blood in which Combrogi soldiers lay in great torment being torn limb from limb by beasts of nightmare. The air was so alive with magic that Ursula wanted to cry with frustration. If only she could still reach the magic she could have destroyed Rhonwen's illusions so simply. She would swap all her Boar Skull strength for one moment of power, when the lightning energies of the magic coursed their wild rhythm through her veins. But, it was not a choice she had. Ursula could see the Aenglisc advancing stealthily beneath the illusion of a sea of blood.

'Do it Dan! They're coming this way – the real Aenglisc. I don't think anyone else can see them.'

The Aenglisc looked uncomfortable as though they themselves expected to be set upon by the beasts of

Rhonwen's conjuring, but they were brave men and they followed their leaders with swords and seaxs drawn.

Dan nodded at Bryn, who shut his eyes against all the horrors and sang. The first tentative notes were swallowed up in the demonic cries that were themselves magically amplified, but as Bryn gained his confidence, his voice grew stronger, until it truly soared as Frontalis had instructed. Dan opened himself to Frontalis's emotions, letting down the guard he'd been so carefully constructing. It was like relaxing a tensed muscle. It was like forcing himself to swim out of his depth for the first time. He had to allow himself to fully experience Frontalis's faith and send it out like a great, invisible psychic blast to hearten the Combrogi and confound the Aenglisc. It was an unnerving experience but quite unlike the bewildering loss of self he had experienced with Ursula. He found it easiest to imagine he was a kind of amplifier taking input from Bryn and Frontalis and projecting it as loudly as possible through the bizarre powers of his mind. It was instinctive. He could not describe what he did, he only knew that it seemed to work, for the effect was immediate and tangible. The Combrogi stopped cowering beneath their shields and straightened their backs. They were still as threatened by the lowering evil above and around them, but their fear was dissipated by the purifying clarity of Bryn's unearthly soprano and Frontalis's unshakeable faith.

Arturus raised his shield, this time in triumph, and his gesture was answered by several hundred Combrogi soldiers who responded by raising their own.

Ursula felt Rhonwen's illusion waver as her confidence was temporarily dented by the impact of Bryn's clarion song. Ursula was not the only one to notice. For one brief moment, the illusion of the sea of blood shimmered like a heat haze and dissolved. It was long enough to reveal the presence of the advancing Aenglisc. The Combrogi let loose a shower of stones. When Arturus gave the word the four men given charge of the precious ballista leapt into action, raining down huge round missiles on the unsuspecting heads of the enemy. Bryn's glorious *Alleluia* became a still more triumphant anthem. The dark cloud overhead paled to grey, and then drifted apart so that fragments of demon floated overhead, becoming gradually less cohesive until they ceased to exist at all. The somewhat cold, wintry sun shocked them all with its sudden, hard brilliance. In the unforgiving morning light the blood river appeared far less convincing and Rhonwen let it go.

Ursula felt the sudden sagging relaxation of her muscles as the magic ceased. She had clenched her whole body against her desire to wield the magic and now that it was gone she felt shaky and tearful. The monstrous shrieks had ended abruptly as if someone had turned off a broadcast from hell. Bryn's song, now solitary and sublime rang in Ursula's inner ear. She was ambushed by an unexpected sense of peace. The Aenglisc had run away and the first attack was over. It was clear that the Aenglisc had abandoned their attempt at capturing the fort by stealth. Even firing blind, the Combrogi archers had struck a large number of the enemy, who had themselves been blinded by Rhonwen's illusion and therefore failed to raise their shields in time. The surrounding fields were stained with fast-congealing blood and the corpses of men, who only minutes before had been as alive as Ursula, littered the ground.

The High King Arturus ordered a ceasefire to allow the dead and wounded to be collected. He had strapped his shield over his back and it caught the sun as he moved – a gold cross on a white ground as clear and unsullied as Bryn's voice. As the sun reached the zenith of midday Dan still amplified Bryn's jubilant *Alleluia* and Bryn sang on.

~ Chapter Twenty-six ~

The Aenglisc retired some distance from the fort to bury their dead. The wind bore the distant sound of their singing into the heart of the Combrogi fortress. They were the Combrogi's enemies but they grieved like any other men. Dan felt the regret, the sorrow and the pride of those who sang war songs for their dead comrades. He was glad when the burials finished sometime between dusk and full darkness. He missed Frontalis's faith. He missed Bryn's voice. In the silence of the night it seemed a colder more brutal world, and Dan wished he and Ursula had a way to leave it. Death was everywhere around him, snapping at his heels, in the last thoughts of his enemies and the first thoughts of his friends. Would this be his last sunset? He breathed in the multi-layered stench of the fortress and longed to be home. Ursula had retired to her tent, exhausted by the tantalising presence of magic beyond her reach. Her nerves were worn raw with the desperation of her need for the magic. It was an addiction she had not known she had acquired. Dan felt for her but there was nothing he could give her but his sympathy and Ursula had little use for that. Arturus had doubled the guard overnight but there seemed to be no need. All was quiet, but for the small sounds of sleeping men and animals, the blast of the horn to signal watch change, the small scufflings and fidgetings and quiet exchange of pleasantries that accompanied each handover. Dan was restless. He and Taliesin had tried to take on the merlin form to spy on the Aenglisc but had been unable to make it work. Dan thought they were both too tired but refrained from saying so. Taliesin's pride would admit no physical weakness, though Dan could not remember him caring much about such things when he'd first met him in Macsen's world.

The morning showed Dan the Aenglisc at their fires, eating their now meagre supplies, and cleaning and sharpening their weapons. Just before noon Rhonwen produced an eerie green mist that rolled like some vile toxic cloud all around the fort. It reeked of sulphur and was clearly created to disguise the activities of the enemy. The fort became an island surrounded by an apparently poisonous sea. Arturus instructed all food to be covered up in the great hall to prevent it spoiling, should the green cloud be harmful. Once more, Arturus stood on the battlements with his white shield aloft and gave the orders to fire occasional volleys of stones into the evil looking mist. He was well aware that he had limited supplies of missiles but he loosed them anyway. Dan wondered at his wisdom. He knew the ballista used specially made pottery spheres, which shattered on impact. These had the double advantage of producing lethally sharp shards once fired which wounded as well as stunned and rendered them unusable to the enemy. It had taken months for the relatively poor craftsmen of Camulodunum to reproduce this Roman trick and Arturus still had fewer examples of the clay shot than he would have wished.

Perhaps Arturus was wiser than Dan realised and the blind shooting worked, because no Aenglisc breached the walls. By late afternoon the mist died away to reveal yet more bodies on the scarp slope. By late evening, the unmistakable stench of sickness reached the hill fort. The men from Cado had done their work; the river was contaminated and most of the Aenglisc were affected, doubled up with cramps or vomiting their guts up and worse. That night was unseasonably warm with thick cloud cover burying the moon. The smell from the Aenglisc camp turned Dan's stomach. Everywhere smelled too badly and the inactivity and strain of being under siege was beginning to affect the men. Everyone was irritable and Dan struggled to retain his own good humour. He sat by the fire with Ursula and helped her sharpen her sword and spear. She was tense and grim looking.

'Dan, what if I die here?'

'What? What can I say? You might die, Ursula, this is war. You'll be a target if the Aenglisc have any sense.' He couldn't think of anything very reassuring to say but continued anyway.

'But the Aenglisc are all ill – they'll be less effective. I think they've got food poisoning or something.'

'It doesn't seem very fair does it – poisoning them first?'

'Like Arturus says, he's High King because he wins, not because he's a hero.'

'I'm scared, Dan.'

'I know.' Dan wanted to touch her, comfort her, but did not know how.

They gazed moodily into the fire together. Waiting was the hardest part. After the evening meal, which no one ate very enthusiastically – it was like eating in a sewer, Arturus gathered everyone together to talk about his battle plan. It was simple – at dawn he intended to charge the Aenglisc and destroy them. Though simple it would involve some reconstruction of the fort itself, as its only entrance and exit was both narrow and inaccessible. Under the cover of darkness the men were to cut new gateways in the fort's fabric, large enough for several men to ride through at once. It was an insane idea and yet Arturus had it all planned out so meticulously that he persuaded them that it could work. They would have to work in shifts through the night. Dan was given the task of disguising the noise of such wholesale building work – with music. Most of the men and Ursula were to be involved in removing the fortifications, so the few who were left were chiefly those who were incapacitated in some way. Dan was left with Bryn, Taliesin, two horsemen injured when they'd lost control of their horses, the lituus and tuba players, and a man with a drum. Dan split the men into two shifts and did what he could to amplify whatever sounds they managed to produce. It seemed to work and those busy labouring joined in when they could, so that it must have sounded to Aenglisc ears like some all night carousel. How those not working slept at all was something of a mystery. By dawn, however, Dan was reduced to teaching the men football chants, Bryn had lost his voice and even Taliesin's calloused fingers were bleeding from playing too much. It was a relief when Arturus called them all together again.

'This is it. This is our chance to finish what I started with the High King Ambrosius ten years ago. Beyond these walls lies the biggest army the Aenglisc have ever produced. We have down there the Bretwalda of Britannia, Hengest's heir and all the most land hungry, power crazed leaders of the Aenglisc. If we kill them all now their ambitions for Britannia will be destroyed. We will be in a position to drive the Aenglisc out of Britannia and restore the Saxon shore. Gather your weapons, mount up, ready the fire drums, and we will be victors before noon!'

It was not the most inspiring speech that Dan had ever heard but it seemed to work. There was no cheering, but then they did not wish to alert the Aenglisc to the imminent attack. Ursula found Dan in amongst the milling men and beasts.

'You will take Braveheart?' Dan said.

She nodded dumbly.

'You will be fine. I know you can do this. You are Boar Skull after all.'

Dan knew she wished he would be by her side, fighting with all his old berserker skill. He shrunk from the thought of all the killing and the pain to come. He pulled his hood over his head as if that would make a difference. He was very afraid that Ursula would die. His fear for her overcame his natural reticence and he hugged her briefly.

'Be lucky, Ursula.'

He could feel her fighting to keep her composure. Her face was the dead pan, sullen one of old. She did not trust herself to speak but nodded again briefly and strode off to mount her horse. Braveheart followed her through the furious activity of the men rushing for their posts. In the makeshift stable she found her horse. The Sarmatians had given her a groom to care for the horse and the fine scale armour with which it had been supplied. The groom bowed when he saw her and she nodded somewhat imperiously. She had to lead these men, these proud, brave men. She was almost as afraid of failing them, as she was afraid of death. Someone darted suddenly from the shadows.

'Bryn!'

'Let me fight with you!'

'Bryn, you know you can't,' Ursula said firmly.

'I can ride as well as Cerdic's men – the light cavalry.'

'I know you can, Bryn, but you must stay with Dan. I fear he may need you.'

'What, to sing again?' Bryn managed to fill those simple words with contempt. 'Brother Frontalis would have me be a monk. I am a sworn warrior. My place is with Braveheart, fighting.'

Ursula choked back her sympathy and put all the steel she could muster into her response.

'Your place, Bryn, is with your liege lord as you swore on the road to Alavna. Would your father have had you abandon your lord because he chooses a difficult road.'

Bryn coloured and Ursula was a little ashamed of her blatant manipulation.

'Go to him, Bryn. Arturus may have need of him and he of you. That is your duty.'

Bryn bowed stiffly and with a stony face replied, 'As you say, Lady Ursa.'

Fury evident in every tense line of his body Bryn did as he was told.

Ursula exhaled slowly, trying to calm herself. She needed to concentrate. She accepted help from the groom and rode to the crowded muddy field that was the hill fort. Tents and cooking pots had been removed and stowed away. They would have no immediate need of them. After the battle they would be dead or victorious and either way they would not sleep at Baddon Hill again. It was still early and everyone was tired after the night's hard labour, but Ursula did not need Dan's special perception to feel the anticipation and the fear.

Arturus found Ursula in the melee. 'Lady Ursa, I am going to remain here with Dan and Taliesin in case Rhonwen tries something unexpected. All my hopes ride with you. Take my shield and hold it high as the signal to ride. I will tell Dan to give you my message. Please take this also.' He handed her a full-face mask of gold, modelled on some idealised Roman god. There were eye-shaped holes through which she could see and two finely modelled nostrils through which she could breathe. He helped her to fasten it around her head with leather bands so that it stood slightly proud from her face, overlapping the front of her helmet. She fought a terrifying sense of claustrophobia.

'It belonged to Ambrosius. It will terrify the Aenglisc and may well preserve your beauty. Go with God, Lady Ursa and all the hopes of Britannia.' He smiled almost wistfully and was gone. She rode slowly to what would become the front of the Sarmatian force, next to Cynfach. Brother Frontalis was busy blessing the men. His sonorous voice giving comfort was the only sound that could be heard above the noise of last minute weapon and kit adjustments. Fantastic. She was not only leading the best horsemen in Britannia down a slope of suicidal steepness but she was also hampered by a vast shield slung across her back while her vision was restricted by some mask. When Frontalis came to her and said, 'Bless you my child,' her 'Amen' had never been more heartfelt. It was time.

~ Chapter Twenty-seven ~

Ursula waited with her contingent of Cataphracts behind her at the newly created south gate. More than two hundred and fifty Sarmatians would ride behind her in the main charge, followed by similar numbers of light cavalry and infantry. Larcius would lead the smallest contingent of one hundred men from the east gate, Cynfach would lead one hundred and fifty Sarmatians from the west gate. All waited on Ursula's signal. It felt suddenly too hot in the layers of padding necessary to prevent the chafing of her mail. Sweat trickled uncomfortably down her nose within her mask, making her whole face itch. Of course it was impossible to scratch. She clutched her horse more firmly with her knees and adjusted her weight. The waiting was unbearable. She checked that her sword could still move freely in its sheath and wiped the sweat off her hands, the better to hold her kontos. She heard the standard bearer with his scarlet and gold draco make similar preparations beside her. He was also wearing a full face mask of burnished bronze, which had the advantage of disguising the wearer's terror from the enemy. She could hear Braveheart's rapid breathing at her side. He too was readying himself. The lituus sounded and infantrymen started to drag away the makeshift crossbeams supporting the hastily constructed gates. It was a complicated business to get them open. Everything had been done so quickly that nothing worked as smoothly or as silently as it might – everything creaked and grated and banged. Ursula feared that the advantage of surprise would be lost. The Aenglisc must now know that something was going on. She prayed they would not have time to organise themselves and seize the initiative. There was another blast of the trumpet and the large barrel-shaped casks that had contained supplies were arranged in a row in front of the heavy cavalry. They had been coated in foul smelling pitch. God, how she wished this was over. Her bowels felt weak and her heart hammered wildly to no rhythm but that of fear.

'Steady, Ursula. Not yet. Wait for the barrels to be fired. Arturus says don't forget – raise the shield. Raise the shield!'

It was a good job Dan's calming voice spoke to her mind. She was not sure she could have heard anything else over the loud drumming of her own pulse. She felt sick and faint and far too hot. She needed to shout to the men when she heard the signal, but she had no saliva left. The shield! She had nearly forgotten the shield. What the hell did she do with her spear if she had to hold the shield? Conscious of her role as hero/leader she tried to make her movements deliberate rather than panicky. She thought about the relaxed way that King Meirchion of Rheged had moved effortlessly in the saddle, thought about her old comrade Kai's confident demeanour. She did her best to copy them, to look relaxed and in control as she casually transferred the kontos, the long fragile looking but lethal spear, to her left hand and balanced the shaft on her booted foot. It was a difficult task as the spear was of such a length that it could not easily be moved across the back of her mount. Then she unstrapped Arturus's shield, which was hooked by a long leather thong over her right shoulder. That too was awkward as her movement was somewhat restricted by her armour and though the shield itself was light the heavy iron central shield boss made it unwieldy to manoeuvre. Her undershirt was damp with sweat. She was frightened that the slender shaft of the kontos would quiver with her nerves. That would not look good. She forced herself to breathe, she had forgotten about breathing. It helped.

There was another short single blast of the lituus. Someone ignited the barrels and kicked away the wooden chocks that kept them from rolling down the precipitous slope. There was the crackle of yellow flame as the barrels suddenly blazed. There was a stench of acrid fumes and burning pitch. Black smoke made Ursula's eyes smart and stream so that for a moment her vision blurred and then she saw the barrels roll away from view through a distorting haze of smoke, tears, and rippling air. Men coughed behind her. Braveheart growled and she heard the standard bearer mutter a muffled oath.

'Get ready, Ursula. You're OK. Arturus says NOW! Raise the shield! GO!'

Dan's voice was clear within her mind and Ursula raised the shield with its triumphant golden cross high over her head and yelled, 'Ride!'

Suddenly, her fear was gone. She cried out a Combrogi war cry and rode. She could do this; she *would* do this. It did not matter that she could hardly see, what with the smoke, the burning heat and the limitations of the mask. She had five hundred men behind her and she would lead them well!

Dan watched Ursula closely. It was hard to recognise his schoolmate in the proud figure, gleaming with gold and silver mail. Her face was lost completely behind the bland serenity of her golden mask and only the odd stray blonde hair escaping the golden helmet identified her as Ursula. It was only when he saw her raise the shield, the gold cross on white ground, the shield of Arturus, that he realised that this anonymity was the point. Arturus had set her up. He wanted the Aenglisc to think Ursula was the High King and War Duke himself.

'You bastard, Arturus, how could you? You want the Aenglisc to think Ursula is you. Don't you?'

Arturus turned to look at Dan with a grim expression.

'Without me the Combrogi will die, Gawain. I win battles – remember that. Ursula is good. I'm not too proud to admit she's a better fighter and a better rider than I am. She stands a better chance of coming out of this alive than I would. She will inspire the troops with her heroism. I could not do a better job than she will. Meanwhile, if anything goes wrong, I'm still here, and no one else, Gawain, *no one else*, can save the Combrogi but me.'

Arturus did not even look shame faced. Dan was at a loss. He had to find out how the battle was progressing. He made a decision.

'Bryn! I need to watch over Braveheart and Ursula. Watch over me, please.'

He thrust Bedewyr's second sword at Bryn, the one Ursula insisted he should carry, then sat down among the foot soldiers still defending the battlements. He had made a decision and by will alone he succeeded where he and Taliesin together had once failed. He sent his consciousness out, like the avatar of a Hindu god he had learned about in Religious Studies. He was a bird – a dove flying above the Aenglisc, seeing from a higher vantage point what they saw, and it was truly terrifying.

The sides of the wooden hill fort had been all but destroyed and on three sides burning barrels streamed comet tails of fire through the unprepared Aenglisc camp. The Aenglisc were no cowards, and they gathered their wits and weapons faster than Dan would have thought possible. Their leaders pulled sick men from their beds as their possessions burned under the crackling flames. Ursula's horse leapt the burning barrels. She was a golden goddess on an armoured horse, screaming fury, as her pale hair streamed behind her. She showed no fear as she charged, holding her long spear and stabbing at anyone who did not get out of her way. The standard bearer's open-mouthed red draco whistled an eerie unearthly shriek. As the Sarmatian Cataphracts charged in their blood-red lacquered armour, their bronze and their silver mail, they either jumped the flaming barrels or charged between them, emerging through the flames like riders from hell. The thunderous thudding of their horses' hooves on the charred grass was enough to terrify. They galloped forward in close formation, no more than a metre or two apart. No foot soldier could stand in their way. The Aenglisc were sick and taken by surprise – they did not have the training or the skills to make a defensive formation against such cavalry. Dan vividly remembered the shield wall demonstrated at the renactment he'd seen with Ursula before they entered the Veil for the first time. These Aenglisc had no time to make such a wall and he was sure it would have been futile anyway, the cavalry charge was a roaring tide of massed muscle-power pounding forward, crushing everything in its path.

Dan heard one of the Aenglisc cry, '*Waelcyrige*!' as they saw Ursula riding through the flames and smoke, and ran. Though running would have been the rational thing to do, few of the Aenglisc did it. They flung spears and throwing axes at their enemies and when that failed they tried to attack with sword and seax, but the advantage lay with the mounted men, with the heavy hooves of the horses who trampled men underfoot, with the spear thrusts of the experienced cavalry, and the arrows of the Sarmatian rear guard. Dan wanted to flee from the pain, the fear, and the horror that gathered all around him like the green mist of Rhonwen's conjuring. He had to see that Ursula was safe. The battle scene was chaotic and Dan struggled to identify Ursula below him. Then he found her stabbing and thrusting with her sword, attacked from several directions at once. She had discarded her face-mask, somehow she'd slid it up so that it rested over the top of her helmet like an impassive second face. Her own face formed another mask – of determined aggression, stained with soot and splattered with gore. She was in danger of being unhorsed as her trained mount reared and stamped, cracking limbs and shattering bones, while by her side Braveheart leapt and tore, wild-eyed and blood-crazed. Dan did not dare distract her as she fought for her life. Then Cynfach, having successfully led the western charge joined the main battle and fought his way to Ursula's side. He dispatched her chief attacker with a spear through the spine and she was out of danger, surrounded now by more of the Cataphracts. She raised the now sullied, bloodied shield in the air to let her men know that she lived still, and then the killing continued. There had been well over one thousand Aenglisc in the field and yet though Dan flew high and wide over the whole area he saw scarcely any still standing. Elsewhere the light cavalry under Cerdic finished off what the Sarmatians had begun. Behind them the infantry killed any survivors with brutal efficiency, slashing throats and plundering the dead. Arturus's war machine had done its work.

Dan turned away from the carnage, grateful that his avatar bird did not perceive emotion with the same intensity as his true self. Overhead he saw a merlin fly, a frail and insubstantial form – and knew it to be Taliesin. He was probably searching for Rhonwen. It was time Dan returned to himself, to his own body, his own perceptions and the horror of the aftermath of battle, the losses, and the stink of death.

~ Chapter Twenty-eight ~

Ursula became gradually aware that there was no one left to kill. The battleground was strewn with the bleeding, the dying and the dead. She turned to Cynfach.

'I think we've won.'

He nodded grimly, exhaustion vying with triumph in his face.

Ursula thought someone should say something. As far as she could tell the Sarmatians were unhurt. There must be casualties but when she looked back there were still several hundred mounted men behind her, still broadly in a column formation.

'Help me up!'

She could not stand in her stirrups – neither the Celts nor the Sarmatians knew of them. Her only recourse was to stand on her mount and wave Arturus's shield high in the air as a signal of their triumph. It was still very early. Ursula estimated that the whole battle had taken less than an hour. Battle seemed too grand a word for it; it had been more like a massacre.

Arturus's force cheered wildly at the raised shield, but Ursula had no words of triumph or praise that she could add – that was for Arturus. She dismounted and hung the stained shield over the pommel of the saddle. She ripped off the heavy, golden helmet and face-mask and secured them to her saddle too. They were splattered with soot and flecks of things she'd rather not identify. Her heart was still pounding and she felt breathless. She stuck the bloodied kontos into the ground with such force that it quivered. There were things under her horse's hooves she did not want to see.

'Cynfach, take control till the High King comes, I need some clean air. Oh, and thank you.' She managed a weak smile, 'I would have had it, if you hadn't ridden to rescue me.'

Cynfach still looked stunned, though whether by the ease of the victory or the carnage all round them, she did not want to know. His smile was warm and genuine.

'Your courage inspired us all, Lady Ursa, if I had not been prepared to lay down my life to save yours, my men would never have forgiven me.'

She could not think of a suitable reply to that, so merely nodded and began to walk away. She had to get away from the smell, the charred, burnt smell that was the fire's last endowment; the smell of blood and slaughter and the lingering scent of sickness.

'Dan?' She sought him out, knowing that he would understand.

'Ursula, you are safe!'

Dan's mental voice sounded weary and strained, what it must have been like to experience the suffering of all those dying Aenglisc did not bear thinking about.

'Ursula, wait for me. Taliesin saw Rhonwen leave the battlefield. There's a chance that she might—' He dare not even finish the thought. He dare not hope that Rhonwen might try to escape the best way she knew how.

Ursula did as she was told and stopped walking. Everything felt unreal. She recalled the soft jolt of impact as her spear had skewered an Aenglisc-man. She could still feel the reverberation of it up her arm and in her memory. Such things were better not remembered. Braveheart bounded to her side and butted her affectionately with his head. She patted the matted hair of his skull absently. It was far worse than she could have imagined. She wanted to go home.

It was not long before Dan rode towards her, his dark robes flowing. He did not pause to explain. 'Get up! I think she's about a mile from here. Taliesin thinks she'll try to get away.'

Ursula did not argue but mounted up behind Dan, hoping his pony, which would not have been used in the charge for a good reason, was up to carrying the additional weight. Neither of them spoke. Braveheart loped beside them, his long legs easily keeping pace with the pony. Ursula knew that Dan was aware of her mixed emotions and her revulsion for the horror she had helped perpetrate. She was grateful that he did not say, 'I told you so.'

The battle stench did not abate perceptibly as they rode. So powerful did the vile stink remain that Ursula began to wonder if it was herself she could smell. Would she ever be able to smell anything else?

Dan saw Rhonwen first, kneeling by a grove of trees. She had put to one side her cloak of skulls and wore only a thin, stained, silk shift. Her luxuriant, dark hair fell to her waist. She was singing, crooning almost, in a low voice and Ursula felt her nerves tingle and jangle at the magic. Rhonwen was raising the Veil.

Ursula and Dan dismounted as quietly as possible, much to the relief of the pony. Rhonwen showed no sign of having heard them. She was deeply involved in the ritual of her own technique for calling the yellow mist, dissolving the barrier between worlds. Ursula closed her eyes against a sudden attack of dizziness. She could feel the Veil pulling at her at some deep level, calling to her and she had not the power to answer. Dan obviously perceived her distress. He did not speak for fear of alerting Rhonwen but reached for her hand and held it. She fought to stay calm. Something began to be visible, metres from Rhonwen's kneeling form. It began as a small yellowish blur, like nicotine tainted air, and then grew until the area of swirling yellow was perhaps two or three metres wide.

'Where do you think she will go? Back to her brother, to King Macsen?' Ursula asked.

'I don't know, but I can't stay here. Taliesin thinks swapping worlds changes your abilities. I would do almost anything to be rid of this bloody empathy.' Dan's mental voice sounded desperate. Ursula sneaked a glance at his shadowed face and was shocked by the pallor and the tension there. She thought about what he said. If, say, they followed Rhonwen back to Macsen's world there was a chance that Ursula would once more be able to wield the magic. Once she had the magic back she could raise the Veil herself and steer them both home.

'What do you think?' Dan was responding to her close scrutiny of him with a hard look of his own.

'I want to risk it,' Ursula said firmly.

'What have we got to lose?'

'Well, we could die.' Honesty required that Ursula did not spare him the truth. Bryn managed to follow them successfully through the Veil, but he might have been exceptionally lucky. Ursula knew that in Macsen's world she had wielded more power than Rhonwen commanded even here. What if Rhonwen's way through the

gate was more unstable, not strong enough to allow the passage of two more people?

'What about Bryn?' Their responsibility for the young Combrogi struck Ursula forcibly and she spoke out loud.

'Taliesin would care for him, I'm sure. He is very gifted. He might be the bard's apprentice Frontalis thinks he's looking for.'

'Would he want that?'

Ursula knew that Bryn would not want that but she hoped by asking the question, Dan would realise it for himself.

'If I go back for him – we'll miss our only chance to get home.'

Dan's face was growing paler by the minute.

'Ursula, I swear, if I stay here I'll die. I cannot endure all this pain. I can show you what it feels like if you want.'

Ursula shook her head. She believed him. She did not need the kind of proof he had in mind.

'Dan, how can we leave a message for Bryn?'

'He can't read.'

'But Arturus can.'

They both looked around wildly for something to write on as the power building in the Veil grew towards a climax. Ursula thought her head might burst with the intensity of it. The mist's power was like an impending storm and they would need to be ready to enter into the eye of it. Braveheart wore a heavy, leather collar that one of the grooms had fashioned from a damaged leather belt. Ursula grabbed and removed it with trembling, eager hands and scratched a message with her belt knife into the soft leather.

'HAD TO GO, BRYN, OR DAN DIES. SORRY.'

'I feel terrible – it will be the third time I have let him down.'

Ursula closed her eyes against the pull of the Veil. Rhonwen was standing and beginning to step through. Ursula could bear it no longer, grabbing Braveheart by the scruff of his neck and Dan by his arm she dragged both of them towards the swirling yellow mist and walked through to its heart. She recoiled from the oiliness of the yellow droplets of mist, from the coldness and the strange way it made her feel. It was wrong to leave Bryn behind. She knew it was wrong and she had no excuse. She wanted the magic again and she wanted Dan to live. That was all there was to it. She was sure, even as the mist engulfed her that those were not good enough reasons to abandon an eight-year-old boy in an alien world.

~ *Chapter Twenty-nine* ~

It was all too familiar. They emerged from the Veil into the unknown, their hands locked. Braveheart sneezed and whined; it must have seemed very strange to a dog. He hung his head and dropped his tail dejectedly between his legs. They emerged sometime in a summer afternoon. Birds sang and trees rustled. They were in a forest glade with dappled golden sunlight dancing around them as a light breeze tossed the leafy branches overhead. There was no sign of Rhonwen. They had no way of knowing when or where she might be and they could have been in their own time or in any other.

'We didn't die then?' Dan said, without noticeable emotion.

Ursula shook her head. For an instant she had almost felt she could control the Veil, but here and now there was still no magic. She couldn't disguise her disappointment. She shook her head again when Dan asked, 'Do you think we're home?' It did not feel like home. 'Can you …?'

Dan looked bleak. 'I know you're disappointed that you couldn't direct the Veil, and a little afraid, so, yes, I can still empathise. What if I'm stuck with that for ever?'

Ursula did not need exceptional empathy to hear the fear in his voice.

'Dan.' She made him meet her eyes. 'One problem at a time! Let's find out where we are. I think we might see more from the top of the hill.'

The forest floor sloped steeply in one direction towards what looked like a ridge. Ursula did not have a good feeling about this. Ursula's riding boots were smooth-soled and gave her little purchase on the dry earth. Dan had to help her up the steep forested slope, which was surprisingly slippery. The air was warm and Ursula was conscious of her own battle filth and the weight of her mail. She did not think it wise to take it off and gripped her sword with her right hand as tightly as she held Dan's hand in her left. Braveheart explored the forest floor excitedly. He shook himself once to be free of the lingering dampness of the mist and now seemed content, racing around in front of them like a puppy. Ursula was panting when they reached the top. She pushed a hand through her hair and was horrified to find it stained with gore.

'Have I been cut?'

Dan looked at her, appraisingly. 'No, I think it's someone else's blood and there's some gunky stuff in your hair as well.'

'What do you mean, *gunky stuff*?'

Dan shrugged. 'You've just fought in a bloody massacre, Ursula – you're splattered with all kinds of stuff, and so is Braveheart. It will wash away.'

The same could not be said of the sensations of pain and loss and anguish that still seemed to pollute his own thoughts.

'Don't complain, Ursula, you didn't hear the men you killed scream inside your head.' Dan sounded uncharacteristically bitter.

He had let her hand go and Ursula wished he hadn't. Climbing up to the ridge had not helped much, all they could see below them was grassland in front of them and forest to both sides.

'We're not home are we?' Dan said heavily. 'There isn't a road in sight.'

'No noise either – just birds. I'm sorry, Dan.'

'At least it got me away from the battle. I don't think I could have endured any more of that. Where should we go?'

'Straight on. Looks like it might be cultivated further over that way.'

Dan's face looked grey in the sunlight and beaded with sweat. He took off his long grey cloak and rolled it into a bundle. Ursula was surprised to see that underneath it he wore the scale armour that Arturus had given him. Bedewyr's sword was at his hip.

He shrugged. 'Frontalis thought it was a good idea – when we were travelling – I didn't get round to taking it off.'

'I can tell,' said Ursula with a delicate wrinkling of her nose, though she knew that she must smell at least as bad.

Dan grinned, and she suddenly realised how unusual that had become.

'At least we're alive and we didn't get separated.' She tried to sound bright but she knew as well as he did that, as she had not recovered her magic, their chances of leaving this new world were virtually nil.

'Let's hope we've landed somewhere peaceful.' Ursula continued in the same rather forced tone. 'Do you think I should try to clean up a bit?'

'Stay as you are. You look terrifying – that might be useful.'

'Do you know something I don't?'

Dan glanced at her quickly, as if gauging her reaction.

'I think I can sense something – soldiers, I think. Over there.'

Ursula worked her sword out of its scabbard. She had sheathed it dirty and it stuck badly. She cleaned it up as best she could. Dan unsheathed his too.

Ursula looked at him questioningly.

'I won't let anyone hurt you,' he said tersely, and Ursula wisely said nothing. Dan called Braveheart to heel.

They walked together more cautiously, keeping to the tree line for cover for as long as possible. There was a road, no more than a cart track running across the grassland, too narrow to be seen from the ridge. They started to walk along it. Tracks had to go somewhere and they could not stay in the middle of nowhere for very long. In the distance they could make out two mounted men.

'What do you think?'

Dan shrugged. 'I don't know, Ursula – we don't know that they're hostile. Let's assume that they're not.'

He sheathed his sword. Reluctantly, Ursula followed suit.

'Can you make out how they're dressed?' Dan asked.

'I think they're wearing helmets.'

'Riding helmets?'

Ursula shot him a look. 'You wish! No, I think they've got ridge helmets on.'

'Like Arturus's men?' Dan squinted up the road but could make out nothing clearly.

'Yes, or Aenglisc – they wore the same sort of thing.'

Ursula's heart was beating too fast again, the familiar tattoo of fear. She was tired and hot and hungry. She felt quite tearful. She knew it for certain now. They were not home.

They stopped then, the three of them, and waited for the riders to come into view. Ursula had the best eyesight – in daylight anyway. She identified them first.

'I think they're Combrogi, light cavalry. Cerdic's men.'

Dan looked shocked. 'We're still in Arturus's world?'

'Don't know – looks like it. What can you sense?'

'I'm trying not to sense anything.'

Dan had never looked less relaxed. He was tensed as if against a blow.

Ursula did not recognise the men who stopped a couple of metres in front of them.

Dan held Braveheart by the loose fur round his neck to prevent him from threatening the mounted men more intimately. As it was he bared his bloodstained teeth menacingly.

The riders were clearly uncertain of what to make of a tall, blood-spattered girl in chain mail and her grim-faced companion and war hound. Neither of the men dismounted.

'State your name and business. You trespass on the High King's land.'

They spoke the heavily inflected Latin they had become used to among Arturus's men.

'You mean the High King Arturus?' Ursula ventured.

'Your name?' repeated the bigger of the two men.

'If you are Cerdic's men you will know me. I am Ursa, and this is Gawain.'

There was a sharp intake of breath from the riders.

'You fought with Cerdic?'

'We did not fight together but for the same side, yes,' said Ursula, uncertain of the reason for their obvious agitation.

'Then you, too, must be a traitor and will suffer a traitor's fate. I suppose you know Medraut too?'

'Do you mean Medraut, Count of the Saxon Shore?'

'He means Medraut, ally of the Aenglisc and traitor to the Combrogi cause – what other Medraut is there?'

Dan spoke for the first time, keeping his voice calm and level. The younger of the two riders was red in the face with outrage at the very name of Medraut. It occurred to Dan that they had emerged from the mist into a world almost like the one they had left, but subtly different in ways likely to get them killed.

'Forgive us,' he said as smoothly as Larcius might have done. 'We have been away and clearly much has changed since our last visit. The High King is?'

'Ursus, as every right thinking Combrogi knows, defender of the faith and champion of Britannia.'

'Ursus?'

'High King Arturus Ursus, known to his soldiers as Ursus, since his triumphant victory at Baddon Hill.

Where can you have been that you don't know of his slaughter of nine hundred Aenglisc at one charge, as he wielded the enchanted blade, Caliburn, torn from the stone of the earth by his own hand?'

The younger rider was now almost puce with passion, as if their ignorance was an insult of the most outrageous kind.

Ursula and Dan exchanged a puzzled look. Were they in Arturus's world or in another very like it in which Arturus really had wielded Caliburn at Baddon Hill?

Dan managed to sound confident nonetheless. 'Of course the High King is known to us and we well remember Baddon Hill. Is Cynfach of the Sarmatians, or Taliesin still serving Arturus?'

The younger man blanched at Cynfach's name but the other glared at him so that he closed his mouth and merely looked uncomfortable.

'I'll ask the questions here. You are our prisoners.'

Dan's voice regained something of its old confident timbre in his reply. 'Really, I had not noticed that we were anybody's prisoners.'

The bigger rider glanced at his companion. 'You want to show these ignorant fools a lesson, Nudd?'

The two men dismounted, rather foolishly in Ursula's view, as that threw away their only advantage. Dan warned Braveheart to wait, as it was not his intention to kill these men unless it was unavoidable.

'You take the big one and I'll deal with Nudd. Don't kill him if you can avoid it.'

Ursula nodded her understanding. Her arm still ached from the famous battle, scant hours earlier but her opponent did not look like a man who had ever fought seriously in his life. His kit gleamed, but he moved clumsily with a swaggering gait that lacked balance. He had a long torso, which looked impressive on a horse, but on the ground he was a head and shoulders shorter than Ursula, a fact that seemed to take him by surprise. He drew his sword with a flourish. Ursula guessed that he was in his late twenties but he was a novice in single combat. With a weary internal sigh Ursula jolted her sword from its still sticky sheath and wiped a stray fleck of gore on her leggings.

'We don't have to do this you know,' she said. She wanted to have a long soak in a bath and follow that with a long meal and an even longer sleep. Her opponent attacked her, slightly tentatively. The vibration as their swords met sent an uncomfortable jolt up her forearm, reminding her of just how tired she really was. She did not have the energy to humour him. She slashed back far more savagely than he had expected, and saw alarm widen his eyes. She aimed not for his body but for his sword, meeting his blade with a well-timed blow with the flat of her sword at his sword's weakest point. His sword flew from his hand and shattered. She kicked him sharply and as he doubled up in pain she pointed her own blade at his neck. A quick glance round told her that Dan had stunned Nudd and was binding his hands with a length of rein.

'You won't get away with this. The Tribune will be back soon.'

'Thanks for telling us. We'll be expecting him,' said Dan with another of his almost forgotten grins, as he secured the hands of Ursula's opponent. The action seemed to have cheered Dan up. He looked less grey.

'Where to now, Ursula? Which horse do you want?'

'I don't mind,' said Ursula, 'but we better choose quickly. I think the Tribune is riding this way.'

~ *Chapter Thirty* ~

'Should we wait?' Dan was clearly uncomfortable about leaving their prisoners in the middle of nowhere.

'He'll find them.'

'Yes, but if these men are on Arturus's side where else do we go? If we wait for the captain and explain that they attacked us we may not be marked down as Arturus's enemy. What else can we do?'

He was right, of course, though Ursula found the thought of mounting a horse and just riding enormously tempting. As if just by riding she might find herself somewhere she wanted to be, instead of wherever she was.

The captain was a tall man with a still, watchful face. He reminded Ursula of someone, though whether in Macsen's world, Arturus's world, or her own, she could not say. He took in the scene in a moment, his calm rather closed face revealing nothing. He noted his men sitting back to back with their wrists tied together on the dusty dirt road, Ursula and Dan and Braveheart looking at him warily. His face darkened and he looked almost shocked.

'We have been away and—' Ursula began by way of explanation.

'I know who you are,' he interrupted, shortly.

He held Ursula's eye for a long second. She struggled to put a name to his face. He knew her so she must have met him in this world – was he one of the Sarmatians? He was fair skinned and dark haired and there were not many of that colouring in the troop – surely she would have remembered. Suddenly, Braveheart left Dan's side and with a joyful bark rushed towards the stranger wagging his tail. The man's dour face creased into a warm smile and he vaulted from the saddle. He knelt and hugged the war dog, permitting him to lick his face, burying his face in the thick bloodstained fur of his neck. Ursula was confused. Braveheart never behaved like that except with Dan and Bryn.

Ursula peered hard at the man. He was tall and well built without being heavily muscled. He looked to be in his late twenties, maybe older, with the creased, weather beaten face of a man much out of doors. He was clean-shaven with his hair cut in neat, Roman military style. He wore the characteristic ridge helmet of the majority of Arturus's men, but his was decorated with silver. His clothing was plain and of earthy greens and browns. He wore no mail or scale armour though his horse was a fine black gelding. She looked at Dan, struck by a sudden unbelievable thought. Dan had blushed a deep scarlet as if evaluating the very same conclusion. It could not be Bryn – could it?

'Do we know you?' Ursula asked haltingly, embarrassed. The man looked at her, when he turned he had screwed up his face against Braveheart's enthusiastic and undoubtedly smelly greeting. She knew – it was the same expression she had seen so many times.

'Yes, long ago, I was Dan's squire. It's me, Bryn.'

Should she too have run to embrace him? He had lived to a fine, well-nourished manhood. She should be glad things had turned out so well. Instead, Ursula swayed in the saddle. She was not inclined to faint, but she felt a sudden heat and dizziness. She would have fallen but Bryn caught her.

'I am so sorry,' she muttered, and then passed out.

She was not out for long. She woke to the sound of Bryn's quiet voice, filling in the lost years.

'Larcius took me on as his squire. I studied a little with Taliesin but my heart was not in it. But all these years I wondered why? Why did you leave me alone?'

Bryn's voice was flat, without emotion. She tried to hear the boy in what he said, but even his accent had changed. He spoke Latin, Bryn who had scarcely spoken a word of any language but his own when they first arrived in Arturus's world.

'You found Braveheart's collar?' Dan sounded acutely uncomfortable.

'Yes, Cynfach found it and told me what it said. He was always loyal to you and of course to Ursula. He tried to explain how it was for you, but you even took Braveheart away. I could not sleep for nights afterwards, though Gwynefa gave me a puppy when she found out what had happened. Poor Cynfach, a good man, he was killed soon after.'

'Cynfach? No. Who by?'

Ursula heard the sadness in Dan's voice and felt tears threaten. She could not think of what they had done to Bryn. She could not believe what had happened to Cynfach. She had spoken to him, just before she went through the Veil. He had looked at her with such confidence, such pride. He could not be dead.

Bryn was speaking again, in the slightly peculiar Latin favoured by Larcius. 'He died in a hunting accident, but there were those who thought his death too convenient.'

'Whatever do you mean?'

Bryn cast a warning glance in the direction of his men still tied up in the road. They were trying to avoid his eye.

'Cynfach knew who led the charge at Baddon and

never tired of praising you. It became ill luck to mention you, and Arturus always talked as if it were he who led the Sarmatian charge at Baddon. He presented himself as a war hero and those who mentioned remembering otherwise soon died. Taliesin has never sung about the Boar Skull and the Bear Sark in all the long years since the victory at Baddon Hill. These are peaceful times, or have been for most of us, but those looking for a fight can still find it. There are still Aenglisc and Pict and Scot around if you look hard enough. Cerdic found common cause with the enemy and now rules the small kingdom of Gewisse, with Aenglisc backing. Medraut sought another way to be king of his old lands and has made an alliance with Rhonwen and her old allies. She returned a couple of months ago. Arturus never managed to get the Saxon Shore back and Medraut did not believe he tried hard enough – or so it is assumed. Anyway, I have ridden out here regularly since Rhonwen's return – I wondered if you would follow Rhonwen back here – as I followed you from Macsen's land when I was a boy.' His voice was briefly coloured by some emotion, sadness, regret?

'Taliesin won't speak of any of it – why you came and how you left – he won't ever discuss you except, sometimes he used to mutter in his sleep.'

'Used to? Taliesin isn't—?' Dan found there was a lump in his throat.

'No. He is unchanged. He cares for Frontalis who is old now and half blind. His order disapprove of his involvement with the 'Devil's Druid'. He's banned from Court, though Arturus still consults with him in secret.'

Dan met this further information with silence. It was very hard to take on so much change in what for them, had seemed like no time at all. When Dan finally spoke, it was in a voice strained and roughened by acute embarrassment and shame. Ursula felt it too.

'Bryn, I am very ashamed. I should not have run – I failed you.'

Bryn shrugged. 'It happened a long time ago. It will be twenty-one years when the winter comes.' He indicated the silver cross he wore round his neck, over his tunic.

'Brother Frontalis taught me that it's better to forgive.'

Dan said nothing. It was hard to equate this large, softly spoken man with the passionate child Bryn had been.

'I'm sorry too, Bryn. I thought Dan would die if we stayed at Baddon, but we should never have left you behind. It was wrong.' Ursula blurted the words out in a tumble of remorse.

Bryn gave Ursula a long appraising glance. It made her deeply uncomfortable.

'Is this how you looked after the battle?' he asked

abruptly, for no particular reason that she could see.

She wiped a dusty, weary hand across her already filthy face.

'I still ache from that battle, Bryn. I am stained with the blood of men who, to me, died only hours ago at Baddon.'

His expression was difficult to read.

'You were courageous.'

It was not a question, more an unequivocal statement, said without praise.

'I would have died but for Cynfach. I can't believe he is dead.'

Bryn nodded. 'Will you release my men?'

'Of course. They tried to take us prisoner. We wouldn't have fought them otherwise.'

'They're not the brightest,' Bryn said calmly. 'Will you come with me to my Lord?'

'Arturus?'

Bryn shook his head. 'I have served Larcius for more than twenty years. You are not far from his seat at Caer-Baddon.'

Ursula felt a momentary panic at the thought of seeing Larcius. She had not seen much of him since their march from Camulodunum. She was more aware than ever of her disreputable state.

'I would like to wash and clean up my armour before I have to meet anyone,' she began, but Bryn forestalled her.

'It would do some people good to be reminded of who actually fought the Battle of Baddon Hill. It has brought us twenty years of peace, but the people who have gained most did not pay the price,' he said cryptically.

Ursula was too much in awe of this man who had once been Bryn to question what he meant.

Once his men were untied, Bryn made them walk behind the horses on the journey to Caer-Baddon. Ursula had dreaded the silence she expected between them but Bryn chatted easily about that and other matters: how Arturus had tried to restore Camulodunum to its former glory and reintroduce the rule of Roman law into the country; how he had given land and property to the church to set up schools for the education of the sons of kings and others; how Bryn himself had managed to overcome his fear of literacy and learned to write and read a little, much to Taliesin's disgust. Taliesin, it seemed, still believed writing damaged the mind. Neither Ursula nor Dan spoke much, other than to ask the odd question. They were not home nor were they any nearer to getting home. There was no magic. There was no respite from Dan's empathy. They had gained nothing in entering the Veil and lost something Ursula had not known was precious – the belief that they had acted from the right motives, the assurance that they had done their best. She had killed because she had believed it was what she had to do, but she had also betrayed someone who had trusted her. There was no way of making up for that, for all that they had done to Bryn, and they all knew it.

~ Chapter Thirty-one ~

The road was largely empty but for a few wagons loaded with foodstuffs. There were distinct signs of smoke from hamlets and sometimes, far from the road, a cluster of thatched structures which must have been Combrogi villages. Fields were well tended and the road was largely free of weeds but there were still guards at the Gate to Caer-Baddon, guards who regarded Ursula's bloodstained finery with frank suspicion.

Caer-Baddon still retained much of its Roman splendour though, as in Camulodunum new and altogether cruder houses replaced many of the original stone buildings. There were market stalls and more permanent shops selling fruit, eggs, strong cheese, and souring milk in wooden pails. Butchered meat hung from hooks surrounded by a mass of plump bluebottles, and fish rotted rankly in the heat. There were stalls selling woven fabrics, leather goods and horse tack, iron goods and even copper jewellery and beads – evidence of a way of life Ursula had never seen, a way of life that was not wholly taken up with the business of war. The warm, wholesome smell of baking bread reminded her that she had eaten little for the last few days as rations had been carefully regulated during the siege of Baddon, and the stench of the Aenglisc sickness had in any case put her off her food. She felt too guilty to ask anything of Bryn.

Passers-by gave Ursula and the war dog wide berth. The taint of death seemed to follow her in a cloud of flies and she rather suspected she had picked up fleas because she itched desperately under her many layers of protective padding. She longed to bathe, but Bryn rode past the still intact Roman Bathhouse, which smelled even from outside of scented oils and clean steam.

Larcius's home was not what she had expected – a plain stone building which had been re-roofed with thatch. It looked incongruous among the finer buildings, a Combrogi chieftain's hall in an ancient Roman setting. Even Ursula, who was not politically astute, recognised such a blatant political gesture that served to differentiate him so clearly from Arturus.

Bryn dismounted and handed his reins to servants who had emerged at their approach. Having used their horse's reins to tie up their prisoners, Ursula and Dan merely dismounted and with Braveheart followed Bryn into the main hall.

'Ah Bryn,' a man's voice spoke in familiar tones and Ursula felt suddenly sick with apprehension.

'You are back later than I expected, and with guests. This is most unusual.'

As the corpulent figure strode towards them Ursula was able to watch the blood drain from his face as he saw her.

'In God's name it cannot be, Lady Ursa?'

Ursula's own shock was scarcely any less. The years of good living had coarsened Larcius's fine features into a parody of his former beauty. His eyes were still bright and piercingly blue, but sunk deeper into now puffy flesh. His aquiline nose had broadened, his once sensuous mouth had slackened into an altogether looser, wetter feature, while his once firm and chiselled chin might still have existed but only as one chin among many. He was old and fat and ugly.

'Larcius!'

Ursula did not know what else to say.

Larcius stepped forward to embrace her, then noticed her bloodstained mail.

'I don't understand – how are you so – unchanged?'

Bryn saved her from that complex explanation.

'The Lady Ursa disappeared through the Veil after the Battle at Baddon Hill. She emerged from the Veil earlier today.'

Larcius was staring at Ursula with a mixture of awe

and revulsion. He paid little attention to Dan.

'By your leave, Larcius, I would dearly love to wash away the stench and stains of battle,' she began somewhat desperately.

'Of course, forgive me. It has been so long, Ursa, since I have looked upon your beauty. You must be tired and hungry.'

He clapped his hands and servants escorted Dan and Ursula to the baths, provided them with clean, woollen garments, and brought them back to Larcius's hall, where a fine meal awaited them. Bryn assured them that he would ensure that their valuable war gear was cleaned and returned to them. Dan had been loath to part with his sword even to enter the cleansing waters of the baths. He was mistrustful of everyone. He sent Ursula a warning as they sat down to eat.

'*Something is wrong, Ursula – his emotions are all muddy. He never thought to see either of us again. I don't trust him.*'

Larcius's gaze was intense as he watched Ursula's every small move.

'You are more beautiful even than I remembered,' he said more than once. His compliments gave her an uncomfortable feeling. She shared some of Dan's unease.

'It is fortunate that you arrived today, for tomorrow the High King pays us his annual visit on his way to his fortress at Cado. He will be very … surprised to see you after so many years.'

There was something in Larcius's tone that startled her, something that sounded very like spite.

It was a strange meal. They ate with many of Larcius's retinue in the main hall. Long, low tables were laden with a variety of strongly spiced meat and fish dishes, thick black bread, and fruit. It was awkward to eat without chairs or couches and Ursula was acutely self-conscious of her long legs in their wool leggings. Larcius could hardly keep his eyes off them and the lasciviousness she had found exciting in a young and handsome companion became something altogether more sinister and obscene in this bloated older man. Larcius had taken no wife and there were no women present at the table, other than the servants who waited on them and avoided Ursula's eyes as deliberately as they avoided Larcius's wandering hands.

It was Bryn who ended it all by suggesting quietly that the guests ought to be shown to their quarters. There were several Roman bedchambers off the main hall and Bryn explained that he had left their kit in one of them. Bryn gently took Dan to one side and in Ursula's hearing said in a low voice. 'You probably already know that Larcius is not to be trusted. He fears you. In many ways, he remains Arturus's rival and he knows that Arturus will find a way to use you once he has got over his embarrassment at seeing the true heroes of Baddon return. Watch over Ursula. When Queen Gwynefa is safely in her husband's bed … Larcius has a certain unsavoury reputation, though with any luck he will be too drunk to try anything.'

Ursula did not want to be excluded from the conversation. She spoke softly but forcefully. 'What has happened to turn Larcius into that?'

Bryn looked saddened. 'Larcius has been good to me and I would not deny him the honour I owe him for the many acts of kindness over the years. He is a weak man. He has wealth and power but Arturus is still High King and still married to Gwynefa. Larcius has never got over either fact.'

'Larcius still loves Gwynefa?'

Bryn gave Ursula a world-weary look.

'Gwynefa is different from you, Ursula. She was born to play the kinds of games—' He looked uncomfortable but continued. 'They are twin souls, Gwynefa and Larcius, they have corrupted each other.'

It was too dark to see, but Ursula had the distinct impression that Bryn was blushing.

'It doesn't matter. You are here again. In the morning I will resign my position.'

'What do you mean?' Dan spoke for the first time.

'I hated you when you left me. When Rhonwen returned I expected you to follow, though Taliesin explained that even if you followed her immediately you might arrive hours, months, or even years later. I planned all the things I would say to you, all the things that have been in my heart all these years. Now you are here, I see what you are and through your eyes I have seen what Larcius has become and I am ashamed. You were my hero, Dan, but now I see you are barely out of childhood. Ursula, you are an innocent – I couldn't even bring myself to explain to you that Gwynefa and Larcius have been lovers for more than twenty years. My vow on the road to Alavna cannot be expunged. Taliesin was right. I pledged you my soul when I was a child and you have it still.'

'But Bryn – I ran away.'

'You tried to go home. Now I have a son of my own I know what that means. You forget I knew about your sister – you told me more than you remember. I am Combrogi. I survived you going. I find that all the Latin speaking in the world cannot change what I am – a man born in a simpler time with simpler rules than Larcius's complex deceits.' He sounded bitter. 'I promised Larcius my total loyalty only until you returned. He did not think you would ever come back. The oath I swore you was the strongest I could ever make. God was my witness, though I did not know it. I am bound to keep my oath to you.' He was speaking now in the language of his childhood.

'Oh Bryn, I don't deserve such loyalty.' Dan's voice broke into a sob then and Bryn comforted him as he might have comforted his son. Ursula could not control her own tears. All the disappointments and the sorrow of the day and the horrible humiliation of the dinner with Larcius found a kind of release. Bryn's strong hand found her shoulder.

'My late wife could not bear to meet Larcius either. She hated the way he looked at her. There is no shame in that, Ursula. Cry it all out – it will all be better in the morning.'

With that, Bryn was gone.

It was not better in the morning, but by morning Ursula had made a decision. She dressed in her mailshirt and shook Dan awake. He started, guiltily. 'Sorry, Ursula, I must have dozed off – why are you dressed like that?'

'I can't stay here, Dan – Larcius is, well you know what Larcius is and I've been thinking. Rhonwen is here, ahead of us – maybe I could persuade her somehow to re-open the Veil and if I could make her do that, I think I know how I could use it to get us home – I really think I could do it this time.'

'Ursula, Rhonwen tried to destroy you with sorcery at Baddon.' He knew by the stubborn set of Ursula's mouth that she was not listening. 'OK – maybe she won't try again but what if Taliesin has had enough time to build up some more power and found a way to raise the Veil? If he had d'you think he'd still be here?'

Ursula scowled. 'I don't know Dan, but if we stay here I'll have to fight again – people will depend on us, we'll get sucked into it again, be dragged into whatever stupid war is coming and you were right, before, when you decided not to fight, it's not what I want either.'

Dan saw the haunted look in her eyes and needed no special empathy to know that she was thinking of the men she'd killed so recently at Baddon. 'Bryn said there was peace.'

'Do you believe that?'

Dan shook his head. There was violence in the air, he could feel it, a growing tension with which he was too familiar. 'No,' he said slowly, 'Something's not right – it doesn't feel like peace.'

'Dan, listen to me – we're not needed here. We have to try to get home. We've done enough. Bryn said that Arturus had made people think *he* led the charge at Baddon, not me. Whatsisname who attacked us yesterday said Arturus called himself Ursus now. If he doesn't even call himself Arturus anymore, just Ursus, he must be taking the prophecy for *himself*! Taliesin will have helped. All Taliesin wanted was a leader who might fulfil the prophecy. He's got his *Bear* now, he doesn't need us. Arturus does not need us – he has the reputation of a hero. Everyone who was at Baddon is dead or doesn't care what really happened.'

Dan nodded thoughtfully, Ursula carried on.

'How pleased do you think Arturus would be to see us?' She looked at Dan, her face set and determined.' On the other hand, Rhonwen might be quite pleased to see the back of us by sending us home. We can't help her enemies if we're ...'

'Dead,' added Dan helpfully. 'You were the one who was so sure that we should get involved with fighting the Aenglisc; are you saying you've changed your mind?' Dan kept his voice carefully neutral. He did not want to precipitate another row.

'Yes, I don't want to get involved again. I want to go home.'

Dan sighed, 'I want to go too, but I don't see how we can. Anyway, I think we're already involved – maybe we came back now for a reason, because we are needed. Ursula, I think that if Arturus is our King Arthur, Larcius is Lancelot. Didn't they fight because of Guinevere? I think you're right – there is going to be a war and we're part of it because somehow we're still part of Arturus's story.'

'I think Arthur and Lancelot did fight, yes, and I'm not sure I care.' She paused before adding, bitterly. 'Arturus used me at Baddon, didn't he?'

Dan had not wanted to tell Ursula how callously Arturus had been prepared to spend her life. He wondered how long she'd known.

'Yes. I swear I didn't know it until I saw what he'd

done. He thought it was for the good of Britannia – or so he said.' Dan did not know why he was defending Arturus but he found he was.

Ursula nodded, as if it no longer mattered, as if she had not nearly died for Arturus's sake the day before. She sounded calm and unutterably weary when she replied, 'He's not a hero, Dan, he's a coward. I wish he was – you know – like he is in the legend, noble and a great leader and all that, but he's not.'

'He's kept the Combrogi safe for twenty years,' Dan pointed out reasonably.

'Maybe, but he would have let me die!'

'You're right,' said Dan, but it was as if the Veil had dampened down his anger, as if he had felt it twenty years ago, not just the day before. 'But I think Arturus is still our King Arthur and, I don't remember the story well, Ursula, but I think it all unravelled, the peace, the Combrogi, everything because of the rivalry between Lancelot and Arthur – maybe if we could warn him ...?'

'No, Dan – we can't change history, and I don't think we should try. We must try to get home.'

'I want to go home, Ursula, you know I do, but I think we're part of history like the sword from the stone thing – like your victorious charge at Baddon. You got the sword and won the battle and then that story got mixed up with Arturus.'

Ursula was stony faced, unimpressed by his theory.

'Does that mean you won't come with me to find Rhonwen?'

'It means that I'm going to stay and meet Arturus.'

'I can't persuade you?' Ursula asked, truculently.

'No, but you could wait with me and, then we could go and find Rhonwen together.'

Ursula shook her head.

'Just promise me one thing,' Dan said and held her gaze for a moment, felt her fight her fury at him for not agreeing with her.

Ursula nodded, tersely.

'Don't go home without me.'

She nodded again and turned her head away from him so he couldn't see how close she was to tears. He knew anyway.

'Do you have a plan for finding her?'

'I'll ask Bryn where Taliesin is. He'll know where Rhonwen is. She's why he's here.'

'And if there was a way of persuading her to raise the Veil, don't you think he'd have already tried it?'

Ursula looked at him in distress. 'Please, Dan, don't be sensible,' she whispered. 'I have to get away from here.' She moved towards him awkwardly and kissed him briefly on the lips. It was such an unexpected, intimate, incomprehensible gesture Dan did not know how to respond.

'See you later,' she said shyly, and hurried from the

room. He had no name for the multi-layered emotion she projected nor for his own bemused reaction.

Dan did not have much time to reflect on Ursula's motives as he was summoned to the main hall to join his host for breakfast.

Larcius's eyes were bloodshot and the skin around them swollen with sleep but they were sharp as ever, calculating, cold.

'Your youth reminds me of a time most of us have all but forgotten.' Larcius ripped a loaf of dark bread savagely and gave a generous portion to Dan. He spread it thickly with the strong sweetness of honeycomb. The powerful aroma and flavour stunned Dan into temporary silence. He had missed sweetness. Only after he had eaten did Larcius speak again.

'You will find the High King little changed. He is older of course, but his monkish spirit has kept him from some of my excesses.' He slapped his enormous belly derisively. 'Life is for living – grab your pleasures while you can, I say. You have a sweet tooth, too, I see?'

Larcius's own teeth were still remarkably well preserved in spite of his love of sweetness. His smile was nearer a snarl and to Dan he reeked of bitterness.

'Where is the Lady Ursa?'

Dan had been wondering how to broach the subject for the duration of the meal. He had decided to tell the truth, or as much of the truth as he thought would be acceptable.

'She wanted me to thank you for your hospitality,' he began carefully. 'But she has ridden out to try and find us a way home. You know we did not come from here and—'

Larcius's eyes grew colder still. 'She is a very foolish young woman. This is not, for all Arturus's many boasts, a safe country. I must have her brought back here immediately.'

'This is Ursa we're talking about. She is well able to take care of herself. She is not your responsibility.'

'On the contrary, the Lady Ursa is very much my responsibility. She must be found.' Larcius directed his last remark at Bryn. His tone was so disrespectful that Dan flinched on Bryn's behalf.

Bryn showed no sign of having noticed the contempt.

'I came to tell you, My Lord, that Arturus has sent a rider ahead. The High King is to be expected at noon.'

Larcius grunted and poured a generous cup of ale from a stone flagon.

'Inform the kitchens, and I want the Lady Ursa found before Arturus gets here.'

Bryn's face was as impassive as Ursula's own.

'My Lord, I thank you for all the many kindnesses you have offered me. I believe I have served you honestly and as well as I knew how, but now I cannot serve you further. The man you call Gawain has a prior claim upon me. So I give you back your sword.'

With a certain melodramatic flourish, which suggested he had not been wholly inattentive to Taliesin's lessons, Bryn drew his sword and handed it, hilt first to Larcius.

Dan noted the edge of violence in the air and tried to resist the urge to rest his hand on his own sword hilt. It was a reflex – he had no intention of fighting, except for Ursula and Braveheart and, it seemed, for Bryn.

~ Chapter Thirty-two ~

Ursula was glad to be riding away from the stink of Caer-Baddon: its decaying food, overripe fruit and the fetid stench of sun-warmed animal dung. She was glad to be free of it, free from Larcius and even free from Dan. She did not know what had possessed her to kiss him – gratitude maybe that he understood, that he did not look at her as Larcius had done, that he was not old and fat. She could not say, and shied away from thinking about it. It was embarrassing.

Bryn had helped her, as she had known he would. He had suggested she borrow one of Larcius's toughest ponies and told her that Taliesin was staying close to Brother Frontalis's religious community, a few hours ride from Arturus's fort at Cado. He had drawn her a map, which he scratched on a scrap of leather. It reminded Ursula too painfully of the message she had left on Braveheart's collar. It clearly reminded Bryn of the same thing because he suddenly disappeared to return moments later with the well-oiled leather collar. It was strange to see the marks she had scratched on it so recently, now faded and aged. Braveheart stayed still long enough to permit the collar to be fastened back around his neck.

There was no Roman road between Caer-Baddon and Fort Cado, only farm tracks and open country. In her own time Ursula would not have dreamed of riding such a distance with the minimum of directions. It was a measure of her desperation that she was prepared to attempt it here. She had an instinct, maybe no more than a hope misconstrued, that she would find her way. She was not remotely surprised when just before midday as she rested and watered her horse and prepared to eat her lunch, she spotted the flecked, brown form of a merlin falcon on a branch nearby.

'Taliesin?'

The bird tilted its head in a questioning way.

'Taliesin, if it's you, can you ...?' She struggled to think of a sign he could give her. 'Oh, fly over to that big tree and back!'

The bird managed to express disdain even as it followed her instructions. Surely it could not be a coincidence? She drank some water from the stream to save her supplies, in case the day grew hotter later, and mounted up.

'Taliesin, I really hope it is you because I'm going to follow you. Let's go!'

*

Bryn's change of status in Larcius's house was the cause of considerable confusion. From what Dan could gather he seemed to have been in charge of almost everything concerning the running of Larcius's life. No one seemed to be able to progress the preparations for Arturus's arrival without consulting Bryn constantly. He was polite but steered all their questions towards Larcius himself, explaining that he himself now served Gawain, once the Bear Sark of the Combrogi. Whatever the title had once meant it was clear from the blank faces of Larcius's retinue it meant nothing in these post-Baddon days.

Larcius was extremely angry and bellowed at anyone who came near him. In the confusion he forgot about finding anyone to follow Ursula until it was too late, and Arturus arrived with two hundred of his Sarmatian troops plus about one hundred light cavalry and rode with great pomp into Caer-Baddon. Time had been less cruel to Arturus than to Larcius Ambrosius. He had matured. His pale hair was paler now with many strands of grey among the gold. He was still slim and fit looking though he moved more stiffly than before. His rather bland face was improved by the lines of aging, they gave him an air of quiet authority that he had formerly lacked. He was clearly startled to see Dan again but quickly regained his composure.

'Gawain, but I thought you long dead, or gone from us.'

'I understand many years have passed.' Dan faltered as he searched for something more to say. 'And there has been peace since the Battle of Baddon Hill.'

Arturus nodded, 'We have fought,' he said, 'but only skirmishes. The Aenglisc have gained no more land.'

Dan could see that, along with the more tangible signs of aging, Arturus at least seemed more regal, more the king history had made him.

'And we have tried to rebuild our Roman heritage. Many of our towns are beginning to thrive again and I am proud to say the rule of law has been restored. But, Dan, you are … as I last saw you. What miracle is this?'

'We went through the Veil – you know?'

'Taliesin spoke to me about it once.'

'Then you know as much as I do.'

There was an awkward silence.

'And how is Taliesin?'

'Difficult, moody and unhelpful, as he has been since Baddon. I don't think he approves of peace. Needless to say his spirits have improved lately, now that we are under threat again.' Arturus gave a wry smile.

So there was war brewing. As Arturus spoke Dan knew that the certainty of it lay in all the emotions eddying as an undercurrent to the flow of conversation. In war, side-taking was inevitable – he chose his on instinct. He was with Arturus still, in spite of everything. He hoped that he was not wrong.

*

Ursula was becoming extremely irritated with the bird that seemed to take delight in leading her across streams, ditches and marshland. This perversity convinced her that the merlin truly was Taliesin as nothing else could. It was getting dark, and Ursula was hungry, exhausted and thoroughly bad tempered, when the bird finally came to rest in a clearing where a round, thatched hut, of the type favoured by Macsen's Combrogi, vented fragrant wood smoke into the cooling air. The wind was blowing towards her and she coughed.

'Lady Ursa?' The voice was tremulous. A figure bent and hesitant appeared at the door, holding on to the wooden door frame for support.

'Brother Frontalis!'

The old man reached out to her and, abandoning both her horse and Braveheart, Ursula dismounted and ran to him. He peered at her through eyes dimmed by cataracts and touched her arm with his still strong, large hands. She gave his arm an answering squeeze.

She followed him into the dark and smoky interior. The smell of stew flavoured by herbs and hops from the beer fermenting in the corner could not quite disguise the faint odour of old age. Taliesin lay like one dead on a bed of sheepskin close to the fire.

Frontalis sat down slowly on a low Roman couch, almost the only furniture in the room. It was covered in animal skins and so its incongruity had not been immediately obvious.

'Would you get Taliesin some ale from that jug there,' he indicated a pitcher with a nod of his head. There are some cups just there. He will be thirsty when he wakes.'

Ursula did as she was asked. Taliesin opened his eyes and grunted something and she obligingly raised the horn cup to his lips as he struggled to sit up.

'What took you so long?' Taliesin sounded surly.

'What do you mean?' Ursula answered, confused.

'I wait twenty-one years to see you and I'm not your first port of call!'

Ursula hung her head. 'Please don't tease me, Taliesin – I've followed you through some pretty hard country, I'm tired, I'm hungry, I've lost my sense of humour, and I want to go home.'

'I'm not teasing. I'm the only one who knows what's going on round here. Arturus thinks he knows it all. Trouble is brewing and you can help.'

Something about his tone irritated Ursula and she found herself replying more aggressively than she'd intended. 'Why, Taliesin? Why should I help? All I want to do is to go home!'

Then she had the somewhat dubious privilege of seeing Taliesin look, for the first time, utterly surprised.

~ *Chapter Thirty-three* ~

Arturus's mood darkened as the day wore on. Gwynefa had gone somewhere with Larcius and returned late. When she finally arrived elaborately dressed and imperious, Dan was shocked at the change in her. He had heard from Bryn that her union with Arturus had been childless. She had miscarried some nine times and it was evident to Dan, if to no one else, that she carried the pain of every one of those lost potential children like a stone in her heart. Her whole being was rooted in grief and bitterness. Dan found it hard to look at her. She was bravely dressed in a Roman chiton of scarlet wool that clung to her voluptuous curves, and a long, floor-length cloak of deep blue interwoven with threads of gold. She was festooned with gold jewellery and wore her jet-black hair in a complicated style, pinned with glittering combs and clips that Dan's sister would have loved. The dark skin of her face was still smooth and plump, and her startling, pale green eyes were accentuated by dark make-up so that they seemed to glitter maniacally. She must have been in her late thirties and had retained a far more youthful appearance than either Arturus or Larcius, yet to Dan she seemed old and world-weary. Her still charming smile did not reach her eyes.

It was obvious to Dan that Arturus still loved and desired her. It was also apparent in her every gesture towards him, that she accepted both emotions as her due – but shared neither. She seemed scarcely warmer towards Larcius, while the sentiments he exuded defied Dan's limited powers of emotional description: not envy, not hate, not irritation, not respect, not quite love, but somehow all of them together. It was more than Dan could grasp.

It all became easier when Gwynefa left early from the dinner Larcius had arranged in Arturus's honour. Arturus explained that she intended to ride out before dawn the next day to negotiate the purchase of some horses from a well known horse breeder a day's ride away and that she intended to meet him back at his Fort at Cado. It seemed to Dan that Arturus was both pleased and irritated by her independence, while Larcius was both excited and disturbed by her plans. Dan was merely bemused. Something was going on but he did not know what. He tried to reduce his sensitivity to the emotional ambience, and following Bryn's example, concentrated on his meal – it was hot and tasty and richly filling, a simple, satisfying pleasure.

Frontalis soothed Ursula with kindness, consideration, and dinner. Taliesin had the good sense to leave aside the tricky topic of Ursula's allegiance until she had finished her supper, cared for the animals, bathed in the nearby river, divested herself of her riding boots and chain mail and was drinking some hot sweet herbal concoction of Frontalis's as she dried her hair by the fire. However, once he did broach it Taliesin leapt straight to the point.

'What did you mean, Ursula, about not helping? I thought you were Combrogi now.'

Ursula sipped her drink and watched the flames dance and destroy a large log of sweet apple wood. It was so good to drink something hot that was not wine or mead or even warm ale. Frontalis had a gift for hospitality. She felt warm and safe and clean and somehow loved. She did not much want to have to justify herself to the old druid.

'Taliesin – why can't you let me be and sing a song or do something soothing? I have only had one night's rest since I fought at Baddon. I still ache from that and from the ride. You have no right to bully me.'

Unexpectedly, Taliesin did pick up his harp from where it was carefully stowed and began to play. He did not choose the melody he'd played at Baddon, as she thought he might or even the saga of Boar Skull and the Bear Sark. He played instead the tune he'd played the night she'd given her warrior's oath to King Macsen, the Combrogi leader. It was a clever choice. That night she had been accepted into a select and much valued band, a girl who had not often been accepted. She found her eyes watering from more than the sweet smoke.

'Taliesin, you are a manipulative old goat,' she said when he had finished. 'Arturus isn't Macsen and you know it.'

'He's not as tall or as handsome.'

'Don't patronise me,' Ursula snapped. 'He is not a worthy leader. He tricked me into bearing his shield at Baddon, then he claimed that he'd led the battle charge and killed my friends who might have contradicted him. Why in God's name should I lift a finger to help him?'

'You are very well informed.'

'I also heard that you pretended that Dan and I had never existed. Thanks Taliesin. Haven't you messed with our lives enough?' Ursula felt ashamed to have lost her temper again in front of Frontalis. She sipped her drink and tried to calm down in the long silence before Taliesin spoke again.

'After Baddon – it was confused. Arturus thought you were dead. Cynfach saw you ride out with Dan and we couldn't find you. A small Aenglisc war band survived the charge down Baddon Hill – they were the Bretwalde's men, Aelle's hand-picked warriors, they set up an ambush. They picked up various Combrogi shields and helms that were lost in battle and scattered them round some Aenglisc bodies and when our men went to check that none of ours were fallen or injured, they killed them. We lost twenty men that way and somehow your helmet and faceplate got mixed up with them.'

'I tied it to my horse's bridle.'

'Well, it must have come loose and fallen and in all the celebration it was some time before Cynfach noticed that you had not returned. When Arturus saw his own face-mask that he'd given you at the ambush site – we all assumed the worst. Then some of the Sarmatians seeing him with the face-mask assumed it was he that had led the charge along with you.'

'And he did not deny it?'

'He is High King of a contentious, territorial, ambitious, self-serving, envious, power hungry group of men. Would you deny you were a hero if it would help you keep that lot united?'

'What about Cynfach?'

'I don't believe Arturus killed him. I don't think Arturus set out to lie either, but he did not discourage the lies and neither did I, Ursula, Arturus's position was not completely secure – Cerdic, Larcius and Medraut all had claims on the title and so I too just stopped talking about you. You were only with us a short time. You were remembered, but many of those who fought at Baddon are dead now, it's been twenty years'.

'And this is good – this is a reason to help Arturus?'

'He is "the Bear", Ursula – I do believe it, though I don't believe he would have come into his own without your help. I justify what I have done with that thought, Ursula. "The Bear" is on the hillside and you helped put him there.' He touched her hand, demanding that she look at him, and she saw in the firelight that his face was damp with tears.

'Ursula, my dear, brave friend, I have been to many worlds, seen many atrocities, the tribes are not perfect but they are my people, they are Macsen's people, your people. Would you see all that they are, die for ever? Would you let all the songs die for ever?'

As he spoke he started to play again, a song of home. Ursula could not prevent the tears from running silently down her own cheeks, but it was not Macsen's people that she cried for but her own: her mother and her classmates and the lost heart's ease of her own home.

~ Chapter Thirty-four ~

There was no one in the hut when Ursula woke. Bright beams of sunlight bored through the gaps between the wooden slats of the shuttered window and she could see silver dust motes whirling in the air. Instinct said it was late morning, later than she had ever slept since leaving home. She got up quietly and slipped out of the hut to go and bathe in the stream. It was hot and insects buzzed around the outbuilding where her horse, Braveheart and Frontalis's livestock had been housed for the night. She heard Taliesin and Frontalis arguing as they fed the chickens.

'You have to tell her. It is her choice not yours. What you are doing is wrong.'

The quavering voice was Brother Frontalis but his strength of feeling was clear.

Taliesin's response was low but his bard's voice carried his words to Ursula's ears: 'She doesn't understand. She just wants to go home. I have spoken to men who know about these things and I believe their prophecies, this world needs Arturus and the Combrogi and Arturus needs Ursula, perhaps more than he needed her at Baddon.'

'I don't doubt you, Taliesin, but you are not God. When will you learn to submit to his will, and not constantly try to force him into a corner? Ursula will choose what she will choose and you must let her.'

'Let me what?'

The two men looked up like guilty schoolboys at her voice.

'Good morning, Ursula.'

'What are you keeping from me Taliesin?'

Taliesin sighed and spoke reluctantly.

'It's Rhonwen, Ursula. She is prepared to raise the Veil. It's possible that you might be able to get home.'

'What!' It was so exactly what Ursula had hoped to hear that she was instantly suspicious. Surely, after all she had been through it couldn't be so simple?

'I don't understand, Taliesin, why would she do that?'

In spite of her argument with Dan, Ursula had not honestly expected Rhonwen to help her.

Taliesin rested his weight on a tree stump before answering her. 'She came to see me when she emerged from the Veil back in the autumn. The Battle of Baddon Hill had frightened her – the carnage was more than she could deal with. I don't know that she had realised how many men would die. She is a princess and she did not shirk her share of the responsibility. She'd given up the dress of a Heahrune and was very much Combrogi royalty again – demanding my aid. She had planned to go home see, back to Macsen's world, butI think whatever I did to twist the Veil to bring youhere has made it more difficult to leave. She can raise the Veil all right but she can't direct it – she never could, actually. She wanted me to help her. I said I would but … not yet. I really believe Arturus is *the Bear* of the prophecy and that I must help him.'

'And?' Ursula could not quite see the point.

'Rhonwen got angry. Her temper hasn't improved. She knew you had followed her. She said if I wouldn't help her, she was prepared to make her peace with you and ask your help to get home. I don't think she knows that you can no longer raise the Veil, as you once did. She thought you were pursuing her into the Veil to punish her for her attempt on your life. She still fears you as the sorceress you were in Macsen's world.'

Ursula was silent for a moment – wondering if that could be true, if Rhonwen could not sense the presence of magic in this world, as she herself could. Perhaps it was possible that she did not know the truth of Ursula's incapacity. After a while, Ursula said slowly, 'And knowing how much I wanted to go home you weren't going to tell me this?'

Taliesin looked away. 'I thought you cared about this

world – it is after all your own world too.'

'No you didn't, you thought I'd opt to go home.'

'And will you?'

She could not say no, not with Taliesin looking at her so intently, and she did not want to say yes. She said nothing and then asked, 'So where is Rhonwen?'

'I can take you to her.'

'As a merlin?'

Taliesin nodded. 'I have improved with much practice – I find it less tiring now. It is a long way – a two-day ride. We could make a start after breakfast.'

Ursula nodded, distractedly, and resumed her walk to the stream. She felt the eyes of the men on her as she walked. Rhonwen could be persuaded to help her get home or, at least, back to Macsen's world where she would have magic again. Her experience in the Veil this last time had convinced her that the power to manipulate the Veil had not entirely left her; she might, after all, actually be able to do as Rhonwen wanted. She shut her eyes as she washed in the cool stream. Her body thrilled at the never to be forgotten memory of the thrum of magic coursing through her again. She knew she had made her decision.

After Ursula had breakfasted on bread and goat's cheese and warm milk, she saddled her horse, accepted Frontalis's generous gift of food for the journey and followed Taliesin's darting merlin form. She said goodbye to Frontalis, uncertain whether she would ever see him again.

'Thank you, Brother Frontalis, for your hospitality and for standing up for me.'

Brother Frontalis turned wise eyes on her. 'Trust to God, Ursula, and obey your conscience. I know that you will do God's will. I will be praying for you.' He thrust a package at her and she was surprised to see that it contained the helmet, Arturus had given her. She accepted it gratefully and understood that he expected her to encounter trouble.

To her surprise she found that his words helped. They rang in her ears as she rode off, Braveheart trotting, panting by her side. It promised to be a hot, summer day and she rode in full armour. Under her helmet her hair was plastered to her head by sweat, which trickled down her face. It was not a comfortable ride. As soon as it grew too dark to continue she found a sheltered spot to eat, care for the animals and sleep. She slept lightly, trusting to the merlin, Braveheart, and her own instincts to keep her safe.

By late afternoon of the next day she was stiff and thoroughly tired of riding. When Ursula stopped to rest, the merlin watched her intently and somehow made her understand that caution was needed for the next stage of her journey. She watered her mount and hobbled it in a shady spot close to a brook. Having drunk their fill of the clean water both she and Braveheart set off more cautiously, following the merlin.

Braveheart smelled it first, the scent of habitation. He growled a low threat from the back of his throat. Ursula drew her sword and gripped Braveheart's collar with her left hand. She knew they were in enemy territory. The land opened up into tended fields and limited cover. Ursula was acutely aware that her armour glinted in the sun. She felt her heart begin to pump like a piston, and tightened her grip on both her sword and Braveheart. They could both be dead in the time it took to fire an arrow, hurl a spear or fire a stone from a slingshot. None of those things happened. As she got closer she could see that the village was ringed by a series of ditches and embankments bristling with sharpened stakes. There was no obvious way in. Keeping as low as possible, which, due to the size of Braveheart and her own sometimes inconvenient height, was not very low at all, she circled the village until she came to a guarded wooden bridge. Two young warriors stood on either side of the bridge, sweating under the weight of their helms. Ursula still did not speak a word of Aenglisc. She did the only thing she could think of and marched confidently up to the boys. They looked at each other in consternation.

'Rhonwen!' Ursula said. 'Heahrune, Rhonwen.'

One of the boys, unhooked a horn that was fastened to his belt and blew the alarm. Ursula stood her ground.

She had not yet been threatened. She had to hold Braveheart back and make him sit without snarling. The response to the horn was immediate; twenty-five heavily armed and bearded Aenglisc warriors emerged from nowhere. Ursula prayed that one of them spoke Latin.

One of them did – it was Gorlois Cerdic, Arturus's half-brother. She clearly recalled twisting his arm until her own ached with the strain the day Arturus was elected High King. Why had Taliesin not warned her? Ursula swore elaborately and inventively to herself while keeping her face impassive.

Cerdic stepped in front of her.

'Lady Ursa?' He spoke wonderingly, unable to take his eyes off her youthful face.

'Cerdic.' She nodded at him as if to confirm her own identity. She hoped her discomfort did not show. She saw him glance down at her hands that had so nearly strangled him and knew that in all the twenty-one years that had passed he had neither forgotten nor forgiven her for belittling him at Arturus's court.

There was a lot of muttering from the assembled men. She heard the word *Waelcryrige* more than once.

'My Aenglisc friends remember you from Baddon – they believe you are a Valkyrie, one whom their great god Woden has given the power to choose who should die on the battlefield. They do not think you very selective. You needn't fear them. They would not kill you – you are too connected with their wyrd, their destiny as warriors. The same cannot be said of me. You are just a young and interfering woman.' Cerdic had aged, but age had brought dignity and a certain gift for contempt. He all but spat out the last remark. He would have liked to have killed her. She had known that even when they had both served Arturus. She kept her voice as emotionless as her face.

'I came to talk with Rhonwen. She is here?'

'She sits in council with another of Arturus's women – Queen Gwynefa.'

It took a lot of self-control not to react to that. But Ursula did not show surprise by so much as a flicker of an eyebrow, nor did she loosen her grip on her sword.

'I have come here alone.'

'But for that hell hound.'

Ursula ignored him.

'I have come here alone to see Rhonwen. There is unfinished business between us. I served her brother. I would see her now.'

Cerdic seemed surprised at that, and in spite of his declared lack of belief in her supernatural powers, he was clearly deeply uncomfortable in her company. He turned to one of his companions and spoke rapidly to him in some Aenglisc language, sending him off with a message.

Ursula waited. While the sweat trickled down her chin, she did not move a muscle and did not take her eyes off Cerdic. He looked away first.

The companion returned and whispered something into Cerdic's ear.

Cerdic appeared displeased and said grudgingly, 'the Heahrune is prepared to see you in the Great Hall, Lady Ursa. We will resume our war council later.'

The men watched silently as Ursula walked forward as proudly and as confidently as she could, Braveheart at her heel. Her back prickled with perspiration and the awareness of many frightened eyes upon her. She walked through the village along a path of baked earth strewn with straw. The buildings were triangular with their steeply-pitched thatched roofs almost touching the ground. They smelled of goose fat and sour milk, bread and hops and charred wood. The Great Hall stood out as the only rectilinear building. The lintel of the door was decorated with runes and brightly painted pictures, but Ursula sensed no magic. She followed calmly in Cerdic's agitated steps.

There was no sign of the merlin, though she knew with a strange certainty that somewhere he watched her. If they killed her there would be a witness to let Dan know. It was not a comforting thought.

~ Chapter Thirty-five ~

Ursula noticed how the guards who waited outside the door of the Great Hall bowed to Cerdic and flinched away from her. If her allies had chosen to forget her, her enemies had not.

It was dark, dank, but pleasantly cool inside the hall after the blinding brightness of the summer daylight. Rhonwen sat at a plain wooden table in a pool of slatted sunlight and shadow. She was unchanged and while the distorted, shiny skin of her burnt cheek remained red and raw looking, the rest of her face remained unblemished and lovely. It took Ursula a moment longer to place the plump dark-haired woman next to Rhonwen. She was wearing some kind of moulded breastplate of archaic design, gilded and encrusted with coloured glass, and a highly decorated golden spangelhelm, from which her long black hair hung loose to her waist. She made a stunning, if extraordinary, figure. It was only when Ursula noticed her pale green, kohl-rimmed eyes that she recognised the parody of a warrior woman as Arturus's young wife, two decades on.

Cerdic stepped forward into the wide space between the door and the table.

'Well?'

'The Lady Ursa is here, Heahrune. We shall talk further of our plans when she is gone.'

'Let us be clear, Cerdic,' – Rhonwen was very much the Combrogi princess here, her new relationship with Medraut clearly entitled her to respect, and she had never taken kindly to being told what to do – 'I come with an offer of an alliance with Medraut. I have invited Gwynefa to discuss a further alliance with the High King's enemies. We will finalise an agreement now. I want the Lady Ursula to know how all her efforts to prop up Arturus, the Raven usurper will come, in the end, to nothing.'

Cerdic swallowed hard as if his pride or his anger stuck in his throat. Dan would have known which. Ursula struggled to guess at the nature of their relationship. Cerdic signalled for a serving woman to hand him a fine golden goblet of Roman design and ostentatiously drunk from it. Ursula guessed it was intended to serve as a small reminder to Rhonwen that Cerdic was as Roman as his brother Arturus. He waved his arm expansively and the two women were also furnished with drinks. Only then did he seat himself at the table.

Ursula remained standing. No one had yet divested her of her weapon. She had a suspicion that none of the Aenglisc would have dared try.

Cerdic signalled to another servant and a vellum map was spread across the wooden table.

'Ursula Alavna ab Helen.' Rhonwen used the title Ursula herself had used when she took Rhonwen's brother, King Macsen's oath. It was a blatant reminder of what they had in common. 'Come and see how Arturus will be crushed.'

Cerdic opened his mouth to say something but closed it again when Rhonwen flashed him a venomous look.

Ursula moved forward awkwardly, indicating for Braveheart to stay. She was surprised how little she wanted Arturus to be crushed at all. She had offered the man Dan's sword, Bright Killer, she had risked her life for his dream. He was King Arthur of legend even if he wasn't all she might have wished. Her residual loyalty surprised her. She moved forward and saw that the map was an old Roman one, of fine quality, showing all the Roman roads and forts, written in a good though fading hand. The more recent additions, the effective boundaries of Aenglisc occupation and the more recent names for places were less elegantly written but it was still a very good map.

Gwynefa spoke for the first time. 'Arturus recognises Medraut's threat. He is riding to Cado to mobilise the body of the troops – to reinforce the small force that remain in Camulodunum. He will use the Icknield Way – it is the only road suitable for Cataphracts.' Rhonwen sketched a line with her finger from Cerdic's own base, marked by a disproportionately large star, and the Icknield Way.

'It is Medraut's intention to ambush him here.' Rhonwen placed an imperious finger at a spot on the map. 'In the crooked valley.'

Gwynefa traced a further line from Caer-Baddon to the chosen valley. 'That will do,' she said quietly.

Rhonwen looked at the apparently older woman with her piercing emerald green look. Rhonwen had abandoned her mantle of skulls for something more conventionally regal, sewn with feathers and semi-precious stones. Even so, Gwynefa flinched from her intense gaze and made the sign of the cross, surreptitiously.

'I do not understand you, Queen Gwynefa and so I find it hard to trust you. Why do you choose to betray your husband? I have never heard that he beats you or mistreats you, only that he has failed to give you a child – but then your lover has not succeeded there either. Why do you want Arturus destroyed?'

Those present who understood Rhonwen's words winced at her bluntness, Gwynefa merely paled. Her voice was bleak, emotionless, without the bitterness Ursula would have expected.

'It is over for the Combrogi. Arturus still believes we can hold out against the invaders for ever. It is not so. We need a leader who will negotiate, who will compromise, who will preserve something of our ways. Arturus would see us dead in our beds before he'd shake an Aenglisc hand.'

The reason did not quite ring true for Ursula; it would not have motivated Ursula herself to such a massive betrayal, but Rhonwen appeared to be satisfied. She nodded and moved on.

'I, Rhonwen, speak for King Medraut. He and I, and our Aenglisc allies, will be there at the crooked valley in six days. That is the auspicious day on which the auguries predict our victory.'

Rhonwen turned to a tall, well-armed Aenglisc behind her. He was obviously her messenger as she slipped a large garnet ring from her finger and gave it to him. Ursula noticed that she was quietly instructing him in the wording of her message in a corrupt form of the language of the Trinovantes. Her servant, like Medraut and like Rhonwen, was Combrogi. That depressed her greatly. Here, just as in Macsen's time, Combrogi would kill Combrogi. When Rhonwen had finished giving her orders she returned abruptly to Cerdic and Gwynefa.

'I have business now with – what do you call her? – "the Lady Ursa". She has had too many names. If I do not return, rest assured that the outcome of this battle is secure. Written in the stars, carved in every rock, carried in the life-blood of every living thing. Arturus will die and Britannia, our Island of the Mighty, will be left for those who dare to forge a new alliance between its peoples.' Rhonwen's voice rang with the prophetic confidence of an Aenglisc Heahrune and Combrogi princess. Ursula shivered at the words; they sounded too much like truth to her.

'If you are in danger from this, this Valkyrie, I will send an escort.' Cerdic regarded Ursula with both dislike and suspicion.

Rhonwen dismissed his concerns with a casual flick of her jewelled hand.

'Lady Ursa will not harm me. We have a common goal. I hope you find what you are looking for, Cerdic. You, too, Queen Gwynefa. Do not worry, Cerdic, the Lady Ursa will not betray your plans – the outcome is certain. Arturus will die.'

With that, Rhonwen bowed graciously and swept from the Great Hall. Ursula followed her, not daring to look at Cerdic and Gwynefa. Rhonwen did not turn to check that Ursula followed, but strode purposefully past the guards, through the village and over the bridge into the meadow beyond.

Ursula did not know what to think. This Rhonwen was so unlike the screaming witch she had last seen at Baddon Hill, it was hard to grasp the change, harder still to interpret it. Was she still in danger from this woman? Then she remembered. Rhonwen did not know that she no longer commanded the magic.

'Are you ready?' Rhonwen's question was both abrupt and incomprehensible. She fixed Ursula with unreadable emerald eyes. Ursula would have liked to have known what emotion Rhonwen was projecting. Should she trust a woman who hated her?

'Ready for what?' Ursula asked.

'For me to raise the Veil. Surely that is why you have come? I assume you spoke to Taliesin.' She managed to squeeze venomous dislike into the four syllables of his name.

'I don't know,' Ursula said flatly. 'I don't understand why you should want to go – you didn't before.'

'I didn't want to do what Taliesin wanted.' Rhonwen tossed her head. 'A princess is not to be brought back through the Veil by a bard, like some errant puppy. I have been a Heahrune here and consort to a king. I have made my mark on the world. I have proved that I could win without Macsen. Now I want to go home. Now it is my choice, on my terms. I want to see the hills of home again, speak my own language, see Macsen – isn't that enough?'

Ursula had to admit that it was.

'Why do you hate Arturus?' Ursula had never understood that.

'He is a Raven. He fights the Raven way. He seeks to remake the Combrogi in the Raven image. They no longer hear the Goddess. We Combrogi have more in common with the Aenglisc than with the Ravens: I will not make a common cause with Ravens. Why Taliesin thinks Arturus is keeping the Combrogi alive I do not understand. The man is no Macsen.' With that, too, Ursula had little quarrel. This was not the way things should be with Rhonwen. Rhonwen was not reasonable.

'It seems wrong that Gwynefa should betray Arturus,' Ursula said thoughtfully.

'Gwynefa? Oh, she just longs for death – it's in her eyes. She's just going to take them all down with her – a tortured soul, Gwynefa.'

She said the last matter of factly, without noticeable compassion.

'And you?' Ursula was intrigued. What was going on inside the head of this woman she had so long regarded as her enemy?

Rhonwen's eyes were as cold and clear and hard as the emeralds their colour resembled.

She spoke softly. 'I am not your friend, Ursula. I pulled you from your world and you have repaid me for that first unkindness many times over.' Honesty obliged her to add, quickly, 'Oh, I know you saved me once, back home when the Ravens took me and I have repaid that debt.'

Ursula nodded. She had always suspected that it was Rhonwen who had called to her and helped her return to her senses after she had shape-shifted into an eagle, back at Macsen's fortress – she did not know how long ago.

Rhonwen continued. 'Have no illusions about me. I don't like you, I would have killed you – would have made you pay for the times you've belittled me. However, one thing a Combrogi princess learns early is that life is compromise. I need you, that is all, if you can tell me how to get home.'

Ursula thought hard and tried to describe the indescribable. Manipulating the Veil was to do with the will and with belief and power. She was sure that even without magic, once inside the Veil she would find the knack again, but to describe it was an impossibility.

'It's how you let the power flow – I don't have the words. I would have to show you.'

'Then you'd better show me or the Goddess alone knows where we'll end up.'

Rhonwen knelt to raise the Veil. She had already prepared herself for the task. A dead chicken had already been laid out on the earth as the blood sacrifice; it had not been necessary after the battle of Baddon when the earth was gorged with blood. Rhonwen began to sway and chant and Ursula suddenly panicked.

'Not now? I can't go now!'

'Why else are you here?'

'To talk about it!' Ursula knew it was a lame answer but she could not think with Rhonwen's magic calling to her as it built, pulling at her, weakening her resolve. She wanted the magic, wanted it more than anything, maybe more even than she wanted to go home. The unnatural dirty yellow mist began to form like smoke from an unseen fire as Rhonwen's power called the Veil into being.

'God, no! I cannot go now. Not without Dan. I promised!'

Ursula turned and, checking that Braveheart was at her heels, ran for the trees, her horse, and the means to put miles between her and the terrible, unearthly, seductive call of the Veil.

~ Chapter Thirty-six ~

Bryn disappeared from Larcius's hall late in the evening of Arturus's first night at Caer-Baddon. Without the situation ever being properly discussed, both Dan and Bryn had assumed that they would leave with Arturus in the morning, and Bryn had his whole life to rearrange. Dan sat uncomfortably while Larcius and the High King discussed strategy. Arturus was determined to put an end to the threat from Medraut in the east as soon as possible. It seemed that Rhonwen's re-emergence from the mist had been the catalyst necessary to turn Medraut from a political adversary, to a full-blown enemy. Dan listened with growing dread as they discussed the detail of troop movements. Something was wrong.

Arturus was intending to move his troops from Cado along the Icknield Way to reinforce his base at Camulodunum and then to march on Medraut's stronghold at Dumnoc. Larcius would meet him at the border between his land and that of Arturus's ally, King Dewi who ruled that land around the former Roman city of Calleva Atrebatum, as it was marked on Arturus's map. They would mobilise at once.

Dan was not interested in the minutiae of rations and camp sites, though it seemed to him that the whole business was even more complex than it had been when they had marched to the fortress at Baddon Hill. The Icknield Way bisected many territories, and safe passages for even the High King's troops had to be negotiated with the rulers of each and every territory. The number of small kingdoms had proliferated over the years and although the High King had a right to levy men and provisions from each of the client kingdoms the process was by no means straightforward. The High Kingship was maintained only by a complex balance of debts and favours, and an assault on Medraut, the former Count of the Saxon Shore, related by blood to many of Arturus's allies, was no mean enterprise. It was obvious to Dan that Arturus had been engaged in preparations for months and that most of the agreements and arrangements had already been made. Arturus's political skills must have improved over the years to hold the many disparate rulers and interest groups together. This ought to have reassured Dan that Arturus knew what he was doing and yet it did not. He could not ignore his own unease. Larcius was difficult, his mood unpredictable. His dominant emotion was one of shame. Dan could not work it out and went to his bed that night disturbed and fearful.

That night he dreamed of death. He saw heaped corpses rotting in the hot sun, skies swarming with fat flies and the recurring vision of a figure with pale blonde hair, who both *was* and *was not* Arturus, being hewn down again and again by mounted men. The scream of the almost-Arturus reverberated through the nightmare. As each blow fell, he screamed out, 'Dan!' while a merlin falcon hovered overhead.

It was a relief when dawn broke and Dan rode with Bryn in the first rank of Arturus's company towards Fort Cado. Bryn was quiet, his feelings muted. He appeared to Dan to feel surprisingly little regret for the position he left behind. Dan found it difficult to adjust to Bryn's changed status. The boy he had known just days before was now older than he was. It was hard to know how to begin again. Dan encouraged Bryn to talk of the intervening years to fill up the awkward silences between them. It helped break the monotony of the journey and distracted Dan from worrying too obsessively about Ursula. Dan prayed she would be safe. He could do nothing else.

They rode hard and arrived at Arturus's military stronghold at dusk. Fort Cado was far from being the Roman castle Dan had expected. It was a Celtic hill fort in which the broad, flat top of the hill had been entirely enclosed by a huge wooden palisade. Within that defensive circle a whole Combrogi village was laid out with dedicated blacksmiths, farriers, potters, weavers, leather workers, and stabling for several hundred horses. Everyone but Dan and Bryn knew where to go. They dismounted, rather overawed by the military efficiency. Grooms took away their horses, and they were led to Aturus's hall.

Dan's nagging concern that there was something very wrong darkened and deepened to conviction. He could feel it as soon as he walked into the Great Hall. Gwynefa had not yet arrived. Arturus was desperate. He was afraid that she had been taken by the Aenglisc for ransom, or worse. None of her bodyguard had returned either and there was no hint as to what might have become of her. Arturus's confessor, a pale, young man dressed in monk's robes hovered behind him intoning prayers for Gwynefa's soul, while Arturus cursed uncharacteristically and ordered someone to send for Taliesin. Bryn sat very still and watched and waited as he had obviously learned to do with the volatile Larcius. Dan's concern for Ursula grew. If Gwynefa with her coterie of well-armed body-guards could be taken then Ursula could be in trouble too. Perhaps he should have taken more notice of Larcius's concerns. Dan could not find Ursula's thoughts. Though he tried, he could sense nothing beyond Arturus's complex distraction, a hard to disentangle combination of worry, guilt and fear. Arturus's cool exterior hid passions on a massive scale. Dan felt the terrible sense of oppression, which had afflicted him so badly after Baddon. He was no better equipped to deal with it now than he had been then.

Ursula ran, all but blindly. She would have closed her eyes and stopped her ears if it would have reduced her awareness of the magic, but nothing did that. Braveheart led her to her horse. She patted his rough head and with her chest still heaving with the effort of running and breathing and doing the opposite of that she most desired, she freed her mount and rode, back the way she'd come, as if the devil were at her heels.

No magical apparition followed her. Maybe Rhonwen dared not use the power, or maybe she had entered the Veil alone. Ursula needed no retribution from Rhonwen, she could not feel worse than she already did. She had ridden away from the magic. She felt insane with the need to feel the magic again. She could taste the magic on her tongue. It buzzed as if she had bitten chilli peppers or sucked on cloves. She began to tremble convulsively. She spurred the horse on until her nerves no longer jangled and she could simply sob at her loss. If only Dan had been with her – they both could have gone home. Braveheart whined in distress when she cried. She had never known him do that before but she stopped because he sounded so pitiful. What did she do now?

Slowly, as her wild grief subsided, she began to think again. She had to find Dan and warn Arturus. She rode listlessly, bearing west, searching for some landmark that she might recognise. In the end it was Taliesin who found her. His merlin form soared above her several times before settling high in the topmost branches of a distant tree and cleaning his feathers. It seemed a self-satisfied gesture to her. Fighting her irritation with Taliesin, and indeed the whole world, she turned her mount to follow the brown speck that was all she could see of the falcon as he winged his way, far ahead of her into the setting sun.

That night she didn't sleep at all but, when she didn't dream of murderous Aenglisc, her night was haunted by images of the Veil and all it meant to her. By the second day of her journey she was tired and irritable and by the time she was discovered in late evening by a group of Arturus's men searching for Queen Gwynefa, she was in no mood to be toyed with. An officious looking Sarmatian wished to arrest her but Braveheart bared his teeth and Ursula drew her sword.

'Listen, I fought with your father and all your uncles at Baddon. Don't you dare touch me – or my dog. If you are returning to the High King Arturus I will ride with you, but you really wouldn't like to take me on in a fight.'

Ursula saw by the man's reaction that he believed her. She probably looked half crazed. She certainly felt it. She did not add that she knew where the Queen was. It did not seem politic to reveal the extent of Gwynefa's perfidy until she had informed Arturus himself. She hoped he would not feel inclined to shoot the messenger who bore such bad news.

Later, when the light faded she felt better disposed towards the Sarmatian. It was too dark to follow the merlin falcon, who had loyally remained in sight, and without the torches of the search party she would have been hopelessly lost. Unfortunately, even though the Sarmatian knew where he was going Ursula still felt hopelessly lost. Rhonwen would never help them now and she was stuck until death in this time that was not her own. In the darkness, hot, bitter tears rolled down her cheeks unchecked. Bloody Dan. It was, after all, his fault.

~ Chapter Thirty-seven ~

The atmosphere in the Great Hall was very tense when Ursula was finally ushered in front of Arturus. Gwynefa had been missing for four fraught days. Braveheart, lightly restrained by Ursula's hand on his collar, launched himself first at Dan and then Bryn.

'*Ursula, you're safe!*' Dan's voice in Ursula's mind rang with relief.

'*Dan, we could have gone home. Rhonwen would have raised the Veil. I could have got us home. Why didn't you come with me?*' Dan could hear her distress, her frustration and the tremulous emotional aftershock of her close contact with magic. What could he say?

'Lady Ursa.' Arturus got at once to his feet.

'Your Highness.' Ursula barely bowed her head. She had not forgiven him.

She was uncomfortable, though only Dan, knowing her so well, could read the subtle signs, the tense way she gripped the hilt of her sword. For some reason she had not been disarmed.

'I have news of Gwynefa, but I would prefer to speak to you alone.'

Foolishly, Arturus spoke chivalrously. 'I cannot imagine that you might have any news of my wife that could not be aired in public.'

Dan watched Ursula discreetly readjust her weight to be ready for trouble and take a deep breath. From the corner of his eye he noticed Bryn perform a similar manoeuvre. A number of servants and men at arms present in the Great Hall chose that moment to look away. That should have told Arturus something but he seemed impervious to it all. It was clear to Dan that Gwynefa's indiscretions were common knowledge.

'I went to talk to the Aenglisc Heahrune, the Princess Rhonwen. She alone has the power to return Dan and myself to our proper place. I found Rhonwen in Cerdic's stronghold where she was holding war council on Medraut's behalf with Cerdic and with …' She visibly steeled herself. 'With Queen Gwynefa.'

'You lie! Guards, seize that troublemaker!'

As two men approached Ursula she unsheathed her sword and they backed away, and Gwynefa chose that precise moment to make an entrance. She was still splendidly dressed in her gilded, jewelled armour. Dan thought she looked ridiculous, like some aging opera singer trying to look like a warrior queen. Ursula looked at her in consternation and surprise. No one else seemed to know what to do.

'Gwyn!' Arturus caught himself, before he rushed to her side. Feeling the waves of love and relief that emanated from the High King, Dan was horribly aware that Ursula was unlikely to be believed. His hand unconsciously found his own sword while he found his eyes drawn to his much superior surrendered blade at Arturus's hip.

'She has besmirched my honour.' Gwynefa said melodramatically. 'Arturus, will you do nothing?'

Arturus gave Ursula his coldest most calculating glance.

'And what would you have me do with our finest fighter on the day before we march to battle?' Arturus's tone was reasonable.

'Someone must fight her. Someone must champion my honour.' Dan wondered if Gwynefa had forgotten who Ursula was. She had bested everyone she fought against prior to the Battle of Baddon Hill

'I choose him.' Gwynefa's glittering, wild eyes picked out Dan.

Dan got to his feet.

'Queen Gwynefa, I regret to say that I cannot be your champion.'

'Arturus, make him!'

'Gwyn, you may have forgotten Gawain. He does not fight.'

'He fought the Aenglisc at Camulodunum – I've forgotten nothing. And he fought Gorlois Cerdic. What kind of fool do you take me for?'

Dan felt everyone's eyes on him. He felt their excitement building.

'Let's give them a show, Dan. Stop at first blood.'

He realised then that Ursula wanted to know; could she be as good as the former Bear Sark? She still felt she had something to prove to him, and he to her.

Dan stood up. Arturus threw him his sword, Caliburn that was once Bright Killer, and Dan caught it easily. It was good to hold it in his hand again. It had melded to the shape of his hand, through Ursula's magic, back in Macsen's land. He was horrified at how suddenly complete holding it still made him feel.

Bryn called Braveheart to his side. Dan had removed his helm some time ago. Ursula removed hers so that her damp hair fell to her shoulders, dark with perspiration. He could feel her sudden excitement, her exhilaration. She had too much frustrated energy to unleash. She needed this.

She attacked, he parried. She was frighteningly strong. His sword arm felt the impact of the blow at his shoulder. He attacked, switching hands to confuse her, but she met every attempt to get past her guard. She was quicker than he remembered. He could feel how good it felt to her, the pleasure she took in her strength, and in her speed. She saw herself as a lioness swift and powerful. Her back ached a little from the ride. She was saddle sore, and lightly bruised, but shifting her weight to thrust her sword forward, it did not matter to her. A part of Dan was becoming alarmed, not only did he begin to feel what she was feeling, he began to know what she would do a moment before she did it. All Arturus's court, his servants and his guards had gathered round the combatants. They began to shout and stamp, even Arturus yelled for his wife's champion. Dan noticed the rumpus peripherally.

'Get out of my head, Dan!'

'Can't!'

It was true he couldn't. Dan had the terrifying sensation of becoming Ursula, while at the same time being himself. Because of the closeness of their connection and their strange experience in helping Taliesin, the fusion happened suddenly, startlingly, completely. Dan no longer knew whose body he controlled. He seemed to see out of two pairs of eyes at once and had no way of processing that vision so that it made sense. The bodies still moved, under whose volition? He felt impact and was afraid; they were going to get hurt.

'We have to stop this, I don't like it!'

He did not know which one of them spoke, or if it

was both screaming mentally with one accord. Dan's body backed away and Ursula's did the same. He bowed and heard himself say in a voice that seemed a long way away.

'If Queen Gwynefa is satisfied, I believe we should call this a draw.'

He felt his own hand on the distorted shape of a sword hilt and knew that he was himself. It took a moment for his equilibrium to be restored. A quick glance in Ursula's direction showed him only that she was breathing heavily. Dan looked round to bow to the Queen and realised, at the same moment as everyone else, that Queen Gwynefa was gone.

Ursula sheathed her sword. She looked unperturbed by their strange experience. It was a gift for coolness that Dan envied.

Bryn spoke. 'I fear the Queen was not so confident of her innocence that she could wait for Gawain to prove it.'

There was a horrible silence. Arturus had gone very pale.

'Secure the gates and let no one out!' His voice was cracked with strain. Men hurried to obey him. It was too late.

Gwynefa had planned it well. As she arrived and generated the diversion, three hundred Sarmatian

Cataphracts, her dowry troops, had left the fortress along with a sizeable proportion of Arturus's campaign supplies, neatly stowed in barrels and crates. She was a princess of Rheged, daughter to Meirchion Gul, and the sons of Cynfach's Cataphracts were men of Rheged first, descendents of the Sarmatians second, and troops of the High King third. It was a bitter blow.

Arturus gathered the remaining men – somewhat less than two hundred, thanked them for their loyalty and instructed them that they would march the next day. Gwynefa had taken few of the officers with her, few of the veterans. She had persuaded young men to join her, men dissatisfied with the slow pace of promotion in the unit. A roll call quickly established that she must have made officers of untried boys. Arturus brightened a little at that. He had hopes that if they could link with Larcius's light cavalry they could defeat the deserters before they could join with Medraut's force. He was further cheered by the arrival of Taliesin and Brother Frontalis. Brother Frontalis was too weak to ride but Taliesin had persuaded the brothers of Frontalis's order to lend them their cart so that Frontalis might go and serve his king for one last time. Arturus's eyes were damp with tears when he saw the old man, indeed Arturus's carefully controlled emotions were threatening to overwhelm both himself and Dan. Brother Frontalis was helped inside Arturus's private chamber in a small rudely screened room to the back of the Main Hall. Arturus sent for food.

Taliesin helped Brother Frontalis drink his wine, his hands trembled from the stress of the journey and he looked weary. Dan tried not to feel the pain in Frontalis's joints, his sorrow at seeing the distress of Arturus, his hope that he might live long enough to help. He spoke wheezily.

'Taliesin saw Gwynefa heading towards Gewisse. That's Cerdic's kingdom,' he added for the benefit of Ursula and Dan. 'I thought you might want to talk to an old friend.' Arturus clasped the old man's bony hands and kissed them.

'Brother Frontalis. What have I done to her? I knew she did not love me but I did not think she hated me.'

Brother Frontalis shook his head. 'We will talk of these things later, in private. For now, you have more pressing concerns. We must talk about how you can deal with the threat of Cerdic and Larcius.'

'Larcius?'

There was a strained silence. Could Arturus truly not know that Gwynefa and Larcius had been lovers for the best part of twenty years? Or had he simply assumed that she was capable of acting alone?

Frontalis's voice was gentle, so soft suddenly that everyone strained to hear it.

'My dear friend, I think it is time you faced what you

have denied for years. This last betrayal of Gwynefa's is but the last of many. She will join her lover and he will abandon you.'

No one dared breath.

To Dan's surprise Arturus's overriding emotion was one of relief as he turned to Taliesin for the first time. 'Well, my merlin, what are the forces arraigned against us? Can we win?'

Taliesin slowly shook his head. 'You cannot ignore them either. Now that they have shown their opposition they cannot but move against you.'

Ursula spoke. 'I was going to tell you – before. They intend to ambush you in the crooked valley off the Icknield Way.'

There was another long pause, as if Arturus was considering their words. With so many factions against him, he could not stay where he was – he had no choice about war – he could only choose to fight now or to fight later. Everyone in the Hall had ceased breathing, waiting. All eyes were on the High King when he finally spoke.

'Then we must hurry to this crooked valley, I know it well, *Camlann*.' He rolled his tongue round the word and smiled. 'So that's where it will end, at Camlann.' The smile died. 'Let us find a way to ensure that we will not die alone.'

~ *Chapter Thirty-eight* ~

Arturus knew the valley of Camlann. Ursula discovered that Arturus knew a lot about a lot, everything it seemed to do with war, his men, his horses, his weapons – in that at least he was the Arthur of legend. She listened while Arturus and Taliesin talked tactics.

'Would Rhonwen have known that you would come to me with what you'd heard?' Arturus's sudden question startled Ursula – she had ceased to listen to the detail of the conversation.

'Where else would I go?'

'Where would *she* go?' Arturus demanded, very much the High King.

'I don't know, she may have raised the Veil.' Ursula knew it was childish but her voice was truculent. She was on Arturus's side but she didn't have to like it.

Taliesin was shaking his head. 'I don't think she'd raise the Veil without Ursula or even me to guide it. You forget that the last time she tried to leave your world she was unsuccessful. That's why she wanted help – she cannot direct the Veil alone and that is risky.'

'She would have gone to Medraut then?' Arturus said gravely.

'And even if she did not, I know she sent him news of her meeting with Gwynefa.' Ursula added quickly. It was a detail she had almost forgotten.

Arturus scowled, though whether at her omission of his Queen's title or at the memory of her betrayal Ursula couldn't say. When he spoke his voice sounded bitter. 'Medraut is a good leader – he knows how I think. He knows what I would do were I to expect an ambush. If Rhonwen left Gewisse today, how would she get to Camlann?' He drummed his fingers on the table thoughtfully. 'Merlin – any ideas? If we don't delay Rhonwen and her messenger we're in trouble. We have a chance *only* if no one knows I will be expecting an ambush.'

Brother Frontalis spoke unexpectedly. Everyone had thought he was asleep. 'The brothers of my order, especially Brother Paulinus, would love to try and convert the Heahrune of the Aenglisc.' He smiled. 'They would not be able to hold her for long, sorceress that she is, but they could surely delay her so that she would arrive too late for Medraut to change his battle plans. If only we could get a message to the brothers.'

'How would they know where to find her, and wouldn't they be terrified of her magic?' Ursula had seen the effect Rhonwen's illusions had on brave fighting men, she was doubtful that monks would be any less terrified.

'The brothers would consider it a blessing to walk through hell to save her soul. They would regard it as a test of faith. They wouldn't fail it.' Frontalis squinted at the map, putting his eyes no more than a centimetre from the vellum.

'If I were an Aenglisc Heahrune I would travel as much as possible in Aenglisc territory. Cerdic's land ends here.' He pointed to a spot on the map. 'She would need to camp overnight. Now, she could either stay the night here, which would give her a long ride tomorrow, or here.' He pointed to another position. 'There is an old Roman villa there, disused, but with a sound roof, still solid walls and a working well in the grounds. It is often used by travellers. It is only a short ride from our chapel – we used some of the villa's stone in the building of it. If I were a betting man – as I'm sure you know I was in my youth, I would bet my old cloak against the King's mantle that she is there even as we speak.'

Arturus grinned and raised a hand in acknowledgement of the bet.

'Done!' he said, and Ursula glimpsed some other less serious man, an Arturus she had never known.

Ursula thought that Frontalis was probably right about Rhonwen and said, 'It's a pity you have no homing pigeons.'

'What?' Arturus asked.

'Pigeons always find their way home – you take them somewhere and tie written messages to their feet and they will take them back to where they came from.'

'Say that again.' Arturus suddenly looked calculating.

'Pigeons always find their way home?'

'No, the message part.'

'You tie the written message to their feet?'

'Merlin?'

'It might be possible, but I haven't unlimited strength and you're going to need me to reconnoitre the battle scene.'

Arturus considered this.

'Gawain, can you not also take on a bird form?'

'I didn't think it was real enough to take a message. I thought it was just a, you know, an imaginary thing.'

Taliesin sighed dramatically. 'I'll do it then, and if I have no strength left, Gawain will have to observe the battle scene.'

'Could you carry my cross too, so that Paulinus will know it is not the devil's work?'

'I'm a bloody bird not a weight lifter,' grumbled Taliesin.

Brother Frontalis wrote something in a large and spidery hand on a small square of precious parchment. He rolled it up, tied it with the leather thong attached to his wooden crucifix, and pressed it into Taliesin's hands. Taliesin grunted and lay down in front of the fire. In moments, his facial muscles loosened into something more than the relaxation of sleep, a kind of slackness, an absence, like death. It was a disconcerting sight. Ursula saw a fleeting, flickering vision of the merlin falcon, then it was gone.'

'This doesn't make any sense,' Dan mumbled, 'the note and the cross are still here. How can it be in two places at once?'

Ursula gave him an amused look. 'What does make sense in this whole situation? I'd like to know, because I can't think of one thing.'

He smiled back and for some reason Ursula wanted to kiss him again, wanted to be close to him. They were probably going to die at Camlann.The awareness of that possibility was fast becoming a doomed belief in its probability. She had only just got away with her life at Baddon – surely her luck had to have run out this time. She did not want to be alone. She edged closer to Dan and slipped her hand into his.

'Why?' He seemed surprised at the sudden intimacy.

'You're the best friend I've ever had, Dan. Do you know that?'

'I've never been so close with anyone – and that sharing thoughts closeness—'

'Dan …'

Ursula didn't finish. It was neither the time nor the

place to say what she wanted to say. Arturus was talking to her, to all of them.

'I'm going to talk to the men. I suggest you all bed down here. We will eat on the march, leaving here at dawn.'

'King Arturus.'

'Lady Ursa.'

'There is one other thing. Cerdic knows I saw the battle plans and so does Gwynefa.'

Arturus's face was suddenly sad. 'Cerdic will not share information with his allies, he will wait to see the outcome of the battle before he commits his troops – I know my half-brother of old. As for Gwynefa – I do not know her at all it seems.'

Then Ursula realised that despite all the evidence he had against his wife, Arturus did not believe that she and Larcius would truly betray him.

'But—'

'Gwynefa believes in heroic gestures, not good planning – she believes that battle goes to the bold. She is not a stupid woman but it is quite possible that she would not think your knowledge important. No, Medraut is the important one – if we can keep our knowledge from him then we have a chance.'

Ursula wished she could believe him, but his words lacked the conviction of Rhonwen's: 'If I do not return, rest assured that the outcome of this battle is secure.

Written in the stars, carved in every rock, carried in the life-blood of every living thing. Arturus will die and Britannia, our Island of the Mighty, will be left for those who dare to forge a new alliance between its peoples.'

It was those words and not Arturus's, that ran through Ursula's mind all night, turning her dreams to nightmares.

In the morning Taliesin's merlin was back. Taliesin was groggy but elated.

'It worked! Frontalis was right. They found her and her messenger and put them both in a cell with Brother Paulinus. I do not know who I feel more sorry for!'

Arturus, grey with fatigue, smiled wanly. 'That will give us a chance. My thanks, Merlin.' He looked around at the sleep-wrinkled faces of Dan and Ursula, the quiet readiness of Bryn, and the red, rheumy eyes of Brother Frontalis. Solemnly he and Frontalis swapped cloaks.

'I should have known better than to bet against you, old friend!' Arturus smiled then said softly, 'Let's go. We have a long ride ahead.'

It was a long ride – three days of discomfort with the dust from the horses' feet blowing in Ursula's eyes, and the bulk and the weight of the chain mail making the horses lather. They took frequent breaks to water themselves and the horses. What was tough on cavalry must have been tougher still on infantry, weighed down with spears and shields and their toughened leather cuirasses and felt-lined helmets. Ursula had little sympathy to share. She was too busy trying not to be afraid. Experience of battle made her fear worse not better. She knew how close she had come to being hacked to death at Baddon. The odds against them at Camlann were bound to be worse. Dan rode at her side, all too aware, she knew, of the emotions boiling all round him. She spoke little so as not to distract him from the task of dealing with them. It was a relief when each night they set up camp. Arturus persisted in the old Roman ways, defences were dug, tents aligned in good order and everyone was fed with prompt efficiency. It was much as it had been on their journey to Baddon and Ursula felt as she had then that Arturus was firmly in control. She knew that the ability to promote such confidence was important.

'Larcius is not going to join us, is he?' Ursula's sharp ears caught Arturus's muttered aside to Taliesin as the senior officers met at Arturus's tent for a briefing. She, Dan and Bryn were included in this elite. She was pleased to see an older wiser Bedewyr also included in this group. Ursula waited in trepidation to hear what impossible task she would be given this time.

Taliesin patted Arturus briefly on the shoulder. 'I'm sorry, but Larcius has never been worthy of the trust you placed in him, Arturus. He is not his father, your beloved Ambrosius, and was never going to be.'

The first watch on picket duty raised the alarm and Arturus with a small coterie of his leading officers hurried to the defences. Ursula saw a brief flicker of hope in Arturus's eyes but it died when he realised that the newcomer was not Larcius but King Dewi's son Prince Mordaf and seventy infantrymen to swell the ranks of Arturus's men.

'That's good, isn't it?' Ursula asked Taliesin as the High King gave them cautious welcome.

'King Dewi is busily hedging his bets. My guess is that Larcius camped on his land last night. Dewi wants to be on the winning side and he will choose it only when it's won.'

'Do you think Larcius will betray Arturus?' She glanced at Bryn who answered before Taliesin had a chance.

'He has betrayed him with Gwynefa for twenty years. He will have left for Camlann already. I am sure of it. He is the High King Ambrosius's son and he believes he should have been High King and that Gwynefa should always have been his. As far as he is concerned Arturus stole his birthright. He does not betray Arturus, he only reclaims what he believes is his own.'

Bryn's speech, long for him, was made without rancour.

'There, you've heard it more or less from the horse's mouth,' said Taliesin. 'It is good to see you again, Bryn. Still practising I trust.'

Bryn grinned. 'I practise with my sword daily, Taliesin, with my harp only when my son was a babe and I sang him to sleep in his crib.'

'Is little Gwyar safe?'

Bryn nodded. 'He is with people I trust. I have left him well enough provided for – if I do not come back.'

Taliesin smiled. 'You will come back, Bryn. Rest assured of it.'

Arturus was cagey about his strategy, preferring not to commit himself until dawn when Dan would be able to see the placement of the enemy's troops from the air. Dan was busily discussing with Taliesin and Arturus how to go about studying the enemy positions. Bryn was with Brother Frontalis, praying along with many of the men in one of the tents that had been painted with the sign of the cross. Ursula felt too shy to join them, though she knew she would have been welcome. Instead, she sat by the fire, stroking Braveheart's rough head and praying in her own way, for survival, for victory and for some miracle that would get her home.

~ *Chapter Thirty-nine* ~

Dan woke when it was still dark. He'd had the dream again: of death, heaped corpses and the figure with the pale blonde hair, who both was and was not Arturus hewn down by mounted men. His heart was thumping and he was drenched in sweat. The memory of where he was and what he was doing there only returned to him in small fragments. It was several hundred rapid heart-beats before he had the whole picture. He remembered then: Arturus was expecting him to somehow project his consciousness into some imaginary bird in order to view the layout of the battle scene. It still seemed mad to him and, even though he'd done it before, impossible.

He got up and stretched. Ursula lay outside, wrapped in a travelling cloak. In the firelight her hair looked pink. Her mouth was slightly open and she snored lightly. He fought the urge to kiss her, to hold her as if she was some sleeping princess in a fairytale. Perhaps that would break the spell and they could both wake up and find this whole doomed enterprise a dream. It wasn't, of course. He ached from riding; he itched where insects had bitten him in the night. He was hungry and he needed to find the latrine.

All round, Dan could sense the muted fears of dreaming men and the less muted fears of those who could not sleep. Birds sang. It was almost time.

Arturus was at the defensive trench, sharpening Caliburn on a small piece of whetstone. It was still too dark to see his features clearly but Dan knew he, too, was afraid.

'Are you ready?' Arturus did not whisper and his voice sounded too loud and harsh.

Dan nodded. His mouth was dry. 'I'll get Taliesin. I'd like him with me.'

They walked towards Taliesin's tent together.

'Do you know what you will do?' Dan asked.

'I have a plan in mind – I need to be sure that Medraut has done what I expect him to. It isn't hopeless – far from it. We can win, but, I've been thinking – about you and the Lady Ursa. If it's a rout, go! Try to get home. This is not your place. Even if we win I fear I have failed. I thought I could bring back the stability of Roman rule – but we Combrogi are not Roman, don't want to be Roman. I know that now.' Arturus sighed and Dan felt his searing sense of disappointment, the pain that betrayal had caused him. Arturus kicked a loose clod of earth.

'It was all for nothing. I've fought for unity for thirty

years and the only time my dearest friends and brother make an alliance, it is against me.' He shook his bowed head in disbelief. 'I had such hope after Baddon – Aelle turned his ships back, you knew? I wonder if I had done things differently could I have got rid of the Aenglisc for good?' Arturus looked directly at Dan, daring him to contradict. 'I will fight, Gawain, but it is with a very heavy heart.'

'You are known even in my time as a great king, Arturus. You will be remembered for a thousand years and more for what you did here.'

Dan hated to feel the distress of this man, the real, unheroic, ruthless, pragmatic, High King Arturus. Dan had never respected him more. Truth was more complicated than myth but over the years Arturus had become a man to honour.

Arturus smiled. 'Taliesin tried to tell me about time, though I'm sure I never grasped it. Tell me, if you know my story – how does it end?'

Dan blanched.

'As I thought, it's how they all end isn't it?' Arturus sheathed his sword, Dan's sword. 'Let's find Taliesin and Frontalis. If I'm to die I will not die unshriven.'

There was no wind, no sensation at all, just the bird's-eye view and the vertigo of flight. Taliesin had told him what to look for, flying east into the rising sun. A flash of something metallic caught his eye. He'd found them. Arturus's enemies. He saw the glint of a gilded helmet straight below where the arrow-straight Roman road crossed the crooked valley. He looked closer and saw more. There were hundreds of them, massed in three separate blocks, hidden by the unusual terrain. He remembered Taliesin's advice and tried to fix their exact formations in his mind.

The crooked valley was formed by three hills, two to the north of the road, one larger hill to the south. The road, formed with Roman singleness of purpose ran in a broadly west–east direction. The valley floor, on the other hand, formed a channel that twisted north then widened into a broad, flat, triangular plain before narrowing to a smaller passageway and turning back towards the south. A large band of light cavalry formed a disciplined block in the apex of the triangular plain, where the two northern hills met. That would be Larcius. His men were not heavily armoured and their horses wore no armour at all but they were light, fast, manoeuvrable and well trained, the Roman way. Dan realised that from the ground they would be hidden by the curve of the nearest hill. Opposite them, halfway up the gentle slope of the largest of the three hills, Gwynefa's Cataphracts were jockeying for position to find shelter under the limited tree cover. Dan could see flashes of their red-lacquered scale armour, like bright birds among the trees. The more he looked the more he saw, like counting stars in the night.

He flew further towards the eastern end of the valley. Medraut's infantry, two hundred or more Aenglisc in no particular order waited, hidden from the road, behind the large hill's eastern side. Dan could see their brightly painted Aenglisc shields, their bronze helms, their axes, their spears and their gleaming swords. He flew back towards Arturus's waiting men with a heavy sense of doom. Were Arturus to ride along the Icknield Way to where the road crossed the wider plain, he would be attacked on his left by Larcius's light cavalry, on his right by Gwynefa's Cataphracts charging down the hill-side. Those men who survived the combined onslaught would meet the Aenglisc horde under Medraut's command as they poured towards them from the eastern side of the valley. It was a classic ambush and Dan could see no way out of it for Arturus or for his men.

Dan woke by the fire outside Taliesin's tent, the scent of one of Frontalis's herbal concoctions and the smoke and crackle of flames bringing him back to earth. Arturus listened to his debriefing carefully, nodding. He made Dan sketch his aerial vision with a stick in the earth, and then gave his orders. He was clear and decisive and had obviously worked it all out in his mind. Ursula was to take a small, hand-picked troop of sixty Cataphracts up the blind, steeper eastern side of the largest hill. They would climb to the hill's highest point to take the higher ground above Gwynefa's men. The entire western side of the hill was gentle enough for Ursula to charge down Gwynefa's men and put them into a state of disarray. Thus ambushing the ambushers.

They would deal with Larcius's light cavalry in the same way. Arturus's remaining Cataphracts would swing wide around the nearest hill, ride through the narrow valley formed by the two smaller hills and emerge to the rear of Larcius's force. Meanwhile, Arturus's own infantry would march in fighting formation so that at the lituus's signal, they would form a defensive double shield wall, presenting a double level of spears to the enemy on four sides. Any of Gwynefa's Cataphracts who succeeded in completing the charge in the valley could not attack the infantry so long as the shield wall held.

'I have good men,' Arturus said proudly. 'Trained the old Roman way – they will hold.'

Ursula bit her lip. 'How steep is that slope?'

'Steep enough to ensure no one will be expecting you from that direction. You want to take the younger more agile horses, but you will have to lead them up on foot. The horses might do better without their mail.' That made sense.

'We won't be silent. What if we are seen?'

'There will be scouts – Medraut's no fool, but if they

are close enough to see what is going on with us – they are a long way from the command group – it will take time to get the message back and by then it will be too late. Gwynefa is inexperienced. She might send her men to charge you down. Believe me, a horse can get up there but a horse cannot get down, not at speed, not with a rider on his back. It would be carnage.' Dan knew he was thinking of the fine Sarmatian horses and the fine Sarmatian soldiers who were about to die – Sarmatians who just days ago were his own, sworn men. Ursula looked grim. It was cold this early in the day and Frontalis had lent her his cloak – Arturus's cloak. She clutched it to her throat for warmth and Dan saw that her fingers were clenched white. She gave no other evident sign of nerves.

'Any of our Cataphracts who successfully make it through to the road must form up in front of our infantry – they will be useful against Medraut's Aenglisc war bands.'

Dan could not tell from Arturus's tone whether he expected most or any of his Cataphracts to make it that far. Arturus's emotions were under tight rein and Dan did not wish to probe them.

'Dan and Taliesin, you will have command of five riders each with golden dracos and horns that can sound the basic commands. If you see some unforeseen disaster looming send out the messengers to divert the troops as you see fit. I trust you to decide.'

Dan did not like the sound of that. He was no military strategist. 'What about you?'

'I will lead the Cataphracts against Larcius. We leave at once. Ursula, pick your men!' Arturus's tone brooked no opposition. Ursula looked distressed. Had Arturus forgotten that she knew none of these people?

'I don't know them. I knew their fathers!'

'Sons are not always of the same mettle it is true – ask for volunteers. You command – they must follow you!'

Dan could feel Ursula's battle nerves steady as she concentrated on her task. She glanced back to smile briefly at Dan, before striding off.

'Lady Ursa!' Arturus's voice halted her in mid stride. 'Take this.' He handed her the gold face-mask she had worn at Baddon Hill. 'For luck!'

She took it thoughtfully, more mistrustful of his motives than she had been at Baddon. Did he wish Gwynefa to believe she was Arturus? It hardly mattered. She did not have to be mistaken for Arturus to stand a very good chance of dying.

The camp dissolved around them with a blast from the tuba. They were to eat on the march. Most of the men were glad to be moving – anything was better than waiting. By the time they arrived at Camlann their enemies would have been waiting for three or four hours. Dan could not help thinking that gave their own men a psychological advantage.

~ Chapter Forty ~

Ursula mounted her war horse. Arturus had given her a good mount, strong but lighter than the norm, handsomely equipped with silver mail. She fastened Arturus's mask to her helmet, but did not put it over her face, and trotted towards the waiting Sarmatian troops. She did not know what she was to say to them. They were ready, of course, though not yet mounted as she rode up to them. Strangely, it seemed as if she should know these men, wearing armour handed down from their fathers. She saw the distinctive mail shirt of Cynfach and had to remind herself that he was long dead and that these men in the same war-worn suits of scale and mail, were strangers. She cleared her throat nervously. She could feel their eyes on her. Most of them were in their late twenties or thirties though she spotted one grizzled veteran and a few younger men whom Gwynefa had not seduced. Ursula dismounted Combrogi fashion. She wanted the earth beneath her feet. She planted herself on the churned grass and stood very straight before them, conscious of her height and her hidden Boar Skull strength but all too aware of how she must appear to them.

'King Arturus has asked me to lead the bravest of you against your former comrades.' She began. Her voice was not loud and scarcely carried beyond the first rank.

'Speak up young 'un – we can't hear at the back.' The voice, speaking heavily accented soldier's Latin was mocking, and Ursula's heart sank.

'You will not remember me.' She began again, more loudly, 'but I fought alongside your fathers, led them in the famous charge at Baddon Hill.'

There was a snort of derision from somewhere and Ursula fought to keep her temper under control.

'That was Arturus – everyone knows that!' someone called out. Then a voice spoke from the front rank – one of the younger men.

'No, it wasn't. It was a woman, my ma told me!'

'Shut up, Caradoc – your ma tell you where babies come from yet?'

There was more laughter but it was not unfriendly and Caradoc ignored it. He was a strong looking youth and addressed his mockers in a clear, ringing voice.

'You all heard of my father, Cynfach, who led us at Baddon, well, he rode with the Lady Ursa. I have told the story before – it was the Lady who led the charge wearing Arturus's face-mask!'

Ursula took her opportunity. She marched towards the youth and dragged him forward to face the troops. She spoke clearly as Caradoc had done, allowing each word to echo and die before continuing.

'This man had a father to be proud of. Cynfach was my friend. Cynfach saved my life too, on Baddon field when the charge was over and the worst of the killing began. I carried this mask then and I carry it now.' She waved Arturus's golden mask before them.

'Baddon was tough, but the task I ask of you now is tougher and I need to know if you are worthy heirs of your fathers.'

The silence of the assembled men had deepened as she spoke. She had their attention at last. Then the veteran she had spotted earlier pushed forward to the front and as he approached she recognised him as one of Cynfach's corps.

'Lady Ursa, I have not forgotten.' He was a big man, heavily muscled and scarred. His voice was as powerful as his frame. 'I have not forgotten those that fell that day and those who have fallen since and I have never forgotten you. I do not know what magic has preserved you unchanged through these long years which have seen my strength fade but, by all the soldier's gods, it is good to see you again.'

'Rhys! You've gained a few pounds, but I do not believe your arm is any the weaker for it.' Ursula was relieved that her voice sounded firm as she grasped his arm.

Rhys spoke to the assembled men.

'Do not be misled by this Lady's beauty, by her youth or, begging your pardon my Lady, the slenderness of her frame, for this is the Lady Ursa, the she-bear of Baddon Hill, and I promise you – you will never see a better fighter!'

There was an instant's silence and then the commander of the Cataphracts stepped forward. He was a handsome man in a blue-grey surcoat of much-mended horn scale. He moved with the easy confidence of command and his voice carried effortlessly in the still cool morning.

'I don't doubt your sincerity, Rhys, but we need more than that. If you are to lead us, Lady, why has Arturus not sent me orders?'

Ursula could not answer that.

'Perhaps he hoped that you would gladly follow a hero,' she said softly, 'or perhaps he wished me to prove myself to you – again.' She sighed. 'There is little time, so let's get it over with. I will fight any two of you if need be, to establish that I'm fit to lead. Who wants to test my mettle.'

She removed her armour so that she stood in just her

tunic, bare-headed and shieldless, her sword in her hand.

Rhys grinned at her and the commander nodded his assent.

'I am Vitus and I will fight you, Lady.' He said courteously.

'Anyone else?' Ursula knew by the men's reaction that Vitus was their best. She was not afraid, indeed her earlier nervousness had disappeared. She wanted this.

She did not take long. He was a good swordsman but she had fought the best and she was angry, not wild and out of control angry, but coldly furious that Arturus had deliberately placed her in this situation again, hours before he expected her to die for him and his doomed cause. Vitus could not parry the blows she rained on him fast enough, she was too quick and too strong. She came at him more fiercely than he anticipated, attacking constantly so that he was unable to think of anything but his own defence. He stumbled and she stopped, reining in her temper before she injured him.

'Anyone else?' Ursula repeated her earlier question. There was silence. She helped Vitus to his feet – he had overbalanced and lay, panting on the ground.

'Right! I am the Lady Ursa, veteran of Baddon Hill and I will lead you well if you will follow me.' No one breathed and she knew that she did not have them yet. She had more to prove. She had made a speech before, in Macsen's Hall on the brink of another battle, the battle of Craigwen. She had found the right words then and she needed to find them again. She took a deep breath and began. She spoke more quietly, but the men listened, strained to hear as she began.

'I know that you are loyal men. I know how it must pain you to lose brothers in arms and I'm sure brothers in blood too, but they are gone, lost to you. They have allied with our enemies. They have allied with the Aenglisc and we have to fight them. We have to fight them, those who were you brothers, because if we don't the Aenglisc will sweep us away. Once, long ago, before Baddon I was there when the Aenglisc burned down a village, cut down those that ran to escape and killed a young girl for sport. King Arturus is all that stands between us and that. We have to fight to keep Arturus's dream of Britannia, our Island of the Mighty, alive. Arturus is Roman and Combrogi both, he carried the hope of all of us at Baddon and after twenty years of peace he carries it still. We walk into an ambush but we can win, must win. We will have victory if you have the heart and guts for a tough fight, more than that, a tough fight against fellow Cataphracts who have betrayed us all.'

She knew when they cheered that she had won them. All of them volunteered to follow her up the steep slope of the nearest hill and down again the other side, follow her through whatever mayhem and carnage lay between. Inwardly, she marvelled at their courage. She did not believe many of them would survive the day.

She allowed Vitus to choose the sixty lightest and strongest for the task ahead and rode with him, at the head of the Sarmatian column, towards Camlann.

When the largest of the three hills came into view Ursula peeled away from the main force, Dan rode over to her side. Her face-mask was up and she looked worried.

'These men don't know me, Dan – they didn't even know I'd led the charge at Baddon. Arturus could have made it easier.'

'Maybe he made it hard on purpose.'

Ursula pulled a face. Dan could feel her fear and her excitement. She was flooded with nervous energy. He wanted to hold her, but she was fully equipped with kontos, sword and bow. The hillside looked too steep for her to climb. There were too many ways she could be killed. There was so much he wanted to say and yet this was not the time to say any of it.

'Good Luck!'

Ursula nodded, gave him a tight, terse smile and swung her mount away to join her men. Dan could sense their fear, too, and the beginnings of that strange adoration Ursula's warrior-woman persona tended to engender. He almost went with her at that moment, to try to keep her safe, but he did not want to fight again and that determination could make him a liability. He returned to the main body of Arturus's force as the High King was instructing his command group, and sought out Bryn and Braveheart.

'Are you going with the High King?'

Bryn shook his head. 'I will not fight my former Lord if I can avoid it and anyway, you have forgotten, Dan, my role is with you.'

'But you think me a coward, for not fighting.'

'I never said that.'

'I knew you felt it.'

'I was a boy then.'

Dan nodded. 'Wouldn't it be wonderful if you could sing it all into oblivion, make it all melt away like Rhonwen's illusion at Baddon?'

Bryn grinned and the moment of awkwardness was over.

'It wouldn't work now – my voice broke some years back!'

They rode together towards Taliesin and Frontalis's cart. Brother Frontalis was with Arturus's confessor, blessing the Christian troops.

'What happens now?' Dan asked Taliesin.

'Bedewyr and the infantry will advance and form their wall when Ursula reaches the top of the hill.'

'And we'll know she's done that when ...?'

'When you tell us, my friend.'

Dan was not at all sure that he wanted to watch Ursula risk herself again. He was beginning to understand those mothers who looked away when their children did anything dangerous. He propped himself up against the cart and let his thoughts fly. He saw Ursula at once using the kontos like a walking stick and leading her reluctant horse. Her troops had spread out around her in a line rather than a column so that one man's lost footing need not signal a major disaster. The ease with which Ursula climbed under the weight of her mail and helmet served to encourage the men. They were not going to be out-climbed by a mere girl. All the horses also appeared to be coping with the sharp incline. They were strong beasts but relatively lightly built, unlike the heavy, mediaeval war horses Dan had seen in pictures. It took perhaps an hour for all the men to reach the summit. Dan saw Ursula signal with a wave of her sword for her men to mount up. He saw her adjust Arturus's cherubic, golden, face-mask. He shivered mentally as he saw the effect as her men fitted their own masks. Sixty human fighters were at once turned into sixty unearthly creatures, with bland, impassive, metal faces that did not register pain or fear. They stood proud, like inhuman centaur gods. They were outlined against the sky and visible to their enemies if not their allies. These sixty Cataphracts, so improbably positioned, were Arturus's message to Medraut. Arturus was still High King, still in the game. It was not over yet.

Dan allowed his consciousness to sink back into his body and opened his eyes.

'Send the infantry!'

One of the standard bearers immediately blew the advance and Arturus's three hundred men marched forward the short distance to the valley. On a second signal the front row (and each of the men in the end column and the rear line) dropped to their knees and rested their oval shields on the ground. They pointed their spears forward at hip height, like the spines of some armoured, mythical beast. The horn blew again and the second row of infantry rested their shields on the shields of their comrades to form a wall as tall as a standing man. They held their spears at shoulder height. This second shield wall appeared on all four sides of the rectangular formation. It was a bizarre sight. A Roman tactic performed by the Combrogi. Each man had his own distinctive war gear. Some had mail shirts, some the battered remnants of antique Roman scale armour. Some wore the protection of boiled, hardened leather, others thickly padded woollen garments. Each man bore a shield painted with a different design, with their war gods or saints, with lucky symbols or sacred words, in every colour that their ingenuity could produce. They looked as different from each other as they did from their Aenglisc enemies but they moved as one.

It was only when Arturus's battle horn sounded that Gwynefa noticed her danger.

Ursula heard the battle horn – it was her signal. Her legs ached from the climb and her tunic stuck to her, damp and itchy with sweat. The dappled, diffused light made the job of spotting the enemy harder, but the screaming of horses and cursing of armoured men told her all that she needed to know. Gwynefa had seen them and begun to recognise her peril and was ordering her men to face Ursula's own force. She did not quite believe that Gwynefa would be so foolish. She lifted her mask briefly to grin confidently at the men nearest to her, Rhys and Caradoc. She had not wanted to bring either of them. She did not want their deaths on her conscience, but Vitus had chosen and was himself at the rear of his chosen men. She lowered her mask and patted the lathered neck of her mount. None of the horses in her troop wore armour now but, like the men, had to trust to speed, skill and the grace of God to stay alive. Ursula sat straighter in the saddle and raised her sword high in her own signal to advance.

Without willing it, Dan found himself flying above Ursula again, drawn by his need to know that she was safe. He heard Gwynefa's shrieked orders. She attempted to send half her force up the hill to face Ursula's smaller force. It was a naïve mistake. Gwynefa's

Cataphracts were too tightly packed to benefit from the limited cover of the trees, each man carried a kontos some two metres long, each horse required more space than was available to turn round and face up hill. There was chaos as the well trained Sarmatians struggled to obey orders that were almost impossible to follow. Men and weapons became entangled with tree branches and each other. For those few who managed the manoeuvre, the prospects were scarcely any better. Gwynefa's horses were armoured and trying to charge up hill, while Ursula's, though unprotected had the advantage of the downward slope, the element of surprise, and a commander who had fought on horseback before. Dan saw Ursula at the moment she raised her sword again in the signal to charge. He saw her ride forward, her golden face lending her a terrible calm assurance. She held her kontos like a lance, to impale anyone who got in her way. There were too many terrified men and horses ahead of her. Dan dreaded the impact, the moment when spear pierced flash and all the pain and animal terror began. Gwynefa's forces panicked. They had not had time to fasten their own masks, and fear was evident in their faces. Half were facing downhill and they rode, without any signal from Gwynefa, to escape the gold-faced goddess who led their former comrades like an avenging angel. Gwynefa's strategic value to Arturus's enemy died at that point. She had lost control of her men, and her men were doomed. Dan did not want to watch as Ursula's men dispatched their former comrades. He did not want to hear the thud as living men, unhorsed, fell onto the rucked ground. He did not want to hear the fear and horror in their primal cries as they were trampled under foot. He did not want to hear the ring of metal against metal, weapon against weapon and worse, the sound of the cracking and splintering of bone, the ending of lives. When he had been a berserker he had never been aware of anything but his own bloody purpose – to watch a battle was a terrible thing and to feel men die was worse.

Less than fifty of the rebel Sarmatians got away. Gwynefa was among them. She charged down the hill screaming words Dan could not hear. She was a princess of Rheged and rode like one, both hands holding the kontos, keeping her seat with superb balance and skill, her black hair like a dark flag, streaming behind her. It was a shock then, when her horse stumbled on a corpse and she fell from the saddle. She landed badly like a doll tossed from a pram, her limbs bent at improbable angles. Dan could not see her move. Dan turned and wheeled away – away from the hillside and the riderless horses stampeding over Arturus's Queen where she lay, bloodied and crushed. She was dead, trampled by her own men fleeing the chaos on the hillside. Dan had felt her dying anguish, her panic, and her sudden peace.

He withdrew instinctively from the screams of combat and the soundless anguish that accompanied them and found himself flying over the plain where Larcius, too, had made Gwynefa's fatal mistake and tried to fight on two fronts at once. Some of his light cavalry had successfully turned to face the bulk of Arturus's Cataphracts, those that Ursula had not chosen, but most were fleeing the charging heavy horses, resplendent in their glimmering armour, fleeing the fierce strength of the armoured riders, with their inhuman metal faces-masks. The greater part of Larcius's force forgot all battle discipline and rode into the growing melee of men and horses across the centre of the plain. There, Bedewyr and the infantry held their square formation. They looked solid as a tank and deadly as a giant porcupine, sprouting spines of metal spears. Bedewyr's men formed a formidable defensive weapon which hampered the movement of the surviving cavalry as they struggled to stay clear of the double row of spears. Larcius's light cavalry were sandwiched between Arturus's Sarmatians, the fleeing remnants of Gwynefa's force and Ursula's cavalry who had now swept down the hill into the central plain. There were horses everywhere rearing and kicking, dying or lying dead. There were bodies everywhere and small desperate battles in a confusion of contorted flesh and armour. All Dan could feel was pain. It almost drove him back to his own form, but he fought his own urgent need to flee: he had to find Ursula. At last, he spotted her golden face-mask and saw her fighting hand-to-hand with some light cavalryman, while her Sarmatians fought to get close enough to protect her. She was alive for now.

He flew away, instinctively, too fearful to watch. He turned and found himself observing the battered form of the High King Arturus, wearing Frontalis's tattered monk's cloak and fighting for his life. He had lost his horse and was bleeding from a blow to the groin. He was coming to the end of his strength and struggling against a gore soaked opponent whom Dan belatedly realised was Larcius. His face was almost unrecognisable, dark with congealing blood from a major wound to his head. He had lost his helmet and seemed scarcely more alive than Arturus. As Dan watched, Arturus staggered forward and thrust his sword through Larcius's chest. He put all his weight, all his anger at betrayal, all his vast disappointment behind it. For a moment it looked as though Larcius would speak, his mouth opened, then Dan felt him die. Dan found himself staring at the dead man through Arturus's battle weary eyes, eyes that stung with salt sweat. Arturus wiped his face and Dan shared with him the hollowness of the victory. Arturus was exhausted, he waited until his breathing became less ragged, resting his hands on his thighs as he knelt on the ground beside his victim. Arturus stretched forward and twisted the hilt of the sword, Caliburn, Dan's own Bright Killer, which still protruded from the chest of Gwynefa's lover. Arturus gazed at his handiwork; and then with a trembling, sigh, ripped Caliburn from the dead man, cleaned it roughly on the grass and moved on through the confusion of bodies, in search of a horse. Dan struggled to separate his consciousness from that of the High King whose thoughts were shadowed with battle lust and a grim, dogged desire for vengeance.

The sun was high now and the battleground reeked of death. The infantry had still not engaged. The only route to the enemy was still blocked with cavalry, fighting to get away, to stay alive, a sea of horseflesh. Ursula was nowhere to be seen. Dan circled, trying to ignore the grim sights and worse emotions that battered at his senses from all sides. It was worse than Baddon and even more difficult to find Ursula by eye alone and he dare not seek her thoughts. Her golden helm was almost invisible among the crowd of bodies. Some few of her men were with her, but there were many more of Larcius's lighter cavalry. The battle no longer had any obvious pattern; men were fighting and dying without purpose, without reason. Ursula was swamped by men, fighting to retain her seat as her horse reared, fighting to parry the slashing swords that surrounded her. She cried out, with all the strength she had left. She knew she could not hold out much longer. Her cry broke through all the ambient pain and fear to deafen him.

'Dan!'

'Ursula! Hold on!'

He woke in his own body, breathing as if he himself had been stabbed. It was his dream made real. Who else could it have been, the Arturus who was not Arturus but Ursula, whose deeds had become entangled with Arturus's own? He had never been more afraid.

'Bryn! Must go to Ursula! Braveheart!'

Bryn reacted instantly, understanding everything, questioning nothing.

It all looked different from the ground. What had seemed like a series of separate skirmishes from the air was from the ground unreadable chaos: a cacophony of noise, a crush of roiling, twisting, dying men. There were bodies underfoot and everywhere the stink of death and dung. Bryn and Dan took the swift horses of two of the messengers. Taliesin flew as Merlin somewhere unseen. Braveheart ran at their side. They rode past the still intact infantry division, past the body of Larcius, closer to the road than Dan had thought it. He rode into the melee hacking at anything that got in his way, except it wasn't anything but anyone, and every blow he dealt he felt. In front of him he saw the battered form of Arturus locked in combat with Medraut.

The veteran was frailer and older than Dan's memory of him, but he was still a wily opponent. Arturus was badly injured and without a horse. Arturus tried valiantly to hamstring Medraut's mount but had not the strength. Dan could feel the life leeching from the King as, with an almighty cry, Medraut launched a frenzied attack on his former comrade. Arturus had found a shield from somewhere and held it above him saving himself from the most vicious of the blows but, weakened from blood loss Arturus fell, only to be crushed by the hooves of Medraut's mount as it reared, and Medraut rode on. Arturus Ursus, High King of Britannia, died there unnoticed by any eye save Dan's. Arturus's face was an unrecognisable ruin, another anonymous corpse on a mortuary field, wrapped in a monk's cloak. Later, there would be deep regret and even sorrow, but there was no time in all that madness, in the bloody maelstrom of battle. Dan dismounted, swinging down from his horse and vaulting straight back up, pausing only to pick up his own blade, Bright Killer, from Arturus's still warm and bloody hand. Dan was so desperate to save Ursula that it did not even seem a callous act.

With single-minded purpose Dan refused to accept the pain he felt in every part of his being. He dared not stop to check whether he was truly bleeding from a hundred wounds, or if it merely felt like it. He could only think about Ursula. Her voice still screamed in his head, weaker but still desperate.

'Dan-Dan-Dan-Dan!'

'Hold on, Ursula!'

He could not tell if she heard. He was dimly conscious of Bryn behind him. Somehow Bryn had acquired an Aenglisc war axe – perhaps it had been in his pack, but he used it to brutal effect at Dan's left while, at his right, Braveheart dodged the hooves of horses, snarled, and savaged, and stayed by Dan's side. Ursula was still in the thick of the fighting. Her gold face-mask was in place but blood was pooling at her neck. A young Sarmatian fought at her right hand, fending off what blows he could but he was himself hard-pressed and tiring. As Dan watched, Ursula despatched a new attacker with a ferocious blow to his groin which sliced an artery. Blood pumped from the wound and only as the man fell did Dan recognise the aged body of Medraut and, riding towards him through all the chaos of battle, Rhonwen.

'Get Rhonwen!' Dan yelled over the battle noise.

Bryn seemed to understand.

A large Sarmatian was closing in on Ursula. Dan slashed Bright Killer's sharpened edge into the man's face and almost passed out with the pain. The world went black for a moment, but he kept upright and got to Ursula. She was barely conscious, only in her seat because one of her men held her there trying to defend her with his own shield. Dan fought to hang on to his own awareness, not to feel Ursula's pain. He concentrated ruthlessly upon action. Dan could not lift her onto his horse but, instead, leaped onto hers. He timed it carefully and slapped his own horse hard so that it reared and startled the throng pressing against Ursula. The young Sarmatian who wore Cynfach's armour, left Ursula's defence to Dan and was able to launch an attack of his own. Between them they made some space and rode free, Braveheart at their heels, Bryn fighting his way after them, herding Rhonwen and her mount, and keeping attackers from their backs. Ursula's mental cry, almost like a mechanical distress beacon, had stopped by the time Dan got her back to Taliesin. Dan hastily sheathed Bright Killer, still sticky with congealing gore. In the distance he knew that the battle still raged. He heard the roar as the Aenglisc infantry charged, and spent their lives on Combrogi spears. It no longer mattered. The one remaining messenger helped Ursula from her horse and between them they carried her to a safe place. Dan ripped off Ursula's mask. Her face was so white he was momentarily afraid that she had died. She was so covered in blood he could not see where she was injured. He made himself think and tried to focus his empathy on her alone. She was in terrible pain and had been cut in many places – the worst being her leg. He fashioned a tourniquet. Brother Frontalis shook his head. She'd lost too much blood.

'I've got to get her to hospital – in my own world – get her a transfusion,' said Dan. 'If I could get her home – she'd be all right.'

Dan tried to do what he had once done with Medraut, tried to focus on his own health, and project that into her consciousness. It was too much. He could feel himself being dragged by the closeness of their rapport into the place of near-death where Ursula lay. He pulled away, physically gasping for air, tears of frustration and grief making it hard for him to see. Rhonwen dismounted and looked dispassionately at Ursula's bloodless face.

'She killed Medraut. She is a brave girl, braver perhaps than he was. She deserved Macsen's trust. And yours,' she added, looking into Dan's haunted face. 'She would not leave you.'

Dan looked at Rhonwen in surprise. She had dropped the illusion that had disguised her scars from all but Ursula. She looked tired, grief-stricken, and suddenly old.

'How many Combrogi dead, Princess?' said Taliesin bitterly. 'You have killed off Macsen's heritage true enough. Are you satisfied?'

Rhonwen said nothing.

Dan was checking Ursula for a pulse. She still had one, but it was weak.

'I don't care about that, Taliesin, this is no time to talk.' Dan's voice was sharp with grief, raw and wretched. He was willing Ursula to hang on, trying to lend her his strength without losing himself in her pain.

'Rhonwen, please, raise the Veil! Please! By all you hold dear, she was never your enemy. Let us go home. We fought for your brother and we've fought for the Combrogi. We did all we could. Help her now! Let us go!'

Rhonwen silently turned her back on Taliesin. Dan thought she was crying; he could spare no empathy for anyone but Ursula, his fear for her blotted out everything. Rhonwen walked a small distance away and began to chant. To Dan's eyes it looked at first as if nothing was happening. Every instant they remained in Arturus's world the life ebbed away from Ursula. Then the first yellow tendrils of mist appeared and began to grow. At the use of magic, Ursula's colour brightened, almost as if she drew strength from Rhonwen's power. She found Dan's hand and squeezed it. It was a weak squeeze, the slightest of pressures but it was something. Dan dared to hope she might live. Taliesin and Dan lifted her between them and carried her into the growing vortex.

'I love you, Dan. You came for me – fought for me?' Her mental voice was quiet but present. He clutched her hand, willing her to hang on, his tears uncontrolled and unnoticed running in rivulets down his face.

'Of course I fought for you. I love you, too, Ursula. Rhonwen's going to get us home. You'll be fine. I'll take you to hospital. You've only lost blood. You'll be fine!'

He'd said what had seemed so impossible to say, now it seemed as easy and natural as breathing. Of course he loved her. He would not let her die. Frontalis and Bryn were on their knees praying.

'Will you come, Bryn?'

He shook his head. 'I have a son and I cannot leave him. God bless you, Dan, and know that in spite of everything I do not regret a moment spent in your service. You have been a worthy Lord.'

Dan could not speak in reply; his throat was constricted by tension and grief. He nodded and hoped that Bryn would understand and forgive as he had understood and forgiven so much else.

Braveheart stepped into the mist to stand beside Dan and pushed his nose into Dan's hand, licking Ursula's bloodied body.

'Rhonwen?' Taliesin met Rhonwen's eye. 'Will you come home?'

She shook her head. 'Who is left to make sure the Combrogi are never forgotten if I go? You are ready to go now aren't you?'

Taliesin, abashed, nodded.

'Arturus is dead, Rhonwen. *The Bear* is no longer on the hillside and I fear it is over for us. We Combrogi had twenty more years because of him. That is better than nothing and perhaps it is enough to keep our memory alive. I have one remaining duty – to help take Ursula home. Her injury is my fault. *She* needs me now.'

Rhonwen nodded. It seemed as if Taliesin and Rhonwen understood each other very well, in spite of their differences.

'You are right – there is no one left here I would trust to boil water. Cerdic cannot even make the battlefield on time. Tell Macsen I will make sure that the Combrogi are remembered here. I made a mistake, I see that now. I have hastened our end.' She sighed, a sorrowful sound. 'The Aenglisc have a word for fate, *wyrd*. It is my *wyrd* to put right what I have helped make wrong. That is what you want isn't it? Isn't that what you said this world needs?'

Taliesin nodded. '*The Bear* must be remembered too, *the Bear* of the prophecy – that's important. He must be remembered as a good man. Maybe the memory is as important as the deeds. *The Bear* must be a beacon, bright in the dark chaos of this new Aenglisc world.'

Rhonwen was ashen faced, but more sincere than Dan had ever heard her. 'I will see to it. Though it seems to me that this Ursula is as much *the Bear* as your Arturus Ursus. She is all that the Combrogi crave in a hero – and more, she leaves the field still breathing – maybe we can call on her again, when next we stand on the brink.'

She spoke with the strange cadences of a prophesying Heahrune, then stopped abruptly. 'Do not worry, Taliesin, I have heard of the prophecy and I will ensure that the Celtic Bear is remembered. You have my triple oath.'

Taliesin nodded again, his eyes misty. 'I will tell Macsen, if I should see him again, that he yet has a sister to be proud of.'

Dan was not interested in Rhonwen's reputation; he only wanted to get Ursula home.

She seemed better, touched by the mist, but even so they had no time to waste.

'We haven't time for this, Taliesin. Can you direct the Veil to get me home?' Dan no longer cared about anything but returning Ursula to their own world.

'Goodbye Rhonwen, my dear Brother Frontalis, Bryn.' Taliesin sounded sad, chastened.

Dan grabbed Braveheart's collar with one hand while, with the other, he helped support Ursula's weight. The sadness was oppressive. Dan's eyes were wet with tears. He would have liked to embrace Bryn and Frontalis, but there was not time. Dan placed his hand on Taliesin's shoulder and thus joined, he allowed Taliesin to lead them all, Ursula, Dan and Braveheart, forward, through the yellow Veil, to home?

~ Afterword ~

No one knows for sure what kind of a man might lie behind the legend of Arthur but if there really was one great leader who turned the tide of the Saxon settlement of Britain in the fifth century he may well have been a War Duke (*Dux Bellorum*) of Britain struggling to maintain the remnants of Roman civilisation after the departure of the legions and much of the Roman hierarchy. It is a period of British history in which hard facts are few and far between. Though *Warriors of Camlann* is definitely fiction, I have tried to re-create the time as realistically as I can and have included historical figures in the story. Hengist and his sons Aelle and Aesc actually existed, as did Cerdic, though he is generally thought to have been a Saxon of Celtic descent and not, as in my story, Arturus's half-brother. He did, however, settle in Gewisse (Southampton). Ambrosius Aurelianus who 'wore the purple' (i.e. was an Emperor) and Vortigern (the British leader who invited the Saxons to

Britain as allies to fight the Picts) are both mentioned by Gildas in *Of the Fall and Destruction of Britain*, a near contemporary history.

I have tried to make the weapons, armour and strategy of the time as accurate as I can and I'm grateful to Dan Shadrake for his help, though he is not in any way responsible for any of my errors! There is a tradition of Arthur being a cavalry leader and from the late Roman *Notitia Digitatum* it is known that Sarmatian armoured cataphracts were stationed at Ribchester in the ancient Kingdom of Rheged in the late Roman period. They carried a dragon standard and brought their own myth of a sacred sword pulled from a stone. They were descendants of the 5,500 cataphracts brought from their native Hungary in AD175. I like to think of them as Arthur's most powerful weapon.

There are many competing theories concerning almost everything about the Arthur story and not least the location of Camelot, but two favourite contenders are Camulodunum and Cadbury Castle, the site of my Fort Cado. No one knows the location of the decisive battle at Mount Baddon either, though it ended the Saxon advance for a generation and is supposed to have lasted three days. There is evidence to suggest that it may have happened where I place the battle site, just outside Bath (Aquae Sulis). I also place the last battle at Camlann (crooked valley), one of the many possible sites, and according to the *Annales Cambriae*, it is where both Medraut and Arthur died. *King Arthur*, *A Military History* by Michael Homes inspired my ideas on the military campaign, though the battles and tactics in the story are my own invention. Arthur's burial site has, of course, never been found.

N. M. Browne